SHIFTER

SHIFTER

THE STONE WARDENS
BOOK 1

By Asher H Boyan

asherhboyan.com

Cover Design and Illustrations by Robyn H: robynh.art

First Edition September 2025

ISBN: 979-8-9995397-1-7 (paperback)
Arcane Sigil: 2-10-105

*To my wife and children, who have listened to many
cycles of storytelling and have yet to grow bored.*

To Alex, Lisa, Kat, and Lori, who encouraged the magic.

*And to Mom, who always believed.
I miss you.*

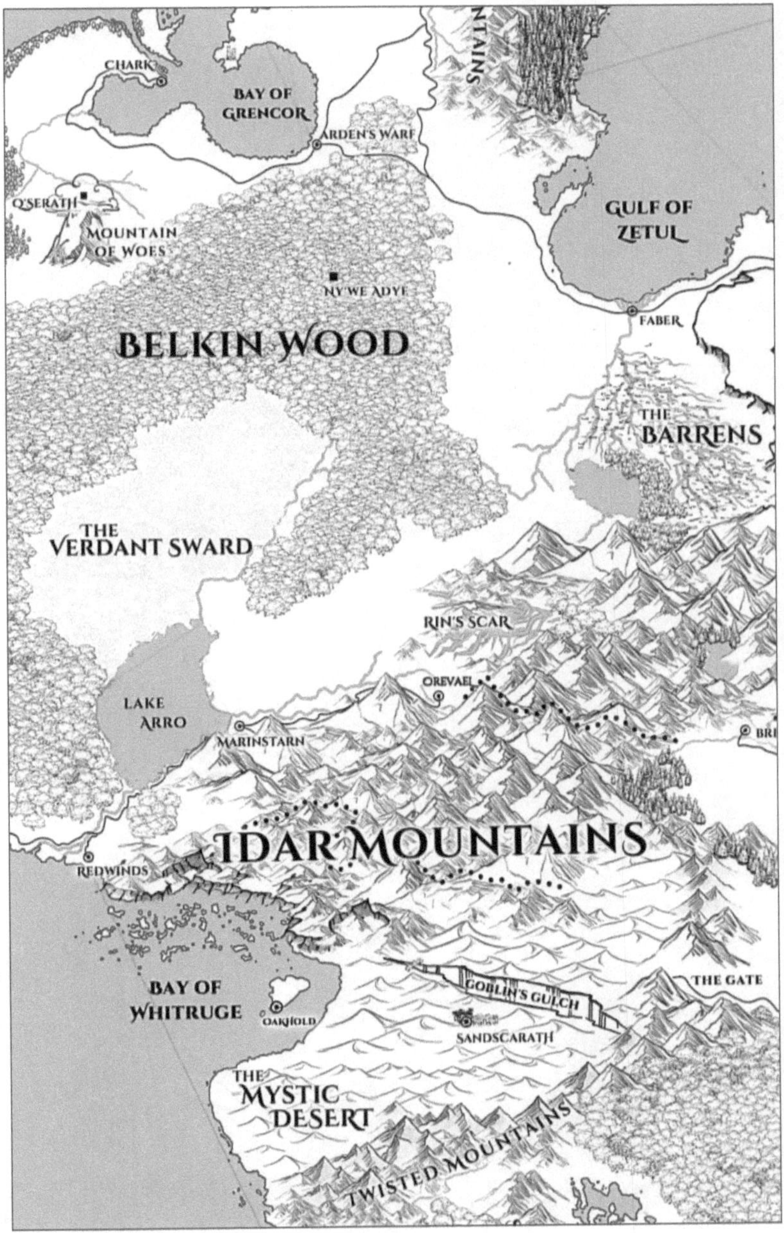

CHARK
BAY OF GRENCOR
ARDEN'S WARF
MOUNTAINS
GULF OF ZETUL
Q'SERATH
MOUNTAIN OF WOES
NY'WE ADYE
FABER
BELKIN WOOD
THE BARRENS
THE VERDANT SWARD
RIN'S SCAR
OREVAEL
BR
LAKE ARRO
MARINSTARN
IDAR MOUNTAINS
REDWINDS
BAY OF WHITRUGE
OAKHOLD
GOBLIN'S GULCH
THE GATE
SANDSCARATH
THE MYSTIC DESERT
TWISTED MOUNTAINS

CHAPTER 1: ADVENT

Cycle 739; Apricity; The Fifth Age.

Arracnoth wiped his eyes and glanced at his friends. The brothers stood beside him, somber and unspeaking, as the cold mist fell around them. It was a chilling drizzle, the kind that sunk into bones. It made saying goodbye to his mother even just that much more miserable. Muted sounds met them from the distance: a dog barking, the clatter of horses on the cobblestone streets, the mournful coo of a dove. Avanstel and Danvaren said nothing, giving him time alone with his thoughts.

He stared at the ground. His mind flooded with a lifetime of memories … thoughts of his childhood, the many cycles with Adine filled with warm embraces and smiles, mixed with more recent memories of her unexpected sickness and wasting away and abrupt death. The moments passed in a long montage of sadness, laughter, joy, anger, and many other emotions – some unfamiliar, unnamable. Arracnoth felt a hand on his shoulder after a time that was only moments but felt like ages.

"We brought your things to the Hall," Danvaren said. He glanced at his older brother.

"We assumed you'd want to stay with us," Avanstel said. "If not, we can make other arrangements." He paused. "Come whenever you're ready, of course."

Arracnoth nodded and placed a hand on his friend's arm. He raised his head and looked into the eyes of his companions. They had walked the same path when their own mother had passed two cycles ago. He had stood beside them then, in this same place. In their faces, he saw both sympathy and resignation. This was the way of things for the *ort*, those half-human children whose Weode blood gave them both the blessing and the curse of outliving the humans they loved for decades, sometimes centuries.

Avanstel stepped forward and embraced Arracnoth. He began to sob again at the touch, flooded with gratitude and grief.

"We will be beside you," Avanstel said softly, giving him a gentle squeeze of reassurance. Arracnoth swallowed hard, pushing down his sadness and attempting to gain control of his emotions. Avanstel held onto him until his sobbing faded and then pulled away, patting him on the back before gently grabbing his shoulders and placing their foreheads together in the Weode manner of pledging.

"*Namartha t'undel*," Avanstel said in Weald-speak.

Arracnoth took a deep breath and sputtered the words back to his friend in reply. Hot tears streak down his cold cheeks. His breath trembled loudly in the space between them. It was a long moment before he felt the strength to release his friend. Danvaren stepped forward and repeated the ritual with Arracnoth. Then the brothers departed, fading into the grey mist and leaving Arracnoth alone. This was their tradition – giving him time to say his parting words to his mother.

But the words wouldn't come.

Not because he didn't want them to, but he simply couldn't find the *right* words to give her. What words were sufficient for the woman who had rescued him from the gutters, had given thirty-six cycles of her life to nurture and care and provide for him, a child who was not her own … and an *ort* child at that? Adine had been a wonderful parent to him despite being a poor human woman living alone in the slums of Chark.

He sighed and shuddered, trying to keep the lump in his throat from escaping and overwhelming him again. What could he say? What could he give her? He waited, wrestling with the thought. The words would not form. His grief-addled mind simply could not be still long enough to compose a soliloquy sufficient to offer her.

He fell to his knees beside the freshly turned earth. His vision blurred with tears once again. "Mother," he managed. "I...." He couldn't finish.

His shoulders slumped. Bleary-eyed, he reached into the leather pocket on his belt with trembling fingers, removing the two silver coins that were inside – a parting gift … and all he had. He clenched them tightly in his hands and forced himself to continue. Fresh tears spilled down his cheeks as he closed his eyes. He kissed the coins and placed them on the dirt mound in front of him.

"Mother," he started, trying again. "I owe you so much. I...." He broke off, shook his head, and wiped his arm across his nose.

He was exhausted. He didn't have the strength to continue and could not bring himself to say the last goodbye. He couldn't find the words to give her and wondered if he would ever find them. He reached out and placed a hand on top of her grave. Was her spirit watching him from afar? Could she see the agony written on his face? Would she even hear the words if he were able to find them?

He closed his fist around the dirt, a sudden flush of anger racing through him at the unfairness of it all. He ground his teeth and felt his neck becoming flushed. *No!* He couldn't give in to the anger. Adine had raised him to control his emotions – to focus on compassion, peace, and kindness. Those were the tenets to focus on in times of distress. He needed control. Anger was to be shed, like an old skin. He wouldn't let his rage spoil this moment.

"*Sere'eden.*" He whispered the word like a prayer. *Peace.* Adine had taught him the elven words. She had made him repeat them, time and time again – whenever he had felt overcome by frustration or rage. He took a deep breath and pushed the outrage from his mind, slowly releasing the pain and recapturing his calm. He looked down at his clenched hand and slowly opened it, staring at the clump of dark soil.

He closed his eyes. "I will find the words someday, Mother."

He pulled a small pouch off his waist that held the remembrance of his mother: a pale blue moonstone pin, enclosed with copper and brass and no bigger than a coin. He took the pin and stuck it securely into the blue leather pouch and slid the handful of earth inside it. He fastened it to his belt and bound it securely. He would take this reminder of Adine with him until he had the right words to give to her – the words she deserved – and then he would release her.

He stood up and slowly turned his back to her grave. His former life was over. He was an orphan now, without a family.

Alone … but not completely alone.

Many of the *ort* in Chark were facing the same situation. The part of them that was elven gave them long life – the ability to outlive their human caregivers. They often became orphans before they were adults … at least by elven measurements. Adine had told him he was born in cycle 703, making him thirty-six cycles old. By human measurements of time, he was an adult. But for a Weode, even a half-Weode like him, he was a mere adolescent – a young boy just starting his transition into adulthood. The *ort* were lost children – not welcomed by their human neighbors, and similarly shunned by the elves for their mixed blood.

The larger *ort* community in Chark had an established system of caring for these 'orphans' until they were independent and could live on their own. Out of necessity – and tradition – orphaned *ort* vacated the homes they had grown up in and moved to the Hall, a sanctuary within the Blundt – the section of the city of Chark where they lived. The Hall was a large dormitory-style building where *ort* could find lodging, companionship, and a 'family' of others who were in the same situation. It was the way things were done within the tight-knit half-elven society; the way they had been done for many cycles now. And it worked well.

Arracnoth navigated the labyrinthine streets, leaving the graveyard behind, as the gloomy day transitioned into a darker night. He crossed the Harbor and Market districts, passing through several of the residential areas as he navigated roughly south, further from the center of the tarn and towards the outskirts where the Blundt was located.

The Blundt was out of the way and separated from the more traveled areas of the city. That kept the *ort* separate – which was the way it had been intended. The proper Citizens of Chark avoided the district – and dealings with *ort* in general – unless they had to. Most considered the *ort* a drain of resources, and a problem thrust on them by their uncultured neighbors, the Weode. Most Citizens wanted the *ort* expelled from Chark entirely and made to find another place to call their home. But the problem of abandoned bastard half-elven children never went away, so the Blundt was the Citizens' solution to the blight of the *ort*.

While the Citizens marginally tolerated the *ort*, the Weode of nearby Belkin Wood outright shunned them. These half-blood children were a dirty secret, a taint on the purity of the elven blood. Thus, the Weode discarded their *ort* children, dropping their bastard babies into Chark's begrudging arms. This tension between the Weode and the Citizens of Chark was the world that Arracnoth was born into, and in which he had spent his early childhood. Unwelcome, unwanted, and unloved, his life would have been one of despair, like so many of his kin.

Except that Adine had rescued him.

Now, as he entered the Blundt, he instinctively turned toward his house, lost in his thoughts. After a time, he found himself standing outside the low wooden gate leading into the place that – until today – he had called home. He paused. Unfamiliar voices came from inside the small house.

His hand reached for the knife at his side, prepared to attack the invaders of his home. He stared at the pale glow that leaked from the greasy windows. Figures moved within. Then there was laughter and the noise of a child crying.

"Arrac," a voice called from the nearby darkness. He spun around as Avanstel stepped into the dim light coming from the neighboring inn. "I figured you might end up here. I did the same when my mother passed. It's a habit … you will adjust."

Arracnoth closed his eyes; his shoulders slumped. He looked down at his feet, fighting off a fresh wave of grief, his hand slipping off his knife and brushing against the pouch of soil at his belt.

"Come on. Let's get something to eat," Avanstel said. "My treat! Anything you want … well, at least, anything that Mabe is serving tonight at The Two Coppers," Avanstel said. He put his arm around Arracnoth's shoulders and steered him away from the shack and towards the inn. "And you can choose light or dark in a game of Haven Chase. You can even play the dragon if you want." He chuckled and grinned. "I might even let you win. And after dinner we will get you settled in. I'll be here with you through this."

The routine of his new life at the Hall, as well as the companionship of his friends, proved a balm for Arracnoth's loneliness. He assumed that was the intended purpose – the reason they had this tradition of moving orphaned *orts* to live together. It gave them all what they needed deep inside – a sense of family.

The Hall wasn't an orphanage per se, but it was a place to find camaraderie with others like them until they were of a sufficient age to provide for themselves. Here, they worked, some doing chores for the Hallmaster and the others who ran the place in exchange for a place to live. If possible, some found outside employment, giving a portion of their wages to the Hall as compensation for their room and board. Some even continued to support the Hall after they had moved out, giving aid to other *ort* children who passed through.

As planned, Arracnoth moved into Danvaren and Avanstel's room. The brothers were a welcome and necessary distraction from his heavy heart. He had been friends with Avanstel for as long as he could remember, but living together and working through his grief intensified their connection. They spent most of their waking time together. They were the same age, and although they were different in many ways, sometimes their differences were what made it so enjoyable to be together.

Avanstel had a job outside the Blundt and had saved enough money for an inexpensive Haven Chase board. They would play long into the night, often by candlelight, after Danvaren had fallen asleep. They were equally matched and enjoyed the game as much as each other's company. Arracnoth preferred the quill token, part of the dark set, while Avanstel typically chose the sword marker in the light set. Avanstel was more competitive than Arracnoth and religiously kept score ... while Arracnoth simply played for fun.

While Danvaren dreamed, Arracnoth and Avanstel would move their pieces around the circular board and speak in hushed tones about the events of their day and what they planned to do the following. Often the conversation would dip into deeper topics: hopes for the future, memories from their childhood, and thoughts about their journeys thus far in the world.

At times, they'd talk about their original parents – wondering who their father and mother were, which one was elven and which was human, and under what circumstances they had met ... and wondering what had driven them to give up their child. Avanstel fancied that his father was a soldier in the Weode army, while his mother had most likely been just a woman traveling through from the east who had fallen in love with that handsome elf. Maybe she had been from as far away as Harper, and maybe she had been a baker – and that's why Avanstel loved pastries so much. Or maybe she had been a scholar at one of the colleges in Faber. Whatever she was, Avanstel was sure that she hadn't left him due to anything short of dire circumstances.

Adine had shared little about Arracnoth's parentage. Every time he had asked, she had skillfully changed the subject or dismissed his inquiry until he had persisted so long, she had to give in. Finally, she had explained to him that his mother was from Stone March. She had met his father there, became pregnant, and had fled to Chark to avoid disgracing her family. She had left Arracnoth in Adine's care when he was newly born, and then she had disappeared. Adine either didn't know or didn't say where she had gone, only revealing that she had traveled by ship. That was the extent of the information she had provided. The rest remained for Arracnoth's imagination to fill in.

It was an all-too-familiar story, echoed by many others like them. Humans found the Weode exotic, different, enchanting, and mysterious – mostly because they knew so little about them. The elves scorned human interaction … except, apparently, for *this* kind of interaction. Unfortunately, many a fair maid's suitors discarded them quickly upon receiving the news of an impending birth.

There *were* some *ort* children who lived with their original mother, or sometimes their father, but abandonment was the norm. The Weode simply couldn't be fouled by the stain of a half-breed child.

So, the three of these orphaned *ort* eventually fell into a routine and established an equilibrium. Danvaren, though cordial to Arracnoth, sometimes felt like the third wheel in their world. When they were younger, Danvaren had always been the annoying little brother that Avanstel and Arracnoth would run and hide from. There were occasions when the three of them had some grand adventures together – such as several memorable hunting trips to Upper Geffam – but Danvaren was usually the outsider to these exploits. With the reintroduction of Arracnoth into their everyday life, some old feelings of jealousy and resentment over the closeness that his brother shared with Arracnoth had reignited. They worked it out, but three was always an odd number, and there wasn't a way around that.

The situation changed, however, when the trio became a foursome and another *ort* showed up in the Hall after losing her parents and needing a place to stay. Her name was Questelle, and she wasn't a native of the Blundt or of Chark – she was from Arden's Wharf, a small tarn across the great bay.

With beautiful auburn hair, a fair complexion, and an endearing smile, she proved a delightful new distraction from the day-to-day regimen of life in the Hall. The young men enjoyed taking turns showing her around the city, explaining the layout and best landmarks by which to navigate, which fishers had the best prices on the daily catch, details on the politics and how to avoid being targeted by the Chark Guard, as well as introducing her to the local characters – of which there were many. She seemed in awe of her new city, which was so much bigger than her small hometown.

Her story was like theirs, and the same as most other *ort*. She shared that before, she had lived with her mother. Her father was an unknown Weode. On her deathbed, her mother had urged Questelle to go to Chark to find other *ort* and make a life for herself among them. So, she had left Arden's Wharf at the tender age of twenty-nine and had arrived here in the Blundt, becoming yet another resident of the Hall, a welcome part of the larger *ort* family. Of the three young men, Danvaren found himself increasingly the object of Questelle's attention, and the two of them paired off quickly and naturally.

"So, Arrac, will you come with me tonight? Fert's expecting you," Avanstel asked as he rolled the die and moved his sword marker eight steps around the circle.

Fert was the proprietor of The Pig & Lamb, a tavern and inn just outside the Blundt. Avanstel had been working there for several months as a barkeep and doing well. Two nights before, a coworker had found himself at the wrong end of a sword after some questionable gambling dealings, and Avanstel had convinced Fert to give Arracnoth the opportunity to fill in.

"You are sure he'll take another *ort?*" Arracnoth rolled a five, and then picked up three of the smaller beads in the neighboring squares and advanced two squares forward.

"Fert's not like the other humans. He doesn't mind our kind. Pays fair wages, too. Haven't seen him treat me any different. I'm sure you will be fine." He tilted his head to the side. "Are you trying to take my tower off the board? You know that won't work."

Arracnoth tried to keep a straight face to not give away his strategy, but Avanstel knew him too well. Avanstel rolled the die and moved his tower out of Arracnoth's reach.

"What does he want me to do? I've never served tables. I'm not sure I have much I can offer him."

"Fert will find something for you. Ah! Haven Chase!" he declared, and picked up two dice and rolled them together. "Twenty total!" He moved his white shield to block Arracnoth's next play. "Cook, clean, serve, split wood or slop the pigs." He paused, arched an eyebrow, and smirked. "Maybe even entertain …"

Arracnoth looked at his friend, unsure whether that last part was a joke. It was often hard to tell with Avanstel, who had a jovial nature and loved to play tricks on him. Arracnoth was skeptical. This sudden opportunity might be a setup for another laughable encounter at his expense. He figured it didn't matter — the opportunity to spend more time with Avanstel was worth the risk. Besides, Danvaren and Questelle spent almost all their time together, so he could either go with Avanstel or sit here alone by himself and continue to do Hall chores. Avanstel was always enjoyable company … even when there was a prank afoot.

"All right, Van," he said, "I'm in." He rolled and moved his token forward. "Quill takes the sword again! Black for the win!"

"I let you have that one."

"Sure, you did," Arracnoth laughed.

Avanstel stood up and stretched. "Let's get cleaned up. If Fert likes the looks of you, he'll hire you on the spot. Best be smelling fresh and looking your best! Here, you can have this shirt. It fits me a little tight in the arms anyway. On you, it will fit nicer … and it's better than anything you have." He reached into his dresser and tossed a cream-colored shirt at Arracnoth. "Fert pays ten coppers a night for the work, but you'll have to sign a contract to lock that in. He wants to know he can depend on the help he hires, and the wages are decent for contract work. You get to keep all your tips — that's where the money is. Take this belt too. It's in better shape than yours. I'll punch another hole there for you. You've got to put some meat on you, Arrac. You're skin and bones!" He patted his stomach and grinned. "All muscle here!"

Arracnoth laughed. "And a lot of Caty's cooking!"

"Speaking of which, be sure to save enough money to pay for your own food and drink. Fert's a good man, but he's smart about his business, so nothing is on the house." He pulled his shirt off over his head and replaced it with a clean one. "And mind yourself," he added. "Don't get suckered into a game of Haven Chase with

Fert. You'll end up losing your entire night's coin and you won't have anything for food the next day."

Arracnoth smiled. "Speaking from experience?"

Avanstel grinned and shook his head. "More than once, friend!"

CHAPTER 2: STRANGERS

Cycle 739; The Blooming; The Fifth Age.

Three months – and many games of Haven Chase – passed, and Arracnoth and Avanstel had fallen into a rhythm at The Pig & Lamb. It was tiring but not overly challenging, and the inn itself was convenient, located just outside the Blundt within a neighboring district. This far out from the city center, the customers of The Pig seemed like they were more focused on getting a mug of ale and a plate of fritters than they were worried about being served by a half-elf. Although the work was sometimes mind-numbing, the young men enjoyed the fast pace, the tips, and, of course, working together.

Avanstel tended the bar, keeping the spirits flowing. Arracnoth had picked up serving duties more quickly than he had expected. He discovered he had a knack for remembering faces, and after just a few visits, he could have drinks in hand for most regular patrons shortly after they crossed the threshold. For the most part, the two were an effective team at the bustling tavern. The speed at which they served the customers led to a heavy coin purse most evenings. Fert was pleased with how well they worked together, so he kept Arracnoth on contract.

"Two mugs of meads and two glasses of wine!" Arracnoth shouted to Avanstel above the din of conversation in the bustling room. Avanstel nodded in acknowledgment while he continued to pour a pint of ale for a customer seated at the overcrowded bar.

The Usher celebration was soon approaching. With the next full moons of the Blooming month only days away, the night was especially busy. Many of the farmers from the surrounding communities came into Chark to celebrate and purchase seeds and supplies for the spring planting. The locals believed that Eunoin, the local deity of fertility and agriculture, would bless their crops if they were planted on the full moons in Blooming – just thirteen days after Usher. If they adhered to the traditions, come the Falling month, the harvest would be bountiful. It was a race to get everything purchased and planted in just under two weeks, but the race was worth it for those who believed in the blessing of Eunoin.

Arracnoth scanned the room and thought to himself that it would be nearly impossible to fit any more people into the space. Just then, Ruct and Igna, a friendly couple who operated a brewery nearby, passed by him as they jostled their way to the door. Ruct flicked a copper in the air at him and dipped his head in thanks. Arracnoth pocketed the coin and returned the nod, watching the couple disappear out of the exit.

Before the door closed, three hooded figures entered. They paused in the entryway, scanning the crowd.

The first man was brawny, draped in a scarlet cloak and standing a head taller than his companions. Even from this distance, strength emanated from his colossal frame. He pulled back his hood, revealing a handsome, clean-shaven face with dark copper skin and shoulder-length raven hair. A long-ago healed scar ran down the left side of his face, from forehead to cheek, cutting a slice out of his left brow. He moved across the room toward the roaring fireplace. His smooth, cat-like movements indicated that he might have had some training in combat, each movement purposeful and efficient.

The second figure, clothed in hues of brown, also removed his hood. His chestnut hair was in a neat knot on top of his head, and a full beard framed his face. Though not as tall or as wide as his companion, Arracnoth noted he also moved with the same grace and fluidity as the raven-haired man. An unfamiliar symbol decorated the man's tabard. These clues, Arracnoth thought, pointed to the bearded stranger being a man living under vows: a cleric, dedicated to some deity unfamiliar in these parts of Halbrun.

The last figure was leaner and slightly shorter than the others. Unlike their companions, this figure did not remove their hood, instead pulling the black and grey cowl further down to shield their face. It was impossible for Arracnoth to make out their features in the shadows. The figure moved across the floor, following the others and quickly blending into the crowded room.

Arracnoth's brow furrowed. There was something about the visitors that seemed out of place. Strangers from the surrounding lands filled the room, but these three didn't fit in with the others. The trio didn't carry themselves like Citizens from Chark, nor like sailors or fishers, nor farmers or working folk. Something in their movements and mannerisms stood out from the locals.

Perhaps they were foreigners who had come in on a ship, Arracnoth thought. But not a ship from the Norlands – from one that came from much farther away – maybe from the south.

"Here you go," Avanstel said as he slid two pints of mead towards Arracnoth, interrupting his thoughts.

"And … ummm …" The piercing flash of a golden-eyed gaze from beneath the third stranger's dark hood distracted Arracnoth again.

"Arrac?" Avanstel asked, giving his friend an inquisitive look.

"Sorry." He paused. "The newcomers," he said without indicating which patrons he was referring to. "Something about them."

Avanstel scanned the room. He picked out the three figures immediately. "Foreigners," he said, agreeing with Arracnoth's suspicions. "Mercenaries, maybe. They've seen battle, in any case." He frowned. "The hooded one …"

"Strange, right?"

Avanstel nodded and turned to Arracnoth. "Take these and come back." He pushed the ale and wine towards him. "The big one looks like he might be from the desert in the south. Let me scrounge around – I think I might have something special for him and his companions." He turned around and disappeared into the room behind the bar.

Arracnoth delivered the order and retrieved several empty tankards, along with some tips left by the boisterous crowd. As he was making his way back across the room, someone grabbed his arm. He turned to see the large raven-haired man standing next to him.

"Rooms?" His voice was thick with an accent that Arracnoth could not place.

"I'm sorry. We are full tonight. Blooming moons."

The man stared back at him blankly. Arracnoth realized the trio wasn't aware of the local holiday, which confirmed they were foreigners to these parts.

"Food?" the man said.

"Yes, we have some chowder, and bread and cheese, and some salted and dried fish … if there's any left. I can check."

The man grunted. "Yes," he said curtly, without specifying what he wanted.

Arracnoth looked at him and frowned.

The bearded man stepped up beside his large companion and smiled politely. "Excuse my friend. He doesn't communicate so well." He winked. "We'll take two bowls of chowder, please."

The large man grumbled something, and the pair slid into a recently vacated table – moving aside the Haven Chase board.

"Only two? What about your …?" Arracnoth looked around the room for the hooded figure, but they had disappeared.

"Two. Thank you," the bearded man said with a hint of finality, cutting off any inquiry about their missing companion. The man's accent was distinct from the first, suggesting they came from different places although they traveled together.

Arracnoth fetched the chowder from the kitchen and returned to the bar where Avanstel was waiting for him.

"What did they say?" Avanstel asked, leaning in.

"Just asked for rooms, and then food."

"That's it?" Avanstel frowned. He had been expecting a more thorough report. "Give them this," he said and handed Arracnoth three tin cups filled with a thick brown liquid that swirled sluggishly around inside.

Arracnoth sniffed the drinks. They smelled both sweet and almost spicy simultaneously. He looked up at Avanstel and raised his eyebrows. "What is it?"

"Fert purchased it off a ship from the south, and it has been sitting here ever since. I think they call it 'Flying Rage'. Those strangers look like the kind who might enjoy it more than our local folk," he said with a grin.

Arracnoth shrugged and returned to the table with the chowder and the strange drinks. He placed the bowls in front of the men, and then apprehensively sat all three tins on the table, looking around once more for the third figure. When the visitors saw the drink, they reacted in surprise, said something to each other that Arracnoth did not understand, and then in unison looked towards the bar where Avanstel stood, waving at them. They each picked up a tin, raised it in salute to Avanstel and promptly downed the drinks in one swallow – gasping and grinning and striking their chests.

"Your friend honors us with the drink of heroes. We are grateful," the bearded man said when he caught his breath.

The dark-haired man reached for the remaining tin and downed it in one gulp. "Yes," he said and pounded his chest a second time.

The bearded man looked again at the bar and said, "Please tell your friend we are grateful." He took Arracnoth's hand, placed a coin in his palm, and closed his fingers around it.

Arracnoth nodded, slipped the coin into his purse, and returned to the bustle of serving the crowded room of ever-hungry, ever-thirsty guests … while also keeping one eye out, watching for the third mysterious stranger.

The rest of the night kept Arracnoth busy as he worked to keep tankards and bellies filled … and the coins flowing into Fert's pouch. Avanstel had his hands full too, emptying a whole barrel of wine and two barrels of ale all in one night. It was a week's worth of business crammed into one evening. As they sent the last visitor out the door, they took stock and discovered they had expended most of their larder. Fert instructed Arracnoth and Avanstel to make a trip to the docks first thing the next morning, to fetch supplies and restock. He expected another busy night and wanted to ensure they would not turn away any guests for lack of provisions. Fert promised them both a silver, in addition to their contracted ten copper, if they retrieved enough to feed the crowd the following night.

They returned to their quarters at the Hall well past the mid-of-night, slipping in as quietly as they could, so as not to disturb Danvaren and Questelle. They were exhausted, but the tips that they had earned that night made the young men giddy. Neither was ready to go to sleep.

"A game?" Avanstel asked.

"Nah. Let's go outside instead," Arracnoth said. He opened the shutters, lifted the window, and slipped out onto the roof. Avanstel followed. They both took a moment to enjoy the cool night air, then Avanstel reached for his pouch.

"How much did you make?" he asked. "I think I have over fifty copper, and at least two silver!"

"I didn't have a moment to count," Arracnoth said. He pulled out his purse, which was almost bursting. "Help me count it, Van."

As they sorted through the night's haul, one of the coins slipped out of his hand and rolled down the slant of the roof. Avanstel leapt after it, catching it before it fell from the rooftop and onto the street below. He laughed and opened his hand to return it to Arracnoth. Looking at it, he gasped. "Where did you get this?" His tone was suddenly serious, and it caught Arracnoth off guard.

"What is it? What's wrong?" Arracnoth asked.

Avanstel handed the coin back to him.

With a flash of recognition, Arracnoth said, "Oh! This was for you, Van. The foreigners …." He paused and examined the coin intently. It was like nothing he had seen before. It was made with the finest craftsmanship and detail of gold, inlaid with silver and copper. The coin featured an intricate carved design, and its surface displayed strange writing etched around the edges. "A wolf?" he asked.

"The White Wolf," Avanstel replied, "Ni'Ilyan, to be exact." His voice was soft and distant. He looked out over the city.

"Ni'Ilyan?"

"The symbol of an ancient hero – the first king of the Weode. Legend says that Ni'Ilyan could transform into a white wolf at will. Allegedly, that's how he snuck into the palace of his father, Lord High Emperor of all Th'arule, and killed him. Then he fled to the north, bringing with him his followers, and establishing the kingdom of the Weode. This one coin is worth more than everything else in your purse. Possibly more than an entire cycle's worth of wages."

Arracnoth flipped the coin over. On the opposite side was an equally intricate engraving of a tree whose roots and branches braided around each other. He looked at his friend. Avanstel's face was clouded and somber.

The prospect of that much coin, of having enough to leave the Hall and start their lives anew, thrilled him. But something about Avanstel's reaction to the odd coin dampened his enthusiasm. A gloom set in and extinguished the moment of joy.

"What is it, Van?"

Avanstel was silent for a long moment. When he answered, he did not turn to his friend but continued to peer into the darkness.

"The strangers," he answered. "They must be here on Weode business. That's the only way one obtains a coin of such value."

When Avanstel didn't offer more, Arracnoth pressed. "And?"

"No good comes to those who pique the interest of the Weode," he said, "Especially a Weode who can give away that kind of coin."

Arracnoth flipped the piece over, his mind jumping to a future where they were no longer living in the Hall – a future where he and his friends were able to leave Chark for other places that might be more friendly to their kind.

"Well, the foreigners weren't mercenaries, Arrac," Avanstel said, bringing Arracnoth back from his daydream. "Mercenaries or assassins would have entered with drawn swords and completed their assigned task. These men might be bounty hunters sent to retrieve an *ort* whose absent parent has suddenly developed a conscience. Or an unusual … and expensive … interest in their bastard child."

"Who do you think they're after?"

"Hard to tell, here in the Blundt," Avanstel said, "But that they took such an interest in me, ensuring that you gave me that coin, doesn't bode well."

Arracnoth followed his friend's gaze, looking out over the dark buildings and toward the ocean. He wondered where these strangers were now – what shadows they might lurk in, and what dark deeds they were scheming … And what they could want with his friend. He reached out and touched Avanstel's arm.

"I will be beside you," he said.

The words brought Avanstel back from his thoughts. He smiled and then turned and clasped his friend's shoulders. Their foreheads met.

"*Namartha t'undel*," Arracnoth said.

"*Namartha t'undel*."

They crept back inside, slipped into bed, and tried to put the strange events of the night behind them. But they were unsuccessful. Their dreams were filled with dread and darkness. Sleep, when it eventually found them, was troubled and fleeting.

The light of the dawn sun struck the room far too early.

CHAPTER 3: MISSING

Avanstel and Arracnoth were tired from a night of fitful sleep. They dragged themselves out of bed, dressed, and made it to the docks as the last boats arrived. The rain had stopped, but the morning was cold and overcast. The dreary weather proved no deterrent for the residents of the city, however: despite the gloomy forecast, there was a bustle of activity all around them.

They maneuvered their way through the crowds, heading for Whitley's familiar table at Dock Eight. Arracnoth kept his head down, trying to avoid eye contact with the Citizens. He bumped into a woman who crossed his path, a basket in one arm, her young son at her side.

"My apologies, ma'am," he said.

The woman looked up at Arracnoth. When she saw his face, her lips tightened. "Mind your way, filthy *rot!*"

Arracnoth winced involuntarily. 'Rot' was cruel slang, a crass term for '*ort*' that was used by those Citizens who considered themselves no friends of the half-elves.

The boy, probably seven cycles of age, looked up at Arracnoth curiously. Upon seeing his pointed ears, he frowned, and echoed his mother's hateful thoughts. "Mommy, it's a nasty *rot!* Go home to your forest, you dirty thing! Get out of here and leave our city alone!" He spat at Arracnoth's feet.

Arracnoth bit his tongue and looked down at his feet, which was the only acceptable thing to do in this situation. A dispute between an *ort* and a Citizen never ended in favor of the *ort*. He stepped away nimbly, extracting himself from the exchange without another word, and hurried to catch up with Avanstel, who was just greeting Whitley.

"What are you after?" the fisher asked.

"Depends on what's your prices," Avanstel responded.

As Avanstel negotiated with Whitley over the cost of whitefish and oysters, Arracnoth feigned attention to the transaction, but his focus was elsewhere. He was feverishly alert, despite having been deprived of sleep the night before. His eyes darted from dark alley to dark doorway and back to the gathering crowds on the dock, searching for the hint of a brown – or scarlet – or black-hooded figure. His nervous actions betrayed where his mind was.

"Relax, friend," he heard Avanstel say in a low voice. "They won't bother us in a crowd. That's why they only gave warning last night. Too many people, and too many possible opposing interests. They will be sure they capture their bounty with the least amount of attention and trouble."

Arracnoth exhaled and fidgeted with his knife. "Maybe so. But still…"

Whitley chuckled. "What's got you all wound up, mate?" the fisher said, bringing another tray to the table for Avanstel to inspect.

Avanstel put his arm around Arracnoth's shoulders and feigned a punch to his chin. "Arrac's spending too much time worried about 'what could be' instead of focusing on 'what is.' We'll take these six of those, Whitley," he said, pointing to a large silver fish. "Bag them up?"

Whitley nodded, and Avanstel dished out the coin for their haul while the fisher handed the sack to Arracnoth.

"Let's get this back before Fert changes his mind about our bonus," Avanstel said. He grabbed a sack full of shellfish, which he slung over his shoulder with ease. He grinned at Arracnoth and nodded toward the road back to The Pig & Lamb.

Whitley clapped them on the shoulders, bid them farewell and told them to return tomorrow for more amazing bounties of the sea … and encouraged them to bring more money to spend next time. Arracnoth liked Whitley; he was one of the vendors he liked to work with on the docks, always offering them a fair price and excellent quality fish. Unlike most vendors, he didn't hold the typical prejudice against *ort* that many of the other townsfolk did. He was one of the rare few who didn't call him '*rot.*'

Avanstel led the way, walking a few paces ahead of Arracnoth, as usual. Even though they were the same age, Avanstel was slightly taller than Arracnoth, with broader shoulders and a longer stride. His ears were less pointed, and his face favored his human parent, while Arracnoth looked more elven. There was no mistaking Avanstel was *ort*, but he looked less so than most. He was good-natured, quick to turn a phrase, easily able to make fast friends, and he had a grin that demanded nothing less than a smile in return. His attractive looks, along with his jovial manner, made people generally like Avanstel, even most humans. Which is probably why Fert put him at the bar.

Arracnoth, in comparison, was more lithe and graceful than Avanstel – more elf-like. Where Avanstel was like a big, happy, perhaps slightly clumsy dog, Arracnoth was more like a cat – sleek and quick to react to the situations around him. Avanstel liked to point out his own muscular build – relishing in the fact that he could always win at arm-wrestling. But Arracnoth was fleet of foot, and in a race, Arracnoth would always claim victory, much to Avanstel's frustration. They complemented each other, and they both knew it.

It was part of what made them close friends – they didn't need to compete against each other. They each had unique talents.

They returned to claim their reward from Fert. "A silver for each," he said with a grin, "Unless you want to go double or nothing in a game?" The question was directed at Arracnoth – Avanstel had firmly stood his ground that he would never play Haven Chase with Fert again.

Arracnoth shook his head. "Maybe another time, Fert. I'm too tired and I think you'd have me at a disadvantage today."

Fert laughed and sent them away with orders to get some proper sleep and to return mid-afternoon to prepare for another busy night. They agreed, welcoming the small reprieve, and made their way back to the Hall.

Danvaren and Questelle were there. A spread of bread and goat cheese was on the table in the center of their small room. Danvaren motioned for Avanstel and Arracnoth to join them. Questelle had pulled her hair into a woven bun at the back of her neck. She wore a cerulean sash, trimmed with silver threads that accented her silver necklace. She had worn that necklace since she had met them – a gift, she said, from her late mother. From the chain hung a single silver stone that was engraved with an elven rune. None of them recognized the symbol, but they agreed it was definitely elven. The entire ensemble made her sparkle beautifully.

Arracnoth raised an eyebrow at her. "New outfit?"

"For tonight's party." She blushed at the attention, her hand going to her neck and touching the stone. She laid her other hand on Danvaren's arm. "Danvaren surprised me with it! I've only just put it on. Do you like it?"

"Lovely. Where did you get it?" Avanstel asked Danvaren.

"A traveling clothier who just came into town," Danvaren replied. "He said it was a popular color with the women of Arden's Wharf. I thought it might remind Questelle of home."

Arracnoth looked at Questelle and, curiously, caught a frown on her face.

Danvaren noticed it too. "Questelle?"

The strange look vanished quickly. "I love it!" she exclaimed, smiling. "Yes, yes, it reminds me of home. Everyone in Arden's Wharf wears this color. Thank you." She turned to Arracnoth quickly and changed the subject. "Will you two be joining us at the square tonight for Usher?"

Arracnoth shook his head. "Got to work," he said. He grabbed another chunk of bread and smeared goat cheese on it.

"And probably another late night," Avanstel added, barely understandable through his mouth full of food.

"We'll miss you," Danvaren said. "I believe the clouds will move off, and we will have a clear night for the celebration. We should be able to see all the stars because both Relos and Eyama will have set by then. It should be lovely."

Arracnoth groaned, "Thirteen more days until the madness ends. I'm not sure I can make it that long." He flopped backwards on his bed.

"The crowds will disappear after tonight," Avanstel said. "Once Usher is over, the farmers will scatter quickly back to their fields to get their crops planted before the full moons. *Then* we can sleep!"

"I think I'm already sleeping," Arracnoth muttered and kicked off his boots, pushing himself further into the mattress.

Avanstel and the others laughed.

"Let's let them rest," Questelle said. She turned to Danvaren. "You and I can go for a walk so you can tell me more about growing up here in Chark. I want to hear more about your childhood."

Danvaren smiled. "Of course! Though I think I've told you everything I know, but if you want to hear it all again …" He chuckled. "I thought by now you'd be bored of hearing about Chark. When are we going to talk about Arden's Wharf?"

"Not a lot to tell," she said. She grabbed his arm and pulled him toward the door.

Arracnoth did not hear them go. He was already asleep.

When he awoke, the sun had slipped past the window. It was afternoon. He stretched and realized his shoulders were sore, but he couldn't remember why. It took him a moment to orient himself. His sleep had been deep and uninterrupted. He replayed the day's events in his mind and remembered the trip to the docks earlier in the day … and then Fert's instructions that he and Avanstel were to return in the early afternoon to help prepare for the evening.

Arracnoth looked over at Avanstel's bed, but the space was empty. He must have already gone ahead. He sat up, stretched again, and walked to the window to look out at the street below as he laced up his boots. Below, the townsfolk were decorating the streets with paper lanterns in the shape of stars, and the neighbors were sweeping their porches and setting out seats on their front stoops to watch the festival. He looked up at the sky and realized he had overslept. He grimaced at his own tardiness – he would be late for his shift at The Pig & Lamb, and that's probably why Avanstel had already left. He was mad at himself for oversleeping, and then at Avanstel for not waking him!

Glancing once more at Avanstel's empty bed, he rushed out of the room and made for the staircase leading to the entrance of the Hall. Danvaren and Questelle were just returning. She had her arm in his. A couple of delicate white flowers decorated her auburn hair, and she was laughing. Danvaren was extremely fortunate to have the attention of such a beautiful woman. He passed by them in a rush, explaining he was late. As he reached the door of the Hall, he turned to ask them if they had seen Avanstel, but they were quite far away now. Questelle was watching him go, a dark look on her face. When she caught him looking, she immediately turned away and pulled Danvaren deeper into the building.

Arracnoth frowned. That glare had been unusual, and he wondered if he had upset her somehow? He'd have to ask her about it tomorrow. Right now, he didn't have time to talk. He needed to get to the Pig & Lamb. He stepped out onto the street and pushed his way through the gathering crowds, admiring the decorations for tonight's festival.

As he made his way to the tavern, a little tug of irritation pulled at his mind. Why hadn't Avanstel woken him? Why had he left him sleeping and let him be late? Surely his friend had only the best of intentions – letting him get the rest he needed. But it still annoyed him. Avanstel probably thought it was better for one of them to be on time than for both of them to be late. Maybe Van was pleading with Fert right now, explaining how exhausted they all were. He worked his way out of his cross mood with this rationalization. He had never seen even a hint of malice in Avanstel.

The door swung open to The Pig & Lamb. Without even looking around, he knew something was not right. He glanced towards the bar and saw Fert behind it, talking with Ogud and Rychel, two regulars. Fert noted his entrance and scowled at him. Ogud and Rychel followed his glance and then hastily returned to their glasses of wine. Arracnoth suspected he had been the topic of their conversation. The barkeep stomped toward Arracnoth.

"Did ya not hear my instructions?" he snorted. "Early afternoon! We are behind now. I need ya to get to the kitchen and help Caty with the oysters! And where is Avanstel?"

Arracnoth paused. "He's not here?"

"Do ya see him?" Fert motioned toward the space beside himself, then crossed his arms over his chest. "He better show up soon, or I'll be docking his full pay tonight – and maybe the next few nights for breach of contract!"

Arracnoth sputtered, "I thought he would be here."

"Well, he ain't. And we got things to get done. Go on, now. Get to the kitchen and shuck the oysters. They ain't gonna jump out their shells themselves! Get!"

Arracnoth tilted his head, confused, then lowered his eyes, and made his way towards the kitchen. Caty was there, in as much of a fit as Fert. She glowered at him.

"Busiest night of the cycle, and you show up late! Here, take this. And those. And I need these peeled too," she said, dropping an armful of potatoes into his arms. Arracnoth sat them down at the table behind him and started working silently while Caty kept ranting about all the work that needed to be done. "Probably won't be able to feed a single living soul with the way things were going today!" she said.

Arracnoth moved his hands rapidly, completing the tasks in a flurry. His mind was racing just as quickly. Where was Avanstel? Why wasn't he here? As he peeled the potatoes, the skins flew everywhere, and he grew increasingly frustrated. He shouldn't be here playing around with vegetables. He should drop everything and return to the Hall and look for Avanstel – or at least clues to where he could be. Maybe he could find Danvaren and Questelle in the crowd that was likely gathered in the square of the Blundt for the Usher celebration. He'd probably have no better luck finding them than locating Avanstel. And Fert would definitely cancel his contract too, if he abandoned The Pig & Lamb tonight. At least if he stayed here and made it through the night, he could appeal to Fert and ask him to honor the contract – even if Avanstel had broken it. If he left, he'd have no leg to stand on and wouldn't be able to advocate for his friend.

He began mentally retracing the day's events. Maybe Avanstel had returned to the docks for more provisions? But surely Caty would have said something. Suddenly, he had a thought that made his stomach sink. What if …

"No," he said aloud.

Caty did not hear him. She was busy clanging pots together and slamming her cleaver down to split the head off a large fish.

Panic rose in his heart. If the strangers were bounty hunters … and if they had taken Avanstel from the room while Arracnoth slept … then they would undoubtedly be professionals, experienced at retrieving their prize without drawing attention. People like that would not have left a trace and were probably already on their way out of town. With the crowds gathered for Usher, there would be no way he could find them, let alone catch them.

Arracnoth swallowed hard, fighting back the sudden prick of tears. He kept his back to Caty so she couldn't see the look of despair that crossed his face. Where would they have taken him?

He slammed down the potatoes and struck the knife violently into the wooden table, frustrated at his situation and his inability to act to change it. Caty jumped in surprise. She turned and looked at him, expecting him to explain himself. He didn't look at her and remained silent, a mix of startlement, grief, and anger bubbling inside of him.

It *must* have been the strangers!

His best friend was gone – probably forever. He had lost another important person in his life.

He was alone.

Again.

CHAPTER 4: NIGHTFALL

Everything about the evening was terrible. He went through the motions like an automaton, doing what was necessary to get through the night. His body was moving blindly; his mind was far away. He just wanted the night to end.

There were just as many people there as the night before, and the noise was deafening inside the little room. Fert was in a foul mood since he had to cover the bar for his missing employee, and Arracnoth had to suffer the worst of his wrath since he had to fetch drinks from the tavern master frequently. The smooth rhythm that he shared with Avanstel, he did not share with Fert – even when it wasn't the busiest night of the cycle. He tried to minimize his trips to the bar, preferring to avoid Fert's glower. It wasn't Arracnoth's fault that Avanstel had not shown up to work, but Arracnoth was a convenient target for Fert's displeasure.

While he worked, he ran through the possibilities in his mind. What did he know about the foreigners? He couldn't be certain that they were bounty hunters, although Avanstel had made a case for that. Why else would they have such a valuable Weode coin? Could it be possible that their arrival the night before was mere coincidence and that the strangers had nothing to do with Avanstel's disappearance? It was possible, but …

What if someone mugged or attacked Avanstel instead? It had happened before – many times to many *ort*. What if his friend was lying in an alley somewhere, and Arracnoth could help him, even save him?

But if that were the case, what events would lead him to leave the Hall alone without Arracnoth? The appearance of the strangers, be they bounty hunters or not, could not be a coincidence.

There were far too many unanswered questions, but he simply could not stop asking them, running through scenarios and outcomes repeatedly in his mind.

Eventually, people consumed all the food, emptied the drink barrels, and left the tavern. Patrons vacated their tables slowly, disappearing out of the inn and joining the stragglers on the streets who were lingering after the big Usher celebration had ended.

Fert, true to their agreement and despite his irritable mood, still paid Arracnoth his wages for the night. He even surprised Arracnoth with an extra silver piece. The two nights of massive business must have exceeded Fert's expectations for the barkeep to be generous enough to part with an extra silver. Maybe Fert had seen the worry etched into Arracnoth's face throughout the maddening night, or maybe he'd inexplicably become empathetic. Although Arracnoth was grateful to Fert for his generosity, regardless of the source, the extra money would not bring back his friend … which is what he wanted most.

Arracnoth stepped out of the tavern and stood on the landing, shivering in the cool air. The sky was clear and dark. Thousands of stars sparkled in the sky, just as Danvaren had predicted. In the distance, he could hear music playing and people laughing.

A couple passed by him. He lowered his head, hoping they would not notice he was an *ort*. Instead of spitting hatred, they nodded and greeted him with a "Good Usher!" It was a small and surprising courtesy, but it was welcomed nonetheless. Everyone was in a bright mood at festival time.

He stepped down onto the cobblestones, inhaling the fresh night air deep into his lungs and putting the tension of the evening at The Pig & Lamb literally and figuratively behind him. He needed sleep so he could think right — and figure out what to do about Avanstel. He rounded the corner and made his way toward the archway that marked the entrance to the Blundt. Suddenly, a figure slid out of the shadows of an alley and matched his steps. He stopped. His hand went reflexively to his knife.

"My apologies, *sondartin*," the figure said in a soft voice, opening their palms to show they were unarmed and intended no harm. "Good Usher to you."

Arracnoth squinted to take in the details of the figure. He couldn't see much in the dim light coming from nearby windows. The edges of the person's black and grey cloak blended with the surrounding shadows. It was hard for him to discern where the shadows ended and the figure began, not just because of the darkness of the moonless night, but something unnatural — or magical — was at work. Then he saw a flicker of golden eyes from beneath the hood. He withdrew his knife quickly and quietly, keeping it at his side.

"*Sondartin*," the figure said. "I truly mean you no harm."

"I'm not so sure," Arracnoth replied. "You came to The Pig & Lamb last night — with the other two." He raised the knife in front of him as a warning and looked around for the others.

The figure stepped back, raising their hands to their hood and removing it. Silver-white hair framed a dark, masculine face, skin tinted with a purple cast. Golden eyes glinted in the light from the nearby window.

"*Drivrid?*" A small gasp escaped Arracnoth's lips. "I ... I ..." He stammered in disbelief. "You ..."

The figure nodded purposefully, a smile curling the edge of his lips. "Yes. I am *drivrid*, a nether-elf." He stood there for a moment while his words sank in. "But I truly mean you no harm. I just wish to speak with you."

Arracnoth's mind was reeling. He was standing here – face-to-face with a *drivrid* … a mythical race from his childhood stories. The shock and disbelief joined his already swirling thoughts of Avanstel's disappearance. He was too tired to think straight, and the weight of it all was too much.

How could this be a *drivrid?* Everyone thought they had died out long ago. Even the tales of fools venturing into the depths of Caerbexsys hadn't mentioned the nether-elves for hundreds, maybe thousands, of cycles. They were fairy tales. An impossibility.

Yet here one stood.

"Deception," Arracnoth sputtered. He rubbed his forehead. "Impossible. The *drivrid* are extinct. Perhaps I am dreaming."

"No, *sondartin*," the nether-elf said, motioning in the direction of the Hall. "I assure you I am quite alive, and you are not dreaming." He smiled disarmingly and bowed. "Please, let us walk … and talk … and perhaps I can convince you of my intentions. Is there any reassurance I can give you that would ease your mind?"

"I'm … not sure." He hesitated. "Where are your friends? The others?" He looked around at the shadows gathered in the alleys and the doorways.

"Ah," the figure said, "They are headed eastward." He stepped slightly backward. "With your friend, Avanstel."

Arracnoth reached out with the knife, striking with instinctive reaction. The *drivrid* reacted quickly, disarming Arracnoth and shoving him backwards towards the middle of the street. The entire thing took only a split second.

"*Sondartin.*" The *drivrid* bowed his head in deference and proffered his hand. Arracnoth's knife rested in his gloved palm.

Arracnoth stood, mouth agape. The gears of his thoughts ground against each other, trying to determine a way out of this predicament. Was the nether-elf speaking the truth? Should he trust him? Or should he shout for help instead? Surely, if the *drivrid* had wanted to hurt him, he would have. After that small display of his prowess, he knew he was no match for the nether-elf. He could be bleeding from many quick wounds and left stunned and dying in the street. The dark elf had had plenty of opportunities to hurt him — even before announcing himself from the shadows in the alley.

Cautiously, Arracnoth took back his knife, clasped it, and placed it back on his hip.

"All right, *drivrid*, you have my attention."

"Nightfall," the nether-elf said, placing his hand on his chest and bowing. "Pleased to meet you."

"Arracnoth."

"Yes," Nightfall said, "I know."

Arracnoth cocked his head. This entire interaction with the stranger had stupefied him. Nightfall, if that was indeed his name, apparently knew much about Arracnoth, while Arracnoth was still trying to wrap his head around the nether-elf's very existence.

"Let's speak about that," Arracnoth said. "How do you know my name? And why do you call me *sondartin?*"

Arracnoth saw the *drivrid's* posture relax. He gestured again towards the Hall. Arracnoth frowned and started walking down the street. Nightfall replaced the cloak over his head and matched Arracnoth's steps.

"*Sondartin* is an honorific in my native tongue. My people use it to address a young person, typically from noble houses. It's meant as a mark of respect — not intended to offend." His tone was measured and calm. Arracnoth sensed no malice or deception so far.

Arracnoth peered curiously at the nether-elf.

"I have been watching you for quite some time," the *drivrid* said. His words lacked the thick accent of his companions, and his inflection was like everyone else who called this part of Halbrun home. "In fact, since before your mother passed. My condolences."

Arracnoth stopped abruptly. Nightfall paused beside him. "Before …?" His voice trailed off.

Nightfall nodded and started walking again. Arracnoth fell in beside him. "I have been observing many of the *ort* children of Chark over the past cycle. That has been my purpose in this city. I believe my time here has come to a close."

"Because you have Avanstel." Arracnoth's tone was sharp – sharper than he intended.

"I do not *have* anyone," Nightfall said. "And neither do my companions. Your friend went along of his own accord."

"I don't believe you. He would never –"

"It was not without great consternation. And he bid me watch over you when he left." The elf paused for emphasis. "And to explain his departure to you, if you would hear me out."

"Explain him willingly leaving without so much as a word? I don't know *any* circumstances that would make that explainable."

"*Sondartin*, there is much to tell, and the night is old. And you are not of a clear mind. I promise you that your friend is safe, and the manner in which he departed was for a just cause. But I would recommend that you take this evening to get what sleep you might. We can talk more on morrow's eve when you are in a better mind."

They rounded a corner, and the oversized doors of the Hall came into view. Arracnoth wanted answers, but the *drivrid* had a good argument. He *was* exhausted, and Avanstel, if the *drivrid* was telling the truth, was in no immediate danger. Despite his confusion and his concern for Avanstel, he was suddenly incredibly sleepy. Perhaps this *would* all make more sense after a night's rest, when his mind was clear.

He paused again and turned to Nightfall. "But I have a contract. I can't meet tomorrow night. I must be at The Pig & Lamb. With Avanstel gone, Fert will depend on me even more."

Nightfall smiled. *"Sondartin,* you no longer need to work. Not tomorrow, and not for quite some time. You already have what you need."

The Ni'Ilyan coin. Nightfall nodded as he saw the recognition on Arracnoth's face. "Return to your employer the wages you received the past two nights, and he will release you from your contract."

Arracnoth slowly reasoned it out – his thoughts moving sluggishly. He nodded his head in agreement. "But Danvaren … he will be concerned for his brother. He'll want to know what happened."

"Everything will be explained on morrow's eve. Tonight, get some rest. There are roads ahead that you will want to travel – if you will trust me – and you'll need your strength for that."

Arracnoth peered into the recesses of the dark hood, catching the glint of the golden eyes again. Although it was difficult to make out his features, the way Nightfall held himself, his gestures, his calm, and disarming voice, inclined him to trust the nether-elf. Or possibly it was the sheer exhaustion overtaking him, lowering his threshold for reason. Why not trust a strange, fabled creature that should not even be standing here before him? *Nothing* made sense right now.

"We will talk on morrow's eve," Arracnoth said, still slightly guarded, but very tired. He yawned.

Nightfall nodded. "Good Usher," he said. He turned away and promptly vanished into the shadows of the night.

Arracnoth stood for a moment in the cool evening, trying to see if he could pick out the figure fading into the darkness, but he could not. He gave up, turned, entered the Hall, and made his way up the stairs. With every step he took, his feet became heavier and harder to move. Exhaustion overtook him, his eyelids heavy. He was barely able to keep them open as he stepped toward his bed, giving one last glance over to the space where Avanstel should be. He collapsed in a heap and was instantly unconscious.

He hadn't even had the energy to see if Danvaren and Questelle were in the room. Sleep overtook him the minute his head hit the pillow, so he failed to notice the faint glittering waves of air curling around each other above him like a miniature aurora. Even an alert observer would have struggled to see the barely visible vapors fade and shimmer out of existence, but that was the way it was with this kind of magic.

The ripples disappeared the moment he started to snore.

CHAPTER 5: LOSS

Questelle was sitting by the window, looking out at the street below, when Arracnoth woke up. Her hair and skin were glowing in the warm yellow light. It took Arracnoth several minutes to orient himself and realize that it was late morning and that he had overslept again. The events of the previous evening rushed back, and he jumped out of bed.

"Avanstel!" he exclaimed, startling her. He rushed to his friend's alcove and looked at all the belongings intently. Everything was as he had left it. Nothing was out of place. Nothing would have given a clue to a confrontation or fight. He looked at where Avanstel hung his cloak and noted it was missing. His travel pack was gone as well.

He remembered very little of the night before, of the conversation he'd had with Nightfall, in his panic. But one small comfort surfaced as he looked over Avanstel's belongings: nothing here hinted that anyone had taken him against his will. It was as the *drivrid* had explained … Avanstel must have left intentionally. But to *where?*

Questelle stepped up beside him. "What is it, Arracnoth?"

He whipped around, the frantic look of panic on his face creating a look of concern in hers.

"Do you know where Avanstel went?"

"No," she shook her head. "I wanted to ask you about that." She stepped closer to him and looked at him directly. Her hand instinctively went to her neck, where she rubbed her silver pendant. "Do *you* know where he went?"

Before he could answer, Danvaren burst into the room, a giant smile on his face. He set a small sack on the table, and turning to them he announced proudly, "The batch of blackberry sour is ready and it's …" He trailed off, noting the serious look on both their faces.

"What?"

"Your brother …" Questelle said.

Danvaren looked over at the empty bed, then at Arracnoth. "I figured he was gone – I received a letter from him just now, and he doesn't squander money on pen and parchment." He held up a paper in front of him. It had a red seal on it. "I haven't opened it yet. He must have left it for me downstairs, and they just gave it to me. I'd recognize his scribbles anywhere."

From the corner of his eye, Arracnoth caught another mild frown flash across Questelle's face. She stepped towards Danvaren, her scowl turning to a coy smile. She pulled him closer. "What does it say, my love?"

Danvaren shrugged. "Let's look together. Knowing Van, he's probably gone to the Cedars on some errand for Fert."

"No," Arracnoth said. "Not for Fert."

Danvaren cocked his head. "Then I don't know what it's about. If he's gone off on a hunting trip and left me here, he will never hear the end of it!"

Questelle took the paper from Danvaren. "Sit here," she said, pointing to the bed. She sat down beside him, perched on the edge of the bed. Her long, slender fingers broke the seal, and she read aloud.

Dearest brother,

Please forgive me for sharing this news with you by letter instead of directly. I am writing this in haste, as I do not have time to say farewell. I must leave the city urgently, and under cover of night, to conceal my departure and direction. I know this is unexpected, but I received information that required immediate action. If I were to stay, there is a risk of consequences to those that I love, and I cannot allow harm to come to you, Arracnoth, or Questelle.

It is important that you do not follow me. Those near me are in danger. You must stay here and care for the children. You must stay in Chark and care for those closest to both your heart and mine. You must be the elder brother now. Ensure the safety of our small family. Be alert and wary! I hope that by leaving, you will be out of harm's way, but I am unsure how far my new adversary will go or if they will dig deep enough to find you.

Under my pillow, you will find several coins. This is enough for you to purchase a home in the upper quadrant. Be wise with your new fortune, brother. Avoid drawing attention to yourself, though I know it will be tempting to live to excess when we've always had so little. Stay modest and blend in as much as you can, even though you now have the means to live extravagantly. Secure a suitable, secluded, and defensible home, away from prying eyes.

I will send for you if it's safe. Otherwise, dear brother, know that I love you and will do all that is in my power to protect you from afar.

Avanstel

Danvaren looked up at Arracnoth, his lips trembling. He looked lost. "He's really gone?" His voice trembled. He placed his head and his hands and wept softly.

Questelle passed the letter to Arracnoth. He read it. He read it again, and a third time, just to be sure he was understanding. He looked at Danvaren in shock. "You can't be serious, Danvaren! We must go after him! We must go now!"

Danvaren hung his head and mumbled. "We can't, Arracnoth. He said I must 'care for the children.'"

Arracnoth exploded. "And?"

"That's a code we have. Whenever there is danger, and we need the other to follow directions to ensure their safety, we would use that code. 'Care for the children.' If I went against his direction, it would put us all in danger. I must stay here and do what he says. We made a promise to each other that if we used those words, we would follow the instructions, even if it made little sense. I have to stay here and wait to hear from him again … just as he said."

Arracnoth rubbed a hand over his face and paced the floor, exasperated. "But he's gone!"

"And where would you go to find him?" Danvaren asked, lifting his face and meeting Arracnoth's gaze. His eyes were red already. "Which direction? To the sea? His ship would have sailed last night, and for where? Or he went north to the Norlands. Or to the west, to the Cedars? Or to the south, to Redwinds or beyond? Which direction would you go, Arrac?"

"I … I …" he stammered.

Questelle took the paper from Arracnoth and folded it up. "Don't worry about Avanstel," she said. "Danvaren is right. We'll stay here. Stay together – all three of us. Remain right where we are. If we leave and chase after him, we will not be here if, or when, he returns."

Arracnoth didn't want to accept it. He couldn't imagine a world without Avanstel. But Danvaren was right – Avanstel had left no clue as to where he went. Searching for him, without even a hint of where they should look, would be futile. Avanstel had disappeared, and though no one had abducted him, the result was the same. He was gone from their lives, and they had no way of finding him, no way of contacting Nightfall and no guarantee that even the *drivrid* knew more than they.

Arracnoth was not sure he could bear the loss. He was used to having Avanstel nearby – both day and night. They were best friends – more than friends. They knew everything about each other. They could finish each other's sentences, knew each other's favorite foods, favorite places in the city. They had shared their deepest secrets with each other; their hopes and dreams. They even nearly shared a birth-day, only a few days apart, down to the same cycle. Life without Avanstel was … unimaginable.

Arracnoth wiped his eyes and glanced at the Haven Chase game board sitting on the table in the center of the room. He picked up Avanstel's favored white sword token and played with it in his hands for a moment, thinking about their last game. He was about to set it back on the board when he noticed something odd. He tilted his head and frowned. The black quill piece was missing from the board.

Avanstel had left him a coded message, too.

There would be no Haven Chase until they were together again … and Avanstel intended that someday they would be.

It took several hours for the three of them to sort out what to do next. Questelle took the lead, stepping in to direct them. Arracnoth was happy he didn't have to think. At first, she seemed irritated by Avanstel's departure, and then at the two of them for not knowing what to do next. Even after time had passed, she seemed annoyed at the situation. Arracnoth couldn't understand her reaction. Danvaren was still here – why did she care so much about Avanstel's departure?

The afternoon faded into evening. As the letter said, Avanstel had left a small fortune of coin under his pillow. They all knew that he could not have earned or saved that much coin, no matter how long he had worked for Fert. If he had, they would have all moved from the Hall long ago. Under what circumstances Avanstel had amassed this much treasure was just another part of the mystery surrounding his disappearance. Another unsettling fact in a story that already made no sense.

Danvaren's grief paralyzed him. He was lying in his bed, staring at the ceiling. Arracnoth did the same. The more he thought about the situation, the more he despaired.

Questelle announced she would take care of things. She gathered the coins and left the room, instructing them to wait there while she was gone. It was hours before she returned. When she entered the room, she brushed her hands as if she had just finished chores.

"The day is waning, isn't it time for you to head out for work?" she asked. Arracnoth looked at her, taking a moment to process her question. "Fert will hold you to your contract. Even if we have funds to buy a house, your contract will require you to work. And what next if we run out of money?"

"Coin," he said, breaking through the cloud of thoughts that filled his head.

"Right," she said. "We'll still need coin when this is gone."

"No," Arracnoth answered. "Sorry … I was …"

He reached for his own purse. Inside were the wages and tips he had earned over the last week. It was more than enough to buy out his contract with Fert, just as the *drivrid* had said. As he grabbed his purse, his hand brushed over the small blue pouch with the moonstone pin sitting next to it. He rested his fingers on it, gently caressing the smooth leather. First Adine, and now Avanstel.

He picked up the azure pouch and tied it to his belt, along with his coin purse. He felt the need to be close to his mother right now.

Avanstel had been his anchor since Adine had passed ... who would be the anchor for him now that Avanstel was gone?

He grabbed his cloak and started toward the door. Questelle gave up waiting for him to make any sense. Arracnoth thought a further response unnecessary, as she seemed preoccupied with other things. They all seemed a little off. Arracnoth chalked it up to Avanstel's disappearance.

He paused at the door. "Don't worry, Dan. It will work out. I'm sure we'll find Avanstel. He's not gone forever. Remember when we lost him on that trip to the Cedars in Upper Geffam, and he left us a trail to find him? We'll be together again. We'll find your brother."

Danvaren nodded silently.

"It's too late for Fert to find someone else to help tonight. I will work my shift and will buy out my contract at the end of the night. Tomorrow, we can figure out what to do next. If the danger is as serious as Avanstel thinks, then let's find somewhere to blend in and not draw attention."

"All right." Danvaren's voice was distant and small.

"Buy out your contract?" Questelle asked.

Arracnoth only nodded. He would rather stay here with Danvaren, to grieve with him. But there wasn't much that would accomplish. He needed to finish his work with Fert. And then figure out what was next for them.

Fert, although not as affable as he could be when business was good, and he *wasn't* missing a barkeep, was not in as foul of a mood as the previous night. The tavern had returned to a normal pace; the city had emptied as the farmers returned to their fields. It was steady, not busy, and Arracnoth was relieved to see that Fert was managing well enough without Avanstel.

At the close of the evening, Fert offered him his ten copper pieces, and Arracnoth declined. He placed his full coin purse on the counter and shared with Fert that he wanted to buy out his contract. Fert wasn't pleased at having to find not just one, but two new employees. His displeasure, however, faded quickly as he looked at the bulging pouch of coins. Recouping his staff expenses, plus all the tips that Arracnoth and Avanstel had earned, seemed like a win to Fert. They shook hands and parted amicably.

Arracnoth said goodbye to Caty, who, despite her gruff and fiery persona, had taken a shine to him. She shed a tear or two as she stood in the doorway waving goodbye.

His heart was heavy. He was saying goodbye not only to Avanstel but also to the comfort of the routine that he had shared with his friend. Which was all he had left — memories of the time they had shared.

Arracnoth made his way through the chilly night back toward the Hall along his normal route, lost in thought and sadness. As he approached the alley where he had met the *drivrid* the night before, he slowed. As if on cue, Nightfall, his face in shadow beneath his hood, emerged from the darkness and fell into step beside him. A wave of mild relief swelled in his chest, followed by doubt.

"Danvaren received the letter," Arracnoth said, "but it doesn't explain it all. I want to know —"

The faint sound of alarm bells started in the distance. The two paused in unison and swiveled in place to discern the direction of the noise. It originated ahead of them. They could hear people shouting at each other, with rising panic in their voices. Arracnoth looked at Nightfall, unsure of what to do. Should they head towards the alarms or flee in the opposite direction? Perhaps someone had seen the *drivrid* slipping between buildings, thus raising the alarm.

"Smoke!" Arracnoth said, picking up the scent in the air. He looked up into the sky and saw an orange glow illuminating the bottoms of the clouds hanging low over the city. Somewhere nearby, there was a fire. He weighed his options.

"This will have to wait," he said. His stomach knotted as he turned toward the frantic noise and started forward again, leaving the *drivrid* to fade back into the darkness.

As he drew nearer the Hall, his concern turned to fear. The clanging of the alarms and the shouts of people grew louder. Doors opened around him, and people stepped out onto the street, running towards the orange glow in the sky. He rounded the corner and drew to a stop with a gasp.

It was the Hall! Large belches of smoke rose into the night sky, and the flames licked at his home.

Someone pushed a bucket into his hands and shoved him toward the fountain at the center of the square. Arracnoth raced ahead, all the while unable to take his eyes off the blaze. He looked to the third floor, locating the room that he shared – used to share – with Avanstel and the others. Flames licked the edges of the window where he had sat that morning. Dread overtook him.

The blaze burned for hours. Mindlessly, he passed buckets of water from left to right as he watched his home burn. Every *ort* in the Blundt was on hand to help in the futile attempt to extinguish the firestorm, but it was a losing battle. Eventually, they shifted their focus from saving the Hall to saving the surrounding buildings, everyone silently and somberly acknowledging the loss of the Hall.

By sunrise, the fire had reduced the building to a charred pile of ash and timber. People filled the square, arms around friends and those who had been displaced, weeping and crying softly in the morning light. Arracnoth sat at the edge of the nearly empty fountain, which was now filled with grey water and debris, gazing blankly at the ground in front of him. He was covered in soot. Streaks of pale skin showed through the black, where his tears mingled with the ash. Were these tears from the sting of smoke or a different loss? He shrugged. It didn't really matter what they were from. He was numb to everything now. It was all too much for him.

Around midday, volunteers distributed food to the many ragged crowds sitting and lying around the square, which the night before had been decorated with lights, laughter, and music. The *ort* of the Blundt were a close community, lending help to those in need, even when there was little to share. Losing the Hall would devastate their neighborhood. It was an incredible loss, made worse by the deaths of those who had perished in the fire.

Arracnoth bit into a piece of bread that someone had handed to him, chewing it methodically and watching whiffs of smoke trail out of the remnants of the Hall. Small hotspots would ignite every now and again, and people would pass by him to retrieve buckets of water to put them out.

As the afternoon passed, his mind shifted to finding his friends and considering where he might get shelter for the night. He still had a few coins left, in addition to the Ni'Ilyan coin. Now that the farmers had returned to their homes, Fert might have mercy on him and allow him to rent a room at The Pig & Lamb – even though he had broken his contract. He did not want to show anyone or use the Weode coin – unless there was no other option.

"Arracnoth! You're alive!" The shout came from across the square. He looked up and saw Danvaren racing toward him, waving his arms. He got to his feet and made his way toward Danvaren, his body moving slowly and stiffly. Danvaren swept him into an embrace and wept. Arracnoth broke down too. At least Danvaren had survived!

He was afraid to ask, but he needed to know. "Questelle?"

Danvaren stepped to the side. Questelle was standing a few steps behind him. Her hair flew around her face. She looked less disheveled than he expected for someone who had been fighting the fire. Perhaps she had been helping somewhere farther away from the blaze.

"Oh!" she said. "You survived? How … fortunate." Her amazement faded quickly. She rubbed the pendant hanging from her neck and smiled politely. There was something in her tone that didn't sit right with Arracnoth, but the moment passed quickly as Danvaren embraced him again.

"I couldn't bear the thought of losing my brother and you both!"

"*Namartha t'undel*," Arracnoth said, and placed his forehead against Danvaren's.

As afternoon turned to evening, Arracnoth shared his thoughts about staying at The Pig & Lamb. Danvaren shook his head, saying that while Arracnoth had been at work last night, he and Questelle had located a small house on the southern side of the Blundt and had purchased it with some of the funds left by Avanstel. The home was unfurnished, save for a small bed and a chair, but Questelle urged Arracnoth to stay with them.

"It's not much, but we will be together," she said. "I think that's what we need tonight … to be together. Right?"

As much as Arracnoth appreciated the offer and would certainly find solace in the commiseration of their circumstances, he didn't want to inconvenience his friends. He desperately needed rest, and he was almost certain he could persuade Fert to rent him a room for the night for what coin he had left.

"I really think you should be here tonight," Questelle said. "With us. With Danvaren. So much has happened." She looked at him, pleading, her hand going to her neck.

He was about to surrender when Danvaren stepped in. "Let him go," he said. "Fert will give him a room. Avanstel always spoke highly of him. Let Arracnoth rest on a comfortable bed tonight at The Pig. We'll see him tomorrow."

Another quick frown crossed her face, but she shrugged. "Of course," she said. "We'll see you tomorrow."

Arracnoth nodded. Danvaren put a coin in his hand. "To cover expenses," he said. "We'll work out everything in the morn."

He attempted to return the coin to Danvaren, but before he could explain that he already possessed a Weode coin and had all he needed, Danvaren closed his hand around Arracnoth's. "Avanstel would want you to have it," he said. And that settled it.

Danvaren assured him they would come to visit him tomorrow at The Pig & Lamb. Together, they would plan what to do next. Questelle offered that there was a loft in the home that they could make into a place for Arracnoth, so the three of them could remain together.

Arracnoth smiled in agreement. That would be something to think about. They embraced farewell. Arracnoth was slow to break the embrace. Given all that had happened in the last two days, he had a sudden fear that this could be the last time he saw Danvaren … or Questelle. Finally, though, they said their goodbyes and headed off into the evening toward their respective destinations.

As he had hoped, Fert was happy to have more coin coming his way, and agreed to rent him a room. He even gave him a small discount – for a week's payment in advance, of course. Arracnoth was more than glad to pay. This would at least get him past his immediate needs.

He retired to his room and slid into the tepid bath that Caty had prepared for him. The dark ash fell off him, and the weariness of his soul seemed to dissolve along with it. He closed his eyes and leaned back, taking in the moment's comfort and grateful for the reprieve.

"Good evening, *sondartin*." The voice came from the shadowy corner of the room behind him.

Arracnoth did not startle; he was too tired to react. He had half-expected a visit from Nightfall, given their unfinished business. And he was getting used to the strange nether-elf's sudden appearances, manifesting from the shadows randomly.

"Nightfall," he said. He didn't turn around.

"A tragedy. I am most sorry, *sondartin*. For the fire, that is."

Arracnoth scooped a handful of water from the bath and ran it over his face. "The tragedy is for the other *ort* who lack the means for a comfortable bed and a warm bath tonight. They have nowhere to go now that the Hall is gone. I am lucky. At least I have a place to rest and rebuild my life, thanks to this … generous *gift* from your traveling companions." He raised an eyebrow, but there was no response from behind him. "I am alive. And so are Danvaren and Questelle. We will figure out what to do next."

"That's the reason I am here."

Arracnoth sighed, slid forward, and sunk his head beneath the water. He didn't want to hear what Nightfall was about to share with him. His world had changed too much, too rapidly. And whatever the nether-elf was about to reveal, he was fairly certain it would bring even more change. He wasn't ready for more. He wanted to return to the days before the strangers entered the tavern, before his world turned upside down.

He couldn't hold his breath any longer. He sat up in the tub, gasping. He turned to see if, by some miracle, Nightfall had dissolved back into the shadows. Golden eyes glinted back at him.

"I don't want to hear it," Arracnoth said flatly.

Nightfall leaned forward, his face coming into the light of the lantern sitting on the small table next to the bed. "*Sondartin*, aside from what my companions believe, what assurances your friend may have given you, I believe that *you* are still in earnest peril. That is why I have remained behind while my fellows have gone on ahead."

Arracnoth didn't respond.

"The events of last night … the fire … support my suspicions. It was no accident that the fire began on the third floor."

Arracnoth frowned. "What are you saying?"

Nightfall stood and produced a clean tunic from somewhere within the darkness of his black cloak. He extended it to Arracnoth. "There isn't much time, *sondartin*. It is important that we depart as soon as we can. By morning, at the very latest." His voice was profoundly serious, tinged with urgency. Although not demanding they leave immediately, he was certainly suggesting it. "We will rendezvous with your friend and my companions. The sooner we depart, the quicker we can rejoin them."

Arracnoth's heart leaped. "Avanstel? You know where he is?"

The *drivrid* nodded.

"You'll take me to him?"

"I will."

Arracnoth stood up, water streaming down his body and back into the grey pool beneath him as he wrung out his dark hair. He stepped out of the tub and reached out for the shirt. The fabric was smooth and fine, nicer than anything that he had worn before. It was an article of clothing whose purchase was beyond his means, or that of Adine, or of anyone he knew in Chark; it was something a wealthy merchant or local noble would own. He turned the cerulean fabric over in his hands, marveling at how soft it was before slipping it over his head. Nightfall offered a pair of accompanying travel trousers in navy dyed leather, as well as a dove grey hooded cape and new black leather boots, all just as fine and expertly crafted as the shirt.

Arracnoth dressed in silence, marveling at each new item he put on. When he finished, he took a moment to look at his reflection in the window. The well-dressed but slightly haunted visage that stared back at him was unrecognizable.

He turned to Nightfall and sighed. "I paid for a week. If I leave now, I am out the coin. I'm guessing that since you were able to secure such fine garments for me, that won't matter. Fert is the beneficiary of yet another windfall at my expense."

Nightfall smiled and bowed his head.

"I also assume you will explain this all to me. Why the urgency, and what is the danger?"

"All will indeed be explained."

"Good. Where are we going? Where is Avanstel headed?"

Nightfall handed Arracnoth one last item: the small blue pouch containing the grave-earth and the moonstone brooch.

"He is on his way to Ny'we Adye," he said. His eyes flashed. "To the capital of the Weode kingdom."

A shiver slid across Arracnoth's back, and the hair rose on his neck. His resolve to find and reunite with his friend faltered for a moment. This was indeed a serious and paramount situation if he and Avanstel were traveling to Ny'we Adye. That was a place where no *ort* was welcome. No human either. And certainly not a *drivrid*.

He absentmindedly placed the pouch on his belt, wondering what he had gotten himself into.

CHAPTER 6: INTRODUCTIONS

Nightfall had a horse stabled outside the city gates — fittingly, matching his cloak, it was a black mare. Their journey through the city in the dark had been uneventful, save for two patrols of the Chark guard they encountered. Strangely, the guards had not noticed them — or they had just ignored the two cloaked figures roaming the street past curfew. Getting over the wall had proven a little more difficult, at least for Arracnoth. Nimble as he was, was no match for the athleticism of the *drivrid*. They climbed the rope that Nightfall had left specifically for their escape and were soon saddling the horse.

"I will go by foot, *sondartin*," Nightfall said. "You can ride."

Arracnoth frowned. He had little experience in riding — just a few occasions when he had journeyed with Avanstel and Danvaren on hunting trips. He knew he would have trouble controlling the creature should she decide to bolt. And if she did, he would lose his new companion — and his guide to Ny'we Adye … and Avanstel.

"You can ride," Arracnoth said. "I can walk." He tried to sound nonchalant.

Nightfall raised an eyebrow and looked at him intently. After a beat, he climbed up into the saddle and reached out a hand. "We will both ride. The mare can hold two elves without trouble. I will sit in front of you. You sit behind me, so you can rest. You will need the sleep."

It sounded like a smart solution. He grabbed the *drivrid's* arm and ungracefully mounted the mare. Nightfall led the horse through the ramshackle outskirts of Chark, and they soon left the city behind them, riding off into the darkness and into the chilly spring night. The city eventually gave way to farmlands, which turned into wide open spaces with no sign of activity. The way became steeper as it wound around the cliffs surrounding Little Grencor Bay. As they continued, the sea fell away until it was far below them. The sound of the waves pounding against the cliffs and the steady movement of the horse beneath, combined with the exhaustion of the day, made him drowsy. He leaned forward against Nightfall, gripping his arms around the nether-elf tightly to steady himself, and fell asleep.

When he woke, the sun was rising. His body was stiff and sore, but he had had a surprisingly deep and peaceful night of sleep. He noted that Nightfall had put a strap around him sometime during the night to keep him on the horse, for which he was grateful. That would have been a harsh awakening! The *drivrid* directed the horse to a small copse of trees on the side of the road.

"Let's stretch our legs," he said. "We made good time overnight, and we are more than halfway to the river. The horse needs a rest." He clicked his tongue, and the horse stopped. "Are you hungry? I have provisions."

"Yes," Arracnoth said. He dismounted from the horse. As soon as he put his weight on his leg, it gave way beneath him, and he grabbed the mare to steady himself before he fell backward.

"Are you ill, *sondartin*?"

"No," Arracnoth answered, "just very sore. I have never been this far from Chark." He forced a smile. "How many days' ride is it?"

"Six to the Wood, if there's no trouble and the weather continues in our favor. Five if we press hard." Nightfall opened a saddlebag and withdrew a turnip and a hunk of salted pork. He offered them to Arracnoth. "And then another four to the capital. We might catch our companions by the morrow if we continue at this pace. I asked them to travel slowly – but to be wary, as there is a risk to Avanstel. I am sure that you are eager to speak with him."

Arracnoth accepted the canteen offered to him and took a big swallow of cider. It was tart but refreshing. "We can continue. I'm fine with the pace."

"This is hard for you." It was a statement, not a question.

"Not at all," Arracnoth replied. He was lying, but he wanted to reunite with Avanstel as quickly as possible. This entire affair was strange and uncomfortable. Having Avanstel by his side would not only ease his worry but would also help to prove that trusting the *drivrid* wasn't a mistake. He was uneasy and tired, and found himself dependent entirely on the word of this stranger. A *drivrid* – whose mere existence had been the stuff of legends just days ago.

Nightfall shrugged. "We will continue then."

They stopped once more as the sun was dropping low in the sky behind them. Ahead lay a small hamlet on the edge of Cedar Creek. A sturdy bridge provided travelers with a means to cross the rushing waters, and the road continued eastward. They dismounted, and Nightfall handed Arracnoth the reins.

"Go into town," he said. "Give the horse to the groomer and fetch supplies. My presence would draw too much attention." He pressed some coins into his hand.

Arracnoth laughed. "I'm an *ort*. Do you think the humans will welcome me?"

"It would not be easy for either of us. Still …"

"I'll go." He was used to brushing up against the prejudice and ridicule of humans. And Nightfall was right – an *ort* might pass through with little notice, but a *drivrid* would cause quite a stir.

The nether-elf slid away from the road and into the shadowy brush, leaving Arracnoth alone. He took the reins of the horse and led it into the town. He located the stables and negotiated a price with the owner to refresh the mare. The price seemed high to him, but since he had little experience with horses, he wasn't sure if it was the standard price, or if it included an *ort*-only tax.

With the mare taken care of, Arracnoth made his way toward the local shops to refresh their provisions. He paused for a moment in the center of the bridge. Stepping to the side, he watched the water rushing below him, marveling at how far it had come and where it was going. The spring rain and melting snow from the surrounding lands fed the river as it made its way across the plains and down to the bay. He had heard stories of a tall, beautiful waterfall where the river met the sea and cascaded over a high cliff. He wished that their route would allow him a chance to see the falls, but it was several hours north of the hamlet, across the flatlands, and the road they were on led east toward Faber … towards Ny'we Adye and Avanstel.

He made his way to the shops. The baker gave him a side-eye when he realized he was *ort*, but he refrained from any comments or disparaging remarks. Although the other merchants were polite, none of them were overly friendly. It was what he expected from the humans. Although the original reason for the hatred had long been forgotten, the prejudice remained – centuries, even millennia, later.

Some humans, like Fert and Caty and Whitley, were kinder than most – and Arracnoth was grateful for that – but he didn't expect it. He had assumed that since the hamlet was closer to Belkin Wood, there would be more *ort* here, but he didn't encounter others. If there were others of his kind here, their presence hadn't altered the humans' attitude toward *ort*. The humans he met had a similar disposition to those in Chark.

After purchasing the required food, he headed back to fetch the mare. Her dark coat glistened; she had been cared for well. He paid the stable manager, packed the provisions into the saddlebags, and led the horse out of the barn and over the bridge, heading eastward. As he strolled, he took notice of the families going about their business – preparing evening meals, caring for their animals, and doing other farmland chores. It was a quaint and peaceful place, but it soon faded behind him as he progressed down the road.

The sun had fallen, and the sky was lit with hues of red, orange, and purple. He continued past the edge of the village and began down the road through the surrounding fields, looking thoughtfully at the idyllic homes speckled across the landscape. Lanterns were being lit inside them. He mused that perhaps some of these farmers had been his customers at The Pig & Lamb just a few days ago – before his world was upended.

Nightfall appeared out of nowhere and fell into step beside him. It was becoming so commonplace that Arracnoth was no longer surprised by it. "Everything well?" he inquired.

"As well as can be," Arracnoth replied.

They walked together in silence for a while longer before Nightfall motioned to a small, faint trail that branched from the main road. He took the reins from Arracnoth.

"We will go this way tonight."

"But I thought that the main road went through Belkin Wood?"

"It does. But we will take this route. We don't want to enter Belkin via the usual ways. It is too dangerous to do so. And the others have gone this way."

Arracnoth shrugged. Nightfall had plans, and Arracnoth had to either agree with them or turn back to Chark. Trusting the elf meant he had a chance of reuniting with Avanstel; his other option wouldn't lead where he wanted to go. And there was also the danger of turning back and facing whatever danger existed back in Chark.

He waited for Nightfall to mount the mare, grabbed his proffered arm, and fell into place behind him. He again fell asleep remarkably fast, wondering in the split second before consciousness slid from him why they had not camped for the night … and just how long a *drivrid* could go without sleep.

Arracnoth woke pre-dawn, and like the previous night, was resting against Nightfall with a strap around him. He felt less sore and stiff than the day before. Their horse plodded ever forward, nickering softly as she picked up the scent of smoke moments before Arracnoth did. Ahead on the horizon, a dark triangular shadow appeared against the dim light of the sky. "Where are we?"

"That is the Mountain of Woes. Our companions have made camp ahead. From the smell of it, they are preparing breakfast."

Arracnoth's stomach grumbled. They hadn't eaten after leaving the river hamlet, and the smells coming from the cookfire before them were heavenly. Several more minutes passed before they rounded the bend and descended to the small riverbank camp. Two figures at the fire stood up as they came near. One was the bearded stranger Arracnoth had served in The Pig & Lamb, and the other –

"Avanstel!"

Arracnoth dismounted as fast as he could manage, slightly less awkwardly than the previous day, but still without much grace. Avanstel was there to catch him, with a powerful embrace.

"Arracnoth!" He was grinning from ear to ear, but his smile faded quickly. "You shouldn't have come." He looked at Nightfall, brows creasing. "Why did you bring him? It's not safe."

"It was necessary. Let me explain."

The bearded man stepped forward, interrupting the conversation. He clasped arms with Nightfall. "Greetings, friend. Come, let's eat before the food gets cold. We have prepared enough for all of us. We can talk while we fill our stomachs with Merce's blessings!" He made a sound, like the whistle of a bird, and the tall stranger with the scarred face and raven hair stepped out from the bushes to their right.

"Friend," the man said in his thick accent, clasping forearms with Nightfall in the same fashion as the bearded one.

Arracnoth followed Nightfall and Avanstel to the campsite. Nightfall perched on stone near the fire and offered Arracnoth a drink from his canteen. As soon as he had finished drinking, the bearded man handed him a plate of eggs and bread. The others took their places around the fire, and they began to eat as the sun peeked above the horizon, illuminating the surrounding landscape.

As he ate, Arracnoth marveled at the enormous, singular mountain that rose in front of them. There were no other mountains or hills around, just the one gargantuan peak that rose out of the flatlands, taller than anything Arracnoth had ever seen. It looked out of place, as if it had fallen accidentally from the pouch of Enos, the god of creation, when he set the foundations of the world. It was so tall that clouds obscured the top.

Nightfall followed his gaze. "Some say there's a city up there, above the clouds."

"Q'Serath. I've heard the stories."

The *drivrid* nodded and took a drink from his canteen. "And below the mountain, the underworld of Caerbexsys."

"Is there truth to the tales? I thought they were all just fables … but I also thought that the *drivrid* were just something mothers made up to encourage their children to behave. I've learned differently."

Nightfall laughed. "Indeed, *sondartin*. I can tell you for certain that both the *drivrid* and Caerbexsys are real! The underworld was my home for over a century before I came to live among the surface dwellers. As far as Q'Serath …" He shrugged and exchanged a look with the raven-haired giant, who shook his head in response and shoved a piece of bread into his mouth.

"Where are my manners. I'm sorry that I haven't introduced you to my companions." He nodded at the bearded man. "This is Hathar, Faithful Brother of Merces."

"Greetings. It is good to have you along with us, Arracnoth. We welcome you."

The nether-elf motioned at the tall, muscular man with the dark skin and scar. "And this is Scorpio."

The warrior nodded politely, but remained silent.

"We are fortunate to have them with us," Avanstel said. He put his arm around Arracnoth's shoulders. "We will need their help."

"How so?" Arracnoth asked.

Avanstel paused, looking at the trio for permission to speak. Hathar nodded. Avanstel drew a deep breath. "I am sure you will have many questions, Arrac. I did myself. And if it were my choice, we would both be back at the Hall with Danvaren and Questelle." He chuckled and pushed at Arracnoth playfully. "And I would be claiming another victory against you in a game of Haven Chase."

"Unlikely," Arracnoth said. He chuckled.

Avanstel suddenly grew serious. "Even more unlikely …" He paused, and Arracnoth could see he wasn't sure where to start. Avanstel opened his mouth to say something but changed his mind. Arracnoth waited, growing more curious as time passed.

"You see …" Avanstel stammered. "It's like this …" He paused again. "Well, let me just … I know it sounds mad, but … they … Hathar, Scorpio, and Nightfall … they think, and maybe they are right, but … they think I am heir to the throne of Ni'Ilyan." He took another deep breath. "I am the next White Wolf." His brows wrinkled as he looked at Arracnoth.

Arracnoth stared at Avanstel incredulously, at a loss for words. "How …?"

"As our new friends tell me, it is a well-kept secret, known only to those in the innermost circles of the Weode royal palace. Supposedly, the Ade Gerent, the ruler of the Weode, sired a child thirty-six cycles ago. They claim the woman was herself a noble, who gave her child to her maid to raise."

He paused, looking at Hathar, who nodded for him to continue.

"The maid left the service of the lady and hid among the families of the Blundt to raise the child."

Arracnoth closed his eyes, processing the information. The story didn't sound all that remarkable. It was a common occurrence – Weode who sired children with human women and left them to fend for themselves. But why would they think Avanstel was any different from any other *ort* child?

"You have a brother, Van. And your mother was poor, just like mine. Wouldn't a noble lady have the means to care for her child?"

"Allegedly, my real mother fled to the Norlands, and no one has heard from her since. And allegedly, the woman who raised me, the maid whom I called mother, took in another *ort* child a couple cycles later – Danvaren. She told everyone we had the same parents to help further her disguise. I always thought Danvaren was my natural brother; however, I remember whispers from my childhood that made no sense then. And just look at us – if we had the same parents, don't you think there would be more similarities between us? I had always pushed those things aside and dismissed them as coincidence because I didn't really want to delve into them any further. When Hathar shared his tale with me, those things came back, and now they make sense in the light of his revelation. What he, what they all believe, answers a lot of questions from my childhood."

He took a drink and finished the piece of bread on his plate, waiting for Arracnoth to work through the information he had shared.

"But if you really are the true heir, why would you be in danger? Wouldn't the Ade send his soldiers to protect you? You would be royalty!"

"There's also many who would want to see me quietly disappear," Avanstel said. "Which is why I had to leave under cover of night and with such haste."

Nightfall cleared his throat, and Avanstel looked at him. "Indeed, *sondartin*. Fire destroyed your lodging just two nights past."

Avanstel glanced at Arracnoth for confirmation, concern flashing over his face. Arracnoth nodded. "Danvaren and Questelle are safe. They are following your instructions in the letter you left."

Avanstel relaxed. "But why did you come, then, Arrac? Why not stay with them and stay in safety?"

Arracnoth looked at Nightfall, who answered, "He is here at my urging. With your lodgings destroyed, I was concerned for your friend. His love for you is strong. It would have been only a brief time before he set out looking for you on his own, and that would put him in even greater danger. I know what he means to you, so I offered to bring him to you directly instead. It reduces the risk to you both."

That wasn't exactly how Arracnoth recalled the events of the night at The Pig & Lamb, but not that terribly far off, either. He wanted to find Avanstel, and he would have sought him on his own, eventually. That much was true.

Avanstel thought for a moment. "There is significant risk for you if you continue on with me," he said. "But there is also risk for you if you return to the Blundt. And my heart has indeed been heavy since leaving you and the others."

He motioned to Hathar and Scorpio. "And although my new allies are adequate conversationalists ... well at least you are,

Hathar." Hathar laughed. Scorpio said nothing. "It would indeed ease my mind, and comfort me to have you here by my side."

"Even were you to send me away, I would refuse to go!" Arracnoth laughed. He looked at Avanstel somberly. "I am beside you."

Avanstel patted him on the back, the smile returning to his face. "I saved this," he said. He reached into a pocket in his cloak and withdrew something. He opened his hand in front of them. The black quill marker from their Haven Chase gameboard rested in his palm.

Arracnoth smiled. "I noticed," he replied. He reached into his cloak and pulled out the white sword token and showed it to Avanstel. "I saved this one for you."

The five of them packed up what little belongings they had and set off again toward Ny'we Adye. Avanstel had his own mount, which had been provided by Nightfall on the night they had left the city. Unlike Arracnoth, Avanstel was skilled at horse riding, having worked for a time at a stable in his youth. Arracnoth opted to ride with Avanstel after being reassured that Nightfall would not take offense.

"Of course, *sondartin*. I would expect as much. I will circle back and do what I can to cover our tracks. I will catch up with you by evening. Hathar and Scorpio will keep you safe."

They forded the river where it was shallow and headed south towards the Mountain of Woes. Arracnoth wasn't looking forward to another long day on horseback, but being with Avanstel made the journey much more bearable. He didn't really care where they were going, as long as they were going together.

CHAPTER 7: GROUNDLING

It was evening when the party found themselves deep in the mountain's shadow. The pace had been slower today than the days before, which was a welcome change, but Arracnoth was hungry and ready to stretch his legs. He had spent the day talking with Avanstel over his shoulder about all that had happened to them and discussing what might lie ahead.

"What do you think he will be like – the Ade, your father?"

"I don't know, really." There was a shift in his tone that surprised Arracnoth. The good-natured and jovial companion of his youth was becoming more serious. An unexpected change in the brief time they had been apart. Arracnoth knew that leaving Danvaren behind, and the possibility of what might lie ahead, weighed heavily on his friend.

"Do you think Ny'we Adye is as big as Chark?"

"I imagine it's bigger. But without a harbor, of course. Hathar tells me they have an entire army there."

"Will the Weode welcome you? You might be the heir, but you are *ort*."

Avanstel took a moment to answer. His hesitation spoke volumes. "I'm not sure."

Arracnoth knew his friend well enough to read the pause before the words. Avanstel was concerned about what awaited him in Ny'we Adye. And about whether the Weode would accept him. "Well, they'd be stupid *not* to welcome you, Van. You'll make a fantastic king someday!"

"I hope so. I will do my best."

"If anyone could do it, it's you. I have no doubt."

Avanstel looked over his shoulder at Arracnoth. "Your faith in me means a lot, Arrac. More than I can say. I am glad you came, even though I told you not to." He winked.

As they rounded a large outcrop, Hathar signaled for them to stop as he continued forward alone. Ahead, they could see the glow of lights from the windows of a small building. Smoke emanated from the chimney and filled the evening air with the smell of burning wood and roasting meat.

They had passed no other dwellings or people on their journey that day. To come upon a lone homestead in the middle of nowhere was odd, and a bit unsettling. Hathar made his way back towards them, motioning for them to remain silent.

Scorpio slid from the back of his horse in one fluid motion and disappeared into the darkness.

As his horse came up beside them, Hathar leaned over and whispered. "We are where Nightfall said we should be, but he did not mention a dwelling. We will wait here for Scorpio to check it out and return."

Arracnoth looked to both sides and glanced back the way they had come, half expecting to see someone coming up from behind them. Although he couldn't make out much in the fading light, he thought he heard the snort of a horse not too far away. Avanstel must have heard it too; Arracnoth felt him tense and turn his head to the side.

Hathar dismounted. He made his way back down the trail they had just come from, removing the large maul he carried across his back. He swung the immense hammer with ease in a display that impressed Arracnoth. He wouldn't want to be on the receiving end of one of those swings! The cleric took a defensive stance, crouching and bracing for an attack.

Arracnoth suddenly felt exposed, sitting atop the horse with Avanstel while their warrior companions had gone in opposite directions. He looked at Avanstel and gestured that they should dismount, but Avanstel shook his head.

The sound of a bird taking flight sounded in the distance and startled him.

Hathar instantly relaxed and swung his hammer once before placing it back into position on his back. He cupped his hands over his mouth and made a sound similar to that of a quail flying. At the sound, Nightfall emerged from the gloom and approached Hathar. The two exchanged whispers and gestured towards the house. Arracnoth couldn't hear what they were discussing, but he could see Hathar nod and smile. The cleric cupped his hands once again and made a whistling sound. It echoed back to them from somewhere in the darkness ahead.

Nightfall pulled his horse up alongside the *ort*.

"Rest easy, *sondartins*. I know this place and the woman who lives here. I trust her, and you can also. She will have food and drink for us and will aid us on our journey."

Arracnoth let out a breath. Avanstel did the same.

Scorpio appeared beside them. "A child," he said, frowning. "Or maybe a very short woman. A groundling?"

"Her name is Arial Stonesplitter," Nightfall answered. "She's an ally of mine from the time before. I will speak with her. I'm sure she knows we are here, and we are fortunate that she has not already sent her arrows after you. She's not used to visitors."

Nightfall strode purposefully toward the small house nestled at the foot of the magnificent mountain. Arracnoth watched him disappear again. He looked up at the inky blackness ahead of them, the dark silhouette of the mount looming overhead. Clouds still shrouded the top, which was unfathomably high above them. He wondered if the stories were true about a city among the clouds. Why not? He had always thought the *drivrid* weren't real, and the groundlings hadn't been seen for centuries. Why couldn't there be a city above the clouds, too?

They heard a whistle. Hathar led the horses toward the small building. Scorpio followed behind them. As they neared the cabin, they could make out the shape of Nightfall and another short figure silhouetted against the warm light coming from the open doorway.

Nightfall and the others exchanged greetings as Arracnoth and Avanstel dismounted. Much to his surprise, he was able to get off the horse without making a fool of himself. Perhaps he was getting the hang of riding horses after all.

"And this is Avanstel and Arracnoth, our *ort* friends." Nightfall said, motioning at the two of them.

Arracnoth tried to mask his surprise as the diminutive woman greeted him. She was the height of a child but was clearly an adult. Her aged and weathered face had faint whiskers, like a man. She wore a patch over one eye, her other eye sparkling blue as she grinned up at him.

"First time seeing a groundling?" she asked. Her voice was full of mirth. "Most haven't. Most never will." She motioned to her doorway. "Welcome. Come in! Friends of Nightfall are welcome. May you find rest and comfort beneath my roof." Her accent was strange, but he understood what she was saying. Her voice, though gruff and graveled, had a singsong quality to it, almost melodic. Despite her odd appearance, Arracnoth felt immediately at ease.

"Come, come." Arial turned, motioning them inside. The five of them funneled into the small house. "I have some rabbit roasting, just caught today, and a loaf here of hard bread … which isn't so bad when you wash it down with some *drekannen*. And I've got plenty of that for all! Several batches I made last cycle and it's just now ready for drinking."

Nightfall motioned for them to sit at the table. The furniture was low to the ground, fashioned for the owner of the house, not five giant-sized men. Hathar sat down first. Avanstel followed his lead and managed to half-sit, half-squat into the small chair. Arracnoth seated himself with ease, looking sideways at Avanstel and hiding a smile. Scorpio remained standing at the doorway, his head tilted slightly to avoid hitting the ceiling. Arracnoth chuckled to himself; it would have been a sight to see the giant try to squeeze himself into one of the child-sized chairs.

Arial produced meat from the spit, bread, and cups filled with *drekannen*. Arracnoth had never heard of the drink before. It wasn't something that was ever served at The Pig & Lamb. He watched Avanstel break off a piece of bread, put it in his mouth, and then take a big swallow from his cup. He smiled, seeming to like the drink. Arracnoth took a swig of the liquid. *Drekannen* seemed similar to mead in its sweetness, but also had a dark, earthy aftertaste that was unlike anything he had had before. He liked it too. He took another bite of the bread. When he reached for his cup, he discovered their host had already refilled it.

"Thank you for your hospitality, Arial," Nightfall said. "But let's hold on more *drekannen*. I have just arrived here and have news to share with my friends. We will need clear heads tonight!"

Arracnoth took a bite of the rabbit. It was succulent. He considered it might be even better than Caty's cooking and wondered where Arial had learned to make such delicious drinks and meat. Fert would give a silver a night to have someone like Arial in his kitchen.

"What news, Nightfall?" Hathar said between bites. He offered some rabbit to the nether-elf, who declined.

"As we anticipated, we are being followed. Our attempt to leave the road and travel on other paths didn't work to throw off our pursuers. They must also have knowledge of the less frequented routes to Ny'we Adye."

"That's not good news," Hathar replied.

"There's more." The *drivrid* cleared his throat. "I'm afraid they are but an hour or two behind us – at most. My attempts to disguise our trail were of no avail."

Scorpio made a noise that sounded like a growl. He turned to look out the window, scanning the darkness for any signs of their pursuers.

"We should go immediately," Hathar said, standing and motioning toward the door. "We have no time to wait. We can't let Avanstel …"

"Or Arracnoth," Nightfall interjected.

"Right." Hathar looked at Arracnoth and shrugged. "Apologies, friend."

"We must keep *both* of the *ort* orphans safe," Nightfall said.

Arial coughed, choking on her drink. When she cleared her throat, she looked at the nether-elf. "Nightfall? Did you say orphans?"

He motioned dismissively. "Let us speak of the Arcana Sephyrie at a different time, friend."

She nodded and took another drink from her cup, staring at Avanstel, then at Arracnoth, and then back at Avanstel. The silence grew awkward.

Hathar cleared his throat. "We must not allow either of our new friends to be endangered. Our oath and our pledge."

"Agreed," Nightfall said.

Avanstel shoved the last piece of hard bread into his mouth and drained his cup. "Then we go. We will ride all night if we must."

"Please, *sondartin*. Let's not be hasty. We won't be able to outrun our adversaries. They know the route we would take into the forest, and they have tracked us – and gained on us – despite our precautions. I am concerned that they will overtake us unless we alter our strategy. Our mounts have had little rest, and we would require fresh and swift rides to stand a chance at outdistancing them on horseback tonight."

Hathar paced the floor, frowning. He spun around and looked at Nightfall. "Surely you are not considering ..."

"There may be no other way, my friend."

Scorpio now turned his attention from the window and looked at Nightfall. "It is very dangerous," the warrior said.

"There is none here, save for Arial, who knows the dangers more than I. But it is a path that our adversaries will definitely not take. There is little doubt about that. I remember the routes and hidden ways. I see no other option."

Arial placed her small hand on Nightfall's arm, a look of concern on her face. "Are you certain?"

Hathar looked down at the floor, lost in deep thought, and resumed pacing. He combed his fingers through his beard nervously.

When several moments had passed with no additional explanation, Avanstel exploded. "What are you all talking about?" He looked at Hathar and Scorpio, then at Nightfall.

"The Shadow Gate," Nightfall said. "Entrance to Caerbexsys. Descent."

A shiver ran up Arracnoth's spine. Caerbexsys? Was there no other way than to travel through the underworld of Halbrun?

Legends described Caerbexsys as a place of eternal darkness and dread; a haunted place populated with ghosts and undead, and thousands of other frightening things that slithered and crawled on many legs through the blackness with their cloudy white eyes – or no eyes at all. Arracnoth recalled tales from his childhood of strange creatures from the underworld who would come to the surface in the night and feast on misbehaving children. It was "where the evil dwells." Should one be so unfortunate as to find themselves there, death was ever at one's heels, chasing farther and farther down.

Chasing you towards the very center of the world and getting you lost forever in the labyrinth of caverns below the surface.

And the Shadow Gate – an ancient and massive portal, created by an unknown race who had long passed from the face of Halbrun – was the most infamous doorway to all the horrors below. The fortress, built into the side of the Mountain of Woes on either side of the gate, was said to be haunted by all those souls who had lost their lives in the torturous building of those primeval gates. It was also said to be a gathering place for the souls of all who had perished in Caerbexsys. Stories told of tortured shades that roamed the place to warn others and prevent them from sharing their fate. Many bards sang songs about the Shadow Gate and those who dared to enter it. People well knew that those who ventured beyond it never returned – alive, at least. Nothing living ever escaped Caerbexsys.

But …

Then there was Nightfall. A *drivrid*, a creature that shouldn't exist. And Arial – a groundling whose people had disappeared three hundred cycles ago. So much he knew of this world had already been proven wrong.

Hathar turned to Nightfall. "I dislike it, but I see no other way."

Scorpio nodded silently.

"I would also prefer to not return to those damned realms. But we have little choice if we are to keep our friends safe," Nightfall said.

"And you can navigate us successfully?" Hathar asked.

"Yes." Nightfall turned to Arial. "Those who dwelled for centuries in the darkness have difficulty escaping the memories of those times … even when they would like to." She squeezed his arm and smiled sadly.

"The Gate will take us down. I will lead us back out. There is egress to the surface within Belkin itself. A half-day from Ny'we Adye. Weode may guard the exit, but we have a better chance of navigating that encounter than taking the risk with what pursues us."

"Arial, friend, should we linger, you may find yourself in danger also. We will depart now and make our way to the Gate. Will you go with us that far? Good. I would ask one more favor. If you take our horses and ride on toward Belkin Wood, it may help to convince our pursuers that we have continued on the expected route. Once they have passed, you can then circle back safely. And, of course, our mounts would be yours to keep, as an expression of our gratitude."

"Of course, Nightfall," she said. "But are you sure about returning to Caerbexsys? I know you don't propose this without weighing all options, but it's not without its own set of dangers. Regardless, whatever I can do to help, I will do it for you and your companions."

"A loyal friend," he said and patted her hand that rested on his arm. "Come all, we must make one last push tonight to the Shadow Gate. Once we cross over, we can seek whatever rest our thoughts allow us. I'm confident no one will follow us beyond the great dark doors. They would be fools to do so."

Hathar and Scorpio fetched the horses. Arial began making a ruckus as she opened and closed cupboards, looking for items she could provide to them to help make the journey to the underworld less burdensome.

Arracnoth swallowed hard and looked at Avanstel. His face was grim. "What danger I have put you in, Arrac? I never ..." His voice broke. He closed his eyes.

Arracnoth took his friend's shoulders and placed his forehead on Avanstel's. "*Namartha t'undel.*"

Avanstel echoed the words back to him, though his voice sounded far away.

CHAPTER 8: DESCENT

The songs and stories about the Shadow Gate did not exaggerate. It was as dark, foreboding, and haunted as the tales had made it out to be. As the party drew nearer to the massive structure, Arracnoth felt his skin prickle and his heart race. He fought against the unreasonable urge to jump off the horse and flee in the opposite direction, which pecked at his brain incessantly. Or was it so unreasonable, after all? It seemed the only logical choice. Get out and get out fast. It was hard to think of anything else.

He could feel Avanstel's shoulders, seated in front of him, grow tense as their horse continued the march forward.

"I don't like it, Van," he whispered. His voice sounded too loud against the stillness.

"I don't either, Arrac. But I trust the others. If they say there's no other way, then …" He didn't need to continue. They truly were out of other options. Still … maybe those who followed them weren't as bad as what was ahead of them.

Someone, or something, had carved the Shadow Gate from the volcanic stone of the mountain – shaping it from the sharp, cragged surface. Two monumental towers jutted from the black rock to either side of the dark gate. They were constructed of massive blocks taller than the height of two men. The gate was a giant opening, hewn from the same stone – a hundred feet tall and just as wide – spanning the space between the towers. The structure altogether was larger than anything Arracnoth had ever seen. While the towers were crude and geometric, with strong angles and flat planes, the gate looked as if it was created by a different artisan – perhaps centuries later … or earlier. The surface of the gate was decorated with thousands of images, symbols, and words from a long-forgotten language. Arracnoth could make out dark and serpentine shapes, faces of creatures that were unknown to him – perhaps unknown anywhere in all the world of Naveis Orthea. Whatever they were, they looked terrifying. Although his logical mind knew they were just carvings, the other part of his brain was convinced the creatures could come alive at any moment and devour him. There was an air of something unnatural and unsettling about the entire place.

"Easy," Avanstel said. Arracnoth wasn't sure if he was attempting to reassure their horse, or if he was hinting that Arracnoth should stop clutching his waist so tightly. Arracnoth relaxed his grip, but found that a moment later, he had tensed again. The area just emanated dread – the kind that you knew made little sense but still gripped your heart with fear.

"*Sere'eden. Sere'eden,*" he repeated over and over again, trying to find the peace and calmness that Adine had taught him to seek. It wasn't working.

Ahead, Nightfall stopped his horse and motioned for them to dismount. "The horses won't go much further. They will throw us and bolt if we push any closer. We will go the rest of the way on foot."

Arracnoth forced himself off the horse but couldn't pull his eyes away from the Shadow Gate. He clutched the saddle, unable to release his grip.

"I'll take the horse," Hathar said, removing Arracnoth's hands gently. He guided the horse over to Arial, who remained astride Nightfall's black mare.

Nightfall reached up and grasped the groundling's arm. "Thank you, old friend. Ride on toward Belkin Wood. Should we succeed in our venture, I will send you word."

Arial grimaced. "You better, dark elf! Or I'll follow you back down into that cursed realm to find your ass and haul you back out!"

Nightfall chuckled.

"Before you go, elf," she said, "I have a gift for your patron … the third volume. I got it a while back in a trade with some of the remnant. I'm sure it will please him to add it to his collection. Perhaps you will read it also and we can discuss it next time we see each other." She glanced over at Avanstel and Arracnoth again, then handed him a small book with a shining silver cover. The unrecognizable creatures carved into the surface reminded Arracnoth of the forms on the Shadow Gate. He wondered if the same person made them both. The *drivrid* slipped it into his tunic without saying more.

Nightfall patted his horse. Arial pulled the mare to the east and kicked, urging her forward. The horse was all too eager to head in any direction that was away from the Shadow Gate. The other horses followed without hesitation. The party watched for a moment until they could no longer make out the horses in the darkness.

Nightfall turned to the others. "Brace yourself. Ancient and powerful magic enchants the Gate. You sense it even now, right?"

Arracnoth nodded and swallowed. His eyes darted to the dark shapes and the towers.

"The disquiet you feel now will grow stronger as we approach it. But once we get past the gate, it will diminish. It will take firm resolve to overcome the panic that will invade your mind and heart. But it *can* be done. I've done it before."

"Who built this place?" Arracnoth asked.

"Unknown," Hathar said. "But it is an infernal place, and I am loath to be here, and reluctant to get closer. Everything within me screams that there is peril ahead. We should be ready to fight."

Nightfall looked at his companions and scowled. "You won't find a battle here, cleric — save for a war against your own will." He turned to Arracnoth and Avanstel. "He is right — no one knows who built the Gate, in what Age, or for what purpose. Some say that it is to keep the creatures of the underworld contained, while others — my people among them — say it is to protect the nether realm from invaders above. Regardless of intent, it has kept the worlds separated. Although there are other routes to the underworld that are far less formidable, this is the only option we have at the moment. There is no other way to escape those that pursue us, and our purposes are of such significance that we cannot risk failure. We must press on."

Nightfall stepped toward the Shadow Gate. He paused after a few steps and looked back at them to confirm they were following. Arracnoth forced his feet to take one step after the other. The *drivrid* continued forward. The ground turned flat and hard. Arracnoth looked down. He could make out black stone pavers broken by brown and dying vegetation. Perhaps the lost civilization that created this place hadn't intended it to be such a desolate and frightening place, and it had merely fallen into disrepair.

He looked up at the massive stone doors, which had grown larger with every step. He could discern more details of the carvings now: serpents, skulls with fire in their eyes, wicked fanged creatures winding around empty skeletons, leathery winged beasts. Arracnoth thought he could perceive a faint red glow emanating from the stone, but he wasn't sure if that was his imagination, or a trick of the moonlight. He clutched the knife at his side instinctively.

Despite Nightfall's reassurance that the danger was only in his mind, he felt certain that something evil lay ahead, waiting in ambush. Behind him, he heard the faint hiss of Scorpio's sword sliding from its scabbard. This place unnerved even the brawny fighter.

"Cursed place!" Hathar said. His voice echoed unnaturally loudly around them. Arracnoth realized that the sounds of the night had disappeared. The hum of crickets had ceased, and even the wind had become still. It was silent, save for the rhythmic noise of their ever-slowing footfalls and the occasional scrape of a boot across the rocky ground.

Ahead, he heard Nightfall's voice, though he could not make out the words. The *drivrid* raised his arm above his head. In his hand, he gripped a large crystal. A faint, cold, white light radiated from it, casting sharp shadows around them that danced as he moved.

"This way," the elf said, and pointed toward the southernmost tower.

The path would lead them directly in front of the macabre stone doors with their frightening images. Arracnoth wiped the sweat from his forehead with his shaking hands and steeled himself, glancing once again at the horrific visages.

Avanstel stepped up beside him. "We'll go together, Arrac."

Arracnoth nodded. Each step toward the massive wall became a contest of wills. He felt Avanstel tug on his arm and realized that he had stopped moving forward – frozen in his tracks. Arracnoth concentrated and forced his feet to move.

They proceeded in this way, silently, for what felt like hours. The air was heavy around them. With every step, their limbs became harder to move. They made their way carefully past the enormous doors with their foreboding images, taking turns encouraging each other to keep moving.

He made the mistake of looking up at the Gate once. An enormous six-legged creature loomed over him. The face was draconic, with sharp, vicious teeth and massive, leathery wings that stretched out behind it. The eyes seemed to glow red, and he could almost feel the hot breath of the creature breathing down on him. A pile of withered corpses lay beneath the creature's massive claws. Their empty, dark eyes stared at him, mouths agape in silent screams carved into the stone. He shuddered again, closed his eyes, and stepped forward, making a note to avoid glancing at the Shadow Gate again.

Eventually, they reached the tower on the other side. Although they had made their way past the grimacing and gruesome images, the dread had not left him. He couldn't get the vision of those black, soulless eyes and the terrifying creature out of his mind. It was burned into his brain.

"We are almost there," Nightfall said.

Arracnoth was relieved, but his relief was short-lived when he noted that there was no entrance to the tower and that the openings – they couldn't quite be called windows – were far above them, unreachable. How would they get past? If they were required to turn back and cross in front of the Gate to find another way through, Arracnoth wasn't sure he would be able to force himself to do so. Once past the gate was more than enough.

As if sensing his doubt, Nightfall motioned to a large, craggy stone that stood between the tower and the doorway. It looked like a fallen piece of the structure that loomed over them. Smaller rocks lay strewn about the base, fragments from the impact. The rubble stood in sharp contrast to the flat and dead ground they had just traversed. Nightfall stopped and held his crystal higher, and the stark shadows cast by its cold light slid across the face of the stone. Arracnoth noticed a darker shadow that did not move along with the others, mostly hidden by fallen pieces of the tower. The nether-elf gestured for the group to keep moving. They advanced around the large block. No one spoke for fear that their words would disturb something – or someone – that was better left sleeping.

The shadow turned out to be a large cleft in the tower's face, about four feet off the ground, hidden from view and seemingly undiscoverable, except by those who had knowledge of its existence. Avanstel paused. Nightfall gestured for him to enter the fissure, but the young *ort* hesitated. Scorpio stepped past Hathar and Arracnoth. Coming to the front of the group, he touched Avanstel's shoulder, motioning for him to step aside. He then clambered up to the dark entrance and disappeared inside. They waited a moment in silence, the pale white light making their faces appear ghostly as they exchanged glances.

Scorpio appeared from the opening and signaled for them to follow. Avanstel climbed up the rock and melted into the darkness. Arracnoth and the others followed suit.

They felt their way forward along the rough walls. The dim light of Nightfall's crystal danced around them. After a while, the walls became smooth, and Scorpio paused. The sound of their steps sounded different. Arracnoth sensed, more than he saw, that they had emerged from the tunnel and had entered a large room. As Nightfall stepped into the space, his light crystal revealed a little more of their location. Arracnoth could discern only a few details of the chamber because the illumination from the crystal fell off unnaturally quickly, leaving much of the place to remain in shadow.

He made out dim shapes that looked like a table and a couple of chairs … maybe a bed, and some crates. The *drivrid* strode across the room, wordlessly taking the lead, and heading for a hole in the wall that had once been a doorway. The remnants of the door lay on the floor. Avanstel glanced back at Arracnoth and then followed Nightfall through the doorway.

On the other side was a stairwell. To the left, a staircase climbed upwards into what he assumed was the rest of the tower. To the right, Nightfall's faint white light was rapidly fading where the stairs curved and descended downward. Knowing that Nightfall was leading them toward Caerbexsys made following the light less appealing than it otherwise would be. But staying here was not an option. They followed him downward.

The stairs ended at a landing every fifty steps or so. At each landing, dark and forbidding tunnels lead off to either side. Occasionally, the tunnels would have doorways – some with doors still intact, though most of the doors had fallen from their hinges. No sound came from the openings – everything was silent. So silent, in fact, that Arracnoth suddenly realized he hadn't heard even the scurry of a rodent or the squeak of a bat. Nightfall ignored the doors and tunnels, continuing relentlessly down the stairs. He never stopped or paused their descent. It was an incessant plod onward – ever forward, ever downward.

The dread and fear that he had felt above faded. Arracnoth began counting the stairs to keep his mind occupied. When he reached four hundred and thirty-four, the stairway stopped, and the stairwell opened into a room. They were in a large, rounded chamber that resembled a prison or dungeon. Eight alcoves lined the walls – some with iron bars, others with remnants of pins where chains and shackles had been anchored. Nightfall moved purposefully to the back of the room, to an alcove directly across from the stairs. He pulled on the door of the cage in front of him. A deafening screech echoed through the room as the rusted iron grated against itself and gave way to Nightfall's insistence. He entered the cell.

At the back of the room, another fissure scarred the wall. On each side of the hole, and lying in piles throughout the cell, Arracnoth could see what may have once been sacks or crates, but were now just rags and boards. Nightfall reached into one of the piles and retrieved a torch. He handed it to Hathar. Scorpio stepped forward and produced a flint to light it, and soon a warm yellow glow lit the room and pushed the darkness further away from them. The cleric stuck the torch into a sconce on the wall.

"We will rest here," Nightfall said in a hushed tone, which still seemed far too loud after so long a silence. "We are far enough away from the Gate that the fear has faded. If anyone follows us here, they will have to check each floor of the tower and every winding hallway we bypassed. And should they do so, we will hear of their approach long before they are upon us." He motioned to the cell behind him. "Rest, *sondartins*. I and the others will take turns keeping watch. Caerbexsys lies through that opening. And although you have already journeyed where few have trod before, what lies ahead may still be the hardest part of this journey."

Hathar distributed provisions of salted meat and a skin of the *drekannen* that Arial had given them. Scorpio took his food and silently made his way back to the bottom of the steps to take first watch. He sat his longsword down beside him and began to eat.

The rest of them cleared space on the floor and arranged their cloaks to sleep on, then sat down and ate in silence. The long day's ride, the flight from Arial's home, and the overwhelming dread of the Gate above were heavy on them all. Although Nightfall said they were far enough from the Gate to be immune to its effects, the experience of it all had left an impression on them. They felt on edge and uneasy.

Arracnoth couldn't help but revisit the images carved into the Gate, and the terror and oppression that had consumed his mind. The descent down the stairwell had also left him out-of-sorts. This was an unearthly place, devoid of rats or spiders or any living thing – save the five of them. He wondered if he would be able to sleep, despite the exhaustion he felt.

As soon as he closed his eyes, however, he was promptly asleep. Avanstel followed suit just seconds later. Neither noticed the twisting waves of faint-colored vapors curled above their heads, dancing in the flickering light of the torch.

The cleric waited for them to fall asleep and then leaned back against the cold stone wall, closed his eyes, and rested his hammer across his lap. "Good decision," he said. "The *ort* will need their sleep."

Nightfall nodded. Caerbexsys awaited. They all would need their strength.

CHAPTER 9: LIGHT

Arracnoth awoke, though he could not tell if it was day or night or how much time had passed. Disoriented, he took a moment to remember he was in the tower, in a cell, at a secret entrance to Caerbexsys. He looked around the room. Hathar and Scorpio had exchanged places; the bearded man now sat at the bottom of the steps where Scorpio had been before. Nightfall was nowhere to be seen – which did not surprise him. The place was silent except for the sound of snoring coming from Avanstel.

He got up and made his way across the room and sat next to Hathar. "How long have we been here?"

"Many hours. It's hard to tell, but surely it is daylight above. How do you feel?"

"Rested," Arracnoth said. "Surprisingly well, for having slept on a hard, cold floor in the bottom of a haunted tower after many days' ride on horseback through a land I've never seen." He smiled and stretched.

Hathar chuckled. "Indeed." He handed Arracnoth an apple.

Arracnoth took a bite and chewed, glad to have something to fill his stomach. "Nightfall?"

Hathar motioned to the cleft in the cell's wall. "Gone to the netherworld. Scouting ahead and confirming that his memory hasn't failed." He smiled.

"How long have you known him?"

Hathar took a deep breath and leaned back against the wall. "Let's see … I met them both nearly five cycles ago. In Redwinds, in an alley behind a tavern." He chuckled again. "They were in a bit of trouble, and I … ah … stepped in to help. Little did I know then that I'd end up being part of their little band and traveling all over Halbrun with the two of them." He shrugged and handed Arracnoth his wineskin. "Though they are good enough company."

"Redwinds? Is that your home? I can tell by your accent that you're Not from Chark, nor the Norlands, or Faber. And I haven't seen this symbol before." He pointed to the emblem on Hathar's tabard: two circles, one nested inside the other, the inner one surrounded by four triangles with their points facing inward to meet it.

Hathar smiled. "This is the symbol of Merces, my god. I have taken vows to serve him – to represent him here in Halbrun. I owe everything I am, and have, and do, to him." His voice was reverent and joyful simultaneously. "Redwinds is where I *used* to call home. Now my home is with my friends." He looked back and up the stairwell. "Tonight, or today, whatever it is … home appears to be at the entrance to the netherworld."

Arracnoth took a swallow of *drekannen* and handed the skin back to Hathar. "Scorpio isn't from Redwinds." It was a statement more than a question.

"No. He's from Sandscarath." The cleric looked over at the large man resting against the wall inside the cell.

Arracnoth grinned. "From the desert! Avanstel was right."

"Yes. But that hasn't been his home for a very long time."

As if on cue, the warrior opened his eyes, yawned, and stood up. He placed his sword against the wall and took off his cloak and tunic. Just by his massive frame, Arracnoth knew Scorpio was strong, but with his cloak and shirt removed, the man was more than impressive. As he rolled up his shirt and placed it in his pack, his back muscles rippled, and his arms flexed. Arracnoth could see the faded marks from many old battles all over the warrior's copper skin, as well as a large tattoo pattern of a stylized sun in the middle of his back. He took his scarlet cloak and wrapped it around his waist. Arracnoth had no doubts that having Scorpio as an ally was much preferable to having him as an adversary. He was a mountain of muscle, yet still somehow as graceful as a cat — a deadly combination in a fight.

Hathar walked across the room. "Rested?"

Scorpio rumbled something. Hathar continued into the cell where Avanstel was stirring and motioned for Arracnoth.

"Well, friends," he said. "Our guide will return momentarily. He has been gone long enough to scout ahead and to retrieve for us some light crystals, like he has. They will help light our way through what lies ahead."

Avanstel stood up, pushed the hair back from his face and brushed himself off. Arracnoth caught a brief flash of surprise cross his face when he looked up at Scorpio. He, too, had been unaware of how well-muscled their companion was underneath his red cloak. Hathar noticed Avanstel's reaction and smiled at them both.

"It will be warmer as we descend," he explained. "As we travel, we may find ourselves in places where the walls are quite close, making it challenging to navigate." He winked at Avanstel. "At least for the ... ah ... bulkier among us."

Scorpio snorted.

As if on cue, Nightfall appeared from the fissure. He had a handful of stones and gave one to each of them. As they touched them, the crystals emitted a cold white light. "Use these, should we get separated," he said ominously.

Hathar frowned. "If that should happen, elf, then I hope that there is more than a light rock to aid us. We will have no means to navigate out!"

"Just a precaution. I assure you I will take us the most expedient, yet safest, route. Attempting to avoid anything that would put our charges in danger and making our time below as short as possible. Although no matter what route we take, Caerbexsys has its own set of unique challenges. There is no path that is perfectly clear. There are shortcuts that would be faster, but those veer too close to *drivrid* realms for my preferences. I will not take that risk with our present company."

"More *drivrid*? I guess I hadn't really thought ..." Arracnoth trailed off, embarrassed by his question. Of course, there were more *drivrid!* Nightfall certainly couldn't be the sole remaining survivor of the branch of that ancient elven tree. Now, he knew, nether-elves were not just stories used to scare children – they were real people. There were possibly entire civilizations of *drivrid* living beneath the ground that he walked upon every day.

Nightfall ignored Arracnoth's comment. "I will lead," he said, changing the topic. The other *drivrid* were either something he didn't want to talk about, or he didn't want to cause further concern.

He stepped through the crevice into the underworld. Scorpio followed next, locking eyes with Hathar for a moment before he disappeared.

Avanstel glanced at Arracnoth as if to confirm that they were going to proceed. Arracnoth shrugged, still a bit embarrassed that he hadn't realized there would be other nether-elves. Avanstel clasped his arm, turned, and then disappeared into the dark rift.

"I will guard the rear," Hathar said, and signaled for Arracnoth to enter the chasm. Arracnoth took a deep breath, held his crystal high, and stepped forward – into darkness.

The crystals helped keep the darkness at bay, though the never-ending and oppressive blackness felt like a massive creature that circled and slithered around them – just beyond the glow of their small lights. They walked for hours in silence, taking their time and navigating the obstacles that stood in their way. There was a general feeling that it was – for some reason – important to keep quiet. Nobody wanted to speak into the gloom or shatter the unending stillness. Perhaps it was best to pass by without disrupting what hadn't been disturbed in ages. The scraping of boots on stone, the creak of leather weapon harnesses and belts, the brush of fabric, and the sounds of breathing provided the only soundscape accompanying their journey downward. These noises mixed with the faint howl of wind moving through the caverns in distant places and the occasional echo of a far-off creature scurrying or screeching into the darkness.

They reached a point where they had to cross a small break in the cave floor. Arracnoth placed his hand against the passage wall to brace himself as he prepared to leap across the space. He noted the walls were becoming warmer, heating the air, and pushing back the chill of the underground world. Although the new clothes that Nightfall had provided him with were comfortable, he felt himself sweating as the temperature crept higher. He considered he might need to follow Scorpio's example ... or at least remove his cloak.

Avanstel cleared the gap. Arracnoth moved to the side of the tunnel to mimic Avanstel's actions. As he jumped over the pit, his left foot struck something that went sliding across the stone floor, tripping him. He wasn't able to get the momentum he needed to clear the hole, and he was certain he was going to fall into the darkness. He gasped and reached out, hoping to grab something to stop him from falling. Avanstel caught him as his right foot landed on the crumbling edge. He pulled Arracnoth toward him, and they both collapsed on the floor, their light crystals flying from their hands and becoming dark.

It took them a moment to untangle themselves. Behind them, Hathar raised his light, peering into the darkness on the opposite side of the break. Ahead, they could hear Scorpio rumble something indiscernible and see his light approaching as he backtracked towards them.

"We are fine," Avanstel said. It was the first words spoken since they had passed from the tower and entered the underworld. The words pierced the air, echoing around them loudly. Arracnoth cringed and held his breath. He was suddenly anxious, peering expectantly into the darkness of the pit he had just traversed.

Nightfall appeared at their side, helping them to their feet and handing them their crystals. The stones flared to life again. He held his light high, directing his gaze over at Hathar. The cleric had bent over and picked up an object from the cave floor. He held it in front of him, holding his light up for them to see what it was. It was a skull – a humanoid skull, either human or elven.

Scorpio made a deep rumbling noise and drew his sword. "Keep close," he said. "We are in someone's hunting grounds."

Arracnoth and Avanstel looked at each other. Hathar moved to the edge of the pit, knelt, and shone his light down into the darkness. Below, they could see a collection of more skulls and bones. Hathar stood up and peered into the darkness above them. Overhead, they could see another break in the cave. Whatever creature lived in this area, it either hunted or trapped its food and used this hole to dispose of the remains of its meals.

"We need to move," Nightfall whispered. "Now." His voice was clear and urgent, and somehow, did not echo around the caverns like Avanstel's had. Hathar nodded. Scorpio turned his back to them and stepped forward down the tunnel again, taking the lead.

Nightfall pushed Avanstel and Arracnoth toward Scorpio. "Follow him. I'll help Hathar across the pit."

Arracnoth followed Avanstel into the darkness. Moments later, he glanced over his shoulder and saw Nightfall and Scorpio closing the distance quickly. They had their weapons in hand. They proceeded like this for several more hours; the urgency faded as they retreated from the pit full of bones. Although the danger seemed to have passed, they were still on alert.

Eventually, the small passage opened into a massive cavern that could fit the entire city of Chark inside. Bioluminescent fungi and lichens illuminated the place, making it brighter than the dark tunnels they had passed through. Reds, blues, purples, yellows, whites, and greens dotted the curving walls of the enormous cavity. A faint blue glow emanated from a large underground lake that filled the bottom of the cave. Glowing man-sized mushrooms and other netherworld vegetation of all different shapes surrounded the edge of the lake. There were even fungi the size of houses dotting the landscape. Each fungus added its own faint glow to the carnival of colors. The sound of crickets and the fluttering of bats echoed through the space. Gentle, teal-colored waves rippled at the shore.

What is this place? Arracnoth wondered silently. He had seen nothing like it before. It was almost peaceful here, not at all what he had expected on a trip into the underworld.

There was a flat terrace before them. Arracnoth could pick out a geometric pattern on the floor, showing that this was not a naturally flat surface. Steps from the terrace led down to the water. There was a long, empty pier extending into the pool, where it looked like a small ship could dock.

Scorpio had taken a defensive stance on the left side of the terrace, opposite the tunnel that they had just exited. Nightfall stepped next to Arracnoth and Avanstel and motioned for them to keep silent and remain where they were. He moved past them to the right side of the terrace. Hathar followed and took a position at the center where the steps led down to the dock.

After a long moment, the *drivrid* stepped towards Hathar and motioned for the others to join them. As they drew close, Nightfall broke the silence. His voice was clear and understandable, without disturbing the world around them. He had a way of speaking that somehow allowed him to talk without his voice carrying more than a few feet away. No one directly involved in the conversation would know that anyone had spoken.

"The Dark Maw is almost halfway between the Shadow Gate and Belkin Wood." He motioned to the water behind them.

Arracnoth looked again at the cave that extended far into the distance and noticed now a mist hovering over the water far away from them. What he had thought was an underground lake could easily be an underground sea.

"The dock? Made by *drivrid*?" Hathar manipulated his voice the way that Nightfall did, though less adeptly.

Nightfall shook his head. "Nor Groundlings. Nor any other known nether races. Although many travel the Maw … for assorted reasons." Nightfall said, pointing to the mushroom forest over the shoulder of Scorpio. "It's safe for now. We will camp here for a rest."

Arracnoth exhaled, though the alien world around him prevented him from completely relaxing. He was hungry, and he felt tired, and the increasing temperatures had made his fine clothes smell bad. It was time for a break, even if the break was in such an unfamiliar and strange-looking place. They moved to the side of the terrace and made a camp at the edge of the mushroom forest. Arracnoth took off his cloak and sat it on the cavern floor. Nightfall did the same and then disrobed completely. He stepped into the blue-glowing lake and continued into the water until he was waist deep, then sat down.

Arracnoth looked over at the others. He felt unsure about leaving the security and protection of the shore and jumping naked into the dark, unfamiliar waters of an underground sea. He could only imagine what creatures lived in these waters … surely nothing that would end up at Whitley's dockside stand.

Scorpio and Hathar were removing their clothes, following the example of their *drivrid* friend. Arracnoth looked at Hathar, unsure what to do.

"If it's good enough for Nightfall, it's good enough for us," the cleric said, his smile flashing beneath his furry face.

Scorpio grunted in agreement.

Arracnoth looked at Avanstel. He shrugged, and with a mischievous grin, he unbuttoned his shirt and started to undress. Avanstel seemed so much more at ease with all the recent events than Arracnoth was, but that wasn't a surprise. Avanstel adapted pretty easily to whatever situation they found themselves in and rarely got upset. Arracnoth wasn't as easygoing as his friend.

Arracnoth was the last to leave the shore. He stepped cautiously into the water and was surprised by the pleasant warmth. Some sort of natural process must heat the sea and keep it warm. It was fascinating … and soothing. The temperature was only slightly cooler than the surrounding air – refreshing, but not brisk and cold like The Deep Brine. He made his way toward his companions, who were sitting in the water up to their necks.

He watched the teal glow swirl around his legs as he walked forward. The glow parted as he moved, as if alive; as if some imperceptibly small creatures on the water's surface were running away, reacting to his presence. He glanced over his shoulder at the beautiful ripples and spirals left in his wake. The bottom of the sea was flat with small regular patterns, like ridges or ripples, that he could feel with his feet. He wondered, had the rock worn smooth over many millennia, or had it always been that way?

The others were relaxing and enjoying themselves and didn't care about what types of nameless watery denizens might slide around beneath the blue surface. Arracnoth did his best to push away his worries and try not to focus on what might be below, looking for an opportunity to snag him and drag him away to drown him in the deeps.

He sat down beside Nightfall. The elf smiled at him. "Not what you expected, *sondartin*?"

Arracnoth shook his head. The water was calm and comforting. The kaleidoscope of colors far above them reflected off the surface of the glowing waters, shimmering as they moved, rippling away from them. He looked at his companions. Scorpio had his eyes closed, as if he were meditating. Hathar and Avanstel were looking up at the myriad colors overhead. It was a pleasant and unexpected respite for the party, a rest from their ceaseless plodding forward – fleeing from the unknown, ever in danger and always alert.

"They say these waters possess magical healing powers." Nightfall cupped his hands in front of him, splashed water on his face, and then leaned back so his long white hair sank beneath the surface. "I'm not sure I believe that, though I have found healing here for my spirit before … in my past life."

Hathar reached up and unfastened the knot that held his hair on top of his head. His umber locks fell around his bearded face. He stood up, his furry chest rising out of the water, then he turned and quickly disappeared beneath the glowing surface. Arracnoth gasped. Had some creature captured him?

He watched the dark patch where the cleric had disappeared. The glowing blue surface slowly reformed. Moments passed, but Hathar did not reappear. Arracnoth scanned the waters around them for signs of a fin, or a wake, or some telltale sign of an aquatic beast that had stolen away their friend. He looked at Scorpio, whose eyes were still closed. Nightfall was admiring the colors on the roof of the cave.

With a splash, Hathar broke the surface right next to Arracnoth, his white teeth flashing beneath his wet beard. He pulled his wet hair back from his face and let out a growl like a wild animal. Arracnoth fell backward in surprise, but Hathar, laughing, caught him before he fell beneath the surface.

"I'm sorry for startling you. I was just playing. We are safe here and you can relax. Nightfall would have warned us if there were anything to be concerned about. Enjoy this moment!"

Hathar slapped the water gently, splashing Arracnoth, who smiled back at him and shook his head. The cleric put a finger to his lips, signaling Arracnoth to be silent. He then turned toward Scorpio, crouched down in the water and then sprung at the warrior, attempting to dunk him beneath the surface. Without opening an eye, Scorpio slid backward, and Hathar plunged into the water clumsily, having missed his target. They both laughed quietly and sprayed water at each other. Avanstel joined in, squirting water from his hands towards the meditating fighter.

The mood was surprisingly lighthearted. Arracnoth realized at that moment that this was the first time that he had been relaxed since Avanstel had disappeared. They had been so occupied with evading their pursuers that there had been no time for trivial matters like this. The others seemed to sense it, too. Even the typically taciturn Scorpio was enjoying the diversion. Now standing waist deep in the strange water, in this strange place, they had finally found rest. Arracnoth smiled, marveling that the irony of being able to find such levity in Caerbexsys of all places. Nightfall maneuvered beside him, moving clear of the rowdiness and splashing that the others were taking part in.

"There are many things in Caerbexsys that would surprise surface dwellers," the nether-elf said, as if reading Arracnoth's mind. "The Dark Maw is just one of them. Not everything in the nether-world is death and danger. We have beauty and pleasure too – just as in the world above." Nightfall looked at Scorpio, whose wet dark hair fell into his face, covering his scar, as he lunged to grab Avanstel. "I have found, in all my journeys, in all my time, that there are very few things in the world – or under it – that are wholly evil … or wholly good. Everything is a mixture of both darkness and light, goodness and wickedness, death and life. We found a moment of light amid the darkness. Let us enjoy it while it remains. Come, we can prepare camp and leave them to their fun."

Arracnoth followed Nightfall to the shore. The *drivrid* picked up his clothing. "Bring your garments," he said. "We'll wash them." He returned to the shore, squatted at the shoreline, and laundered his clothes, washing the sweat and dirt from them.

Arracnoth picked up his clothes, carefully setting aside the blue pouch with the moonstone pin and the white sword Haven Chase token. He joined the nether-elf at the shore and put his tunic into the blue water. As he washed his outfit, he wondered if the healing powers in the water could somehow wash away the weariness of their flight from Chark.

When they finished, they placed their wet clothing on the warm rocks at the side of the terrace to dry. Nightfall assured him they would be dry by the time they were ready to depart the Maw. They opened their packs and found the food Arial had provided for them. Eventually, the others made their way to the shore, wringing out their hair and shaking the water from their bodies. They sat on their cloaks, ate the food, and drank the remaining *drekannen*. Nightfall and Hathar shared a few words in their muted speech as they planned for the rest of the journey ahead of them, discussing the best route to avoid the *drivrid* settlements and other known dangers. When everyone was done, they leaned back on their cloaks and admired the glittering roof of the cave while Scorpio picked up his large sword and moved to the edge of the mushroom forest for first watch.

Avanstel fell asleep first, snoring lightly.

Arracnoth, however, couldn't sleep. Resting on the cavern floor and looking up at the glowing fungi, his mind could not let go of what Nightfall had said about darkness and light existing everywhere together. The *drivrid* had seen much more of the world – and netherworld – than Arracnoth had ever dreamed of. The nether-elf's age and experiences also gave him a measure of wisdom that Arracnoth hadn't gained yet. But there was something more in the thought that Arracnoth couldn't unlock. Something deeper than mere light and dark coexisting. What was it?

The concept of light and darkness was not new to him. He had known both in Chark. The cruelty and mistreatment of the *ort* by the human Citizens … and the care and concern for those who saw beyond his mixed heritage. Like Adine, Whitley, and even Fert.

Here in Caerbexsys, there was darkness, danger, and death … as well as beauty and joy … and laughter. He never thought goodness could exist in a place like the Caerbexsys, in the dark recesses of the underworld.

He rolled onto his side. The pouch and token were directly in front of his face. Avanstel was beyond them, breathing in a steady rhythm. He picked up the Haven Chase piece and rubbed the smooth token in his hand. Since they had first learned to play, it had always been Avanstel's piece of choice. He knew why – the white sword represented goodness, strength, and virtue. It fit how Avanstel thought about himself … and if he were honest, it was how Arracnoth thought of Avanstel, too.

But of course, you couldn't play Haven Chase with only the white pieces. The black pieces were part of the board, too. You needed both the light and the dark pieces to play. Nightfall was right – there were few things in this world that were completely one or the other. Most things were a mix of good and bad, light and dark.

Perhaps there was both light and darkness in Belkin Wood, too. He had always thought that the Weode were dark. They despised the *ort*, considered them to be shameful hidden secrets that were best disposed of, discarded, or denied. But could there be light there, too? Everything he knew of the Weode was darkness, but he didn't know it all. And maybe if there wasn't light there yet, maybe someday there would be … and maybe Avanstel would be the one to bring light to that darkness. He was certainly capable – charming and easy-going and virtuous and strong. Avanstel had all the qualities of a great man … and of a great king. He was good. He was light. If Avanstel could bring light to the darkness, maybe he could change things for all the *ort*, everywhere.

Eventually, his eyelids closed, and he drifted off to sleep, dreaming of the day when Avanstel would set things right.

CHAPTER 10: BEAST

Avanstel shook Arracnoth awake. He motioned to the others, who were silently changing into their newly washed clothing. As Nightfall had said, enough time had passed for the clothes to dry against the hot rocks, though it was hard to know in the night-black cavern exactly how long they had been asleep.

Hathar, his long hair fastened once again in a knot atop his head, handed Arracnoth dried fruit and offered him his canteen. "Nightfall tells me we have just one more day in the nether realm and we should be back on the surface in Belkin Wood."

Arracnoth nodded in understanding. He strapped his belt around his waist and attached his knife and small blue pouch with the moonstone pin. He slid the Haven Chase piece into a pocket. As he pulled on his shirt, he once again marveled at the craftsmanship. They had spent the last several days traveling, having ridden hard and long, and had spent the last days scrambling and scraping through long-abandoned tunnels in the earth to arrive here. The garments had been soiled and abused during that time, yet they looked as if they had just come off the loom. There wasn't a single tear or smudge of dirt visible on it – and the pristine appearance was not due to his incredible laundering skills. He noticed Avanstel's tunic looked as fresh as his own.

Avanstel tucked his cream-colored shirt into his belt and donned his olive-green vest. He looked at Arracnoth quizzically. Arracnoth smiled and shook his head.

"The clothes," he said quietly.

"They're nice. Better than anything I've had before. What do you think? Do they make me look dashing?"

Arracnoth laughed. "As dashing as one can be in Caerbexsys."

Avanstel shrugged, smiled, and then wrapped his cloak around his waist the way they had seen Scorpio do the day before. Arracnoth did the same. They were ready to depart the Dark Maw and continue their journey through the underworld.

Nightfall took the lead, and the rest followed their friend from the edge of the mushroom forest toward another tunnel carved into the opposite wall. As they reached the opening, Nightfall took his light crystal from his pouch, signaling for the rest of them to do the same, and then stepped inside. The first few yards of the egress were lit with the same colorful fungi and lichen as the cavern they were leaving, but as they moved further away from the Maw, the glow grew dimmer, and soon the only light was the cold white illumination from their crystals.

They moved on in silence for several hours. The tunnel's walls and floor were almost identical to those they went through on their flight down from the tower, except Arracnoth thought he could perceive a slight ascent to their path. He also noted that the walls felt a little cooler than they had on the way down. He was grateful for the change in the temperature. Although it had been soothing to soak his muscles in the warm waters of the Maw, the heat of this deep place had been a little suffocating. He expected as they climbed back to the surface it would be easier going, and he looked forward to breathing the cool air above ground again.

They came to a place where Arracnoth felt a slight movement of air against his cheek and heard the faint rush of a breeze blowing past him. It grew steadily louder, and soon Arracnoth could feel the air pushing at him from behind as it moved through the tunnels, seeking escape. Suddenly, they broke through the whistling confines and entered another cavern, large but still only a fraction of the size of the Dark Maw. They continued into the space.

Arracnoth could hear the chittering and screeching of bats far above them. Large stone columns rose from the cavern floor and disappeared into the darkness overhead. Stalagmites of various shapes and sizes surrounded them – some slick with moisture, others dry and ancient. The party silently wound their way through the maze of obstacles, following Nightfall's lead.

As they passed through the cavern, Arracnoth wondered how the *drivrid* learned the way through these dark and seemingly random passages, and how they kept their sense of direction in this strange world. Everything looked identical to Arracnoth: just another pillar of melting stone; or another pile of broken rocks, the same grey-brown color as every other. How Nightfall had charted his way through these places and, more impressively, retained that knowledge after so long, was just one of the many things about the nether-elf that Arracnoth hoped to ask him one day.

At one point, Scorpio and Nightfall exchanged places, and the *drivrid* motioned for them to move quickly and quietly behind an enormous column. He placed his light crystal in a pouch, and its light went out. The others did the same. The moment before he let go of his crystal, Arracnoth saw Scorpio, crouched down, peering into the darkness in front of them. The warrior took a step backward toward the huddled party, one large hand sliding along the stone of the column until he felt Nightfall's shoulder. Then everything went dark.

Over the sound of his own breathing and the distant chatter of the bats above, Arracnoth thought he heard a scuff of motion nearby. Small stones went scattering across the cavern floor, sending echoes through the darkness. The ground beneath him seemed to throb, as if some large, monstrous beast were walking nearby. Pebbles and dirt fell from above with each rhythmic thump. He felt Avanstel shift his weight and press backwards into him and against the column. He then felt Hathar's firm hand grab his arm to steady him and squeeze a warning.

The shaking of the ground stopped. He could clearly hear the measured sounds of breathing from something enormous nearby. Arracnoth held his breath and closed his eyes.

"Sere'eden!" he said to himself, and willed his beating heart to slow.

Suddenly, there was a deafening roar above him. The noise reverberated through the cavern, and the shrill of bats rose to a crescendo with it. Arracnoth clutched his ears, trying to block the noise. He felt Hathar's other hand on his shoulder, grabbing him and shoving him backward. He collided with something hard, knocking the wind out of him.

Scorpio let out a booming shout. Arracnoth could hear the warrior's blade whistling through the darkness, followed by the sound of it hitting something fleshy. There was another, louder roar from the creature, this time mixed with rage. Arracnoth staggered to his feet, clutching the wall he had fallen against.

A blinding flash of purple light sizzled through the darkness in front of him. It lasted only a moment, but it was so intense that the shapes of the world had burned into the back of his eyes. In that split second, he had seen Hathar swinging his giant hammer in an arc over his head with a grimace of determination on his face. Scorpio was beside him, covered in a dark liquid, using both hands to pull his sword from a large tentacle above him. Opposite him was Nightfall, his arm frozen midair as he launched a dagger at something on the other side of the large stone column that blocked Arracnoth's view of the creature. Avanstel was nowhere to be seen. Did the beast get him, or did he get knocked away from the fight?

He shouted for Avanstel, but the sounds around him echoing through the cavern drowned out his call. Then, a blast of hot air exploded in front of him, knocking him back against the wall. As he stumbled to stand up, the floor gave way, and he tumbled backward into the void. His arms flailed, trying to find purchase, as he bounced against the rock walls of the pit several times on the way down. He finally landed on a hard stone cavern floor, where he lay, slumped and unconscious.

He woke up in darkness. His left arm and right side hurt. A sharp pain shot through his head. He reached a trembling hand to his temple and felt a sticky wetness there. Blood? His?

His hands shook as he reached for his light crystal and brushed against the pouch with the earth from his mother's grave. "*Sere'eden*," he said to himself, almost as if in prayer. Finally, he found the light stone, and it flared to life with its strange white light. He looked at his fingers. It *was* blood. He stood up, his entire body aching from the effort, his arms and legs shuddering. He leaned back against the wall, gulping air, and held his light above him.

To his right, he could see a sharp incline where he had fallen from somewhere above. On the left, the floor banked to the side and disappeared. He could only assume he was in another tunnel, which was only slightly better than a pit. He rested there for a moment, assessing whether he had any broken bones or was bleeding from any place other than his head. Although battered and bruised, he was in one piece, and aside from the head wound, it didn't appear he had suffered any severe damage.

Arracnoth grabbed his cloak and tugged at it, trying to tear a bandage from it for his head, but the cloth did not give. He retrieved his knife and managed, with some difficulty, to shred a large enough portion to wrap his head and staunch the flow of blood from his temple. Slowly, he got to his feet and looked up at the shaft. The hole ascended upward, but there didn't seem to be any purchase that he could use to climb back up. How far had he fallen? How much time had passed?

Above, it was silent. He considered calling out for help. But he wasn't sure if that was wise. Even if his friends were up there, they might not hear him … and he might instead draw the attention of someone, or something, else. Other than his small knife, he was defenseless against anything dwelling in the nether dark. He decided remaining silent was probably the better choice.

He leaned against the tunnel wall and slid down to the floor. Perhaps if he waited here, his friends would come to find him. He didn't know the others that well, but he knew Avanstel wouldn't abandon him here in the darkness of Caerbexsys. Unless Avanstel hadn't made it … or the others …

He waited for an eternity, listening intently for any noise other than the sound of his beating heart, loud in his ears. Eventually, his eyelids drooped, and he fell asleep. The light crystal slipped from his hand and faded out.

Somehow, he was standing before the Shadow Gate once again. It was night, and everything was oppressively still. The ominous figures carved into the black stone peered down at him. Their malice was almost tangible. This time, he was certain the eyes of the massive creature were glowing red, and he could feel the hot breath of the beast.

How had he gotten there? Where were the others? He looked around for them, but he was alone, standing small before the enormous doors.

He forced his gaze upward to the face of the monster with the enormous leather wings. It spoke to him, but without moving its mouth. It said strange words he couldn't understand – in a language he had never heard before, but was somehow familiar at the same time. Although the words didn't make sense to him, he knew they were awful, and they filled him with dread.

The withered figures in the clutches of the beast seemed to twist and move, their faces distorting disturbingly. Their frozen screams warped into frightening visages of terror. They reached out to him, their skeletal hands trying to grab him, to pull him into their torment. He felt drawn to them, unable to break free of their power, unable to control his own movement.

As an emaciated hand touched his forehead, he screamed.

He jerked awake. Everything was dark around him, and he panicked for a moment, wondering if the entire thing had been a dream, or if he was now imprisoned within the Shadow Gate.

His temple throbbed. He touched it, feeling the bandage, and then recalling where he was and what had transpired. He reached blindly around the floor near him and located the light crystal, setting it aglow once again. His situation had not changed.

He had been asleep long enough for his head to stop bleeding. His side and arm still ached. Nothing else had changed during his time unconscious, and there was still no sign of the others.

Gathering himself, he pushed against the rock and stood up, studying the shaft and again listening intently, straining in the silence. There was nothing. He turned to his left and shone the light down the corridor. His stomach growled. He was hungry.

If he waited here, there still could be a chance that Avanstel and the others would come for him, but if they did, they'd have to descend the same tunnel he had fallen through, and there was no way back up for anyone.

He considered briefly the possibility that the others were dead. What if they were all maimed or injured, or in need of help? What if Avanstel was lying there, gasping his last breath…

"No!" he said aloud, startling himself. The exclamation echoed down the tunnel and bounced back to him.

He raised his light and looked down the tunnel once again, back at the shaft, and decided that if he were to make it to the surface, or find his companions, it would have to be by his own actions. If he stayed here, he could be here for days, or weeks, and would end up starving to death, growing weaker with each passing hour. He made an inventory and discovered he still had a canteen but no food. He had his knife, the pin and pouch of earth from Adine's grave, the game token, and the light crystal that Nightfall had given him.

Peering up into the shaft one last time, he turned to the wall and used his knife to scratch an arrow and an "A" into the stone – just in case his friends somehow followed him down here. He then turned and shuffled forward down the open passage. The ache in his leg told him it was bruised badly, but thankfully, it wasn't a sprain or fracture. He was thankful for that small thing.

He walked for what seemed like hours, limping along and carefully navigating obstacles. After a long time, he sensed the tunnel was pitching upwards, and he felt the slightest movement of air from behind him. He took that as a positive sign he was traveling in the right direction – up and out. The air would only move if it had some place to go, which meant an egress to the surface. Wherever the air was escaping was a potential escape for him, too. He pressed forward, a little more hopeful.

Sometime later, he noticed that the temperature was growing cooler, and the wind was now coming toward him, not pushing from behind. He must have passed the place where the air was escaping the tunnels. He paused and considered the options. He could retrace his steps and try to find where the breeze exited the underworld, but that might be far above him, in some unreachable place. And he wasn't sure that moving back down the corridor and deeper into the ground was really the direction he wanted to go.

If cool air were moving toward him, that meant that it was from the surface, which would still be an escape from the underground. He inhaled deeply, trying to determine whether the air was stale or fresh. It smelled damp and cool and slightly musty. He continued on his current path. With luck, the cave would open to the surface, and he would soon find himself in Belkin Wood. He quickened his pace, pushing ahead with as much energy as he could muster.

As he rounded a corner, he drew up sharply. The passage he had been following ended at a wall. A large crevasse scarred the surface from top to bottom, and a lone skeleton, its bones visible amidst tattered scraps of cloth, sprawled before him in front of the split. Arracnoth raised his light. He could see that the figure's skeletal foot was lodged in the cleft. It appeared the figure had come through the crevice and had become trapped, unable to free itself. The bony remnants of an arm extended outwards across the tunnel floor, indicating the figure had tried to claw their way out of the predicament – but had apparently failed.

Arracnoth lowered his light, bathing the still bones in a white glow. Beneath the finger bones of the outstretched hand, he caught a glint of metal. He crouched down to inspect it. Buried in the dirt beneath the fingers, he could discern the shape of a small weapon. He paused for a moment, considering whether he should disturb the remains. Would he bring a curse upon himself if he were to violate its final resting place?

He slid the hand bones aside and pulled the weapon gingerly from the dirt, still wary. Standing up to examine it, he could tell immediately that whoever had created the dagger had been an expert weaponsmith. The blade was serpentine and forged of a metal unlike anything he had seen before. It was blue-silver in color, highly polished, almost ornamental. It was wide at the base and tapered to a point; both sides of the dagger were razor sharp. It was an extraordinarily crafted piece, etched with unknown symbols from an unknown language. He wrapped his hand around the hilt to test its weight and balance. He had never held a blade so fine. The grip conformed to his hand as if it were custom made for him. He turned it over, scrutinizing it with awe. This was not something to be left behind here in this cave, buried in the dirt. It was a fine weapon, and a shame to leave it in a forgotten tunnel in the underworld. He looked back down at the skeleton.

"Won't do *you* much good," he said. "I hope you don't mind." He stuck the blade in his belt and squatted down to examine the rest of the figure. "I wonder who you were and what brought you to this place."

He shifted through the pile of dirt, rags, and bones, looking for anything that might give him a clue. He checked the hand for a ring, and the neck for an amulet, but found nothing. Time had destroyed any symbols or crests on the shredded clothing that might have revealed a story.

He moved down the body to the waist. Another glint of metal flashed at him from the dirt below the skeleton. He blew the dirt away, thinking, at first, that he might have found a coin that would provide a clue as to where the person had come from. What he discovered instead was another dagger forged from the same blue-silver metal, and as expertly finished as the first one. Arracnoth took the grip and felt the same smooth fit as the other blade as it formed comfortably in his hand.

Aside from being made from the same material and having the same form-fitting grip, this second dagger was of a completely unique design. The sai lacked the wide, winding curves of the first blade. It was markedly straight and narrow. The crosspieces extended forward, toward the blade tip, and ended in sharp points; a three-pointed blade that was surely as deadly as any double-edged sword.

Since the two blades were of distinct designs, though without a doubt made by the same craftsman, Arracnoth wondered if they had belonged to different owners. Typically, someone able to afford such fine weapons would have a matching set. It was odd to see them so similar, yet so different. He placed the second blade in his belt on the opposite side and finished examining the rest of the remains. Aside from the two blades, there were no other hints that could help him determine the identity of the skeleton. Even the leather boots had deteriorated so badly they were useless.

He stood up and considered the crack in the wall. Cool air was flowing from the other side, and he could smell dampness and age. He thought about the situation that had brought the previous traveler to his end. He reasoned that if the figure had made it through the cleft, only to be trapped on *this* side, that perhaps beyond the entrance the gap must grow wider. If Arracnoth could squeeze through the narrows, he stood a good chance of making it to whatever lay beyond.

Also, he thought, if the figure had come through from the other side, and assuming they were not a denizen of the netherworld, then that meant there was a route to the surface on the other side of the wall. A way out of the darkness. A way to freedom, rest, and light!

Arracnoth removed his cloak, placing it on the ground next to the skeletal figure. Hopefully, Nightfall would forgive him for leaving such a fine garment behind, but he wanted the least amount of material to catch on anything while he pushed his way through the narrow entrance. He didn't want to end up like the last person attempting to make their way through the opening.

He adjusted his new daggers on his belt and stepped over the remains of the corpse. Turning sideways and exhaling, he carefully squeezed himself through the opening. Once inside the wall, he pushed himself forward with his uninjured leg while clutching a jagged piece of the wall with his free hand and pulled himself through. It was a tight fit, but the breach was only a few feet deep and grew slightly wider inside. He gave one last push and freed himself from the rock, spilling forward out into an open space. He landed face-first on the floor, his light crystal flying out of his hand and blinking out.

He rested for a moment, gasping and shaking at the thought of how close he had come to being trapped. When his strength returned, he pushed himself up, crawled forward, and felt around on the ground again for his light. The floor here felt much different from the rough stone passageways he had been walking through for the last few days. The ground was smooth with regular joints, like pavers, and was not cluttered with loose stones and debris like the netherworld. His hands finally found the crystal, and the space flashed into light.

He was in a small room, or rather, an alcove that opened to a dark hallway beyond. Unfamiliar symbols in a strange language adorned the walls. They resembled the etching on the blades but were slightly different. Faded murals depicting forest scenery hung between the symbols. In the middle of the room, on a dais, sat a white stone sarcophagus.

Arracnoth raised his light over the figure carved into the pale slab of stone. She had long, wavy hair and a flowing gown. As he moved his light over her, the lady's hair and gown appeared as if they were rippling in a breeze. Aside from the alabaster color, her realism was so incredible that he had to touch her to confirm she was made of stone. The surface was icy and smooth.

He leaned over her, examining the delicate features. She was thin and elegant with a serene look on her face — as if she were merely sleeping peacefully. Small, pale flowers decorated her hair. Her ears, he noticed with a start, came to a well-defined point.

"Weode!" he said. The word echoed in the otherwise still space. The echo startled him, and he reached for his knife reflexively. His hand landed on the grip of the serpentine blade.

He heard a whisper from nearby. He pulled the dagger from his belt and moved around the room, putting his back to the wall so no one could sneak up behind him. "Hello? Who's there?"

The whisper grew louder, though it was still soft and distant. It was a woman's voice, speaking in a language he didn't know. What was she saying?

"Hello?" he called again.

The voice stopped suddenly.

With the blade in hand, he crept around the room, peering behind the dais to check for anyone hidden there. But the place was empty.

"Who's there? Show yourself."

There was no response. The voice had disappeared.

He turned to the sculpture and touched its arm again to confirm once more that it was not alive. Her lips and eyes remained closed, her face unmoving. Had he just heard the voice of her ghost? Or perhaps the echoes of those who had brought her here so long ago? He shivered. He didn't like this place at all. He needed to get out of here as quickly as possible.

He gathered his courage, keeping the blade in his hand, and stepped into the corridor. He stood there only long enough to figure out which direction the air was moving and turned toward its source. He held his light crystal high and limped forward, eager to leave the underworld behind him.

CHAPTER 11: ARE

Arracnoth found himself in a maze of tunnels filled with random alcoves and hallways of stone shelves, stacked with bodies wrapped in fine linens. Most of the recesses contained figures carved of the same white stone as the elven lady in the area where he had arrived. Some statuettes were effigies of soldiers. Others resembled nobles, garbed in flowing robes. All of them had the same pointed ears as the first. This was definitely a Weode burial site.

He paused frequently, smelling the air and hoping to feel even the slightest breeze that would confirm he was still heading toward the surface and away from Caerbexsys.

He stopped to examine an impressive statue of a man in an elegant alcove. On either side of the entrance were tall pillars carved with delicate vines of ivy and large white roses. The statue stood upright, looming over him. A dog – or wolf – stood at his side. He was an imposing figure, older looking, with a stern and somewhat foreboding look on his face. A diadem circled his head. Arracnoth attempted to decipher the inscription at the figure's feet, but the characters differed from anything he had learned about the Weode language as a child.

He heard a whisper near him. Arracnoth's heart leaped. He spun around, raising his light and peering into the darkness.

"*This one we knew well.*" The woman's voice was clear now, not distant and muted, but he still could not tell where it came from.

"Who is there?" Arracnoth said. "Show yourself!"

He thought he heard her laugh. "*E'Vestren, he was. Cruel and blood-thirsty … firstborn son of the betrayer. We knew him well.*" The voice was regal and refined, like someone educated in a noble's house. But the sound was also ethereal, lacking depth in a way that he found hard to explain.

"Come into the light, so I may see you."

She laughed again, her voice fading away as if she were walking past him and down the hallway.

He stood motionless. His wide eyes darted around the alcove and peered into the shadows. He waited there, still like the statue before him, waiting for something to happen. "*Sere'eden!*" he repeated to himself until the sound of his racing heart ceased pounding in his ears. There was no further response from the disembodied voice.

Was he hallucinating? Or was he simply fatigued beyond sense? Or perhaps the voice was a ghost of one of those long-dead Weode. Giving one last glance at the menacing statue, he marked an arrow on the wall with the blade, placed it in his belt, and continued on.

The path slanted upward until he reached a place where wide stairs were carved into the stone floor. Here, the walls were in better repair and didn't have the lichens and cobwebs that covered the walls below. As he climbed, he came upon an intersection. Five other passages branched from the one he had been ascending. To the right, nestled between the tunnel openings, was a nook that contained a sarcophagus with a small metal box on top of it.

Arracnoth smelled the air and tried to determine if he could feel the air moving, but he couldn't sense anything. He waited a while, peering into the darkness, listening intently for any clue that would give him a hint of which of the tunnels might lead him to the surface. Silence answered him.

Unwilling to take a false route and have to backtrack, he retreated to the alcove and sat down on the ornate stone bench that faced the grave. He figured he'd wait for the air to shift again, a change of the weather on the surface perhaps, and then he could continue his journey upwards. But for now, he was at a standstill.

In the pale light of his crystal, he looked at the white stone box before him. This tomb was like the first he had encountered, but it was missing the carved figure. It was simply a large rectangle with a family crest carved into the top, along with some writing.

Arracnoth found, to his surprise, that he could read these words. They were similar to the letters on the dais of the foreboding man, but he recognized these as Weode. It was the grave of a Weode child named K'Athela. They had passed away from a sickness at the early age of thirty-nine – just three cycles older than he was.

He knew that full-blooded Weode were longer lived than he was because they had more *accentation* in their veins. He had asked Adine how long a Weode might live, but being human, she could only relay stories she had heard. She knew they lived for several centuries – maybe even a thousand cycles – but she wasn't certain. The Weode were a mystery to all those living outside Belkin Wood. What he knew of his ancestors, he had learned from other *ort*, who mostly also lacked first-hand knowledge of their kin. In truth, he knew little about the Weode, other than their obvious lack of care for their half-breed illegitimate children. In his eyes, and the eyes of many other *ort*, that made the Weode contemptible.

He picked up the small metal box off the stone and tried to open it. It was locked. He reached for the sai to pry it open.

"*A flower lost at too young an age,*" he heard a man's voice say over his right shoulder. The voice was deep and resonant. He dropped the metal box, and it clattered to the ground. He swung the dagger to his right, but the space where the voice had come from was empty.

"I am tired of the games!" he shouted. "If you are ghosts or spirits that haunt this place, let me alone. I have nothing for you. I am tired and alone and am only trying to find a way out of this cursed darkness."

"*We can show you the way, if you can trust in us,*" the man said.

"Trust you?" He spun around. "I don't think I should trust anyone who speaks to me from the shadows and refuses to show themselves."

There was a pause. The voice answered back gently and calmly. "*My apologies. It has been ... difficult ... for us to speak. We have been struggling to find the words you might understand. It has been so many cycles, and you are ... different ... than those we have known before. But we have revealed ourselves to you. We know the way.*"

"Come forward, then!"

There was another pause.

"*We are,*" the voice answered.

Arracnoth pulled the other dagger from his belt and put his back against the wall. He had never held a weapon other than a small knife before, but he knew he didn't want these strangers, or whatever they were, sneaking up behind him. He would defend himself against these undead spirits as best he could.

"*We are. We are ... with you,*" the feminine voice from before said.

Arracnoth looked around him, on either side. He could see no one, just the stone walls, the plain coffin, and the bench he had been sitting on. The metal box lay on the floor where he had dropped it.

"*We are ... we have put ourselves in your hands,*" the masculine voice added.

Arracnoth's brow knotted as he became frustrated at their riddles. The ghosts were talking nonsense, and he was tired of their game. "Speak plainly, spirits!"

"Perhaps he is not worthy of this call after all. He is lost and will remain lost, and he will die here. Let the earth claim him as it has those before him." The feminine voice was sharp.

The masculine voice responded. His tone was soothing. *"He needs to be shown the way. We can lead him."*

"He will not listen. He will not follow you. He doubts."

Arracnoth flinched at the bitterness in the voice. It was almost physically cutting.

"It is, and always will be, his choice. Darkness or light."

Silence.

The voices ceased, leaving Arracnoth alone in the dark catacombs. He placed the serpentine blade back in his belt and picked up the light crystal, keeping the sai in his other hand. "Where did you go?"

"We are beside you," the male voice answered.

Arracnoth stiffened. The voice had spoken the Weode oath, reserved only for the closest friends for whom you'd give your life. *"Namartha t'undel."* The words tumbled from his lips before he realized what he had said.

"Namartha t'undel," the deep voice answered. There was such richness and sincerity in the voice that Arracnoth was a little taken aback. The voice spoke with authority, compassion, and strength. Even when he had shared those words with Avanstel and Danvaren, powerful though they were, they did not compare to the emotion behind this voice – from a spirit he could not even see. He fought back a tear, thinking of his friends and how far away and how long ago that moment at Adine's grave had been.

"I don't know who you are, and I cannot see you. I am not sure I can trust you." He cleared his throat. "But ... you spoke ... the words. You are Weode?"

"We are ... but we are not. We are ancient, and we are now. We are not ... Weode, we predate the Weode, but we share ... a connection ... with the Weode. We are what we are."

More riddles! Arracnoth scowled. "Are you beside me? Are you friends? *Namartha t'undel?*"

"*We are.*" The voice was powerful and reassuring.

"If you know the ancient words, and what they mean, you would not have said them if you meant me harm. I will trust you … for now." He raised his light crystal high again. "You will lead me out? To the surface?"

"*We will.*"

"How can I follow you if I can't see you?"

"*Take the second tunnel,*" the voice said.

Arracnoth swallowed, stepped cautiously out of the nook, and crossed the open space toward the second tunnel on his right. He stopped at the entrance. He raised the crystal and noticed the floor seemed to tilt slightly upwards, but there was no breeze or scent of fresh air coming to him. He took another step forward. "This one?" he asked.

"*Continue on. I will guide you, but you must follow me if you want to reach the surface.*"

Arracnoth nodded. He clutched the sai, raising it in front of him, and stepped into the tunnel. He continued forward, passing more statues and tombs and shelves of wrapped bodies. When he reached another split in the passage, he saw two flights of stairs leading upwards in different directions. He paused.

"*To the right,*" the voice said.

Arracnoth hesitated, eyeing the staircase to the left. "Who are you? And how do you know the way?" He turned and looked at the tunnel behind him.

"*Many people have given me many names over the ages.*" There was a lightness in the answer. "*My most recent name was Marek, and if that suits you, you may use it … or you may choose another if you like.*"

"Marek," Arracnoth mused. He stepped forward and climbed the stairs to his right. "That will be fine. And the other voice, is that you also?"

"*Not I, but we are,*" Marek answered. "*We are the same, but we are not the same.*"

"So, there are two of you spirits?"

"*There are … two of us. Yes, we are.*"

He reached another landing, with three staircases leading in different directions.

"*The middle staircase,*" Marek directed. Arracnoth followed. He could tell they were getting closer to the surface. A strong breeze of fresh air was coming from ahead. He breathed it in.

"Who is the other spirit? Why have they stopped talking? Are they still with us?"

"*They are. We are. Up the last flight of stairs to the left.*"

He climbed the last flight of stairs and found himself in an enormous circular chamber. In the center was a large, raised platform with steps leading to the top, where several braziers burned, bathing the massive room in a warm orange glow. Arracnoth could see passages around the circumference of the room, leading off to what he supposed were other tunnels that descended to the catacombs, like the one he had emerged from. Unlit sconces hung on the walls between each of the passages. An intricate mosaic tile pattern of a massive tree with branches spiraling and arching outwards covered the floor. It was the same design from the back of the strange coin Hathar had given him at The Pig & Lamb what felt like forever ago, and it covered the entire room, stretching from the center dais to the cavern's edge. He looked around, taking it all in, and placed the light crystal back into his pouch.

He withdrew the other weapon and stepped cautiously into the room.

"The burial place of the Weode?" he asked Marek.

"*It is,*" the feminine voice answered. Arracnoth instinctively turned to his left, where he thought the voice had come from.

"You're here?"

"I never left. We are."

Arracnoth was too tired to play more games. "What do I call you?"

"Adesh was my most recent name. You may choose another if you prefer. Whatever pleases you."

"Adesh and Marek," Arracnoth said. "Is there a way out of here?"

Then he saw it. On the far side of the room was an open doorway, the doors themselves the height of three or four men. From beyond the doorway came a dim light – the promise of an exit. He didn't wait for the spirits to answer.

He crossed the room and walked toward the opening. As he approached, he could see moonlight from Relos and Eyama shining in the distance. Ahead of him lay a path of crushed white stone that led to a fountain that trickled softly. Beyond that, he could see the dark shapes of massive tree trunks.

All this, and his freedom, lay on the other side of a massive gate. He stepped back and looked at the barrier. The rails made it impossible for him to pass through, decorated with vines and leaves made of sturdy metal. The locking mechanism in the middle of the gate looked like a trunk, and it held the exit shut. He put the daggers in his belt and pushed against the gate with all the strength he had, but the lock held firm. He tried again, straining with everything he could muster, but nothing happened. He was so close – yet still trapped. He looked around him for something he could bash the mechanism with but saw nothing.

The only thing he had was …

He pulled the sai from his belt and placed it into the small opening in the lock. The blade in his hand was much too wide to fit into the hole to do any good, but in his desperation, he would try anything. Suddenly there was a click, and the gates swung open. Arracnoth stared in disbelief, looking at the dagger and back at the open gate. How had that worked?

It didn't matter – he was finally free! Finally out of the under-world! He stumbled past the gate and through the last bit of the overhang and onto the gravel pathway, falling down next to the fountain.

The air was fresh, and the sounds of the night fell sweetly on his ears. He heard an owl hoot in the distance. He rolled over and looked up at the two moons hanging amidst the millions of stars. Streaks of dark clouds blotted the light out randomly as they crawled across the sky. He sobbed – relief flooding his hungry, tired, injured body. He had escaped. He was free.

"*Rest now*," Marek said. "*We will watch over you. We are.*"

Arracnoth bolted upright. "You – you are here? Aren't dead spirits bound to the haunted places? To the burial grounds?"

Marek's voice was comforting. "*We are. We are not bound to anything or anyone or any place. We are. Rest now. There will be time for you to know us. All will come in time.*" His voice faded away.

The sounds of the forest night returned. Arracnoth placed the sai into his belt and leveraged himself up onto the edge of the fountain, where he drank deeply of the cool water. When he finished, he collapsed from exhaustion and closed his eyes. He would figure out where he was in the morning, and then he would begin the search for his friends.

Sleep, deeper than he had had in many nights, overtook him.

Marek and Adesh lay beside him in the green grass, but *they* did not sleep. They never slept. They remained watching over their newest ward.

It had been thousands and thousands of cycles since they had had someone to watch over, and though this one wasn't like the others they had served, he held so much promise.

CHAPTER 12: REUNION

Cycle 739; The Brother; The Fifth Age.

Arracnoth opened his eyes. The light was blinding. He winced, closing them again, and turned away. His head was throbbing, and his entire body ached.

"Can you hear me, friend? How are you feeling?"

He attempted to sit up, but a firm hand pushed him back down.

"Rest. I don't know how you did it, but you have made it from the netherworld and are back with us, now." He knew the voice.

"Hathar…?" He opened his eyes again, squinting at the sharp sunlight pouring in from a tall window. He saw the warm, dark eyes of a bearded man leaning over him. "Hathar … I … I thought …"

"You must rest, friend. I can tell by your injuries that your journey has been difficult. I am eager to hear your tale – when you are feeling better, of course."

Arracnoth licked his dry lips. "Avanstel?" he croaked.

The cleric pressed a cup to his mouth, and he drank deeply. The liquid was cool and soothing, similar to the water from the fountain. He grabbed Hathar's arm. "Where are we? Where is Avanstel?"

Hathar's hand covered Arracnoth's. "He is safe. He's with our *drivrid* companion and our warrior friend. Our patron has summoned them. I stayed here to watch over you." Hathar gave Arracnoth another drink of the liquid. "We are in Ny'we Adye, mother city of the Weode kingdom."

"How long…?"

"They found you three days past, at the garden fountain outside the Undercroft. I dare say if you had gone yet another day you may have been beyond my ability to help. I have *some* skills in the divine art of healing, but you, friend, have put those skills to the test. You have been sleeping since you arrived, and I was worried that you might not wake up again. Your leg is an impressive tapestry of yellow and purple, but it will mend. How is your head? You hit it hard. It's a wonder you didn't knock the sense clear out of you."

Arracnoth managed to smile and reached up to touch his head. There were fresh bandages there. "It still hurts."

"It will for a while, friend. It is best if you rest now. The sun is getting low and soon it will be eventide, which comes to this forest sooner than you may be used to. Tomorrow, we will get you up out of this bed and get you something more substantial to eat. Weode water has restorative properties, but it is no replacement for a meal, and you have gone without for too long."

Arracnoth sank back into the soft bed. He was glad that he had reached Ny'we Adye, and that Avanstel and the others had found their way out of the netherworld. Although he did not remember being transported here, or anything else from the last three days, he was glad to have Hathar taking care of him. He thought about his strange experience in the caverns after he got separated from his friends, but it all seemed like a faraway dream – like something he had imagined.

He touched his head again. *Had* he imagined it? Had he hallucinated the voices, the spirits, guiding him? It was completely possible that it had all been a stupor brought on by starvation and thirst and darkness and solitude – or even his head injury.

"Close your eyes and receive Merces' blessing." The cleric put his hand on Arracnoth's head and murmured some soft words. Peace, comfort, and warmth flooded over him. Hathar's voice was real, and he was sure of it – so different from the ethereal whispering voices of the spirits in the caves. He let himself slip under again.

There was a blinding blue light all around him. Was it lightning? It spread across the sky in a jagged web over the city. Along with it was a horrific sound – not thunder ... and not just one sound, but many. The sound of hundreds, maybe thousands, of voices wailing in pain and suffering.

Then, an enormous bolt of blue lightning fell from the sky with an earth-shattering crack that split the night. The world shook, and the wailing suddenly ceased. A moment of silence ensued, then the night erupted with growls, snarls, and howls. The sounds raised the hair on his neck. The air filled with the noise of a multitude of creatures moving through the darkness as they began to scamper and crawl towards him.

He stood at the zenith of the city, in a tower that overlooked everything. The city stretched for leagues, and beyond that, he could see farmlands and three different rivers. There was no forest surrounding the city. This was not Ny'we Adye.

And then he heard the voice – the voice of the creature on the Shadow Gate doors – whispering the words again that filled him with fear. Except this time, *he* was saying them ... and it was *his* voice. The creatures lumbered toward him. His words enraged them. They were coming for him, to kill him, to devour him. They climbed the tower, flowing over buildings below him in a wave of limbs, fur, teeth, claws. They crawled over each other in their desperation to stop him from speaking, to silence him forever.

He opened his mouth to scream, and what came out was more like a low, mournful wail – a sound of sadness, despair, remorse beyond anything known in this world. And then they were upon him.

He woke up in a cold sweat and looked frantically at the room around him. He was safe – at the house in Ny'we Adye. Suddenly, there was a crack of lightning that lit the room. The thunder rolled away and faded into a low rumble. He couldn't go back to sleep – he didn't *want* to go back to sleep, to risk a return to the dream. He lay awake for hours, listening to the sound of the storm rolling across the sky and watching the flashes of lightning that lit up his room.

Eventually, the storm passed, and he fell back asleep. The dreams did not return.

Avanstel was the first to greet him in the morning, his face beaming with a wide grin. He wrapped his arms around Arracnoth and squeezed tightly. Arracnoth moaned in protest. "It hurts. My arm!"

Avanstel drew back, his face turning serious. "I'm sorry, I forgot! I am so happy to see you. I was so worried. I was afraid …"

"It's all right, Van. I'm glad to see you too." Arracnoth smiled. "It settles my heart to know you are safe."

Avanstel grabbed his shoulders and brought their foreheads together. He was uncharacteristically somber. "My heart is at rest now, too," he said. "I don't know how I could have …" Their eyes met. He didn't need to say anything more.

The seriousness of the moment lasted only a second before Avanstel sprung from the bed and began pacing about the room. "I have so much to tell you, Arrac! You won't believe what has happened." He gestured wildly. "Our patron, Lord Omaga, has arranged for me to meet with the Ade Gerent tomorrow. I've already met with some of the Lords and Ladies of the more important Weode Houses. Everyone is curious about me. I can tell some of them don't like me … which is to be expected, I guess, since I am *ort*, and this entire thing about an unknown heir has surely got everyone wondering what is really going on. But Lady Alle and Lady Shaal'Elonthra seem to be friendly. They're of the Founding Houses. There's five of them, you know … Founding Houses, that is. They're called Elders and they advise the Ade …"

Arracnoth's attention wandered from the conversation as he looked about the room, taking in the surroundings in the daylight. The darkness of the storm had passed, and the room looked more welcoming than it had during the night. The chamber was stately. Rich, dark wood panels covered the walls. There were two tall arched windows with filigree insets of flowers and leaves, from which bright morning light poured. Between them was a large bookcase. The shelves overflowed with ancient-looking tomes, gilded in silver and gold and bound in warm blues and greens and browns. Other objects nestled among them: a large cluster of purple crystals the size of his hand, a bleached white skull from some creature he didn't recognize, a polished stone sphere resting on a bronze stand. A large ornate armoire stood to his right, brimming with tunics, trousers, and cloaks of assorted colors, each worth a cycle's wages at The Pig & Lamb.

He rested on a cushioned bed, nicer than anything he had ever slept in. Above him was a canopy, and dark drapes hung on either side. Multiple blankets and pillows, each more luxurious than the last, surrounded him. An elegant chaise lounge covered in dark scarlet velvet with metallic gold threads sat to the left of the bed. Avanstel plopped himself down on it as he finished his story.

"So, what do you think?" Avanstel raised an eyebrow in expectation.

"I think you'll do just fine," he said, doing his best to disguise that he hadn't been paying much attention to Avanstel's narrative. "And I think that whoever owns this house, I bet they are wealthier than all of the Citizens in Chark combined!"

"This is Lord Selyndar Omaga's home," Avanstel replied. He sat back and put his feet up on the low table that sat in front of the chaise. "He's the one who sent Nightfall and the others to find me and bring me here to meet the Ade. Though what is to come of it after tomorrow is anyone's guess."

Just then, the doors to the room swung open. Nightfall entered with the others, followed by a young elven housekeeper who was bearing a large tray of fruits, sweetened breads, and cheeses. She scowled at Avanstel, who immediately removed his feet from the table and stood up, looking abashed. She placed the large tray on the table and looked at Nightfall.

"Thank you, Y'Zelle," the nether-elf said. The housekeeper nodded, made a curtsy, and left the room. She closed the large doors behind her.

Hathar moved to the bedside. "You look like you've regained some color." He took Arracnoth's head in his hands and turned it to the side. "The wound looks to be healing well. How are you feeling, friend?"

"Much better, though I am a little hungry…" He peered around Hathar at the tray.

Avanstel grabbed a selection of the sugary breads and some fruits that Arracnoth had never seen. "Try these orange ones. They are incredible!" He bit into one himself as he offered the others to Arracnoth.

Nightfall stood at the foot of the bed. "Do you feel well enough to tell us how you ended up in the Undercroft gardens?"

Arracnoth took the fruit and nodded. Between bites, he recounted the tale of falling down the shaft and being unable to get back up, and the long journey through the tunnels, finding the cleft in the rock, and making his way through the elven catacombs. The others listened with rapt attention. When he talked about finding the daggers on the skeleton, Nightfall leaned forward.

"Daggers, you say?"

Arracnoth nodded. "I ... I had them with me when I left the caverns."

Nightfall glanced at Scorpio. The warrior shook his head.

"They weren't on you when the Green Guard brought you to House Omaga," the *drivrid* said. "Those who found you may have taken them ... a normal procedure when armed strangers appear out of nowhere brandishing weapons. I will inquire about them. I would like to see these blades. Though, I'm concerned that if they are as artfully crafted as you have shared, they may have found their way into another owner's belt already."

Arracnoth shrugged. "What about *your* journey?"

Nightfall, Hathar, and Avanstel took turns sharing the story of their fight against the strange beast in the cavern. They had stumbled into a nest of the creatures and soon found themselves surrounded, vastly outnumbered, and suffering some serious injuries. They had lost track of Arracnoth during the battle. They quickly realized that if they were to survive, they would have to retreat and return to find Arracnoth later. Nightfall had led them away from the place and further into the caves where the creatures couldn't pursue. However, in their hasty flight, they took routes that led them into an ambush, and they ended up prisoners of a group of *drivrid*.

The nether-elves captured them and held them for a few days as they discussed what to do with their captives. Some wanted to slaughter them outright for trespassing in their territory. Others thought it better to sell them to the miners harvesting the mountain copper from the Radix. Their leader wanted to deliver them to the

Empress and allow her to decide their fate. As the days passed and they debated, Nightfall engaged their leader, a she-elf who had taken a fancy to her *drivrid* prisoner. He convinced her to have the other nether-elves search for Arracnoth, but they had returned empty-handed and had found no sign of him.

After days of discussion with their captors, Nightfall negotiated their release — but only after pledging to pay a considerable ransom, and only on the condition that they would immediately remove themselves from *drivrid* territory. Unfortunately, this also included the cavern where they had separated from Arracnoth. Unable to backtrack to search for him, they begrudgingly continued their journey, all with heavy hearts over the loss of their friend. Eventually, they emerged north of Ny'we Adye in the ruins of an old Weode fortress, just as Nightfall had planned.

Under the cover of night, they had stolen into the city and made their way to House Omaga, Selyndar's home. Selyndar was a friend and advisor to the Ade Gerent, the ruler of the Weode. And he was Nightfall, Scorpio, and Hathar's employer, their fabled patron — he had been for several cycles, now.

Arracnoth appeared in the Undercroft gardens only a day after the four of them had arrived, though it had been another three days since. Hathar tended to him and healed his wounds while Avanstel, advised by Nightfall and guarded by Scorpio, became entangled in the intrigue and politics of being the recently discovered heir to the Ade Gerent.

"So now what?" Arracnoth asked when silence settled over the party.

"I am sure our patron will want to meet you, if you feel up to it, *sondartin*. Perhaps a walk in the gardens, some fresh air, and sunlight will encourage your healing." Nightfall turned to Avanstel. "And tomorrow we meet with the Ade Gerent. I must warn you I do not foresee this to be a simple path forward. It was not the Ade that asked us to find his heir, but Selyndar. An *ort* child's appearance may displease the Ade and the court even more than it has unsettled some of the other noble Houses. There is much at risk here … for all of us. We will need to walk cautiously."

Arracnoth and Avanstel looked at each other. This was more of an adventure than either of them had ever imagined they would take part in. But they were together again, and for now, that was more important than anything else.

CHAPTER 13: SELYNDAR

The Weode were a guarded people. Distrustful of each other – but even more suspicious of outsiders. They did not tolerate foreigners infringing on their borders, and outright forbade them from entering their capital, Ny'we Adye.

Selyndar, however, was Lord of House Omaga, one of the founding Houses of the Weode. His grandfather, Kaelen, had come to Belkin Wood with Ni'Ilyan when he had split from the Th'arule. As a Weode Elder, a position of authority granted only to the heads of the five founding houses, Selyndar had special rights and privileges, one being the power to declare *taven'sanct*, or 'friend of the Weode.' This status allowed Arracnoth and the others to remain in the city without fear of being executed on sight for trespassing on Weode lands.

Taven'sanct did not exempt them from the other laws of the land, and held Selyndar accountable, even punishable, for their actions – lawful or otherwise. Although they arrived in Ny'we Adye under the protection of *taven'sanct*, it remained best to avoid drawing attention, so they moved by ways less traveled when they needed to go about the city.

Unlike the others, Arracnoth had appeared mysteriously in a secured, sacred space within the city – and he had been armed with strange, ancient weapons. *And* he was an *ort*. Selyndar exercised his influence to secure Arracnoth's release from prison. He had negotiated with the Captain of the Green Guard, who discharged Arracnoth to House Omaga under what amounted to 'house arrest.' For the Elder, openly associating with – even welcoming – a suspicious *ort* trespasser into his home was a risk to his reputation. Add Avanstel's sudden presence into the mix, and it was quite a scandal. Many a Weode raised their eyebrows and whispered to each other about the developments, speculating on why an Elder would do something so outrageous.

Although being trapped at House Omaga was not how Arracnoth had envisioned his first trip to Ny'we Adye, he didn't have other options. And there were certainly less comfortable places to be held captive than the palatial estate of Lord Selyndar Omaga.

After an incredibly rejuvenating soak in the private bath attached to his room, Arracnoth browsed through the outfits in his wardrobe. He selected a sleek grey tunic made of a fabric he had never seen before; it shimmered in the fading sunlight and felt impossibly soft against his skin. He thought back to the night at The Pig & Lamb when Nightfall gave him the first set of fine clothing and how their quality and beauty awed him. Here, before him, there was an entire closet full of such finery! He doubted anyone would miss the cloak he had left in the cave, though he still felt guilty for leaving it behind.

There was a knock at the door, and it swung open. Scorpio entered, dressed in a rich, red ensemble with an intricate golden-threaded pattern. Arracnoth tried to hide his look of surprise. Freshly groomed, the burly man looked radically different from the warrior of their flight from Chark. He'd trimmed his raven-dark hair to shoulder length and slicked it back like a noble. His freshly shaven face still sported a shadow, and he smelled of sandalwood and spice.

Arracnoth thought Scorpio looked ruggedly handsome, but he could tell that the warrior was uncomfortable in the garb by the way he fidgeted and couldn't find a place for his hands to rest. "Wow! You are hardly recognizable!" he said with a smile.

Scorpio grunted. "Nightfall insisted."

"I'm sure he did," Arracnoth chuckled. "He seems to know our patron best. I'm sure he has a reason. Do you know Selyndar Omaga?"

"A little."

Arracnoth knew it would be a challenge to carry on a conversation with the solemn giant. Although his appearance had changed, his demeanor had not. True to his nature, Scorpio was a man of few words. Arracnoth sighed. He would have to rely on Nightfall or Hathar to explain how the trio had settled into the employment of a Weode noble on their quest for a previously unknown royal heir. "Shall we go then?" he asked. "I am looking forward to meeting him."

Scorpio nodded and turned from the room. He led Arracnoth out to the entry hall and along the balcony that overlooked the main floor. Enormous windows set in the far wall filled the gallery with warm sunlight. Tall banners, decorated with what Arracnoth assumed was the crest of House Omaga, hung from the three-story ceiling. They descended the oversized stairs and then made their way to a richly decorated hall lined with intricately woven tapestries and gilt-framed paintings of forest scenes filled with flora and fauna. To his right, tall, elegant windows overlooked the gardens at the back of the house. Flowers in a plethora of colors dotted the landscape, surrounding an open green space. A majestic stone gazebo rested on an island in the middle of a small pond fed by a slowly flowing river. He marveled at the beauty of the place.

Finally, they entered a modest-sized dining hall with a large, dark wooden table. Here they found the others, all dressed as finely as Scorpio, along with a tall, elderly elven man Arracnoth assumed was their benefactor. Although his face was thin and stern, when he saw Arracnoth, a smile softened his expression and lit up his eyes.

"It is good to see you are well enough to join us this evening." He spoke the common tongue, and although he spoke it fluently, his accent was thick with Weald-speak. His voice was pleasant and almost musical. "I am Lord Selyndar Omaga. Welcome to my home."

Arracnoth bowed slightly. "I am in your debt."

Selyndar waved his hand dismissively. "Your presence here is of great import to our people. There are stirrings within Ny'we Adye, and I fear swift action may be needed to prevent dire consequences for all Weode. I am pleased to have you and your friend here under my protection." He paused and then shook his head. "But there is time for discussion of such things after we eat. Come, you must be hungry. I offer you my finest. Y'Zelle, please send for the meal."

The young elven maid disappeared through a door at the back of the room. A moment later, several servants brought forth large trays filled with freshly roasted wild game, rich creamy soups that would put Caty's chowder to shame, piles of fruits that Arracnoth had never seen, and an array of colorful desserts.

Selyndar moved to the head of the table and motioned for Arracnoth to sit at his side. Avanstel took the seat across from Arracnoth. Their eyes met, and Avanstel grinned and winked. The others found their places around the large table. The servants set plates heaping with food before them. Elegant glasses appeared, filled with the sweetest wine Arracnoth had ever tasted. He downed his glass and found it promptly refilled.

Nightfall tugged at his arm. "Go easy, *sondartin*. This is unlike the drink in Chark, and you will soon find yourself asleep again if you continue at that pace."

Selyndar laughed, a baritone melody. "Indeed," he said, and raised his glass, downing it in the same manner as Arracnoth.

Few words passed for the rest of the meal, as they were all focused on the rich and succulent flavors of the masterfully prepared food. When they finished, Selyndar pushed himself from the table and stood up. "Come, let us enjoy the evening in the garden. Y'Zelle, please have more drink delivered to the terrace."

As Nightfall had predicted, Arracnoth found he was feeling very relaxed and slightly drowsy. The food and drink, as well as the company, had been so rejuvenating, and he wanted even more and wasn't ready to retire. He followed their host to the terrace, which led to an incredibly beautiful piazza that ended in a circular gazebo covered in purple flowers. Their fragrance filled the night air.

"Please, sit and rest." Selyndar motioned to a comfortable bench and took his place in a tall-backed chair. "Now that we are all gathered, and your companion has recovered, I will relate to you our present situation. Of course, my agents know some of the story, but not all of it. And there is still some story to be revealed in the coming days."

Arracnoth leaned forward and noticed Avanstel had done the same.

"Your friend, the nether-elf, is no stranger to Ny'we Adye. He has been in my employ several times over the cycles. As a Weode, and a very public figure, I am ... let's say, 'restricted,' in ways that would seem absurd to those who have the freedom to roam as they choose. Many in Ny'we Adye observe my movements and actions, and the wrong behaviors could have undesirable effects on my standing and ability to influence the direction of our kingdom. I sometimes require other parties to act on my behalf." He gestured at Nightfall.

"I am not content, as some of the Weode are, to simply waste away the gift of long life merely in the taking of pleasures. Nor, like others of my people, do I find delight in the malicious games of royal politics, removing enemies and maneuvering for positions in the

Ade's favor … though in this instance, events drew me in for the good of all our people … well, *my* people."

He took a long drink and looked out over the gardens. Arracnoth followed his gaze and noticed that fireflies were appearing within a dark copse of pines that sat beside a slow-moving river. Hushed sounds of doves in the trees and the gurgle of a waterfall filled the night. Overhead, the bright white light of Relos was showing over the edge of the trees. Selyndar sighed and returned to the conversation.

"House Omaga is one of the five Founding Houses that can trace our lineage to the very beginning of the Weode kingdom. My grandfather came to Belkin Wood with Ni'Ilyan when he freed us from the tyranny of the Th'arule. The Omagas have been loyal subjects, our fates intertwined with the fates of House J'Onsal, Ni'Ilyan's descendants, for over five thousand cycles.

"The Ade Gerent and I were contemporaries, growing up together in the royal palace. My father served his father, Ade E'Vestren, as the Captain of the Green Guard, and I served Ade N'Athero, first as his friend, then as his personal Protector, and then finally as an advisor. We know each other well, and I have been by his side through all our long lives. I am privy to many of his secrets and have maintained his confidence all these many cycles. I pledged to serve him, until either he or I make our journey to Parvanor and rest with our ancestors. We were inseparable … until recently.

"A cycle or so ago, the Ade took a new lover. This is nothing unusual for him; he has had many over the centuries, and as the Ade, there are many who seek his favor and use it to their advantage. My friend has a weakness for pleasures of the flesh." He looked at the floor in silence, lost in thought. Everyone waited without speaking.

Selyndar cleared his throat and continued. "Soon after she entered his life, I noted that my old friend had become paler, frailer looking. He is aged, like me, but he seems to me to have now aged beyond his cycles. Perhaps … unnaturally.

"When I asked the Ade if he was well, he dismissed my concerns, making excuses for his weakness and fatigue and quickly changing the subject. I did not press him for answers then, as there were others present, and these things are best discussed privately. Those in the court could, and would, use signs of weakness for political advantage, so it is best to hide such things.

"The next day when I attempted to visit him and privately address my concerns over his health, I found myself barred from seeing him. His new lover gave orders to the guard to keep me away. Since then, he has become a bit of a recluse, secluding himself in his private apartments for days on end with only his lover coming and going. He rarely shows himself in court or other parts of the palace … and to be honest, it's been months since I've even seen *her*, and there are questions amongst the Houses about her pedigree from since none will claim her as their own.

"Rumors have circulated, of course. There are those who question if the Ade is at the end of his rule, though he should have a century or more ahead of him before his rest in Parvanor. Two of the Founding families, House Y'Vellian and House Kellendaer, have talked of moving to replace the Ade with his son and heir, Dredaius."

Avanstel shifted uncomfortably. Arracnoth looked at his friend and saw the surprise on his face. He hadn't known before this that there was another heir. It was as much of a surprise to Avanstel as it was to Arracnoth.

"I thought …" Avanstel began.

Selyndar raised his hand. "Rest easy. The lineage of the heir-apparent is not without question. Although there are some who believe Dredaius to be of royal blood, there are others, myself included, who believe this to be a deceit originating from those who would assume the throne through lies and cunning. The Ade has acknowledged Dredaius as his child because he can bring no proof against the claim. Dredaius' mother, although departed from this realm now, had been the Ade's consort at the time of her pregnancy. The Ade wishes to be seen as a benevolent ruler by his people and so did not challenge her allegation. He took in the whelp and raised him and declared him as heir to the throne.

"But those who know of Dredaius' true nature see things in him that are dissimilar to our great and kind Ade. The Aetheling, the heir-apparent, has displayed concerning behavior for one who could become the leader of our kingdom. His eyes are cold, and his tongue is sharp. He is impulsive, known for his wicked bent, violent and vicious and conniving. A serpent in the beautiful garden of Ny'we Adye.

"Expecting that our Ade is failing, and fearing for the future of our realm, I am burdened to discover the source of his rapid decline and work to bring him back to health. Or, alternately, should he be unable to recover, to reveal a little-known truth to my people: that there is another potential heir to the Weode throne, perhaps with a more legitimate claim than Dredaius has."

Selyndar paused, taking a drink from his cup and allowing them a moment to process all that he had shared. Then he continued, "It is my suspicion that the Ade's new mistress is poisoning his mind and possibly his body, too. Though by what means, it is yet to be uncovered. And without the recourse to intervene peacefully, my options are to either to start a civil war within the kingdom – which is not something that I would remotely consider – or to use my knowledge of the Ade's ... ah ... previous *indiscretions* to locate the child I believe he may have sired. Thus, I sent my agent, Nightfall, to Chark to find the child I believe to be an heir of the Ade Gerent."

He sat back in his chair and folded his hands in his lap, nodding to Nightfall to continue the narrative.

"My colleagues and I were in Chark many moons before the night we showed up at the tavern." The *drivrid* fixed his golden gaze on both Avanstel and Arracnoth as he spoke. "As you know, there are many abandoned half-elven children in Chark, most with unknown lineage. Finding a child with a deliberately concealed heritage is even more difficult. And looking for threads after thirty cycles is nearly impossible. It took us time to narrow down who we were looking for. We discovered that there was another interested party who was also looking for an *ort* child born around the same time. We had to operate discreetly to not draw attention and ensure that we succeeded before they did."

"But we found you!" Hathar exclaimed loudly. He clapped Avanstel on the shoulder. The sudden outburst surprised Arracnoth, who had been hanging on Nightfall's every word. "And you know the rest, friend!"

Avanstel looked at Selyndar seriously, unfazed by the cleric's rowdy eruption. "Do you think Dredaius sent men to find me … and kill me?"

"It is possible he, or others, could have set such events in motion. Ny'we Adye is full of cunning parties vying for the political power and favor of the next Ade." He looked out into the gardens, lost in thought again. "Though I am uncertain how they knew I had sent my agent to Chark. That remains a mystery, as I have not been to the palace in months. I am still unwelcomed there."

He shrugged and looked back at Avanstel. "Dredaius has many resources at his disposal; many Weode are loyal to him and eager to do his bidding. And possibly other allies and tools are yet to be discovered."

There was a long silence. Arracnoth looked around at the others. Hathar was scratching his beard, deep in thought. Scorpio shifted in his seat, peering into every shadow in the garden and looking ever-ready for a fight. Avanstel looked concerned at the revelation of Dredaius and the political spiderweb he had unknowingly stepped into. Nightfall met Arracnoth's gaze, his face unreadable, golden eyes glinting.

"Come now." Selyndar stood up. Y'Zelle appeared instantly, as if out of nowhere, to take his glass from his hands. She stepped back, waiting patiently behind her employer. Arracnoth thought he saw a look of disdain on her face when she glanced at him and Avanstel, but it disappeared quickly. He wondered if they were keeping her away from her own retirement, and she resented it. Or perhaps she held the same prejudices as those in Chark and thought it distasteful to have to serve so many outsiders – including *ort* ... though she hadn't seemed that way previously.

Selyndar motioned towards the main house. "Let us retire for the night. Tomorrow we will speak with the Ade Gerent. It will be the first time in a long time that I have visited with my old friend. I am looking forward to seeing him again, though I have a heavy heart thinking about what I may find when I again look into his eyes. The fate of our realm could well lie in the events of tomorrow."

CHAPTER 14: DUPLICITY

The light coming in through the window was diffuse and dull. It was morning, but something grey and cold had replaced the bright warm sunshine that Arracnoth had expected in this place. He could tell instantly that something was wrong. There was a strange feeling hanging at the edge of his perception that prompted him to swing his legs over the edge of his massive bed and grab a robe to investigate. As his hand touched the doorknob to his room, he realized that the birdsong that usually greeted him in the morning was missing.

The knob turned beneath his hand, and the door opened. Nightfall was standing before him with a serious look on his face.

"Come quickly, *sondartin*. The others are gathering downstairs. There is news from the palace." Arracnoth followed Nightfall out of the room and down the hall. As they approached the balcony overlooking the main entrance and made their way to the stairs, they heard voices from below echoing through the massive two-story entry hall. Arracnoth recognized Selyndar's voice, raised with an urgent tone.

"When did this happen, N'Khael? How?"

"Father, I came as fast as I could." The voice was light and lilting, with the same accent and cadence as their patron. "There are few details, and I have told you all I know. I left as soon as I heard it so that I could get to you before others found out. Word will spread within the hour, and I knew it was urgent for you to be briefed. You must ready yourself and get to the palace before the other Elders arrive."

Nightfall and Arracnoth had circled the room and reached the top of the staircase. Hathar and Avanstel arrived. Avanstel looked as bewildered as Arracnoth felt. The four of them descended the large stairs to the entry hall below. Arracnoth could see Scorpio standing next to an elven woman clad in exquisite, green-tinted armor. Her emerald helmet was resting in the crook of her arm. Long, fiery red hair framed a pale and elegant face, and warm chestnut-brown eyes flecked with gold looked up at him briefly.

She frowned and looked back at Selyndar. "Your guests. They … complicate things."

Selyndar followed her gaze. "N'Khael," he scolded. "They are – all of them – under the protection of House Omaga. I have declared *taven'sanct*, in keeping with the laws of our people and my rights as an Elder."

"But father … *ort?* Do you know what they are saying?"

Selyndar's voice boomed with unexpected power. "I don't concern myself with the whispers of the commoners and neither should you."

A fire sprang up in her eyes. Arracnoth could see the red rising on her neck. "It's not just the commoners, father. The palace is alight with—"

"Enough, N'Khael!" Selyndar roared. "House Omaga opens its arms to all in need. You know that better than anyone."

She looked down, unwilling to meet his eyes. Selyndar stood still, waiting for her to respond, and giving himself a moment to get control over his own emotions.

"I understand," she said after a time. There was a tone in her voice that reflected resignation, more than approval or agreement.

Selyndar straightened his back. "You have served House Omaga well, daughter. Return to the palace before they miss you. I will arrive as soon as I can and will look for you inside the Great Hall. You can share with me any additional information you are able to obtain."

She nodded, looked up at him, shook her head briefly, and then exited through the large main doors at the far end of the room. As they slammed behind her, the sound echoed through the enormous open space.

Selyndar turned back towards them. He looked at Avanstel and Arracnoth. "I must apologize for my daughter. I fear that she has spent too much time at the palace, and it has influenced her perspective, and not in a manner that aligns with her upbringing. I sometimes must remind her of that."

Arracnoth felt uneasy, having observed such a private family matter, and didn't know how to respond.

Selyndar noted their discomfort and changed the subject. "We have grave news, I am afraid." His voice was weary and trembling – a drastic change from the powerful boom that had filled the space just moments before. He walked to the side of the room and sat on one of the stone benches that lined the walls. "The Ade has departed this realm and has begun his journey to Parvanor, the resting place of our people. As I am sure you heard, there are few details to share. My heart is heavy by the loss of my friend ... though I fear I truly lost my friend long ago."

Hathar stepped towards Selyndar and placed a tentative hand on the elder elf's shoulder. He whispered some words in a language that Arracnoth didn't understand, but he recognized a similarity to the healing words that Hathar had spoken over him when he had first arrived at Selyndar's home. Selyndar looked up at the cleric and nodded in appreciation.

"We must get to the palace," Selyndar declared. "It is not the audience that we were expecting, but it is even more critical now that the Ade has departed. There will be those who will want to move rapidly to place Dredaius on the throne, despite the lingering doubts surrounding his heritage." He looked at Avanstel. "Although, this could also be said of others. Quickly, let us prepare ourselves and depart. The city will wake up to this news, and the streets will flood with Weode looking for answers. It is best to be secured inside the palace before it fills up and the doors are closed."

The news had spread as rapidly as N'Khael had predicted, and the streets were almost impassable by the time they reached the entrance to the palace. Arracnoth wasn't able to take in much of the grand city in their hurried rush from House Omaga to the palace. He hoped that someday he would get to know this place better — someday when he wasn't under house arrest, and when Avanstel was on the throne.

Nightfall had given him a grey cloak and instructed him to keep his hood up, his head down, and his eyes fixed on Avanstel's back to avoid getting lost. It was easy enough for him to blend into the crowd as they followed Selyndar through the winding passages and around the gathering crowds. Even Hathar and Nightfall were able to avoid attention for the most part. Scorpio, however, could not help but stand out wherever he went. The hulking mass of muscle stood over a foot taller than even the tallest denizens of Ny'we Adye. His insistence on wearing his own scarlet cloak only heightened the attention he drew, as most of the Weode were dressed in blues, greys, browns, and greens. The sight of him was followed by many surprised gasps and pointing fingers. One child even screamed when she saw the copper-skinned giant lumbering in their direction.

Arracnoth stifled a laugh at the absurdity of Scorpio trying to blend in. He was sure the warrior wouldn't appreciate the humor of their situation.

At the palace, two Green Guards stopped them, holding up their hands to signal that no more visitors could enter. They took one look at Scorpio, shock registering on their faces, and stepped aside. The doors of the palace were closed behind them. They had made it just in time.

The Great Hall was bustling with people. Most visitors gathered in groups, chatting, whispering, and pointing in various directions. The conversation near the door ceased when they entered. At first, Arracnoth assumed Scorpio caused the silence, but he looked up and saw that Selyndar had removed his hood.

A young elf rushed up to the group. "Lord Omaga!" He bowed.

"Greetings, Tretarilus. What troubles the Steward today?"

"The Ade requests your presence in the throne room."

"The Ade? I thought …" He paused. "I see. You mean Dredaius."

Tretarilus stammered. "Sir." That was all he could manage.

"The other Elders?"

"Lord Y'Vellian, Lord Kellendaer, and Lady Alle are there now with the …" He cleared his throat. "In the throne room. Lady Shaal'Elonthra has not yet arrived."

"Be sure to alert the Guard to allow her entrance when she arrives, Tretarilus."

The Steward nodded and stepped aside, motioning them forward.

As Selyndar strode through the hall, the silence spread like a ripple over water. Arracnoth could feel the weight of all the eyes upon their party, though he could not see their faces. He risked a quick glance at his companions and saw N'Khael at the far end of the hall, leaning against the wall, watching them cross the room. The hint of a smile tugged at her lips.

"Daughter," Selyndar said as they passed her.

"Father." She inclined her head, the smirk still on her face. "That was quite the entrance. You have the attention of the entire Hall." She glanced at Scorpio. "So much for arriving unnoticed." She ignored the others.

Selyndar waved his hand dismissively. "News?"

"As expected, Dredaius declared himself Ade Gerent moments after the death of the … ah … his father. He is with the Elders now in the throne room. You are on the way there? Good. I will join you. I know it will raise eyebrows, but I want to be there should there be any trouble."

They proceeded towards a pair of large arched doors. A hush had fallen over the entire room. The guards opened the doors to the throne room as Selyndar approached. As soon as the doors closed behind them, Arracnoth heard the buzz of conversation start up again on the other side.

"You may remove your head coverings," Selyndar said. Arracnoth slid the grey cloak off his head and looked around the room. It was smaller than the Great Hall and much more ornately decorated. Carved forest scenes made of mosaic and pale stone covered the walls. It reminded him of the tombs of the Undercroft, but brighter, with vivid, almost lifelike colors, and in much better repair. Gold, silver, and copper gilded the carvings and sconces lining the room in intricate interwoven designs. At the far end of the room, the design of an elaborate tree decorated the wall behind the throne. Arracnoth recognized it as the tree from the mosaic in the Undercroft, and from the coin that Hathar had given him the night the strangers had come to Chark. It was even more beautiful here than its rendering on the face of the coin.

Before the tree, centered on a dais, sat a tall throne, the height of two men. It was crafted from pale stone, gilded in matching metals. A wolf's head, carved into the back of the chair, menacingly glared down at those who stood before it. Silver flickered in its dull eyes and from its threatening teeth. The chair's arms, crafted to resemble two sitting wolves, almost matched the ferocity of the one on the back of the chair. They were so lifelike that Arracnoth had to look twice to confirm they were made of stone. This was without a doubt where the White Wolf sat, the Ade Gerent, the leader of Belkin Wood, ruler of the elven kingdom and descendant of Ni'Ilyan, the founder of the Weode.

To the right of the massive throne, a step down, rested a smaller throne. The smaller throne looked almost out of place, as if someone had put it there as an afterthought; its craftsmanship and design didn't seem to match the rest of the room and lacked the inlays of shining metals.

Several figures stood at the foot of the dais in heated discussion. Selyndar and N'Khael stepped towards the group. Avanstel and Arracnoth followed behind them. Arracnoth caught a whiff of lavender in the air. The scent was pleasant, and it seemed out of place here inside the dark room with the impending meeting. The others brought up the rear of the procession. As they approached, the discussion paused, and the group turned to them.

"Lord Omaga," one of them said. The man was hunched over and looked like he was in the slow process of caving in on himself. Dark circles hung under his eyes, and his dark hair was thin and scraggly.

"Lord Y'Vellian," Selyndar replied, bowing. "And Lord Kellendaer." He turned and addressed the man next to the first. This man had dark eyes, set deep in his face, and a severe nose like the beak of a raptor. Lord Kellendaer nodded. He looked past Selyndar and over at the rest of the visitors, a sneer tickling the edge of his lip. His expression immediately turned to surprise when he saw Arracnoth and Avanstel, then quickly to concern, and then to indignation. He opened his mouth to speak, but an elderly woman next to him interrupted.

"Lord Omaga," she said. Her hands extended forward toward him, grasping the air in front of her. "Thank you for coming. Our people need your wisdom."

Selyndar stepped forward, taking her hands and placing them gently on his arm. Arracnoth looked at the old elf woman and noticed her eyes were milky white, her pupils completely obscured.

"Indeed, Lady Alle. They need the wisdom of *all* of us. It is an important day for our nation. I think we should all take a moment and pause before ..."

A man pushed Lord Kellendaer aside and stepped forward, stopping a few inches in front of Selyndar. "It is done! All of it is done. There's nothing more to discuss."

Selyndar took a step backwards and bowed, giving Arracnoth a clear look at the figure. He was younger than the others, with wavy dark hair combed back from his forehead. He might have been attractive, if it were not for the look of disgust contorting his face. He had high elven cheekbones and smooth tanned skin, emerald-green eyes flashing out beneath his arched brows. His gaze shifted from Selyndar to Arracnoth and Avanstel.

"*Ort?* You bring *ort* here? Into the palace? To the very heart of Ny'we Adye? To the center of *my* kingdom? You have gone too far, old man. I will have your head, Elder or not! Guards!"

N'Khael shifted her weight beside her father, her hand resting on her sword.

"Cease this nonsense, Dredaius!" Selyndar's voice boomed through the room, just like it had at House Omaga. This time, it was even more forceful. Even Arracnoth took a step backwards, surprised by how the elderly elf commanded the place. He hadn't expected Selyndar to speak with such authority and power. "I have declared *taven'sanct*, Friend of Weode, over these guests. As an Elder, it is my right!" The guards around the dais released their hands from their swords.

"It is his right," Lady Alle echoed.

Dredaius scoffed and turned around, nearly knocking Lord Y'Vellian over as he climbed the dais stairs two at a time and threw himself casually onto the grand throne, resting one leg over the arm. "Your right or not … it is distasteful," Dredaius said. "I heard the rumors but dismissed them, not believing that an Elder would do something so scandalous. We've been patient with your oddities, Lord Omaga. We've tolerated your humans and your *drivrid*. But even this is beyond anything. My father would not have stood for such disrespect."

"Your father …" Selyndar said. He stopped, looked at his feet, and took a deep breath. Arracnoth could see that the Lady's arm gripped Selyndar's tightly, encouraging restraint.

"Yes?"

"Your father was a good friend, Dredaius. And a good ruler." He sighed. "Right now, our people need a moment to grieve our loss. Let us not make decisions in haste. Let us complete the Week of Mourning, as is our tradition, and then the Elder Council can reunite and decide together what is best for our people."

"Wise counsel," Lady Alle said, and patted Selyndar's arm.

"*I* know what is best for our people," Dredaius said. "I am the Ade now and I say there will be no further discussion. I have the support of Lord Y'Vellian and Lord Kellendaer. We have discussed matters at great length and have come to agreement. Will you not align your thoughts to that of your peers? Or would you rather throw our people into a conflict where brother is against brother and father against son?"

"Dredaius," Selyndar said. "Please …"

"Then you want war amongst the Weode?"

"There will not be war amongst our people!" The voice came from behind them. Arracnoth and the others turned around in unison to see an elven woman walking toward them, another of the Green Guard in tow behind her. The woman wore a white and gold gown that floated behind her as if blowing in a breeze. Her wavy, silver-blonde hair seemed to reflect sunlight, though there was neither a breeze nor sunlight here in the throne room. She stopped beside Selyndar. "The Elders will be in unity ... for the sake of all of Weode."

"Ah! *There* is wise counsel," Dredaius said. He sneered at Lady Alle, which Arracnoth thought was odd, since the woman couldn't see him. But his tone conveyed his insult. "I'm glad you could join us, Lady Shaal'Elonthra. Someone needs to explain to Lord Omaga and Seer Alle what is at stake here should my right to the throne be challenged."

Selyndar looked at Lady Shaal'Elonthra, his brow furrowing. She placed her hand gently on his other arm and looked at him meaningfully. "It is as you say," she said, not taking her eyes from Selyndar's. "We will not challenge your right as Ade Gerent of the Weode. For the good of our people."

"Good, then!" Dredaius swung his legs around and stood up. "Then we shall have the Week of Mourning for the passing of my father, as Lord Omaga has requested. I will allow it." He turned to leave the room but paused, turned back, and locked eyes with Selyndar. "And we shall have no more of these ... *whispers* of long-lost bastard *ort* claiming to be a child of my father. There will be no future challenges to the throne. Agreed?"

Arracnoth saw Selyndar clench his jaw as Lady Shaal'Elonthra squeezed his arm. "As you wish," he said. His voice was low and broken.

Dredaius resumed his stride toward the door. He snapped his fingers and spun toward them again. "Oh, and one more thing that I almost forgot to mention: as soon as the Week of Mourning is over, I will be wed."

"Wed? To whom?" Lady Alle asked. "The preparations alone ... and there are alliances to consider ... and your father is just passed."

A smile crept across Dredaius' face. "Oh dear, sweet Tallayah. If only you had your sight, you could see the things right in front of you. Let me introduce you all to my bride-to-be. She is beautiful and cunning. A sharp mind … and a sharp tongue when she wants to use it. She will rule this kingdom at my side as Adelyn of the Weode. A position well-earned for all she has done, and will do, for our people." He turned and opened the door at the side of the dais. "Come, my dearest, let us share our news with the Elders before we announce it to all of Ny'we Adye."

A figure stepped through the open door. The woman was indeed beautiful. A chignon held her dark auburn hair at the back of her head. She seemed … familiar, but Arracnoth could not place where he had seen her before. Something tugged at the edge of his mind. He almost had it, but the memory wasn't quite right.

Selyndar inhaled sharply. "You! I am not surprised that you've gone from one Ade's consort to another! And within just hours of his passing!"

"N'Athero was an old fool," the woman said.

Arracnoth knew her voice. It was familiar … but it didn't belong to the woman standing before them. A gasp came from Avanstel. He heard Nightfall hiss and Scorpio growl behind them.

"Hello, *friends*." The woman's voice dripped with impertinence. She reached for the charm that hung around her neck and fiddled with it. A familiar smile on her lips was now filled with menace and vile.

"Questelle?" Arracnoth blanched. "How did you get here? You … you look … different …"

She laughed. It wasn't the laugh of delight and innocence he had heard so many times when the four of them had shared a room in the Blundt. This laugh was bitter and cutting.

"Of course I do!" she snapped. "I am no half-breed *ort!*" Arracnoth saw it then. She was an older, harsher version of Questelle. Her features were sharper, her ears more pointed and prominent ... like those of a full-blooded Weode. Her thin, dour lips were curled in a way that frightened Arracnoth. She was nothing like the Questelle he remembered.

Arracnoth frowned. "I don't understand. How did you get here? Is Danvaren with you?"

She laughed again. "Danvaren? He's ... well ... he's gone."

"What is this about?" Avanstel said. His voice was sharper than Arracnoth had ever heard it before. "Speak plainly, Questelle."

"Young, naïve *ort*," she said, shaking her head. "So easily swayed by the charms of a beautiful newcomer. So readily welcoming a stranger from Arden's Wharf. Welcoming me right into your midst." She toyed with the silver pendant on her neck. "You had no clue about what was going on around you. Completely oblivious to the game ... not even aware you were pieces on the board."

"Game?"

"Not that foolish game of Haven Chase, Avanstel." Her tone dripped with condescension. "*This* game is grander and more serious ... and I have a worthy opponent. It's more of a race, you see, to figure out which one of you is the rumored bastard child of old N'Athero."

She looked at Selyndar and sneered. "When it was brought to my attention that Lord Omaga had sent his agents to Chark to locate a challenger to the throne, I followed. I wasn't sure which one of the three of you they were most interested in, so I charmed my way into your lives, until I could figure out which one they were after. I thought it was Danvaren, until Avanstel disappeared, and I suspected I had been bested – though I wasn't confident that my opponent had chosen correctly. Then you escaped, too." She looked at Arracnoth. "Which made me sure that Danvaren was just a nothing *ort*. Not at all special. So, I disposed of him."

Arracnoth's stomach dropped. His ears rang, and his vision grew dark at the edges.

"Danvaren!" Avanstel cried. He bent over, and Arracnoth grabbed him before he fell to the ground.

"Don't grieve, Avanstel," she said with a smirk. "I let him die quickly."

Arracnoth gasped, despair welling up in him. "Questelle? You … You *killed* him?"

Questelle grinned. "Welcome to your first lesson in the game, *Arracnoth*."

The way she said his name sounded like a curse. It rang in his ears and made him feel sick to his stomach. Such callous wickedness. How could she have killed Danvaren? He had done nothing wrong. Done nothing but … love her … buy her things … treat her like the princess he thought she was! And she had simply just … killed him? He couldn't comprehend it. He had known no one this – this cruel, this evil. Even the Citizens who despised the *ort* would never …

Avanstel fell from Arracnoth's arms, weeping. One of the Green Guards who was with Lady Shaal'Elonthra stepped in quickly and held him up, so he didn't fall over. She looked at N'Khael, unsure what to do next.

"Thank you, Nephinae," N'Khael said. Her voice was taut with concern. "Hathar, Nightfall, take him home."

They stepped forward, grabbed Avanstel, and took him, weeping, back toward the entrance.

Arracnoth looked at the woman who had helped Avanstel. He wanted to thank her, but his thoughts were muddled, and he couldn't form the words. She nodded to him; her bright blue eyes were filled with empathy and sadness.

Scorpio stepped beside him and took Arracnoth's arm. He looked up at the giant. The fierce, strong face had melted away to reveal compassion and concern. "Scorpio? What do we do?"

"We will sort this out at House Omaga. Nightfall will know what to do. We are beside you. Beside you – and Avanstel."

The words brought Arracnoth back from the brink of complete despair. Did Scorpio realize what he had said? Did he understand the significance of those words?

"*Namartha t'undel.*" Scorpio repeated, as if to clarify. He knew.

"*Namartha t'undel.*" Arracnoth replied numbly and leaned into the warrior.

CHAPTER 15: LESSONS

Avanstel did not leave his room for days. Y'Zelle brought food to him regularly, but he ate little of it. The once dapper, jovial, and hearty young half-elf had become pale and withdrawn. He looked thin and haggard, and he had not spoken since the events at the palace. He spent most of the time sleeping, often waking from his dreams with a shout or cry. These terrors would rouse the house, depriving the others of sleep. After several nights of this, Arracnoth decided he would spend the nights with Avanstel, hoping his presence would give him some comfort. It felt like old times, at the Hall in Chark, being together, just the two of them. Although the terrors did not abate completely, Avanstel became a little more sociable and began to interact.

The funeral procession for the Ade occurred on the evening of the last day of the Week of Mourning. Arracnoth watched from the second-floor balcony at the front of House Omaga, overlooking the street below. The sun had just slipped beyond the tops of the trees when the streets flooded with hooded figures dressed in pale shades, carrying large white pillared candles. He heard the sounds of the sad, quiet song coming from the Weode who trailed along behind a wagon drawn by four white horses. On the wagon, surrounded by glowing candles, rested a large sarcophagus. An artisan had chiseled the top to resemble an older elven man, his hands resting peacefully on the hilt of a sword that lay atop his still body. An intricately carved crown held his long, straight hair in place.

"Like in the Undercroft," Arracnoth said.

"Yes." Selyndar had appeared behind him. "That is our tradition. Many have gone before him, and I fear many are yet to follow with Dredaius and Questelle on the throne."

Arracnoth turned to the elder elf and studied him. The warm glow from the hundreds of candles below lit his face. "What is to become of us now?"

Selyndar stared at the scene below in silence for a long moment before responding. "Things are still in motion, and their full revelation remains unseen. You are, of course, free to return to your city, should you choose to." He turned to Arracnoth. "Or remain, as you would like."

Arracnoth watched the last of the candle bearers disappear around the corner at the end of the street. The soft hum of their song faded into the night.

What was there to return to in Chark? His mother was gone. He had no family there. The Hall had burned. Danvaren was …

"There's nothing for me there. I will go wherever Avanstel goes."

Selyndar turned, placed his arms behind him, and walked thoughtfully back to the doors leading into the house. "I fear Avanstel's role in the events to come is hard to discern." He paused and turned back to Arracnoth. "And, perhaps, yours also."

The next morning, N'Khael appeared as they were eating breakfast. She greeted her father and then turned to the rest of them. "Blessed morn," she said to the others. Her gaze landed on Arracnoth. He saw a change in her eyes from the last time they had met. Something had softened there, though he wasn't sure what had caused the change. She nodded, and he nodded back.

Although she was not wearing the green armor that he had seen her dressed in a week ago, she carried herself with the rigidity of a soldier. Her demeanor was more welcoming than before, but she was, by nature, a direct person. She was used to taking and giving commands, and the manner in which she spoke reflected that. She had no time for idle conversation. She was a woman of action, used to diving directly into what needed to be done or said. "I bring news from the palace."

Selyndar motioned for her to sit. She took the empty seat next to Arracnoth. The scent of lavender filled the air, and Arracnoth realized it was coming from N'Khael. She placed a cloth-wrapped bundle on the table beside her before looking over the bowl of fruit sitting in the middle of the table. She selected a yellowish-green one from the pile. "The Ade … Dredaius… wed Questelle last night, immediately after the ceremony at the Undercroft. *At* the Undercroft." She bit into the fruit and sat back in the chair.

Selyndar slammed his hands down on the table, pushed his chair back, and stood up. "At the Undercroft? The place where we bury our dead? Unbelievable! And without notice?" His face was flushed.

"Would you have attended had you received an invitation?"

"The Council should –"

"Father, your position as an Elder is not in question. But perhaps it is better for you *not* to have received an invitation. That way, you would not have to deal with the consequences of rejecting it. Dredaius knows where you and the other Elders stand. He knows that you supported him only at the urging of Seer Alle and Lady Shaal'Elonthra. You have the attention of the Ade, now, because of your actions." She looked around the table. "Where is the other …?"

Hathar cleared his throat. "He's resting. He has been unwell since learning of his brother's death. We are caring for him."

N'Khael nodded. "The Ade has requested his presence."

"He is in no condition …"

"When he's ready," she said calmly, and took another bite of the fruit. She turned to Arracnoth and looked at him intently. She didn't speak for a long moment, and he could read a struggle within her by the expressions on her face. Eventually, she pushed the cloth-wrapped package across the table towards him. "This is for you."

"Me?"

"Yes," she said, while chewing on the fruit. "My colleague Nephinae suggested that I find them and bring them to you."

He carefully untied the bundle, curious about what could be inside. As he tentatively parted the cloth, he saw a flash of silver-blue metal and looked up at N'Khael in surprise.

"I convinced the captain to give them to me. They are fine blades, although not a matched set, and nothing that a Weode would use. They found them with you at the Undercroft. Nephinae thought you might want them back."

"Thank you."

Nightfall, Hathar, and Scorpio leaned in to get a look at the daggers. Hathar whistled. "I have never seen such craftsmanship!"

"They look elven, but we would never use that metal," N'Khael said.

Selyndar nodded in agreement. "But old. Incredibly old. In Weald-speak, we call the metal *estrayaed*. It translates roughly as 'star ore.' We have little of it here, in Belkin Wood. What exists is from ancient things, brought from the Ivy Forest when we fled our oppressors. Weode prefer steel, gold, silver, and other metals. The *estrayaed* reminds us of times long ago … times our peoples would like to forget."

"Likely the reason the Guard didn't care to keep them for themselves. They aren't of value to us," N'Khael said. She took another bite of her fruit. "Do you know how to use them?"

Arracnoth looked at her sheepishly. "No, I had only just acquired them."

She stared at him again. Another long silence sat between them as she sorted something out inside her mind. "I will teach you," she said. She looked at Selyndar expectantly.

He smiled at her and nodded.

"We will start lessons tomorrow morning. You will need to learn to defend yourself. Although you are *taven'sanct*, Belkin Wood is not friendly to outsiders, especially *ort*. My father's protection is of no good to you in a dark alley or tavern, where others would not bring testimony against a fellow Weode." She stood up, turned to Selyndar, and bowed. "Father, I take my leave." And she was gone as fast as she had appeared.

Arracnoth looked at Selyndar. "I have only ever used a knife. These weapons are …"

"N'Khael will be an excellent teacher."

Arracnoth looked at Nightfall for confirmation, who said, "Because of his religious vows, Hathar will not touch sharpened weapons. Scorpio is a master of the long blade and has limited experience in daggers. I could teach you the Dance of the Daggers, but I think it would be beneficial for you to learn the Weode style of engagement. The enemies you may face in Belkin Wood will attack you in the manner of the Weode. A Green Guard, especially one as skilled as N'Khael, is well-versed in these tactics and will give you excellent training."

Arracnoth nodded, giving a slight shrug. It was decided. Whatever her original thoughts about him, she was extending a peace offering, and he needed to accept it, whether or not he was prepared for the lessons ahead.

"Besides," Nightfall continued, turning to Selyndar. "I will need to take my leave. Here in Ny'we Adye there are many eyes on us, and my next errand for our patron takes me far away."

Selyndar stood up from the table. "It does," he said. "Let us talk more in private." He turned toward the door that led to the gardens. Nightfall followed.

While the Weode mourned the passing of their beloved Ade with public ceremony, Arracnoth and Avanstel mourned the loss of Danvaren in private. He had been a friend to Arracnoth, and losing this friendship brought him a lot of sorrow. But Avanstel had lost a brother. The two had spent their entire lives together, sharing a bond only brothers could. Losing Danvaren had left Avanstel in ruins. He was a shadow of the vibrant man Arracnoth had known him to be in Chark. And as the days passed, he looked weaker and weaker. He didn't even show an interest in playing Haven Chase with Arracnoth on the beautiful board that Lord Omaga had.

Arracnoth was concerned that Avanstel may never recover from his sadness, and his heart ached to see his friend so overcome with grief. He asked Hathar to visit Avanstel to see if there was anything the cleric might offer him. When Hathar entered their room and saw Avanstel, Arracnoth caught the look of concern that flashed across his face. "Has he eaten?"

"Y'Zelle brings him a tray each day. He eats a little, but not much."

Hathar left the room and returned with a cup filled with a red-colored drink. He held Avanstel's head up and murmured some words over him as Avanstel took a sip, closed his eyes, and fell asleep. Arracnoth looked at Hathar. The cleric held up a finger. "Give it some time," he said.

After a few silent minutes, Avanstel opened his eyes again. His face had some color that hadn't been there before, and his eyes lit up when he saw Arracnoth. "I'm hungry," he said. "What's for dinner?"

"Really? What is in that drink, Hathar? He hasn't had an appetite in days."

Hathar frowned. "I need to speak to Lord Omaga immediately. Get Avanstel up and dressed. We will meet you downstairs."

Arracnoth helped his weak friend wash and dress and make his way to the dark-paneled dining room on the first floor of the manor. It was slow going, especially on the stairs. Avanstel had become feeble after so many days in bed and leaned heavily on Arracnoth for support.

When they reached the dining room, they saw Selyndar and N'Khael in a corner of the room, talking in hushed tones. The conversation ended abruptly as they saw Avanstel's emaciated form. He glanced at Hathar, who was standing near the kitchen door with Scorpio, and nodded. Hathar turned and disappeared through the doors to the kitchen.

Scorpio stepped forward and wrapped a large arm around Avanstel, helping him into a chair. Arracnoth sat down beside his friend and pulled the plate in front of them closer. It was full of fruit and bread. Avanstel reached for it.

Hathar returned from the kitchen with a small glass vial in his hand. He held it up to the light. Inside was a yellow, sluggish liquid.

"As I suspected," Hathar said. His voice was serious. "Poison."

Selyndar closed his eyes and shook his head. "In my own house." He placed his hands on the table, his shoulders slumped forward. "Can you heal him?"

"Yes. It will take time, but yes."

"Like the Ade," N'Khael said.

"Perhaps. But faster acting. More potent." Hathar set the vial down on the table.

"I don't understand. Who would want to poison Avanstel?" Arracnoth asked. But inside, he already knew the answer. "Questelle." He grimaced.

"Someone in my own home has violated the *taven'sanct.*" Selyndar's voice was louder than Arracnoth expected. "They will pay for the harm they have caused your friend!" Selyndar spun on his heels and pushed through the doors to the kitchen.

N'Khael's face was dark with echoes of her father's anger. "Justice will be swift. Fear not, this will not happen again under this roof. Let's postpone today's lesson, Arracnoth. We should focus on Avanstel." She turned to Hathar. "Is there anything further you need, cleric?"

"My elixir is working. I will make more. By tomorrow morning, he will feel more like himself. The best thing now is to give him food and drink … and perhaps a sit in the gardens in the sun would be beneficial."

"Hear, hear!" Avanstel said. He popped a berry into his mouth and grinned. He was definitely acting more like the Avanstel that Arracnoth knew.

As Hathar had predicted, Avanstel was feeling better the next morning. Cut off now from the continuous drip of poison, his appetite had returned. Soon, he was able to walk on his own. He was still gaunt, but Arracnoth could see that he was on the mend, at least from his physical sickness. He still mourned his brother, but Arracnoth knew grief took its own path and followed its own timeline, not a predefined set of rules. Avanstel would move forward, and his heart would mend when it should.

A week had passed, and N'Khael was ready to start Arracnoth's lessons. Avanstel asked if he could join them in the garden so he could watch. Arracnoth caught a hint of mischief in his eye and was glad to see his friend's jovial nature returning. Before Arracnoth could object to the idea, N'Khael had agreed. Arracnoth prepared himself for an afternoon of harassment. He would prefer not to serve as entertainment, but if it made Avanstel laugh, then it was worth it.

Avanstel sat on the terrace overlooking the open green space where N'Khael would teach Arracnoth the Dance of the Daggers. He was nervous. Both about his ability to learn – he had never had more than a knife, so lacked any experience in fighting maneuvers – but also about interacting so closely with Lord Omaga's daughter. Their first meeting hadn't been very cordial, and although he no longer sensed her dislike of him, or the *ort*, her direct manner took a little getting used to.

He placed the daggers on a stone at the edge of the green and unwrapped them carefully. The weapons glistened in the sunlight. He picked them up, feeling their grips mold to his hands as he touched them. He lifted them and felt their weight again. Perfectly balanced.

"*We can teach him. He doesn't need the she-elf.*"

Arracnoth dropped the blades abruptly. They clattered to the ground.

N'Khael laughed. "You've given up already? You haven't even started your first lesson!"

"Doesn't even know how to hold the blades!" Avanstel shouted from the terrace. "You *are* going to need a lot of training!"

"Did you hear that?" Arracnoth asked N'Khael, ignoring Avanstel's jest.

"Hear what?"

"Adesh … I mean … a voice. Did you hear a voice? Did you hear anything?"

N'Khael looked around the garden, her forehead wrinkled in confusion.

Avanstel shouted, "What is going on out there? Why the delay? I am waiting for the show! Come on, Arrac, show me your skills!"

Arracnoth was getting flustered. He reached down and picked up the daggers from the grass and turned to face N'Khael.

"Good, yes. Feel the anger. Let it be your fuel. Use it to move swift and strike hard!"

"There!" Arracnoth said. "Did you hear that?"

N'Khael dropped her arms to her side. "What game is this? Do you want to learn, or do you want to play?"

"Learn!" Arracnoth said. "I ... I just hear ... something."

"What do you hear?" N'Khael looked around again.

"A voice. A woman's voice. I've heard it before ... in the Undercroft."

N'Khael squinted at him from the corner of her eye. "What does the voice say?"

"It wants to teach me to fight you, to strike you."

She laughed. "A woman wants you to strike me? Let her come forward, and I will fight her directly. We will see who wins this challenge."

Arracnoth shook his head. "No ... it's not a woman. It's a ... voice."

N'Khael stepped toward him, a puzzled frown on her face. The smell of lavender was strong on her.

"We are. But they will not understand. They don't have ears to hear or eyes to see," Marek said.

Arracnoth raised his hand to N'Khael. "Wait! Just a minute. I ... I think ... it's the daggers, maybe."

"The daggers?"

"Yes. I think they are speaking to me. There are two voices. Adesh and Marek. I heard them in the Undercroft when I found the weapons. They led me out of the catacombs."

N'Khael placed her blades in her belt and crossed the green. He stood, arms wide, palms up, a blade in each hand. She looked at them closely. "The daggers speak to you?"

Arracnoth nodded. "I believe so."

"May I?"

Arracnoth extended his hands to her. She took the weapons and held them, fixing her grip around them. "They are nice blades, as I have said. Well made. But … I hear nothing."

"They said you wouldn't hear them."

She laughed. "Of course! How convenient that you are the only one to hear them. Maybe we should have the cleric whip up a potion for *you*. Perhaps you are the one in need of some of his aid, though I'm not sure if he can heal the mind as well as the body."

Arracnoth shrugged. "It's possible. But I think … May I?" She placed the blades back in his hands. Arracnoth closed his eyes and focused.

"*We told you,*" Adesh chided. "*The she-elf doesn't have the blood. Let us strike her down.*"

"*No,*" Marek answered. "*He has much to learn, and she can teach him. We are, we can be more effective with her instruction. He needs others on his journey.*"

He opened his eyes and looked at N'Khael. "I'm not mad. It's the daggers. They are … alive."

She scrutinized him, but saw no deception in his eyes. "*Estrayaed* weapons that are possessed by spirits?" She whistled. "Perhaps this is indeed beyond the cleric. Let's visit Seer Alle. She oversees the archives of the Weode and knows the histories of when the five families followed Ni'Ilyan to Belkin Wood. If anyone in the kingdom could tell you more about these strange daggers, it would be her. Maybe there is a record of these weapons in the histories from the Ivy Forest, or maybe an explanation on how they ended up in the Undercroft."

"*Yes, the Seer,*" Marek said. "*She will have information that will be helpful to you.*"

Arracnoth nodded. "Yes. She might be able to help. The voices say so."

N'Khael frowned at him again and shook her head. "Stranger every day," she said. "I will take you to the Seer. Make yourself ready."

CHAPTER 16: SEER

N'Khael guided Arracnoth through a maze of alleys and passages, avoiding the main streets as they made their way from House Omaga to House Alle. Following instructions, Arracnoth did his best to blend in, resisting the urge to look around in wonder at the splendid city of Ny'we Adye. His only previous excursion from Selyndar's home had been directly to the palace and had ended in the confrontation with Dredaius and Questelle. He hoped that this time, his visit would be more fortuitous, though he held no delusions of being welcomed by the Weode. He was an *ort*, and that would never change.

"Here we are," N'Khael said, pointing at the steps ahead of them. Long, wide stairs rose to a pleasant portico, which overflowed with vines and greenery mixed with orange and pink flowers. Above them stood a square building that rose four or five stories high. Purple banners rested against the stone walls on either side of a balcony that overlooked the street, similar to the ones at House Omaga, but with a different crest and of a different color.

"Come, quickly," she urged. "The fewer eyes on us the better." Her comment was for his benefit as much as her own. It bothered him, but he was used to it. Thirty-six cycles of ridicule didn't disappear overnight, and the Weode disliked the half-elves even more than the Citizens of Chark.

Arracnoth put his head down and ducked into the shadows of the porch. A formidable, pointed arch doorway stood before him. Symbols and intricate designs carved the twin doors, but they were different from what he had seen at the palace. The symbols looked older, more rudimentary – more utilitarian and less decorative. N'Khael reached for the large metal doorknocker. It was in the shape of an animal Arracnoth did not recognize. He wondered if it was mythical or if it was a real animal from another part of Halbrun. The doors swung open unexpectedly, throwing N'Khael off guard.

"Greetings, Thelyn Omaga." A young elven boy stood inside the doorway.

"Hello T'Antalius," she responded, recovering.

"Lady Alle is expecting you. She bid me to show you the way to her workshop."

"Of course. Please lead on."

As they entered the main hall, Arracnoth looked at N'Khael and frowned. "Thelyn?"

"The Elders of the Founding houses are Lords and Ladies," she explained. "Their heirs hold the honorific titles of Thel, or Thelyn."

He nodded in understanding. "Lady Alle expected us?"

N'Khael nodded. "It doesn't surprise me. The Seer is … well, you will see for yourself."

The boy led them through the main entry hall, reminiscent of the entry hall of House Omaga, but much smaller. At the back of the room, to the left of an enormous staircase that led to the upper floors, was a stone door bearing more elven symbols and etchings. These markings seemed to shimmer with a pale purple light. T'Antalius placed his hand on the symbol carved in the middle of the door and whispered something in Weald-speak. The door moved backwards and then slid up, disappearing into the ceiling. A staircase descended downward, the stone walls on either side carved with the same glinting lavender-colored symbols. An orange glow flickered up from the bottom of the long stairwell.

The boy stepped to the side. "Lady Alle awaits you."

Arracnoth glanced at N'Khael. He could tell by her expression that none of this was playing out quite the way she was expecting. She stepped forward and made her way down the stairs, Arracnoth following silently.

"Come in, come in!" they heard her call from below.

The passage opened up onto a large, cluttered room. Piles of books littered the floor, balanced precariously on several of the many tables, and crammed into the shelves circling the room. To the right was a table overflowing with crystals and stones of varying colors and sizes and shapes. Arracnoth noticed a section of the wall filled with a collection of bottles – each containing different colored liquids or powders, some even housing small living creatures. Thick wooden planks formed the room's ceiling, from which hung bunches of drying herbs, flowers, and other vegetation. A huge fireplace sat against the wall to the side of the room, the warm orange glow illuminating everything. The smell of spices and something earthy but unfamiliar mixed with the faint hint of lavender that he had grown accustomed to when N'Khael was near him.

Sitting on a stool in front of a large open tome was the woman that Arracnoth recognized from the palace. "Please forgive me for the way my workshop looks," she said. "This place is my refuge and retreat; it's not designed to receive visitors."

N'Khael cleared her throat. "My apologies, Lady Alle, we did not mean to intrude. We could have waited for you in the hall, but T'Antalius directed us here."

"No, no. Not at all, dear N'Khael. A visit from Thelyn Omaga is never an intrusion. Indeed, the last time you came to visit you were about the same age as young T'Antalius, so you are long past due."

The Seer turned towards Arracnoth. Her white eyes focused on him. Arracnoth felt her intense scrutiny, as though she was looking at him, or perhaps through him, though her gaze did not move. The old woman's brow furrowed. "And you bring with you a visitor, a handsome young half-elf … with questions."

N'Khael motioned for Arracnoth to answer. "Yes, Lady Alle. I …"

"Please," she said, "call me Tallayah or Seer. Lady Alle is so formal, and we are friends – House Omaga and House Alle." She placed her hands on her lap and smiled brightly at him. Her welcome surprised him. He figured that because she was blind, she did not realize he was *ort*. Maybe that explained her hospitality … but she had just called him a half-elf. How did she know?

"What can I help you with?" she asked.

"I found these daggers, and I –"

"Do show!" she exclaimed. She hopped off the stool and turned to a small table. She picked up a parchment and a mortar and pestle and moved them to the side.

Arracnoth removed the daggers from his belt and felt their warm hilts conform to his hands. He placed them gently on the table. The old woman reached forward to feel them.

"They are very sharp," he cautioned.

Seer Alle placed her hands on her hips, looked at him, and smiled wryly. "I may be blind, but I *do* see. Do not mistake my lack of physical vision for a weakness or an impairment." Arracnoth shot N'Khael a glance of concern, afraid he had offended, but she shook her head, dismissing it.

She reached forward again, touching the pommels of the first dagger, the straight three-tipped sai. "Oh!" she exclaimed, as if shocked, and withdrew her hand.

N'Khael stepped forward, putting her hand on the elbow of the elderly elf. "What is it?"

"Magic! And …" she hesitated, cocking her head to the side as if hearing something strange. "And something else …"

"Did it speak to you?" N'Khael asked. "He says they speak to him."

The Seer's face grew serious. "That is not impossible to believe." She reached for the second blade, touching the handle of the serpentine dagger. "This one too. The same, but …"

"Different," Arracnoth finished.

"Yes!"

"Do you know of these blades? Are there any recordings of them in the archives?" N'Khael asked. "They are *estrayaed* blades. I wondered if …"

"From the Ivy Forest. Indeed. I don't recall reading of blades such as these, but this magic is … old. Older than the memories of the Weode peoples, and perhaps older than the memories of our Th'arule brethren. There are few writings from that time that are still in existence. They may even be from the times of the First Peoples."

"How?"

"How indeed." Seer Alle leaned back, lost in thought. "Where did you acquire them?"

Arracnoth relayed the story of his escape from the Undercroft to the Seer, explaining how he had found the daggers on a body that seemed to have been escaping from the catacombs and how the voices had led him out to the surface.

"Interesting," the Seer said. "They must have been buried with a Weode. That would explain how they ended up here. Someone in the past must have attempted to steal them but had the misfortune of becoming stuck and unable to escape."

"You said they are magic? Can you tell me more?" Arracnoth asked.

"Ahhhh," she said with a smile. She snapped her fingers. "A pupil who is interested in the ancient arts. I haven't had a pupil in decades! Most Weode children don't value old knowledge. I suspect your curious nature is from your mother's side."

She turned around and walked across the room, deftly avoiding several obstacles in her path. "Come, let us sit by the fire. The mystery of these blades has chilled me, and I crave the comfort of my favorite place." She eased herself into a large, cushioned chair next to the blazing fireplace. "Find a seat where you can."

N'Khael grabbed a stool that stood before the shelf of bottles and moved it next to the fireplace. Arracnoth perched himself on the stool that Seer Alle had vacated. As he was arranging himself on the stool, he glanced at the book she had been reading when they came in. The pages were blank – there was no writing on them. He frowned. An old blind woman, reading a book with no words? Seer Alle became more interesting by the moment.

"Magic," she began, "is not like it used to be. When the world was young, there was *akan'gott* – or what we now call 'old magic.' It was the first magic, and it was part of the fabric of everything. All the world was full of *akan'gott*. The rocks, the water, the air, the plants, and the creatures. It was the lifeblood of the world and nothing existed without *akan'gott*."

"And then a great cataclysm came upon the world. What happened is unknown and unrecorded. It remains a mystery of ancient times. But whatever happened, the old magic became inaccessible. People and creatures could not sense it like they had before. It was still there, but hidden, and unusable. The trees stopped flowing with it. The rocks no longer sang with it. And the world was bereft of what once flowed so freely from all things, connected all things, and was in, and through, and with all things.

"The Th'arule, the eldest of the races of the Third Age, sought to access the old magic and to return the world to the way it had been before the calamity. The wisest of the Th'arule quested through the many lands of Naveis Orthea in search of ways to access the *akan'gott* again, but returned empty handed. Their scientists and wise men worked for centuries and could not bring back the *akan'gott*. But they did figure out a way to extract a little of the first magic that remained in the natural things – the stone, the water, the air, the fire. And through extremely intense work, they found they could draw out the remnants, or essence, of it, and with that residue, they created the second magic, the *omu'gott*."

A grey cat brushed up against Arracnoth's feet, startling him. The cat regarded him with large blue eyes for a moment, then turned away and made its way to the chair where Seer Alle sat. She turned to face it, patted her knee, and the cat leaped into her lap where it curled into a ball. The Seer stroked the cat until it purred.

"The second magic was not like the first," she continued. "It was not as powerful as the *akan'gott*, and it was ephemeral, fading quickly. It was *created* magic, not natural or innate like the first magic. And creating *omu'gott* came at a price to its creators; it required use of their *accentation*, their life force. The more *omu'gott* they extracted from the natural things, the more they sought, and the harder they worked, the sooner they passed from this world to Parvanor as their *accentation* was pulled from their blood. It is unlikely that any *omu'gott* still exists, since its nature is so fleeting. Just like those who sought it and gave their lives to create it."

Arracnoth looked at the blades sitting on the table. The orange glow from the fire danced off their silver-blue metal edges and raced along the carved runes. "So, the blades are not *omu'gott*?"

Seer Alle slowly shook her head. "No, surely not. Nor are they the third magic, *creer'gott*, which is what we have now in this world. Simple magic. Small magic. Magic that does not originate from natural things and instead is *placed* inside natural things. Perhaps … like a charm that would allow a Weode to disguise themselves as an *ort*, so they could go about their business unnoticed."

Ah, so that must have been how she did it. Arracnoth frowned at the reminder of how Questelle had fooled him, and how Danvaren had paid the price. But then, his mother's voice was there in his mind. *"Sere'eden,"* Adine said, reminding him that to give in to anger was to become its servant. He took a deep breath and released it, letting go of his rage against Questelle. A time would come when she would pay for her violation and for Danvaren's life … and for the attempt on Avanstel's.

The old woman seemed to sense his thoughts. She stood up, gently placing the cat down on the floor. It wandered away, getting lost among the stacks of books. She stepped toward Arracnoth.

"May I?"

Arracnoth jumped off the stool and stood to the side of the large book. The woman took the seat and thumbed through the blank pages, tracing her fingers down them as if she were reading invisible words there. She flipped to the next page, muttered to herself, and then flipped to another. Arracnoth watched her eyes scan across each page. She was truly reading something that he could not see.

"There are rumors of a fourth magic – the *kramen'gott*." Her finger again traced down the blank page. "It is nothing more than whispers and suspicions …" She shut the book with a loud thud, jumped off the stool and walked over to a pile of tightly wound scrolls. She sorted through them, her blind eyes darting over each.

"Words that have floated on the wind. Words spoken by the rustling of trees or the gurgle of a brook as it makes its way to the sea. Whispers are all they are. Whispers of arcane truths that were lost to time recently rediscovered, and stones with new magic unlike the other magics before them. But these blades are not new magic, they are ancient magic. The Embers have mentioned such things, but the Embers are not elven, so they lack the understanding that the elder races have."

Arracnoth had heard of the Embers – wise men and women who lived in cities and did research and provided knowledge to those who could pay for it. Chark didn't have an Ember, so he had never seen one in person – perhaps someday he would travel to a city where an Ember lived.

Seer Alle tossed the scroll back onto the shelf and put her hands on her hips. "I will need to do more research, and this will take some time. Speak of this to no one. Not your companions, not anyone. This room is the only place where it is safe to speak of these things. I have woven protection over this place with ancient runes that keep my workshop from prying eyes – and ears. With all that is going on, we never know who could be listening … or where our enemies may be hiding."

Her eyes moved to N'Khael. "Send your father to me. I need to speak with him. If Lord Omaga will lend the warrior to me, I have an errand for him that might help me unravel the mystery of these blades."

"I will send him this very day, Lady Alle. Whatever you need, House Omaga stands ready."

The old woman reached out and grabbed N'Khael's hands in hers and gripped them. "You must keep them safe. Whatever you do, keep them safe."

N'Khael glanced at Arracnoth, unsure if the old woman was referring to the blades or to Avanstel and Arracnoth. "I will."

"Indeed." She released N'Khael's hands. "Take your blades. They are potent weapons – with or without the magic inside them. It would be to your benefit to be instructed in their use. Listen well to the words of your teacher, for she is one of the best in Ny'we Adye. Follow her instructions closely. I will see you soon." She smiled at the irony of her own words.

Arracnoth and N'Khael climbed the stairs and made their way back toward House Omaga. He was eager to share all he had learned with Avanstel, but the Seer's warnings echoed in his ears. He would have to keep this to himself until there was a safe opportunity to tell Avanstel about the magics and the blades.

Hopefully, the Seer would discover their origins and solve the mystery of what they were – or who originally owned them.

And maybe even what the voices were.

And why he was the only one who could hear them.

CHAPTER 17: ALONE

That evening, Seer Alle dispatched Scorpio on an errand. Arracnoth wanted to know more about his mission, but as expected, the warrior said little. Even if his assignment hadn't been covert, the giant wouldn't have said much. Without words, Scorpio placed his large hand on Arracnoth's shoulder, smiled, and then slid out the doorway and into the darkness.

After seeing him off, Arracnoth turned to Avanstel and Hathar, the only remaining members of their team. The cleric put his arm around Arracnoth's shoulders. "He will return," he said. "And our *drivrid* friend as well. We have parted many times, and we always reunite. And often with remarkable stories to share of our adventures!" He laughed. "Although the last time Scorpio was gone, he brought back with him more than a story. He had purchased a small kaiko that would make this horrible screeching sound all night long. I didn't get sleep for weeks!"

"A kaiko?"

"A desert lizard. About as big as a loaf of bread, with a mouth full of razor-sharp teeth. Fast little thing too. I tried to catch it several times just to put it in a box so I could sleep, but the little monster moved with lightning speed.

"Scorpio had bought it during his trip to Sandscarath. He said that the 'songs' it made at night reminded him of home … and helped him sleep. He was the only one that thought those shrieks were soothing! Nightfall and I eventually pooled our coins and gave a merchant fifty koara to purchase the kaiko from Scorpio." Hathar cracked a big smile. "He never figured out that we paid the man to buy the little beast to get rid of it so we could get some sleep! And speaking of sleep …" Hathar motioned they should retire for the night, but just as the trio were making their way to the stairs up to their rooms, there was a loud knocking at the front door. Arracnoth paused, wondering if Scorpio had forgotten something.

Anafelen, the head of Selyndar's staff after Y'Zelle had been dismissed for her involvement in Avanstel's poisoning, appeared from a door at the side of the entry hall. He opened the door and spoke with someone on the other side, and then softly closed it. Arracnoth shrugged, assuming it was house business, and turned back to climb the steps.

"Sirs?" Anafelen said. "If you wouldn't mind, could you wait here a moment while I fetch Lord Omaga?" He slipped back through the door and was gone for a long moment before reappearing from another door that Arracnoth had not noticed before. He held the door open, and Selyndar strode briskly out of it, moving swiftly to the main doorway and flinging it open. Outside stood three figures lit by a yellow glow from a lantern. Arracnoth recognized one of them as Tretarilus, the Steward from the palace.

"What is this?" Selyndar demanded. "I have declared *taven'sanct* over my visitors. They cannot be harmed."

"Lord Omaga." Tretarilus bowed. His voice quavered, and Arracnoth could see there was sweat on his forehead. The Steward didn't really want to be here — that much was obvious. "The Ade has requested that the … that your visitor, Avanstel, I believe his name is, accept his invitation to come stay at the palace." He cleared his throat. "As his guest, of course. Not as a prisoner."

"Nonsense. What is Dredaius on about?"

"Lord Omaga, if you will …"

One of the Green Guard behind Tretarilus placed his hand on the hilt of his sword. The Steward noticed the movement and shifted uncomfortably. He cleared his throat again. "The Ade wishes to *honor* Avanstel."

Selyndar made a low rumbling sound. The other guard reached down and placed his hand on his belt, next to his sword. Hathar took a couple of steps towards them, reaching for his hammer and realizing that it was upstairs in his room. Arracnoth and Avanstel stepped behind the cleric.

N'Khael appeared in the doorway beside the Steward. She was panting. Her red hair clung to her face in damp strands. The familiar fragrance of lavender filled the space between them.

"Wait," she said. She held up a hand and then bent over to catch her breath. The guards stepped backwards and relaxed their stances. "I came … as quickly … as I could," she panted. "Father … don't challenge the Ade."

Selyndar folded his arms across his chest. "I have declared *taven'sanct*. It is my —"

"Yes, it is. Your right. You are right." N'Khael stood up and placed her hands on her hips, and breathed deeply. "Please, give us a moment, Tretarilus. I need to speak with my father." She took Selyndar's arm and stepped inside, away from the door, and crossed the room toward the others. By the time she reached the awaiting trio, she had caught her breath.

"Lady Shaal'Elonthra came to the palace today and met with Dredaius." She looked back over her shoulder. "I don't know what passed between them, but the Ade went immediately to speak with the Adelyn. There was shouting and the sound of things crashing in their apartments, and when it was done, Dredaius emerged and sent for Tretarilus. I lingered nearby to see if I could discover what they were about, which is why it took so long for me to get here."

"The rumor is that Dredaius is going to acknowledge Avanstel as his half-brother and that he will have a place at the palace as next-in-line to the throne, as the Aetheling. He ordered the Steward to fetch Avanstel and bring him to the palace before he makes the announcement. He wants to ensure his safety, knowing the sentiment of the city toward *ort*. His announcement will surely stir up unrest, and it is best for Avanstel to be within the palace, protected by the Green Guard when the proclamation is made."

Arracnoth looked at Avanstel. Shock and confusion twisted his face.

"There is more going on here," Selyndar said. His deep baritone voice resonated.

"I agree, Father. That's why I spoke with the captain. I have gotten myself assigned as Avanstel's Protector. I won't leave his side, and I will ensure his safety at all times. Though it may be helpful to have another experienced fighter as a Second. Someone who understands what is at stake and might feel more friendly toward *ort*." She looked at Hathar pointedly.

He nodded. "Yes, of course!"

"I will go too," Arracnoth said.

"No, you cannot. A Protector and a Second may accompany the Aetheling, but no others. You can visit when the Ade approves. But you won't be able to stay. The Ade's blessing is required for outsiders to enter the palace, and the announcement will cause unrest in the city, so it may be a while before it is safe for you to leave House Omaga."

Selyndar frowned. "I don't like this."

"I knew you wouldn't. Dredaius and Questelle are not to be trusted, but to refuse this invitation, to go against the wishes of the Ade, would mean prison for you ... or worse. This is the best way, Father. Isn't this what you wanted? For Avanstel to be recognized? For his lineage to be acknowledged?"

Selyndar closed his eyes and rubbed his temples. N'Khael gently placed her hand on his arm.

"Speak with Lady Shaal'Elonthra tomorrow and see what you can glean from her yourself. I will ask Nephinae if she knows the Lady's mind or has a hint of what is going on. If you discover anything, send word. I will do the same. Tonight, we should do as the Ade wishes. No blood needs to be shed over this. Father, you know you are much more valuable to our people on this side of the dungeon bars. It would serve the Weode no good to have an Elder locked away, especially you. If you fall, then there is only the Seer and the Lady to stand against whatever is going on."

"Very well," the old elf relented.

N'Khael looked at Avanstel and Hathar. "Retrieve your things. Do it quickly. I will speak with the Steward. The guards will stand down and wait for you. Gather only what you need now. We can send for the rest tomorrow." They nodded and disappeared up the staircase.

She glanced over her shoulder to ensure Tretarilus was still waiting at the door, and then looked at Arracnoth. "I will not be able to continue our lessons," she said. "But my father knows the Dance."

Selyndar put his hand up to dismiss her suggestion. "It has been a long time."

"It has indeed been a while, Father," she said. She smiled at Arracnoth. "Perhaps you can coax him to teach you. After all, he's the one who taught me, and there is no better bladesmaster in all Ny'we Adye. If he hasn't told you yet, he was once the Protector of the Ade."

"He has."

"Good. I am sorry that I will not get to spend more time with you. I was looking forward to getting to know you better. Perhaps, when you are able to visit the palace … or when I'm able to return to visit."

Avanstel and Hathar appeared at the top of the stairs, each carrying a bag over his shoulder.

"Let's not keep the Ade waiting," N'Khael said. She met Selyndar's gaze, nodded curtly, and stepped toward the entrance.

Arracnoth locked eyes with Avanstel as he passed by. There were so many things he wanted to say, but there was not enough time to say them. Avanstel grabbed Arracnoth's shoulders and brought their foreheads together.

"*Namartha t'undel*," Arracnoth said, fighting back tears.

"*Namartha t'undel*," Avanstel replied quietly. "I will see you soon. I may even bring back a kaiko!"

Arracnoth managed to smile. "Please don't."

N'Khael, Avanstel, and Hathar left with the Green Guard, disappearing into the night in the same manner that Scorpio had just minutes before.

Arracnoth stood in the large, dark room with Selyndar beside him. They both stared at the closed front door for a long moment in silence, each of them lost in their thoughts.

Selyndar finally broke the silence. "I will," he said.

"I'm sorry?"

"I will teach you the Dance. Lady Alle has shared that your blades are … unique. I believe I can teach you how to effectively wield your weapons. Though my daughter attempts to flatter me and distract me from the situation, she speaks the truth. Only, *she* is my better at the Dance."

Arracnoth thought for a long moment. If he had known how to use the daggers as well as N'Khael or even had been a fighter like Hathar or Scorpio or Nightfall, he would have been able to accompany Avanstel to the palace and serve as his Protector, or at least his Second. Without knowing how to fight, he had little to offer Avanstel other than companionship. How could he help, or protect, or defend Avanstel in this treacherous game of Questelle's without having something useful to offer him?

Up to this point in his life, he had been at the mercy of fate and circumstance. His childhood, losing Adine, the burning of the Hall, fleeing from Chark, the creatures, and the labyrinth of Caerbexsys. Even here in Ny'we Adye, he had little power over his future. Like a boat without a sail, the currents carried him wherever they wanted. No oars or rudder to steer his fate.

No more.

"I will learn," Arracnoth said, but did not look away from the door. His mind was on the growing distance, and the situation separating him from Avanstel.

Selyndar studied Arracnoth, noting his intensity both in his face and voice. He saw something there that had not been there before: a hunger, a thirst for something. A drive that had been missing before.

He touched Arracnoth's shoulder. "You will do well," he said. "I will make sure of it."

CHAPTER 18: LUINEDHEL

Cycle 739; The Sisters; The Fifth Age.

It was almost a week before the Ade approved for them to visit the palace. As N'Khael had predicted, the announcement of Avanstel becoming the Aetheling caused a lot of uproar in Ny'we Adye. While the Weode refrained from protesting or rioting – unlike what might happen in Chark given a similar upheaval of their political system – there was unrest and a general uneasiness in the city. It was almost too much change, too fast, for such methodical and long-lived people, almost as if having the humans in their midst had spread some contagion of immediacy and instability that the Weode had been free of for millennia. First, the death of N'Athero, then the rapid ascension of Dredaius, his marriage to Questelle in the Undercroft, and now the endorsement of an *ort* as heir to the Weode kingdom … Belkin Wood had never seen such chaos in such a short time.

For several days after the decree went out, many elves, from nobles to beggars, had congregated at the palace gates, first requesting, and then demanding, to talk with their Ade. But the gates had remained shut, and everyone had been turned away. Eventually, the drama died down as it became clear that Dredaius' proclamation was not up for discussion and the number of those gathered at the gates dwindled.

Without recourse or access to their leader, the attention of the people had turned to House Omaga. Lady Shaal'Elonthra visited them and informed Selyndar that public opinion had turned against him. Most of the Weode blamed him for introducing such chaotic elements into their society. The events of recent days reinforced the traditional notions of isolationism and separatism that had been the standard for the Weode for ages. There were even discussions and a request concerning a review of the Elders' authority to declare *taven'sanct*, a power that had been established at the kingdom's inception.

N'Khael was right. It was better for Avanstel to be at the palace, and for Arracnoth to remain within the walls of House Omaga.

Eventually, the activity at the palace returned to normal, and the gates reopened … although with double the soldiers in attendance. N'Khael showed up shortly afterwards, with her old abettor, Nephinae.

"It is good to see you again, Nephinae," Selyndar said.

Arracnoth recognized her as the Green Guard who had accompanied Lady Shaal'Elonthra on their first visit to the palace when Questelle announced that she had … "*Sere'eden*," Arracnoth thought to himself.

Nephinae smiled at Selyndar. "It is good to see you also, Lord Omaga. Lady asked me to accompany you to the palace. She is concerned for your safety, and that of your ward."

"These *are* troubling times. Please tell the Lady that I am in her debt."

Nephinae nodded and then looked over at Arracnoth. He expected to see disgust or disdain on her face, but was pleasantly surprised to see neither. Her blue eyes were kind, as was her smile.

He smiled back at her.

"Let's go," N'Khael said, cutting off further conversation.

They left the safety of House Omaga and made their way through the city and towards the palace. There was no point in trying to disguise themselves this time. Anyone being escorted by two of the elite Green Guard was sure to draw attention, regardless of who they were. Selyndar did not cover his head as he marched proudly beside his daughter. Arracnoth could hear the whispers from the crowd. Lord Omaga was a well-known figure, and by proxy, any intelligent person could surmise that Arracnoth was one of the unwelcome *ort*.

He felt their glares on his back and heard the whispers and chatter as they passed. It felt like being back in Chark again, although it hurt more because he wanted desperately to be accepted by these people. He knew he didn't belong in Chark, and he had hoped, maybe too optimistically, that he might find a home in Ny'we Adye.

Dredaius had given Avanstel a fine apartment in the east wing – the side reserved for guests, not the royal family. Selyndar noted that Avanstel's rooms were not as luxurious as those in the west wing where the Ade lived, but it was an honor to be given rooms at all. They had nicely furnished Avanstel's place, so he needed nothing. N'Khael and Hathar had adjacent rooms with connecting doors that opened into Avanstel's reception area, allowing them quick and easy access should the need arise. This certainly wasn't the prison Arracnoth had imagined his friend being taken to.

Avanstel received privileges akin to a royal family member, surprising Arracnoth. He had a dedicated staff who would appear if he called for them and who had access to the entire palace – save for the west wing. He also had a private chef to cook his meals, although Hathar insisted on testing everything first, given their previous experiences at House Omaga. A tailor and butler provided Avanstel with the finest clothes, befitting a royal heir. Arracnoth thought Selyndar had exceptionally crafted garments, but the fabrics Avanstel wore surpassed any finery Arracnoth had ever seen.

It seemed everything was in order, though everyone was still cautious about the sudden change in the situation. Trust was something that would have to come over time.

"Do you have all you need?" Arracnoth asked.

Avanstel swung his arms in a wide arc and spun around. "I couldn't ask for anything more," he said with a grin. "This is beyond anything I ever thought might happen to me, Arrac." He grabbed Arracnoth and hugged him tightly. "The only thing that I could need now is to have you here with me." He broke the embrace and turned to open the large glass doors at the far side of the room, motioning Arracnoth to follow him out to the balcony that overlooked the private gardens. "I've already made inquiry. I want you to move to the palace, too. But Tretarilus said that I will have to go directly to the Ade to get his permission. I have an audience scheduled with him this afternoon and it will be the first thing I talk with him about. I will send for you as soon as I have the approval. It's lonely without you here."

"I feel the same." He reached into his pocket, feeling for the white sword token he had brought with him. He intended to give it back to Avanstel, both as a reminder of their time together, and as an encouragement to continue to be a light in the darkness here at the palace.

"Besides," Avanstel said, brushing aside the seriousness. "I can't play Haven Chase alone. And you should see the new board I have. The pieces are quartz and obsidian. It's beautiful."

Arracnoth let go of the token, leaving it in his pocket. Avanstel didn't need it now that Dredaius had supplied him with a much nicer game board. Their rustic set from Chark would look embarrassingly cheap compared to what the palace could offer.

N'Khael stepped out onto the balcony with them. "Avanstel, your tutor is here."

"Tutor?" Arracnoth asked.

"They have my entire schedule already full of meetings and appointments. I am to be trained in the ways of the court, educated in the genealogies and the important families of the Weode, schooled in diplomacy, learn how to read and speak Weald-speak. There's a never-ending list of things that I need to know … and I know so little of it." He laughed. "I don't even know the route to the throne room or the main entry hall. I couldn't navigate this labyrinth of a palace if my life depended on it! I have to be taught so much!" He turned to N'Khael. "Please show him to my study. I will meet with him there."

"Her," N'Khael corrected. "V'Deliah."

"V'Deliah," Avanstel repeated. "Another new name. Another thing to remember."

N'Khael disappeared back inside the apartment. Avanstel turned to Arracnoth. "I am so sorry, Arrac. I have to …"

"No need to apologize, Van. I understand. I will return to House Omaga with Selyndar and will await your word. You have N'Khael and Hathar here with you; I rest easier knowing you have wise and capable companions who will ensure your safety. The events have stirred up the city, and it's important you aren't in any danger. Not just for me, though you know how I feel, but for the entire kingdom. When you take the throne, you can change it all."

When they walked back inside, several palace servants immediately surrounded Avanstel. They presented him with issues that required his response, decisions, or choices. He did his best to fend them off as he made his way to a doorway lined with dark wood on the far side of the room. The door was ajar, and Arracnoth could see an elegantly dressed, dark-haired elf standing inside. She examined the spines of several large tomes before placing them onto the table and arranging them in a sequence that only she would know. Avanstel entered the room, and she looked up at him. Arracnoth saw an expected flash of disapproval cross her face, but she hid it quickly. There was so much to change – so much prejudice against the *ort* that existed for no reason. Avanstel had a big job ahead of him. He turned, waved goodbye, and closed the door.

"He will be fine," Hathar said, stepping up behind Arracnoth. "We will make sure of it."

Arracnoth smiled. "I am in your debt. He is all I have left of a family."

Hathar nodded. "Rest easy, friend."

"That is something easier said than done," Arracnoth mused. "But I have no say in what has happened, so I will try to accept it and figure out how to continue on."

Cycle 739; The Falling; The Fifth Age.

Three months passed faster than he expected.

Dredaius denied Avanstel's request for Arracnoth to join him at the palace. The way Avanstel explained it, only the royal family, or those deemed to have a purpose for the throne, were to live in the palace. He was free to visit, when necessary, with an escort, of course, but was told not to be a distraction to Avanstel. His regimented studies and activities within the court were strictly monitored and scheduled.

Arracnoth doubted the conversation had occurred in the polite manner that Avanstel had relayed to him. However, he didn't have a choice in the decision. He was to remain at House Omaga and be mindful of his visits to the palace so that Avanstel could focus on his royal duties as the successor to the throne.

It was disappointing news, but Arracnoth did his best to take it in stride. He missed Avanstel's smile, his laugh, and his quick wit.

He missed his presence at meals, and talking together late into the night about everything they had experienced during the day. And, of course, their games of Haven Chase. But other than being his friend, Arracnoth had nothing to offer Avanstel in the way of courtly advice, education on the Weode, or as someone who could protect him from physical harm.

This made him even more determined to master the blades, to prove he could be of some practical use to Avanstel. He vowed to dedicate every spare moment that they were apart to his training with Selyndar, and to learn everything about the Dance and anything else the old bladesmaster was able to teach him.

Lessons occurred daily, early in the morning, before the sun appeared above the forest canopy. The garden usually had a coating of dew. In the cool, dark pre-dawn, Selyndar would explain that part of learning the blades was to not rely on sight to determine where or how to move, but to anticipate your opponent's movements through the other senses — the sound of their clothing or hair moving, the feel of the air around you as they lunged or withdrew or slashed, the smell of them that became stronger the closer they moved toward you. It wasn't a straightforward way to 'see' what was happening, but Arracnoth found that the more sessions they had, the more he could rely on his other senses to inform him of Selyndar's movements around him. He wondered if this was how the Seer was able to 'see' the things around her.

Of course, Adesh and Marek were also advising and prompting.

"*To your right,*" Marek would warn.

"*Slash up! Drive forward swiftly!*" Adesh would urge.

The days turned to weeks … and weeks to months. Over time, the pace at which Arracnoth was able to pick up the Dance surprised Selyndar. The elder elf grew more curious about the *estrayaed* weapons. At one point, Selyndar asked to use them for a couple of exercises, and although they were balanced and sliced through the air with a keen whistle, he heard no voices when he held them. It was as if the blades refused to speak to anyone but Arracnoth.

After this, Selyndar made Arracnoth swap out the *estrayaed* daggers and practice with standard ones. The Weode weapons master lent Arracnoth a pair from his personal collection. They were a matched set, and well-crafted, but Arracnoth preferred the ones he had found in the Undercroft. Selyndar explained that he didn't want Arracnoth to become dependent upon the mystical voices. Arracnoth needed to learn the technical moves of the Dance of Daggers for what it was – without additional help from Adesh and Marek.

"You may not always have your *estrayaed* blades at your side. You must learn to use normal weapons, so you learn the right ways. Those strange tools aid you, no doubt, but it's better to have the skills without their help." He paused. "Although using your special blades … gives you an edge and makes your movements sharper."

Arracnoth dropped his stance and chuckled at Selyndar's pun. He stopped himself instantly and glanced at his teacher to determine whether he was making a joke or had done it unintentionally. Selyndar had his face turned away, but Arracnoth could see the edge of a smirk and noticed his shoulders tremble with silent laughter. Arracnoth laughed, and Selyndar joined him, amused by his own wit.

"I mean no disrespect, Lord Omaga," Arracnoth said, regaining his composure and bowing.

Selyndar wiped a tear from the corner of his eye. "I'm not offended. You are indeed learning the Dance of the Daggers swiftly. Quicker than I expected. What would normally take a student cycles to master, you have learned in just a month. I believe that the instructions you hear from your blades have helped you progress swiftly. Even without their help, with standard blades, you are becoming a formidable opponent … although I can clearly see that you do better with your own."

Arracnoth bowed his head. "Thank you for teaching me."

Selyndar nodded and turned toward the house. The sun was falling in the sky; it was time for lessons to end and for dinner to be served.

"You are a good student," the elder elf said. "It is easy to instruct one who is so eager to master the lessons. Let us see if we can get N'Khael to break away from her duties long enough for you to show her how you have advanced. You will surprise her with what you have learned in these weeks."

Arracnoth stopped and turned to face Selyndar. "I would like that. Perhaps, Avanstel ..." Arracnoth could see in the old elf's eyes that it would be highly doubtful Dredaius would let Avanstel out of the palace, out of his sight.

"Maybe," Selyndar said. "We can inquire." But the look of sadness remained in his eyes. He stepped up the stairs to the portico. Arracnoth followed.

"When do you think Nightfall and Scorpio will return?" Arracnoth changed the subject to avoid dwelling on the unlikelihood of being reunited with his friend.

"I am afraid Lady Alle has sent the warrior to a place few – if any – have ever traveled, so it may still be some time before he returns." There was a sadness in his tone that Arracnoth did not understand, but Selyndar changed the subject quickly. "As for the *drivrid*, he has been gone almost three months now. I would expect him any day, but he won't return until he has achieved his goal. He is very thorough; I have never needed to send him on return trips for stones he had left unturned. He will come when he has the information needed."

"I look forward to having them back ... not to imply that your company has not been exceptional."

Selyndar smiled. "I have also enjoyed our time together, Arracnoth ... may I call you Arracnoth?"

Arracnoth suddenly realized that over the months they had trained together, the elder elf had never used his name, and he himself had never used Selyndar's name directly. It was surprising.

They had grown close over the time, having spent every day together from sunrise to sunset. They had shared many meals together, trained daily – several times a day – and spent countless evenings in the garden sipping the fine Weode wine from Selyndar's cellars while discussing the politics and events of Ny'we Adye over a game of Haven Chase.

Arracnoth treasured the time spent together. He had become extremely fond of the Weode Elder. He admired Selyndar, cared about his well-being, was grateful for all he had done to provide a home for him, fed him, even clothed him in the extravagant manner that those in the Omaga household enjoyed. For all intents and purposes, Selyndar had treated Arracnoth much like one would a member of his own family.

He had begun to view Selyndar, stately and kind as he was, almost as a father. Certainly, Selyndar had given him as much as Adine had, not simply in material things, but also in friendship, care, and educating him in both the world around them and how to defend and protect himself. Selyndar had shown genuine concern for his welfare and had been there when Arracnoth found himself alone.

"Lord Omaga, I ..." Arracnoth looked down at his feet.

"I'm sorry, I shouldn't have presumed. I just thought ..." Selyndar looked away.

"No, it's not that." Arracnoth shook his head but could not raise his eyes. His voice trembled. "When we were at the palace that first time. When Dredaius threatened you and Questelle revealed ..." Arracnoth felt a lump rising in his throat and fought against it. "She said my name." He swallowed hard. "She said it like it was a curse. I can still hear it echoing around me sometimes at night while

I lay in my bed, reliving that moment when she told us she had killed Danvaren.”

Selyndar placed a calming hand on Arracnoth’s forearm.

Arracnoth raised his head and looked into Selyndar’s eyes. “I … I think I would like a new name. It is time for me to let go of my life in Chark and embrace my life ahead. I know I am *ort*, and I cannot change that. But my future is here, with these people, your people. I want to be more than *taven’sanct*. I want to be Weode … or as Weode as I can be.” He paused, gathering the courage to ask his question. “Would you bless me with a new name? A Weode name?”

“A Weode name?” he said, surprised. He turned to Arracnoth. “A name does not change who you are.”

Arracnoth nodded. “I know. But this place … this time I’ve spent with you. It feels … it feels like home now.”

Selyndar did not respond for a long moment, and Arracnoth worried he had overstepped. Then he turned and said, “Come with me. I want to show you the chapel.”

“The chapel?”

“It is there,” Selyndar said. He pointed to a part of the large manor that sat opposite the garden from them, next to the grove of pines and across the pond. Arracnoth had never ventured to that part of House Omaga. There were many places on the estate that he had not explored. He didn’t want to intrude where he was not welcome, and honestly, he had everything he needed between his room upstairs and the library off the dining area. He had occasionally visited Selyndar in his study, and had seen the ballroom once, but the north end of the manor was where Selyndar lived and, out of respect, Arracnoth had not intruded there.

They walked across the gardens and toward the large doors in the stone wall. Selyndar opened them and motioned Arracnoth inside. At the end of a long hall, lined with tapestries and paintings of beautiful scenes of nature, was another door. Selyndar removed a key from his tunic and opened the locked door.

The room was large, and the ceiling stretched three stories high, with windows on each side. Between each window was an immaculately carved, lifelike statue, each more impressive than the other. Women and men, all Weode, in various poses. Some with swords, or lutes, or cradling flowers. One was in a full suit of armor.

"My family," Selyndar said. "The Omagas."

Arracnoth wandered from one to the next, taking time to study them. Selyndar lit a candle and stood next to Arracnoth, silently walking beside him along the gallery. Arracnoth could see the Omaga family resemblance. They all looked noble and kind – regal almost, but in a benign way. These figurines were different from the ones in the Undercroft but crafted with the same expertise. Each figurine looked alive, as though it were frozen in time.

As they walked by each one, Selyndar would tell a little about them. First, his grandfather Kaelen and grandmother Cellecia, who had come with Ni'Ilyan to Belkin Wood. His uncle Kirion – one who had built the gardens and the great gazebo at House Omaga, and another who had been a cartographer and had mapped out the southern portions of the forest near Stone Havens. His aunt was a Grand Master Bowman and could best anyone in the entire kingdom. His father, Gaelethin, was an architect and had built the Summer Tower at the palace. His mother, Sylvana, who was an accomplished horse breeder and supplied horses for the Ade's use – which is where she had met his father.

He paused at the last one. A woman dressed more casually than the others. She wore traveler's clothing and carried a pack on her back. There was a distant look in her eyes.

"My wife," Selyndar said. "Elisryn."

"N'Khael's mother."

"Yes, but also no," Selyndar answered softly. "We were unable to have children." He turned away and sat on a bench in the middle of the room, facing an enormous stained-glass window at the front of the space. Arracnoth could make out the pattern of the Omaga crest, the same that was on the banners in front of the house: three vertical circles intertwined in front of an enormous tree.

"That is why I brought you here. I wanted to share this with you, so you could understand." He looked at Arracnoth. "Elisryn and I adopted N'Khael into our family. A ceremony the Weode call *anneming*. I suppose you had something like that with your mother, Adine. No? Unfortunate, it is a beautiful ceremony. My parents were unable to have children also. I had the *anneming* myself — they adopted me. It has become somewhat of a tradition now for the Omagas to welcome others into our family through *anneming*. Some may call in misfortune, but we do not see it that way. It is a gift, a choice, a decision backed by intention … and love."

"I don't …"

"I would do more than give you a name, Arracnoth. I would give you a family … if you chose."

Arracnoth felt a lump in his throat, and his eyes watered. He had longed for a family ever since Adine's death. He had it momentarily with Avanstel and Danvaren before this adventure had taken that away. And now, with Avanstel at the palace — and, officially, part of the J'Onsal family — he was without even *that* family. What Selyndar was offering him was beyond anything he could have imagined. Not just a Weode name, but to be part of a Weode family — one of the Founding families. An Omaga!

He swallowed back the tears. His voice cracked. "I would like that very much."

Selyndar's eyes welled over. "I would too." He embraced Arracnoth, first tentatively and then strongly, as Arracnoth embraced him back.

"Then we shall plan for the ceremony," Selyndar said. "But first, let us go tomorrow to see N'Khael and inform her of your desire. When she was young, she would always pester her mother and I to give her a brother. I'm sure this is not what she was expecting, but I have no doubt that she will welcome you into our family … with open arms."

The sun was high in the sky. The stained-glass windows made the chapel glow. Oranges and blues, reds and greens illuminated everything around them. The Seer stood to one side of Arracnoth, a paper rolled in her hand. On the other side was Lady Shaal'Elonthra. He could see her gown moving ever so slightly, animated by a breeze that always seemed to surround her wherever she went.

N'Khael stood to the right and slightly behind Selyndar. Arracnoth kneeled before them at the front of the Omaga chapel. The place was filled with the house staff, who sat on the benches or stood at the back of the room. Anticipation and excitement were in the air. Those who knew the Omaga's history knew that this was a significant event – and one that held deep meaning for this family. There was no criticism, no condemnation, no disgust over an *ort* in this room. Nobody glared down their noses. They were delighted, happy, that Selyndar was about to gain a son.

He looked around the room to see if perhaps Dredaius had changed his mind and allowed Avanstel to leave the palace with Hathar, but they were nowhere to be seen. He wanted Avanstel to be here, wished he could be here, but once again, the politics of the nation interfered and blocked him from connecting with Avanstel. He began to feel discouraged.

He looked up and caught N'Khael's eye. She winked at him and smiled. Her acceptance, even enthusiasm, over his *annening* overwhelmed him. She had every right to be hurt, angry, or spiteful, but instead she had accepted him immediately – *ort* or not – and that meant a lot to him. The sadness he felt over Avanstel's absence faded.

Selyndar stepped forward and placed his hands on Arracnoth's head. He nodded, and the room grew quiet. Then he felt another hand on his shoulder and smelled the familiar scent of lavender. He smiled at himself and kept his eyes downcast to keep from tearing up. He was grateful to his new father and sister.

His eyes went to the blue pouch tied to his belt and the moonstone pin. He wished Adine were here. He wondered whether she'd be happy about the event. She always wanted what was best for him, had given everything for him — and this was what he wanted, what he thought was best now. A way to become a Weode, a way to embrace this part of his heritage.

Lady Alle and Lady Shaal'Elonthra spoke in unison. Their voices were musical, elegant, and beautiful.

The branches of the Great Tree weave,
Strong grey boughs and silver leaves,
A child has come, not born, but found,
Where fate and love in hearts are bound.

A path now changed, destiny untold,
Forged not of flesh but made of gold.
From root to leaf, from ash to flame,
New life is born and takes a name.

"Have you chosen a name?" Lady Shaal'Elonthra asked.

"I have," Selyndar responded. "A strong name. A name fitting for the newest member of the Omaga family, who has journeyed far, and has yet farther to go on his travels. I give you the name Luinedhel, which means 'overcomer' in Weald-speak. He who perseveres."

"A fitting name," Seer Alle said.

"Agreed," Lady Shaal'Elonthra responded. "All here hold witness to the right of *anneming*." She motioned to the crowd filling the room.

"We are witness," they responded in unison. N'Khael's trembling voice was loudest in his ear. She squeezed his shoulder.

"We present to you the document," Seer Alle said. She handed Selyndar the paper in her hand. "Under the laws of the Weode, this binding is permanent and unbreakable. Witnessed by all gathered here. Rise, Luinedhel Omaga. We welcome you to your new family."

There was a cheer that erupted from those in the room. Selyndar stepped forward and embraced him.

Arracnoth returned the embrace. "Thank you … Father."

Selyndar warmly squeezed his shoulders in response, and they were both soon wrapped in the powerful hug of N'Khael.

"Thank you, Father, for finally giving me the brother I always wanted. You're going to have to live up to your name, you know. Both the Luinedhel part and the Omaga part. I have high expectations."

He laughed. "I will do my very best," he said through his tears.

Family.

He was not alone.

CHAPTER 19: INVASION

Cycle 739; The Falling; The Fifth Age.

It was a quiet evening at House Omaga. A warm fire of hillstonas wood burned in the library's fireplace off the side of the dining room. The earthy, aromatic scent filled the room. Arracnoth had grown familiar with the warm, rich smell that was so different from the hardwood that was burned in Chark and much less smoky. It was a smell he associated with the feeling of 'home' now, with being cozy and safe and comfortable.

Outside, it was raining. The sound of the rain hitting the window mixed with the crackle of the fire and made the room a welcome retreat from the cool, wet autumn evening. Between them, on the low table, sat a Haven Chase board. Luinedhel hadn't originally wanted to play – it reminded him too much of Avanstel. But Selyndar had encouraged him to do so, knowing that it was something he had enjoyed in the past. He obliged for Selyndar's sake, but soon found that he enjoyed playing with his adoptive father just as much as he had enjoyed playing with Avanstel.

The set wasn't as elegant as the one Avanstel had, but it was nicer than the one they had in Chark. Luinedhel had left Avanstel's bone-carved token upstairs, hoping someday that Avanstel would ask for it, though it seemed more unlikely as the days passed. Selyndar preferred the black horse token. He shared that one of his favorite horses in his stable was of a similar black hue, a gelding named Nyx. And that was why he chose that marker. This left Luinedhel to choose from the white set. He opted for the white wolf – which amused him … and reminded him of Avanstel.

Selyndar took a sip of warmed spiced wine and rolled the dice. "Two," he said and moved his token around the board. "Give me the name of the two children of Ni'Vahyan J'Onsal."

"Oh, come on now! That one is far too easy," Luinedhel said. "Ni'Ilyan, the White Wolf, the father of the Weode."

"And?"

"Ni'Ilyan's sister, Ni'Shashti, who vanished shortly after he left Tyshin'Dael and was never heard from again."

Luinedhel rolled his die. "Three." He sighed. "You take my tower."

Selyndar moved the white tower off the board. "One." The dark horse advanced forward. "Ni'Ilyan's descendants?"

"E'Vestren, the first son of the Ade Gerent." Luinedhel paused, a memory of his trip through the Undercroft and standing before E'Vestren's tomb flashed through his mind. He remembered Adesh's voice in his mind, biting and distant. He had grown so used to that voice now that it no longer surprised him. "And then his son, N'Athero. Your friend."

Luinedhel rolled again. "Eight. Haven Chase!" He picked up two dice and rolled them together. "Eleven. Excellent!"

"I concede," Selyndar said. "You win. Well played." He took a sip of his wine and looked at the fire.

Luinedhel picked up the pieces of the board and reset them. He sat back in the chair, watching the flames lick the air and inhaling the warmth, his own thoughts wandering to Avanstel and wondering what he was doing this evening at the palace. Perhaps he was sitting by a fire with his tutor, learning much the same things that Selyndar was teaching Luinedhel.

There was a knock at the door. "Lord Omaga?"

Selyndar turned. "Yes, Anafelen? What is it?"

"A visitor, my Lord. From the palace."

Luinedhel stood up and shot a hopeful glance at Selyndar.

"Show them in." Selyndar rose from his chair much more slowly than Luinedhel had.

Hathar entered the study, a wide grin on his face, and crossed the room, gathering Luinedhel up in his arms and wrapping him in a big bear hug in one swift motion. His beard, as well as much of his clothing, was wet from the rain, but Luinedhel was delighted to see him. He looked over Hathar's shoulder in the embrace, but sadly, Avanstel did not follow.

"What brings you on such a rainy evening?" Selyndar asked.

"Lord Omaga." Hathar turned to the elder Weode and bowed. "I have come at the behest of Thelyn Omaga. She has sent me with a message for you ... the both of you."

Selyndar gestured toward the fire. "Warm yourself, cleric. Anafelen, please bring a glass for our friend."

Anafelen left the room, shutting the door behind him. Selyndar and Luinedhel returned to their high-backed chairs as Hathar moved to the fire, placing his back towards the flames. His brawny figure cast long shadows over the room. "Thank you, Lord Omaga. It is indeed chilly this evening. Unusual for this early in the season but perhaps fitting for the news I bring."

"Go on."

"My Lord, messengers have delivered news to the palace. The Ade's scouts around Orevael report an invasion by the Th'arule of the Ivy Forest. A Council is to be called tomorrow to share the news, but N'Khael urged me to get word to you this night."

"An invasion?" Selyndar frowned. "That is unthinkable. The Th'arule would have to amass an entire army and march through

Grevyn Pass. The Idar Mountains have ensured isolation from our enslavers for nearly five millennium. The Weode could no more invade the Ivy Forest than the Th'arule could invade Belkin Wood."

Anafelen returned and handed Hathar a warm mug. He cupped his hand around it and took a sip, nodding thankfully to Anafelen. "N'Khael said the same. Even the Ade questions the report, but the scouts have all confirmed the story. A massive elven force is gathering in the valley near Brinca and preparing for the long and difficult journey through the pass."

A dark cloud came over Selyndar's face. "If N'Khael has sent you, then there is cause for concern. She would not have asked you to come if these were mere rumors. What of the other Elders?"

"You are the first, my Lord. I will visit Lady Alle next." Hathar turned sideways to the fire, and the room brightened.

"Lady Shaal'Elonthra would have already heard the news. Her surveillance network reaches farther and penetrates deeper than mine." Selyndar paused, musing. "I will meet with her in the morning before the palace summons us. I'm sure she will expect me. We will find out what additional information she has to share and her thoughts on how we should align." He shifted in his chair. "I'm curious …"

"My Lord?"

"Dredaius … The Ade … has he spoken of this to Avanstel?"

"He has, my Lord. The Ade invited him to dinner in his apartments this evening. I was on duty tonight and heard the conversation."

"Our young Aetheling's thoughts?"

Hathar cleared his throat, shifted his weight uncomfortably, and cast a glance at Luinedhel.

"No need to be concerned," Selyndar said. "Arracnoth, or as he has chosen to be called now, Luinedhel, has become Thel of House Omaga. He is family. What is mine is his. My name, my home. Even my secrets … what few there are to be had."

The cleric smiled warmly; he clasped Luinedhel's shoulder. "N'Khael told me. I am sad that I could not attend the *anneming*. My apologies to both of you. My heart is warmed ... and not solely from this wine, nor the delightful fire!" He raised his glass. Luinedhel and Selyndar did the same.

"Avanstel is concerned, my Lord," he continued. "He is still learning the palace politics, and, as you know Ny'we Adye does not find itself short of machinations of state."

"Any thoughts on the mind of the Ade?"

"Unfortunately, no. Once convinced the reports were not false, his demeanor became much more pensive. I'm sure that tomorrow's council will be of import to all."

"Indeed." Selyndar placed his cup on the small wooden table beside him. "Thank you for coming. I shall not delay you further. Lady Alle will have many questions, so make haste to her home and hurry back to the shelter of the palace before the night grows colder."

Selyndar bowed to Hathar. He returned the gesture and made his way towards the exit, pausing to give Luinedhel another bear hug. "I'm so happy that you have found a good home," he breathed, and then slipped out of the room.

They stood in silence for a moment, Luinedhel watching the expressions on Selyndar's face.

"What is it?" Luinedhel asked.

"It doesn't seem right. It seems impossible. If the *drivrid* or the warrior were here, I would send them to confirm these rumors, or even Hathar, if I could send him." Selyndar sat back in his chair and placed a slender finger on his temple. "I will have to rely on Lady Shaal'Elonthra's resources as I trust none other. We shall learn tomorrow what Dredaius has to say about this. And perhaps we will be able to have some private council with Avanstel too. He will need our wisdom and the advice of the Elders ... without the influence of the Ade and the Adelyn."

Luinedhel smiled. "I would like that."

"We will see what we can do to pull your friend away from his royal duties and trainings. He will need a friend with insight to help navigate him through this statecraft. Let us hope we are able to provide that to him."

Luinedhel sat in one of the many wooden chairs that lined the edges of the circular council chamber. Most of the seats in the room remained empty, save for those around the large meeting table. The typical crowd of House Lords and Ladies that would have filled the seats had been barred from attending this meeting. It was only for the Elders, the Ade, and those deemed privileged enough to attend.

He noticed Tretarilus, the Ade's Steward, sitting several chairs to his right, staring stiffly ahead, focused on the discussion at the table. T'Antalius from House Alle had accompanied the Seer into the chamber and, after nodding to Luinedhel in greeting, had taken his place in one of the chairs to Luinedhel's left. In the chair across the room, Nephinae sat behind Lady Shaal'Elonthra. She smiled at him as their eyes met. Beside her, he could see Hathar and N'Khael and a few other people he recognized from his rare visits to Avanstel's apartments.

An immense table of dark wood, inlaid with silver and gold, occupied the center of the chamber, in keeping with the palace's decor. The overall pattern was of a giant tree – the same as in the throne room, the same as on the coin that Hathar had given him so many months ago at The Pig & Lamb. Around the branches of the tree sat the Elders, each in a chair of the same dark wood. The seat at the base of the tree, the Ade's place, was taller than the rest, itself carved to match the tree, inset into the table and threaded with gold and silver branches and leaves. The chair next to him, where the

Adelyn would sit, was notably empty. Luinedhel wondered what other business she was at that could be more important, but he didn't dwell on it long. He was glad she wasn't here. He'd rather not see her ever again.

"This is dire news, my Ade. We must take swift action."

"I agree with Lord Kellendaer. House Y'Vellian stands ready to defend the kingdom. We should direct the army to meet them in the pass and send the Unwritten skittering back under the rock from which they crawled from."

Dredaius nodded. "Thank you, Lord Kellendaer and Lord Y'Vellian."

Lady Shaal'Elonthra cleared her throat. "Should our kingdom be under threat, I would agree. But before we send any of our people out from the Wood and marching across the realm, let's take the time to confirm these reports, Ade."

"Lady," Dredaius said. The tone of condescension was perceptible even to those unfamiliar with the inner workings of the Elder Council. "While I appreciate your willingness, yea, *eagerness*, to assist with assessing the precarious situation our kingdom is in, you certainly do not mean to question our abilities or that of the agents which are employed by House J'Onsal?"

"No, my Lord. Not at all what I meant."

"Ade, if I may …" Selyndar interjected. "I'm sure Lady Shaal'Elonthra's offer is only to reinforce and support your actions … to prevent further questions. Her network's reputation is known throughout the kingdom and highly regarded. Should she corroborate the findings of the royal house, there would be none that would bring objections. It is in the interest of all for these rumors and findings to be verified."

Dredaius tried to keep the look of disapproval from his face, but his dislike for the Lady and Selyndar was obvious. "I see we are a house divided again," he spat. He turned in his seat to look at the Seer. "And your thoughts? Though I don't see the need to ask as I suspect you've already decided to support House Omaga and House Shaal'Elonthra against me."

Lady Alle placed her hands quietly on the table. "My Ade. These matters are no light issues. Should the Th'arule truly be gathering for an assault on the Weode, it would be an event of incredible portent. The Weode and Th'arule have lived apart for almost five thousand cycles, and we have had little contact in that time with that branch of the great tree. Should you pause and allow time to gather more information before deciding on a course of action, it would be credited to you as acting with great discernment. Your subjects would praise you for prudence."

Dredaius slammed his fists down on the table. Even from this distance, Luinedhel could see the red rise on his neck. "And you, *brother?*" His voice echoed with the strains of Questelle when she had spat out 'Arracnoth,' in the throne room so many months ago. The tone set Luinedhel on edge.

Avanstel cleared his throat. "Ade, I have only been with the Weode for mere months, not decades or centuries, like those on the council before me. Although I seek what is best for the kingdom, I cannot, nor would I presume to be able to provide you with any counsel on such a matter as this. You have more experience and wisdom than I. Any decisions that are made will have an enormous impact on our people, so I would only urge us to make the right decisions when there is sufficient information available. If you feel that sufficient information has been obtained, brother, then I support you. If you think we can get more information, I recommend we do so before deciding. Whatever you see as best for the kingdom, I will support."

Although Luinedhel had seen changes in his friend over the previous months, the formal, regal, and insightful speech from his light-hearted, fun-loving childhood friend still surprised him. Their time in Ny'we Adye was changing Avanstel just as it was changing Luinedhel. Avanstel, the Aetheling, next-in-line, was becoming the future Ade. The quick wit that had served Avanstel so well in Chark had been honed into a sharp eloquence that allowed him to produce politically astute responses to questions that seemed to have no real acceptable answers. He was becoming a man who had the potential to guide the Weode in the centuries to come. Perhaps despite the influence that Dredaius had over him, Avanstel may still be able to bring light to the darkness. He was still the white sword – just as he had always been.

Luinedhel could see Dredaius turn over Avanstel's answer in his mind. Avanstel's words had played to Dredaius' pride, flattered him, and yet also given Dredaius enough room to maneuver to change his course of action should he second-guess his impulsive move to send them to war. He sat back in his chair, considering.

"If I may, Ade …" Seer Alle spoke gently, hoping she could steer the conversation in a more productive direction. "We would surely be outnumbered if we were to war with the Th'arule. Although our lands are vast and our army fierce, the woods of our ancestors are thick with their kind. Their kingdom is older with deeper roots, and thus they have greater resources for which to wage war. To ensure our success against them, we may need to seek alliances or pursue other strategies that would ensure our victory. Perhaps, should you find wisdom in withholding a decision … even for a few days … the Council could come back with thoughts on ways to ensure we are the ruin of those who would come against our kingdom."

Luinedhel smiled. The old woman's insightful understanding of the issues and seeming ability to read others' thoughts granted her remarkable vision. He could sense the shift in the room. Even Lords Kellendaer and Y'Vellian sat back in their chairs.

"A few days …" Dredaius mused. He folded his hands in front of his face, his gaze looking at something distant, not in the room. There was silence as they waited to see what Dredaius's response would be. Across the room, Luinedhel could see N'Khael shifting in her seat, uneasy with the delay. She was better suited for action than for diplomacy.

"Yes," Dredaius said finally. "Let us meet again on Drift Leaf eve. That will give everyone a week to gather whatever information that you can, and thoughts on alliances we might forge, should the need arise. Lady Alle, I want you to scour the archives for anything you could find that might be of aid. Lady Shaal'Elonthra, send word to your spies by whatever means you may have. It is a five-day ride to Orevael on our swiftest mounts, so we can't expect to send out new agents to the other side of the Idar and have them back in such a time. We will need to rely on those already in place."

Dredaius turned to Selyndar. "Your *drivrid* operative, he has not been in Belkin Wood for some time, correct? Perhaps you can contact him and send him through to the other side of the mountains to confirm the numbers that come against us."

"I will do what I can, Ade." Selyndar bowed his head. Luinedhel knew that Nightfall was unreachable, but now wasn't the time for such discussions. What Dredaius was asking wasn't possible, but Selyndar was playing this game as cautiously as the Seer. One wrong word could set Dredaius off in another direction, and nobody wanted that.

Dredaius motioned to Lord Kellendaer. "Send your best man to Faber to treat with the Governor. I will provide the letter with my seal upon it that will grant the authority to begin discussions on an alliance between elf and men. Have him remain there and send word back to whether there is a welcome hand extended. It would be to their benefit for us to remain here in Belkin Wood. Perhaps that is enough to encourage them to come to our aid. Lord Y'Vellian, the same with our neighbors to the south – Stone March and Redwinds. Although it may empty our treasury, I will not see our people enslaved to the Th'arule again." He paused, taking a deep breath. "Are there other matters that need to be discussed?"

There was a moment of silence before Lord Y'Vellian cleared his throat. "I do have one thing to bring to your attention, my Lord." He hesitated. "Perhaps we should discuss it in private."

Dredaius glared at him and huffed. "Out with it, Lord Y'Vellian. We have important things to be about. Our kingdom is at stake."

He paused, looking around the room at the other Council Elders and then back to Dredaius. "Very well, my Ade." He cleared his throat again. "More bodies have been discovered."

Dredaius did not respond.

Luinedhel saw Selyndar exchange glances with Lady Shaal'Elonthra and noticed the slight shake of her head. Neither of them knew what this was about.

Lord Y'Vellian shifted in his seat and pulled on his shirt. He stammered for a moment and then blurted out. "They were found in the city, not in the forest this time. In alleys in the Lower South District and Kettle's Hill area. It's the same as last cycle; young people, none older than six hundred cycles, and yet all aged beyond the norm and turned ashy grey. Withered and dried out like a grape left in the sun too long."

Dredaius took a deep breath, his eyes still fixed on the floor. "Within the city? How many?"

"A couple a month, over the last five months."

There was a long silence. "How many total?"

"Fourteen from last cycle, twelve from this. Twenty-six in total."

"I thought this had ended. You told me no further bodies had been found."

Lord Y'Vellian coughed into his hand. "That was true, my Ade. We had found none for several months, and then they started showing up again. This time within the city."

"The Peytriad?"

"It is possible. But these deaths have no relation to you or House J'Onsal. They seem almost random."

Dredaius nodded. He looked up and turned toward the Seer. "Lady Alle, can you offer any insights?"

"I have only just heard of this, my Ade. Lord Y'Vellian did not share this discovery prior to just now. Had I known of these events when they had first occurred, I might have been able to provide some information for you." The scowl on her face matched her biting tone. She turned toward Lord Y'Vellian, even though they all knew she couldn't see him.

"The Peytriad need to be stopped," Dredaius said, looking at Selyndar. "Their attempt on the life of the Aetheling was inexcusable. And now they are killing randomly? Lord Kellendaer, since Lord Y'Vellian seems unable to deal with the Peytriad himself, I want you to take care of them. I don't have the time, nor the patience for this." Dredaius pushed his chair back from the table, turned swiftly, and exited the room through a tall door at the back of the chamber, followed by several of the Green Guard.

Tretarilus remained seated behind Avanstel and did not leave with the Ade. Luinedhel frowned. It was unusual for the Steward not to accompany the Ade wherever he went, but the others seemed to take no notice. Lord Y'Vellian, Lord Kellendaer, and their entourage departed, muttering in hushed tones to each other and looking unhappy about the way things had transpired. They cast unfriendly glances at Selyndar as they passed by.

Selyndar stood up and bowed to Lady Shaal'Elonthra. "I will be most interested to hear what you discover," he said. "I know your reach is far, but even in one week's time, what he asks is …"

"Come now, Lord Omaga," she said, standing and moving to place her arm in his. She glanced back at Tretarilus before returning her attention to Selyndar. "We all have our kingdom's best interest in mind, and our wise Ade most of all. Let us be about the tasks he has set for us as swiftly as possible." Luinedhel saw the squeeze that she gave his arm, just like she had in the throne room so many months ago. She glanced over at Avanstel, who was sitting in his chair silently, and then at Luinedhel, and then back at Selyndar. "Let us speak in the entry hall to see if we can coordinate efforts effectively."

"Yes," Seer Alle said as she got up from her chair. T'Antalius appeared at her side, placing her hand on his arm, and leading her towards the door. "I have much research to do. I will see if Lord Y'Vellian can deliver one of these bodies to me so that I can determine the cause of death. We don't need additional distractions at a time like this. I shall be in contact should I require any assistance, my Lord, and my Lady." Slowly bowing, the Seer left the room, escorted by T'Antalius. Selyndar and Lady Shaal'Elonthra followed her out.

The closing of the doors startled Avanstel from his reverie. He looked up, as if noticing for the first time that the room had emptied. He caught Luinedhel's eye, and a wide smile crossed his face, the worry and fatigue fading instantly. He crossed the room in four quick strides and grabbed his friend in an embrace.

"It is so good to see you," he said.

"The same," Luinedhel said. "I was hoping to talk with you, to find out how you have been, and to share news with you."

Avanstel stepped back and looked at Luinedhel. The warmth and kindness in his eyes were still the same as Luinedhel remembered them to be – untouched by the months apart and different paths they had traveled. "N'Khael told me! An Omaga! One of the Founding families. What an amazing thing for you." He paused, looked over his shoulder toward the door that the Ade had disappeared through. His eyes rested for a moment on Tretarilus and then he turned back to Luinedhel. "We both have new families now." His voice was hushed and almost sad.

Luinedhel frowned. "Are you all right, Avanstel?"

N'Khael and Hathar had crossed the room during the exchange and now stood beside Avanstel. "Yes, yes, of course," he said. His voice returned to a cheerful tone. "Come, Arrac … I mean, Luinedhel … I will cancel any remaining appointments this afternoon so we can spend some time together. Your new family is something to talk about, right, N'Khael?"

"My father can be as impulsive as the Ade, but he did not make this decision lightly. Luinedhel is an Omaga through and through, and I am blessed to have him join our family. He may help to temper some of our father's more passionate nature. And besides, who better knows the welcome of a family than he and I, as we both have gone through the *anneming* to join the Omaga family. This is a cause for joy in these dark days." She laughed and slapped Luinedhel on the back. "I have always wanted a little brother to duel with."

"But this name … Luinedhel sounds too old fashioned for my taste. I want to pick my *own* name for my new sibling, the Thel Omaga." She brightened. "Thel Omaga … hmmm … I think I'll call you Thelo instead. Rolls off the tongue easier!" She swung at him playfully, but he anticipated the strike and dodged deftly to the side. Her fist met the empty air.

"Oh ho!" she exclaimed. "I see Thelo has had some training with father! These events have suddenly become even more interesting. Not only did I gain a brother, but perhaps a worthy sparring partner. I will have to schedule some time to visit, so you can show me what you've learned with those blades of yours."

Luinedhel grinned. "Happily!"

Avanstel put his arm around Luinedhel, and the four of them moved out of the room.

Tretarilus sat a moment longer and then stood up and moved toward the wall of the chamber. He touched a disguised panel and slid through a hidden entrance, disappearing back into the interior of the palace and heading toward the west wing.

He … they … weren't too distraught about the delays. They had waited an extraordinarily long time. Imprisoned for millennia. Another week would not hamper their inevitable plans. Things were unfolding just as they had wished. They had secured two of their line to help with the ritual. Retrieval of the weapon was next.

The discovery of the bodies and the open discussion of the Peytriad were things they hadn't expected. It might cause more problems than they wanted. They would have to be more cautious in the future.

CHAPTER 20: MISSION

There was a knock on the door that interrupted the laughter from within. Avanstel got up from the chaise lounge in front of the fireplace and made his way towards the door. "I think I've lost track of time. It must be late. You were right, Luin. We shouldn't have started that last game, but a tie-breaker was necessary to keep my standing." Avanstel, in a matter of hours, had shortened Luinedhel's new Weode name to a familiar nickname. Luinedhel chuckled at how fast they had fallen back into their old patterns, as if no time had passed. "It must be well past the time I should have returned to House Omaga. Perhaps that is Selyndar here to fetch me."

Avanstel opened the door to his private apartments. The warm glow from the lanterns around the room spilled into the dark hallway, illuminating the face of the visitor.

"Ade!" Avanstel said in surprise. "I … I did not receive your summons. I would have come immediately, my Lord."

Dredaius waved his hand dismissively and stepped into the room. "I did not send for you. I wanted to speak with you directly, here, away from prying eyes."

A door on the side of the room opened, and Hathar appeared from the darkness within. "My Lord?"

"It is fine, Hathar," Avanstel said. "Return to your rest." Hathar bowed and retreated, closing the door softly behind him.

As he stepped into the room, Dredaius noticed Luinedhel standing by the fire. "I didn't know you had company," he said. The sarcasm that Luinedhel was accustomed to was missing from his voice.

"I can go, my Lord." Luinedhel looked about for his cloak. "I have lost track of the time, and I have overstayed."

Dredaius glanced around the room. "You have no escort," he stated bluntly.

"I can have Hathar —" Avanstel said.

"No need." Dredaius crossed the room to the large glass doors on the opposite side and looked out at the soft lights coming from the rooms of the palace across the private garden. "You may stay, Thel Omaga."

Luinedhel exchanged a quizzical glance with Avanstel. This was the first time he had been invited to stay at the palace. Dredaius had never been so ... *not* Dredaius. Avanstel stepped towards the Ade Gerent. "Ade, are you well?"

Dredaius crossed the room to a table next to the door of Avanstel's study. "I am not." He poured wine from a bottle into an elegant glass and then moved to sit in a chair next to the fire. His gaze fell across the Haven Chase board, noting that the game was still in progress. He picked up Avanstel's token, the white sword, and played with it in his hands, turning it over and looking at it from various angles.

"Perhaps, as your Ade ... and your brother ... you would allow me to speak with you a moment about that which weighs heavy upon me. And perhaps ... in exchange for my kindnesses to you and Thel Omaga, you will accept what I must ask of you."

"Whatever I can do for you, my Ade." Avanstel sat down again on the lounge and leaned forward. He motioned for Luinedhel to sit next to him.

Dredaius placed the token back on the board and sank back in the chair, his face slipping into the dark shadows and out of the firelight. He took a long drink from the glass and then lost himself, watching the flickering of the fire in the fireplace. A shiver ran up Luinedhel's spine. The flames reflected in Dredaius' eyes were like two piercing lights peering out at him from the darkness. The Ade was silent for a long time. Luinedhel could hear his heart beating in his own ears. "*Sere'eden,*" he thought, and took a deep breath. He wasn't sure what was going on, but whatever it was, it was unsettling.

Finally, Dredaius spoke. His voice was grave. "Should the Th'arule come against our kingdom, we will fall."

Avanstel leaned back, as if the weight of those words were a physical strike. "But, Ade, surely …"

"It is very unlikely we will be successful in forming an alliance with Faber, or Chark, or Stone March or Redwinds or any other city of men. The loyalty of men takes a long time to earn and is easily lost. Almost as swiftly as the flames of their lives are snuffed out." He looked at both Avanstel and Luinedhel, realizing that he had spoken against their human heritage. He did not make an apology.

"The treaties will fail. The scouts will not return in time. Lord Omaga will not be able to reach his agent. I have been told all of this by … by someone I trust. Try as I may to position the kingdom against the enemy, I will be unable to ensure our victory. The Weode will fall. Save for one hope."

He took another long drink of the dark liquid, emptying the cup. "This is the reason that I have come in such a peculiar manner and at a peculiar time to speak with you, brother."

"What can I do?" Avanstel leaned in.

"To the east of Belkin Wood lies the Barrens."

"Yes," Avanstel answered, "V'Deliah has shared the maps of Halbrun with me. I have studied them thoroughly and know the place of which you speak. It is a vast marshland."

Dredaius placed his glass down on the floor beside the chair. It made a clink as it scraped against the stone. He placed his hands in front of him, his fingertips forming a small mountain.

"It was not always a marsh, though there's nobody alive that can recall those days."

"What do you mean?"

"Deep within the Barrens, now impenetrable, lies the ruins of a forgotten city. It was the capital of a long-lost empire that spanned the width and breadth of the entire northern half of Halbrun. A kingdom of elven people, the ancestors of the Weode, that reached from Harper to Chark and all the way north, to Norport at the top of the Glimmer Sea. Hemel was the city's name, although history has forgotten the names of the kingdom and its people. It is the place where the feet of the elven race first stepped upon the soil of Halbrun. When the empire failed, the remnants of those people built the kingdom of the Th'arule in the south.

"Knowledge of the lost city, and other secrets, were passed down to their children throughout the centuries, from one generation to the next. To the Th'arule and all the way to Ni'Ilyan himself, and to the Weode … to my grandfather, father, and then to me.

"I expect Lady Alle may find references in her ancient scrolls of the city of Hemel. Maybe even tales of its demise. What started as stories became fables, and then legends, and are now only faint whispers, its existence reduced to scribbled marks in dusty tomes. She may regard such things as rumors lost to the mists of time, but the bloodline of J'Onsal knows the truth of the matter."

Dredaius leaned forward. His face came into the light, illuminated brightly on the left side, still clouded in darkness on the right. "I am sending you there, brother … heir of J'Onsal."

Avanstel tilted his head and frowned. "To the ruins of a lost city in the heart of a swamp?"

"Yes. I need you to retrieve something from Hemel and bring it to me. It may be the one thing that would give us a chance against the Th'arule, our only hope to be victorious against our enemies. I don't trust anyone else to do this. It must be you, my brother, heir to the throne of Ni'Ilyan, the White Wolf. Will you go?"

Avanstel leaned back and looked down at his hands for a moment and then back up at Dredaius. "Of course, I will go, Ade. I serve our kingdom's needs. Whatever they may be."

Dredaius leaned back in the chair, his face fading again into the shadows. "Good, brother. I had hoped you would do this for me, for your kingdom. I will speak with you more about this errand tomorrow. For now, I leave you to enjoy your evening with your friend – an expression of my gratitude."

He stood up and moved toward the door, pausing and turning back to them. "And I hope I don't need to explain to you that this is to be kept among the three of us. The Peytriad are everywhere, possibly even within the walls of the palace. Should our enemies learn of your trip to the Barrens, it would put you in unnecessary peril. Your Protector and your Second will travel with you, but it will be under cover, by secret ways, and no one else should know of your purposes. I only speak of this in the presence of your friend, because I believe he has absolute loyalty to you. Based on what I know, I have no concerns that he would act to put you in danger."

Avanstel bowed his head. "As you wish, Ade." Luinedhel nodded in acknowledgement. Dredaius was right – he would do nothing to harm Avanstel, nothing. At least the ruler was observant enough to read the truth of the matter, despite all his other failings.

Dredaius left the room, closing the door behind him.

Luinedhel let out a long sigh and looked at his friend. "Do you trust him, Van?"

Avanstel shrugged. "He has been good to me thus far. He brought me to the palace; kept me safe from the Peytriad, and from those who are opposed to our mixed heritage; provided education; allowed me to be at his side to learn and see and experience. I think he's genuine about his concerns for the kingdom."

"And Questelle?"

"To tell the truth, I have only seen her a few times. She keeps herself busy elsewhere. Occasionally I spotted her coming and going across the palace grounds, but only a couple times inside the palace. When our paths happen to cross, I excuse myself. It's a dance we do to avoid each other. If it was necessary to speak with her, I'm not sure what I would say ... or do."

Avanstel stood up and stepped toward the paneled glass doors. He stood looking out at the palace light just like the Ade had. Luinedhel noticed how closely Avanstel's actions mirrored those of Dredaius. Avanstel was fitting nicely into his new role as heir-apparent.

"I still grieve his loss, Arrac ... I mean Luin." They both knew he was referring to Danvaren. Neither spoke his name, worried that a fresh wave of grief might rush back in.

Luinedhel stepped beside Avanstel and placed his hand on his shoulder. "I know. I feel it too. He will always be part of us. She cannot take that away. Time and busyness have dulled the ache, but sometimes when I'm alone ... when my mind is at rest ... I just can't believe he's gone. That she ..."

Avanstel turned and looked at Luinedhel. His face creased with sorrow. "I know. Me neither."

Luinedhel touched Avanstel's arm. "I worry for you, Van. I had not heard of the Peytriad until the Council meeting. And now Dredaius says they might be here in the palace? And with Questelle here, and knowing what she is capable of ..."

"I am fine. I have N'Khael and Hathar with me. And I'm the Aetheling now. There's no question about that."

Luinedhel searched Avanstel's face. "What about these bodies that are showing up? I've never heard of this, and neither did Selyndar or the Lady. Why hasn't that been shared with the Council before? Do you *really* trust Dredaius?"

Avanstel bowed his head for a moment. "You know the Weode are a secretive people, Luin. Palace politics only compounds that. Considering everything that has happened, Dredaius has given me no reason to doubt his word. As he said, he has no one else he can trust. I understand that as perhaps nobody else can. That's why he's sending me on this mission. He really *can't* trust anyone else." He turned away from the windows and sat down on the divan. He picked up his token and played with it in his hand.

Luinedhel watched him for a moment. He missed his friend. He missed spending time together. "I should go with you," Luinedhel said and sat across from him.

Avanstel shook his head. "No, you can't. Dredaius would not allow it. We will go by cover. No one must know we are gone. Your disappearance, along with mine, would raise questions. Please, Luin, do this for me. Please stay here."

Luinedhel hesitated. He did not trust Dredaius, and he disliked all the secrecy and machinations of the palace, and of the Weode in general: spies and assassins and deceit everywhere. He had known that the Weode were dark and sly, but he had underestimated how deeply and widely their nature ran. It was almost part of their blood, their *accentation*.

He looked directly into Avanstel's eyes. "I will stay, Avanstel. And I will keep your secret."

Avanstel smiled, his face lighting up, the joy returning. "You are a true friend," he said. "Let me inform Hathar that you will stay here tonight, and he can have word sent to Selyndar so that there is nothing to cause him concern. I want to hear more about your training and about these strange blades of yours! And I want to prove that I can still best you at Haven Chase. I believe I lead?"

"You do." Luinedhel grinned. "But not for long. It's my turn." He picked up the die, rolled it, and moved the dark quill forward by three. "I take your shield," he said.

Avanstel laughed. "But I take your tower." He picked up the black tower piece and moved it off the board.

The sparkle of the firelight on the obsidian game piece caught Luinedhel's eye. How far they had come from the simple games they had played back in Chark.

And how far they had come on their separate journeys. So different, but still together. And that was what was important.

The air was warm and oppressive, almost smothering. Before him was a dark tower – shimmering and pulsing in a slow rhythm, as if it was breathing. As if it were alive, and not made of stone or glass, but it was a creature – or creatures – with thoughts and will and desires. Animate, though inanimate at the same time.

Something was moving inside the tower, pushing against the confinement. Trying to escape and failing. Trying again and failing. And again. And again. It would not cease; it would never stop fighting against the cruel bands of steel that were wrapped around it. Rings that held it in; wards and powers that would not allow it to be free.

Luinedhel peered closer, and he saw a flower. Petals unfolded, layer after layer of petals that reached outward from the center in a never-ending and almost hypnotic pattern. He wanted to touch the flower, the beautiful dark flower, but the bands spinning around it would not allow him through.

Then suddenly, something happened. After thousands of cycles and millions of attempts, something gave way within the whirling rings. It was just a slight change, but where it had found resistance before, there was suddenly a give. Something small, but something that wasn't there before. An opportunity … for freedom.

The possibility of walking away from this prison, of seeing the sun and the moon and the stars once again. Of breathing the air, the scent of forests and oceans, of cities. The promise of hope excited it, and the others with it. It tried again, confirming that the small break was there … and it was.

It continued and continued. The progress was slow, almost imperceptible. But having been here for as long as they had been, they all knew the barrier well … and something had changed, without a doubt. So, they would continue to push, continue to try — until they succeeded.

Luinedhel watched as one of the five spinning rings fell to the floor with a tremendous clang. The blue glowing runes carved over the surface of the ring faded, and it was now simply a metal band. The power it had held faded away.

Part of the dark flower broke away and flew out of the spinning circles. There was a roar that filled his ears and a voice speaking words he knew but didn't understand. The words filled him with terror. The darkness wrapped around him, binding him, pinning down his arms and stopping him from fighting against it. He screamed, knowing that there was little else he could do.

"Arrac! Wake up! It's a dream! Wake up!" He opened his eyes. Avanstel stood in front of him, holding him tightly as he flailed his arms.

"Van?" Luinedhel's heart was racing, and he was breathing as if he had just sprinted the length of House Omaga. His eyes darted around the unfamiliar room. He didn't recognize anything. "Where am I?"

"You're here – with me. In my room at the palace. It was just a dream. You are safe. You were only dreaming."

Luinedhel touched Avanstel's face. "Van! Thank Enos!" He relaxed, letting the adrenaline flood from his body, and fell backwards onto the soft bed as Avanstel released him.

"Are you ok, Luin?"

He looked at Avanstel and saw the concern written on his face. "I get these nightmares sometime … ever since we left Chark. They're dark and frightening. I don't know why. I'm sorry I woke you."

Avanstel smiled. "No need to be sorry. You helped *me* through many a night terror when we were at House Omaga, after we found out that Danvaren …"

There was a knock on the door, and it opened. The light from the fireplace illuminated the room with an orange glow. "Everything ok, Aetheling?" Hathar stood in the doorway in his breeches. He looked like a woodland creature, with his furry chest and long brown hair that fell around his bearded face.

"Luinedhel had a nightmare. I think he is all right. Thank you, Hathar."

"I will bring a draught."

"No need, I am fine." Luinedhel looked at Avanstel. "Just maybe a little too much sweet wine and too many games of Haven Chase with Avanstel." He grinned. "For the record, Hathar, I beat him five games to four."

Hathar chuckled. "An impressive feat, indeed. Rest well, friends." He stepped out of the room and closed the door behind him.

The room became dark again, but this darkness did not compare to the darkness in his dreams. And Avanstel was beside him. That was enough to keep the nightmares at bay for the remainder of the night.

CHAPTER 21: RETURN

Selyndar appeared in the morning to retrieve Luinedhel. His demeanor was solemn, and Luinedhel picked up immediately that something was troubling him. The elder elf didn't share the reason, and Luinedhel did not press. True to his promise to Avanstel, Luinedhel did not discuss the information that Dredaius had shared the night before, nor Avanstel's mission to the Barrens. The conversation between the three was brief and polite, and Luinedhel felt torn between saying a meaningful goodbye to Avanstel and turning his attention to what was troubling Selyndar. He embraced Avanstel briefly.

"I will see you soon."

"Yes." Avanstel broke the embrace, meeting Luinedhel's eyes. "As soon as I can return to my normal schedule, I will catch up with you. And I want a rematch."

"I look forward to that. Though this time, no sweet wine." He laughed. "Until then."

"Lord Omaga." Avanstel nodded at Selyndar. "Please keep watch over my friend. Thank you for all you have done for him."

"Of course, Aetheling. I consider him my son, now, and love him equally as you do. I will protect him with my life." Selyndar put his hand on Luinedhel's shoulder.

Avanstel squeezed Luinedhel's arm one last time. The unspoken words lingered a moment between them before they parted.

Luinedhel followed Selyndar in silence through the maze of corridors and rooms and through the palace gardens. The scent of lavender hung heavily in the air, reminding him of N'Khael.

His thoughts were on the journey that lay ahead for Avanstel. Although Dredaius seemed committed to Avanstel's safety, and Luinedhel understood the reasons for the secrecy, it was still unsettling. Something was gnawing at the back of Luinedhel's mind about the entire thing, and he really wanted to discuss it with Selyndar — but did not want to break his promise.

It wasn't until they were clear of the palace that Luinedhel realized Selyndar had taken them via a different route than normal.

"Father?"

Selyndar shot Luinedhel a quick glance. "Not yet." His voice was tense and hushed. His eyes darted from side to side, and he kept looking back over his shoulder. His manner concerned Luinedhel, and the fact that he wouldn't speak of it made it even more worrisome.

They took circuitous routes through the city, avoiding House Omaga. Selyndar was taking Luinedhel to the out-of-the-way places in Ny'we Adye where the Elders didn't frequent. The homes looked rundown; the alleys grew darker, and the Weode that lingered in them looked less friendly. He felt eyes on him and caught sideways glances as he passed by. He remembered what Questelle had said about *taven'sanct*, and how it wouldn't always protect him. Her veiled threat felt very real here. He wasn't sure if he was feeling the scrutiny because he was *ort* — something 'other' and unwanted by those around him — or if Selyndar was the focus of their unwelcoming glares. Luinedhel instinctively lifted his hood over his head to cover his less-than-Weode looking ears, hoping to at least remove that reason for their attention.

Selyndar paused at an open doorway. Although Luinedhel couldn't see inside the dark building, he heard the sounds of raucous off-key singing mixed with the clink of glasses and the roar of laughter. The Weald-speak inscription above the door read, "The Lopsided Tankard." A drunken Weode stumbled out of the entry, paused a moment, and then vomited on the pavement stones in front of them. Another equally inebriated elf emerged and helped the first to his feet. They stumbled down the street singing a discordant tune.

"There," Selyndar said, pointing to a flash of light in the shadows of the alley across the street. He stepped forward, making his way toward the passage.

"Wait!" Luinedhel said. He grabbed Selyndar's arm and pulled him backward. "Please, father, tell me what is going on."

Selyndar looked up and down the street and then pulled Luinedhel behind a stack of empty barrels outside the tavern. He glanced over his shoulder once again before leaning in.

"Nightfall sent word to meet him here."

"Here? Why did he not come directly to House Omaga?"

"Why indeed! We met here before, but it was long ago, in the early days of his employment. For him to want to meet me here, means he cannot come to House Omaga. Maybe more of the Peytriad have infiltrated my walls and Y'Zelle was not operating alone as we had previously thought."

Luinedhel frowned. "Hathar would have discovered any remaining Peytriad within your household. Dredaius even told Avanstel that none remain at your home." He paused. He was drifting close to revealing the conversation the night prior and wanted to avoid that discussion. "We haven't had any trouble in months. Do you think this is related to the bodies that were discovered? We are in that part of the city, right?"

"We are, yes. This is Kettle's Hill. Perhaps Nightfall has uncovered something and wants to show me in person, though I sent him to discover more about the invasion, not the deaths – we've only recently learned of those. Let's go see what it is he wants to tell us." Selyndar stepped out from behind the barrels and headed toward the alley. Luinedhel followed close behind. As they slipped into the dark corridor, Luinedhel instinctively reached for the dagger on his right hip.

As he touched the handle, Marek's voice echoed in his head instantaneously. *"It's a trap!"*

Luinedhel reached out to grab Selyndar and pull him back, but it was too late. A dark figure rushed at them from the side, catching both of them off guard and slamming them into the wall of the building on their right. Luinedhel swung the sai in an arc, the way that Selyndar had trained him, but the figure adeptly stepped aside, and the blade sliced through the air where the figure had been. He heard the swoosh of his opponent's blade slashing towards him and moved to the right and crouched. The blade caught his bicep, cutting sharply through his shirt and scratching across his skin. He gasped in surprise.

Selyndar regained his footing and held his dagger up, ready to attack, but the figure had vanished. There was the sound of metal on stone. Luinedhel looked and saw a small grate that led to the under-workings of the city slide into place with a clank.

Luinedhel pulled Adesh from his belt, ready to pursue their attacker into the sewers.

"Too late," Adesh's biting voice scolded. *"The poison is already at work in your blood."*

"Poison?"

"What?" Selyndar said.

"Adesh says the blade was poisoned."

"Are you certain?"

"I don't know … she says…"

Selyndar groaned. "This is no good, son." There was something in his voice that Luinedhel had not heard before … a note of fear, almost.

"What is it?"

"We have to get to Lady Alle quickly."

Luinedhel wanted nothing more than to leave this place, but he was concerned about another attack. What if whoever had slipped into the sewers came back to finish the job? He heard another clank of metal on stone, but this one was lighter. He looked toward the noise and saw Selyndar's dagger on the ground. His father fell backwards onto him.

"We have to go, son." There was an urgency in his tone, but the words were sluggish and slurred. Selyndar was clutching his left side. A dark stain of blood was spreading across his tunic and running between his fingers. The elf stumbled and clutched Luinedhel's shoulder.

"You're struck! Sit here and let me go fetch help."

"No. I won't make it."

Luinedhel tucked the daggers into his belt and grabbed Selyndar's shoulders, pulling him to his feet. "What do you mean?"

"The wound is deep." He was having trouble holding his head up. His skin had become pale and clammy. He was rapidly losing blood, and if the blade was poisoned …

"Father, I don't know the way to the Seer's home from here. I don't even really know where we are. We can go now; I can help you … but I need you to show me the way."

Selyndar's eyes fluttered. "No time … Luinedhel, you must … I am so sorry. I dreamed of a wonderful future together."

Luinedhel shook his head. "Come on, Father! Don't talk that way. You will be fine once we get to the Seer. We just need to get help."

"Luinedhel … son … I … *You* are House Omaga now." Selyndar's body was limp, and his feet gave way beneath him. His full weight fell on Luinedhel, bringing them both to the ground. Luinedhel turned so that he could cushion Selyndar's fall. They slammed onto the pavers. Selyndar's head came to rest in his lap. The old elf's breathing was slow and jagged.

"Father! Wake up! I can get help!"

Suddenly there was the slightest sound of a footfall next to him. Luinedhel grabbed Selyndar's dagger off the ground and struck toward the sound.

"*Sondartin!*" The voice was familiar, though Luinedhel couldn't immediately place it. His ears were ringing, and his mind was working slowly.

"Nightfall?"

"I'm here."

Luinedhel felt the weight of Selyndar lift off him. He looked down and saw the dark shadow of Nightfall moving Selyndar aside and propping him against the wall. His father's eyes were pale and lifeless, his mouth agape. A small drop of blood rested in the corner of his mouth.

"Father … Selyndar …" Luinedhel tried to focus on the figure that was wrapping their arms around him and lifting him off the ground, but his vision blurred, his eyes wavering.

"Why did you lure us here?"

"The message wasn't from me. I saw you enter the alley. I was up the street, but too far away to reach you in time. They ambushed you – whomever it was. They probably used the sewers. There is access here, in this alley. I know it because I've used it before. That must be why they brought you here."

"Poison," was all Luinedhel could manage.

"Indeed, *sondartin*. And a powerful one at that. Thankfully, the weapon only scratched you, although we need to get you to the Seer immediately. He lifted Luinedhel up and stepped into the daylight of the street before them.

"Selyndar …"

Nightfall did not respond. Luinedhel watched the shadow of the alley fade away behind them as Nightfall ran down the street, carrying the *ort* in his arms.

"Father …"

Darkness claimed him.

Moments of lucidity punctuated the darkness. There were sounds and lights, although none of them made any sense, and they would fade as quickly as they came, leaving him back in the silent black alone. Eventually, the scattered and momentary visions coalesced into something that made sense … though Luinedhel couldn't tell how much time had passed between the events.

He was safe. He recognized Seer Alle's workshop. He was in bed, in a corner near the fireplace. There were lanterns set about the room. Occasionally, there were smells other than that of the burning hillstonas wood. And sometimes there were foul liquids, or sweet liquids, that Seer Alle or Nightfall would force him to drink. Eventually, there was food, and he was hungry. And then, he was able to sit up, and speak, and understand what was going on.

"How long was I asleep?"

Nightfall was removing the bandage on his arm where the poisoned blade had cut him. "Four days." He grimaced as he pulled the bandage away. "Lady Alle, the wound is still dark."

The Seer shuffled over to the bed. "Hmmm," she said, her familiar, scrutinizing, sightless gaze sweeping over Luinedhel's arm. "T'Antalius, mix up some more of the salve. This is stronger than anything I know. It's no wonder that Lord Omaga ..." she trailed off, realizing too late her misstep.

"Selyndar?" Luinedhel asked. He looked at the blind woman and then back to Nightfall. "Did you get him from the alley? Where is he?"

Nightfall slowly shook his head. "I'm sorry, *sondartin*." The gravity of his words fell heavily on Luinedhel. He saw sorrow cloud Nightfall's golden eyes – compassion and understanding, an echo of a deeper loss of his own from long ago.

T'Antalius appeared with a piece of leather smeared with a pungent-smelling grease. Nightfall took some and rubbed it into the cut on Luinedhel's arm. Luinedhel did not wince. He was numb to everything. He turned his face away from them.

Selyndar ... Father! How could they have taken him down so easily, so quickly? The man was a master of the blades. He had been Protector of the Ade, an Elder of a Founding House. He was part of the fabric of the Weode – it was impossible for Luinedhel to even consider that he was ...

"Who?"

Nightfall wrapped a clean bandage around Luinedhel's arm and bound it, then handed the rest of the salve back to T'Antalius.

"Rest. We will talk later. It's important that you sleep and heal."

"Nightfall ... I ..."

Heavy tears leaked from Luinedhel's eyes, try as he might to keep them in. He tried to meditate on the words Adine had taught him – s*ere'eden* – but they were not enough. Nothing was enough. To have gained a father, and to have lost him in such a brief time. It was more than he could bear.

Nightfall placed a hand on his chest. "*Namartha t'undel*," he said.

Luinedhel reached up and clasped the *drivrid's* dark hand, squeezing it tightly. "*Namartha t'undel*," he replied. His voice was hoarse. He turned his head further away to hide the steady tears that were flowing freely down his face.

"Let him have his rest before we share your news," the Seer said. "All of this is heavy, and he will need his strength."

Nightfall patted Luinedhel's chest. "Rest, *sondartin*. We will tend to you. You are safe. I will watch over you."

The dreams were incoherent and made no sense, but they came anyway. Images of death and tortured people, like those withered corpses carved into the stone of the Shadow Gate – like what he imagined the bodies looked like, the ones they had spoken of in the Council. Leather-winged creatures with red glowing eyes, and fangs that dripped with poison. Pulsing and swirling black smoke flowers that undulated with a rhythmic throb and called out to him for freedom.

And, of course, the pale face of Selyndar slumped against the wall in a darkened alley, blood on his lips. Who was then also his mother, clutching her moonstone pin, wasting away, and breathing her last breath. And then was Avanstel ... which he cried out for but was unable to save.

And a silver-plated book he had seen before, somewhere ... perhaps in Selyndar's study, or perhaps something Nightfall had tucked away somewhere.

Then the obsidian tower, glinting in the firelight. And words in the language he knew and did not understand. And Adesh saying, *"The she-elf doesn't have the blood."* The blood ... so much blood. Rivers of it. And cries of anguish and torment and pain, a city of people crying out in unison.

It was several more days before Luinedhel felt like speaking. The grief of losing Selyndar hit him almost as hard as the loss of Adine. In the months they had shared, he had grown incredibly close to the elder Weode, and the thought of living without his new father became a giant cloud that hung over his heart. He would miss their conversations that lasted long into the night and their games of Haven Chase. He would miss the sparring and the instruction in the Dance. He would miss Selyndar's soft words and kind face and his overwhelming generosity, his wisdom. He would even miss the passion Selyndar had for life – and his deep commitment to the Weode people. Life here in Ny'we Adye without Selyndar seemed … impossible.

Finally, when he had both the physical and emotional strength to talk about the matter, he inquired after N'Khael.

"I sent word immediately to the palace, but received no response," Nightfall answered. "After several days, I reached out to Lady Shaal'Elonthra and asked her to connect with Nephinae. She had not seen Thelyn Omaga in a week. Nor Hathar. Apparently, a disease has sickened Avanstel's entire staff, and they are quarantined in their apartments. Word of their sickness has not spread beyond the palace for fear of concerns of a plague – the last thing Dredaius needs at this moment as he's preparing for war."

"She's not at the palace," Luinedhel said. His voice sounded flat even to himself.

Nightfall frowned. "Why do you say that, *sondartin?* They assured me she's just ill and didn't want to spread the sickness."

"She's not there," Luinedhel repeated. "She's with Avanstel, and Hathar, on a mission for Dredaius. They have left Ny'we Adye."

"What's this?" Seer Alle said, moving closer to Luinedhel's bedside. "What mission?"

Luinedhel sat up in the bed and moved his feet around, resting them on the floor. A moment of vertigo swept over him, and he closed his eyes against it.

"I was not supposed to tell anyone. The Ade, and Avanstel, swore me to secrecy."

"You *must* tell us." Seer Alle turned around one of the chairs that faced the fireplace and sat down. "The Ade has too many secrets. We must expose them to the light." She glanced over at Nightfall, her blank eyes expressive.

Luinedhel swallowed. "Dredaius sent Avanstel to the Barrens. To the ruins of a city named Hemel. To fetch *something* that will help him in the battle against the Th'arule."

The old woman made a peculiar noise that sounded somewhere between a whistle and a woot and sat back in her chair. "To the Barrens, to the fabled city of Hemel," she said, rubbing her chin.

"Why the Barrens?" Nightfall asked. "It is nothing but endless swamp. And what is Hemel?"

"Hemel, indeed." She snorted. "It is a myth. Though if our Ade is sending the Aetheling there, then perhaps there's more to the stories …"

"He said you would say as much," Luinedhel said.

"Well tell us then, Thel Omaga, what new game does Dredaius play with the fate of our kingdom and the heir-apparent?"

Luinedhel shared everything Dredaius had said to them of Hemel, forgotten and hidden deep in the swamplands. And how most believed it was a myth – if they knew of it at all. And how the truth had been passed down the line of J'Onsal to Dredaius, and now to Avanstel.

The old woman listened intently through it all, nodding and prompting him with more questions when he paused. Nightfall looked lost in his own thoughts throughout the story, raising an eyebrow occasionally to show he was still listening. Eventually, the Seer felt she had received all the information she needed. She stood up and turned toward a shelf of old scrolls hidden in the back of the room.

"Share *your* news with him, *drivrid*. This makes for an even more interesting situation."

Nightfall returned from his thoughts. "It does indeed, Lady Alle. Let me tell you where I have been, *sondartin*. As you know, I served our late Lord Omaga for many cycles, undertaking many missions for him. I had just returned from my latest errand with urgent information. When I arrived at House Omaga, I was told by Anafelen that Lord Omaga had gone to the palace to retrieve you, so you could meet me in the alley near The Lopsided Tankard. Since I had left no such message for Lord Omaga, I knew something foul was afoot. Unfortunately, I arrived too late to be of any help."

Luinedhel looked down at his hands, trying to push away the wave of grief that came over him. Nightfall paused too, and then he cleared his throat and continued.

"The mission I had gone on for Lord Omaga was to find out more about our Adelyn and to see if I could discern the truth behind her schemes. As you would expect, there is much more than meets the eye here. Questelle is not only *not* an *ort*, as she originally led us all to believe, but neither is she Weode as she pretends to be."

Luinedhel frowned. "I don't understand. She's not Weode? Then what is she?"

Nightfall nodded his head. "What indeed." He leaned forward. "I traveled across the Idar. I went through Caerbexsys and found my way to Brinca, on the other side of the mountains. From there, I worked my way down the Twisted Mountains and past the Gate that leads to the Mystic Desert and to the lands north of the Ivy Forest itself."

"It was there that I heard rumors of an elf woman who had come to Tyshin'Dael in search of something – though no one knew what, and after a cycle, she had left the Ivy Forest headed north across the mountains. There were tales of her leaving death in her wake wherever she went. Bodies discovered withered and shriveled by something unnatural. Some said she had spoken about destroying the Weode, though nobody put that much weight to it. What could one woman do against an entire elven nation? It might have been any Th'arule, for all of them have a general dislike for their Weode brethren. I did not think there was much to note in the gossip, until I heard a song one night in a tavern in Hadron's Ford."

"It was like other tales of the split between the Th'arule and the Weode, but this one included some references to a woman with talents with poisons. I recalled the rumors of N'Athero's rapid decline and death, and Lord Omaga's suspicions of poisoning, and thought I should investigate further before returning to Ny'we Adye. I could find no other mentions of this woman, and I dared not travel all the way to Tyshin'Dael, for if these rumors were true and there were attempts to kill Weode royalty, I could not waste time and delay warning to Avanstel, and even Dredaius. I immediately turned back to Ny'we Adye."

"And the armies. Tell him about the armies," the Seer prompted as she spilled an armful of scrolls across the table in front of her.

Luinedhel looked at Nightfall expectantly. The *drivrid* shrugged, placing his hands in front of him.

"There are no armies, nor any signs of them. If they exist, I did not find any mention of them. It's not impossible, but the timing of everything doesn't match up. I'm sure I would have heard rumblings of war coming, and there was no talk of such things in the south. From what I could tell, other than this lone woman bent on the destruction of the Weode, the rest of the Ivy Forest has no intent of wiping Ny'we Adye from the map."

"So, the coming war … is a lie?"

Nightfall nodded, his golden eyes flashing. "It appears to be."

"No doubt orchestrated by our Adelyn!" the Seer said.

"Though for what purpose has yet to be discerned." Nightfall leaned back in his chair.

"I may know," the Seer said. "I remember an old scroll about Hemel, the fabled First City. More importantly, about the fall of Hemel at the hand of its ambitious ruler. And I think our Adelyn has intentions beyond the throne of Weode. I wouldn't be surprised if these Peytriad are her followers, and she is doing what she can to snuff out the line of J'Onsal. The Aetheling is in danger. Indeed, we all are."

Luinedhel bolted up. "Then Avanstel is also in danger!"

"If Dredaius and the Adelyn have sent Avanstel to Hemel, then yes, he is in danger."

"I am going after him!"

Nightfall stood up and raised a hand in caution. "Hold, *sondartin*. You are just healing. You are in no state to —"

"Nightfall," Luinedhel interrupted. He stared unwaveringly into the *drivrid's* eyes. "I am going after him."

The nether-elf was silent as he considered what he could say to dissuade Luinedhel. He came up with nothing — he knew he couldn't change Luinedhel's mind. "I will go with you," he said. "We will go together to protect Avanstel. If the Peytriad are cunning enough to infiltrate the palace and poison the Ade and bold enough to attack one of the Elders in broad daylight, there's no telling what lengths they may go to accomplish their goals."

Luinedhel let out a breath. "Thank you."

"I am beside you."

Luinedhel nodded. They would find Avanstel and put an end to Questelle and Dredaius' plans — whatever those may be. For Selyndar.

CHAPTER 22: PURSUIT

In the hours that passed, the Seer had only been able to gather a few scattered pieces of information – references in several unrelated ancient texts regarding Hemel and its fall. There were mentions of a vast kingdom, and a few references to a magical artifact that the emperor possessed – which ensured his triumph over his enemies. Allegedly, the artifact gave him the power to conquer lands and maintain dominance over the realm, but there were few details about the attributes of the relic, its origin, or how it worked. Some small references mentioned it caused the destruction of the entire city and the collapse of the empire, but it was all vague and nothing certain, as all the stories were incredibly old.

"It makes little sense," Seer Alle said. "*Akan'gott* would have faded from the world during the time of these histories. If this arcane weapon still exists, it must have been *omu'gott* … but that magic would have faded from it long ago. *Omu'gott* was very temporary. What good could it serve now? And if there truly is no advancing Th'arule army, why would Dredaius or Questelle have need of an old trophy anyway? Why send *Avanstel* after it? They could have sent any of the Green Guard to fetch it." She flittered about the room, pushing scrolls across tables, and sorting through her dusty tomes, scanning words on pages with her unseeing eyes. "I must dig deeper. I might have to consult with Ember Wynn or see if one of the Mystics will come down off their high mountain to share some of their knowledge with us mere mortals."

Luinedhel chuckled to himself. Because of *accentation*, the life of a Weode spanned many centuries, long enough for most humans to consider elf-kind immortal. The thought that the wizened Seer considered herself a 'mortal' when compared to these people was amusing. "The Mystics?"

She waved her hand at him dismissively, though Luinedhel caught a quick glance that passed between her and Nightfall. "Do not concern yourself with my ramblings. At some point, the recordings become so old that they're vague and nonsensical – even hard to decipher – leaving only stories that someone heard from others long dead, and which someone else captured third-hand."

Nightfall and Luinedhel left Seer Alle bustling around her room, mumbling to herself. They headed to the east side of Ny'we Adye to meet Anafelen, keeping their cowls pulled around their heads. Even so, Luinedhel caught an occasional sound of disgust from some of the Weode who recognized him or Nightfall. There was little sympathy for him here among the elves. It didn't matter that he had just lost his father. It didn't matter that he was of House Omaga. To the average Weode, he was and always would be just an *ort*.

When they reached the stable on the east side of the city, Anafelen was there with T'Antalius. The boy had gathered the supplies they had requested for the journey while they were visiting with the Seer. "Here's everything you requested," he said. "Should you need anything further, please let me know, and I will fetch it right away."

Nightfall checked the bags. "Everything looks good," he said. "Thank you again, T'Antalius. You and Lady Alle have been most helpful." He turned to look at Anafelen. "And the horses?"

"There are four here. If none of them suit you, there are two others stabled on the north side of the city."

Nightfall stepped toward a black gelding. "Hello, Nyx," he said. "It has been a while since I've had the pleasure of your company. Do you remember me?"

The horse nudged Nightfall's hand and chuffed.

Luinedhel thought about Selyndar, remembering how he favored the black horse token because it reminded him of his horse, Nyx. How he missed his adopted father. Having Nightfall ride Nyx felt almost like Selyndar was coming along with them on the journey. His smile was sadness, mixed with joy.

Luinedhel stepped forward and touched the neck of a grey mare that had drawn his eye.

"One of Lord Omaga's favorites." Anafelen said. "She's a strong one."

"She is perfect," Luinedhel said. "What's her name?"

"Her name? She doesn't have a name yet. You may name her if you'd like, Thel … I mean *Lord* Omaga."

"Thel," he said. "Just Thel."

"Very well."

The grey mare touched her nose to his forehead. She had chosen him as much as he had chosen her. "I will take her," Luinedhel said and patted her neck.

They packed the supplies and said farewell to T'Antalius and Anafelen and left Ny'we Adye under the cover of darkness, making their way eastward, beyond the walls of the city and into the forest.

The way started as a clear and well-worn path, but it soon dissolved, leaving them to pick their way carefully between the trees. The Weode did not have many visitors to their city. The unkept roads and secret paths were an obvious sign of the Weode's insulation from everyone.

Neither moon shed its light that evening, and even if they had, little of it would have penetrated the dense canopy of leaves to reach the forest floor. They rode beside each other where they could, and when the way wasn't wide enough, Nightfall took the lead, deftly weaving Nyx between the large dark trunks and over the broken ground. They passed by ruins occasionally, and Luinedhel realized that there was so much about the Weode that he still had to learn. What were these buildings, and why were they there? And why had they been abandoned?

"Do you still have those light crystals?" Luinedhel asked, squinting to make out Nightfall's cloaked form ahead of him.

"I do indeed. Though I think it's best to pass through the woods with as few eyes upon us as possible. I kept news of Lord Omaga's passing restricted to the Seer and the Lady – and their households, of course – but should our travels create reason for inquiry, our allies may have to answer questions that are best left unasked. Lord Omaga's death, and the absence of N'Khael, would shift the balance of the Elder Council, and that's best something to deal with after this matter is sorted."

"Understood."

They rode in silence for a while, leaving Luinedhel to his own thoughts about what Selyndar's death meant for N'Khael, and what implications it had for him. His adoption officially made him Thel of the Omaga family, granting him and N'Khael joint authority over all of Selyndar's possessions and wealth. But his addition to the Omagas did not change the fact that he was *ort*. N'Khael was Thelyn, and a Weode, and a Green Guard. She was respected even among the nobility and elder families of the Weode. Despite his position, he was still an outsider in this place. House Omaga and all that it represented truly belonged to N'Khael, and her alone. He would love to stay if she allowed it, but as far as he was concerned, she was the uncontested Lady Omaga now, and he was still just the Thel.

Ahead of them, through the trees, Luinedhel made out a thin line of a moonlit field. Nightfall turned to him. "From what I can determine, Avanstel and the others have two days' start on us. We need to travel faster if we are to catch them before they enter the Barrens. I don't know Hemel's location, so we need to find them before they disappear into the swamps."

Nightfall kicked his horse into a canter as they emerged from the cover of the forest and into the long meadow. Luinedhel followed. When they reentered the trees, they only slowed their pace as was necessary, pushing their rides forward as quickly as they dared in the darkness.

The rest of the night and the following day passed in the same manner. They rested occasionally to allow their horses to drink or eat for a brief period and then would press on. It was the following evening before they broke free from the gloom of Belkin Wood. Open grasslands stretched before them; groves of trees and small scrub brushes dotted the landscape. The light of Relos shone down on the scene, illuminating everything in its cold, white light. The breath of the horses was like silver smoke drifting off into the crisp night air, the grass painted in glittering frost. Luinedhel squinted to see if he could pick out the edge of the grasslands in the far distance.

"It is still too far away," Nightfall said from beside him. "We are fortunate though that Lord Omaga owns such fine creatures as these. They have allowed us to travel quickly through the wood." He reached down and patted the neck of his horse. It nickered in response. "They still have a substantial lead on us. If we press hard, we could catch them in a little over a day. How is your riding skill?"

"Selyndar taught me to ride," Luinedhel said, patting his own horse's neck in turn. "So, I am better than I was the last time we rode together, but still not as skilled as you. Though my comfort means little. I will endure whatever is necessary and go until I am spent. We must get to Avanstel."

Nightfall nodded. "Then we ride." He clicked his tongue and kicked Nyx into a gallop, setting out across the open grassland. The frosty grass bent before him as he blazed a dark trail like a swath across the field.

Luinedhel bent over and whispered in the ear of his mount. *"Like the wind,"* he said in Weald-speak. A pang of sadness plucked at his heart. It was something Selyndar had taught all his horses — a way to tell them they were to run as if set free from everything in the world. The grey mare lurched after Nightfall.

"Aelduin t'shalanta. Like the wind," Luinedhel repeated to himself, his voice swept away in the rush of air that whipped across his face and dried the tears that flowed from his eyes. "I miss you, father." He closed his eyes, leaned forward, and lost himself in the rhythm of his horse racing across the grasslands. Toward the Barrens. Toward Avanstel.

Sunrise brought streams of pink and orange clouds that streaked across the sky, chasing away the darkness. The horses were at a trot, having run full-out most of the previous day and the night before. Crossing from Belkin Wood to the edge of the Barrens in a day and a half was an incredible feat. However, as well-bred as Selyndar's horses were, they were not inexhaustible. Luinedhel was relieved to see the darkness rising on the horizon, and the glow of the sky above them reflected in a lake nestled in the lowlands directly ahead. On the far side of the lake, he could see the dark outline of a forest — not as vast as the woodlands that lay behind them, but more substantial than the fragmented copses that littered the grassland.

"There." Nightfall pointed to the river that exited the lake. Luinedhel knew from his studies that the river was part of a network that drained the lake and the swamp, flowing north to the Glimmer

Sea. He recalled from the maps he'd memorized that a vast delta, upon which the great city of Faber was built, lay at the river's end.

"What do you see?" Luinedhel squinted into the dim light, trying to discern what the *drivrid* was pointing at.

"Their camp. There at the river's edge."

"That far away?"

"Indeed, *sondartin*. I have the advantage of my blood, although this advantage over my Weode and Th'arule cousins disappears with the sunrise. Our arrival here at this time is fortuitous. Does your mount have anything left to give?"

Luinedhel patted the neck of his horse. "Aelduin will give us everything she has left in her."

"The Weode word for 'wind.' A good name."

"*Aelduin'elanelis*. Grey wind. Aelduin for short."

Nightfall nodded in silent agreement and pulled the reins of his horse to the right, kicking him to a full gallop. Luinedhel nudged Aelduin to follow, and the grey mare rapidly caught up with the black gelding and his nether-elf rider. They crossed the remaining grasslands as the sun appeared on the horizon and began its climb into the sky. Orange and pink faded to bright blue and white, and the warmth of the daylight melted the frost that coated the grass below them.

As they raced toward the river, Luinedhel could discern the dark outlines of a small encampment. He kicked Aelduin and urged her on. The horse leaped to life, seeming to pull from a deep reserve, racing ahead of Nyx. The distance between the riders grew rapidly, and Luinedhel let Aelduin go free. He could sense that the horse wanted to reach their destination almost as much as he did – perhaps to rest, perhaps to put an end to this journey, or perhaps Aelduin could sense Luinedhel's own yearnings. Regardless of the reason, she closed the gap quickly. Luinedhel slowed her to a canter and then to a walk as they pulled closer.

N'Khael was there, at the edge of their camp, daggers drawn in the viper's pose — the first defensive position that Selyndar had taught him. He smiled to himself, remembering those early lessons and how many cuts and bruises he had received at the hands of the gentle teacher who would become his father.

"Hail, sister!" Luinedhel called. He looked around and did not see Hathar or Avanstel.

N'Khael lowered her weapons. "Thelo? I wasn't expecting you." She placed the daggers in their sheaths on her belt. Brown and grey leather had replaced the Green Guard's emerald armor, and her bright red hair was braided and coiled at the back of her head. "What news do you bring? Are we too late? Have the Th'arule stormed Ny'we Adye?"

Luinedhel raised his hand for a pause. "No, sister. The Weode kingdom stands, though the news I have may be just as dire. Call for the others, there is much to tell."

Hathar and Avanstel appeared from the tall grasses to either side of N'Khael just as Nightfall arrived.

"Ho, friends!" Hathar exclaimed, his wide grin stretching across his bearded face. "The nether-elf returns! This is too familiar, *drivrid*. I, with Avanstel, days ahead of you, and you, racing to catch me with Arrac … Luinedhel, in tow! Though this time, he arrived first. Certainly, he has not bested you as a rider! Are you having a troublesome day?"

Luinedhel and Nightfall dismounted. Luinedhel found himself immediately wrapped in Avanstel's embrace. "Luin! It's so good to…" He pulled back. "What is wrong?"

Nightfall gathered the horse's reins and handed them to Hathar. "Would you take the horses to the water? We have been riding full-out for two days to catch you, and these incredible steeds have carried us swifter than we could have hoped. They need some care."

"What is it?" Avanstel prodded, reading the look of concern written on his friend's face.

."There is so much to tell." Luinedhel looked at N'Khael. "None of it is good."

"Then come," she said. "Tell us what has happened over breakfast. This morning our cleric found a nest of goose eggs, and a few fish may remain in the trap. We had a feast last night. I admire his skill with the hammer, yet I am even more impressed with his ability to fill our bellies. No doubt one of the reasons you have kept him in your company these many cycles."

"I heard that," Hathar shouted over his shoulder from the edge of the river. "Indeed, I have saved us from dying of hunger on more than one occasion, right, my friend?" He chuckled and pulled the trap in from the water. "There are two. Should be enough to feed our small army ... along with our eggs and bread."

As they ate their breakfast, Luinedhel shared with them the news that Nightfall had discovered in the south — that there was no sign of an army marching on Belkin Wood.

When he got to the attack on Selyndar, he paused. He wasn't ready to relive that event, and he didn't want to break the news to N'Khael that her ... their ... father had died. But it wouldn't be right to shirk the responsibility and put that onto Nightfall. He swallowed, inhaled, and then told of the trip to The Lopsided Tankard and the ambush with the poisoned blades.

"What are you saying?" N'Khael said. She had sensed it coming, but couldn't believe what she was hearing. "Father is ..."

Luinedhel had tears in his eyes. "I'm sorry." His voice cracked.

"No!" She stood up abruptly, her fists clenched, her face clouded with rage. "No! This is not possible! How could ... He had not even reached seven hundred and fifty cycles! He had at least two more centuries ahead of him. He ..." She pivoted on her heels and wheeled on him. "You! You caused this ..."

"Lady, please," Nightfall said. He stood up and stepped in front of Luinedhel. "I assure you, Lady, I was there. Luinedhel was a target, too. It's only because of the lessons that your father taught him — and his blades — that he was able to move swift enough to avoid the same fate."

"You — you!" Her shout became a wail as she collapsed onto the ground. "It can't be so. It just can't be..." She sank in upon herself, sobbing.

Hathar stepped forward, lifted her up, and helped her back onto the stone beside Luinedhel. She collapsed into him, burying her face in his shoulder. He put his arm around her, gently at first, and then firmly as his own tears streaked down his face and into her hair.

"Father. Father," she gasped between sobs. "It isn't fair. He was a good man, an honest man. He was ..."

"I know," Luinedhel said. "I know. I'm so sorry, N'Khael. So deeply sorry." They stayed that way for a long time, the two of them lost in their shared grief, holding and consoling each other.

Respectfully, the others remained silent, each staring into the fire, lost in their own thoughts. Eventually, N'Khael's sobs diminished, and she regained her natural demeanor. She pulled back from Luinedhel and looked up at him. Tears stained her ruddy face. "And you, Thelo, brother? Are you okay? You're healed from the poison?"

Luinedhel wiped the tears from his face and managed a small smile. "I am. Thanks to Nightfall and Seer Alle. Apart from the pain that still aches deep within my heart, I have healed."

"I'm here," she said. No further words were necessary. They would go through this grief together — as brother and sister — in the loss of their father.

Avanstel placed his hand on Luinedhel's arm and looked sadly into his eyes. Luinedhel grasped his hand and squeezed. Unspoken words passed between them. The loss of their loved ones had marked them both since the cycle began: first Adine, then Danvaren, and now Selyndar. As *ort*, they were familiar with suffering and acquainted with grief, but these hardships were a heavier burden than they had ever experienced before, and it got no easier with each hardship.

Hathar cleared his throat, then spoke softly. "It's the Peytriad?"

"It's possible," Nightfall answered. "That is the story that Dredaius spun for Avanstel and Luinedhel. Poison seems to be their preference. But the tale I uncovered in the southland points to our Adelyn."

"Perhaps they are the same," Hathar offered. "The poisons that Y'Zelle used on Avanstel were potent, and knowledge of recipes for such things aren't common. The attack on Lord Omaga and Luinedhel appears to have involved similar alchemy. Perhaps Questelle is part of this dark guild. Maybe even leading it, as you suspect."

"But to what end?" Avanstel asked.

"We wondered the same," Nightfall answered. He turned to N'Khael and Hathar. "Were you followed? Do others know of your quest?"

"I don't believe so," Hathar answered. "It's hard to hide our passing from someone as keen at tracking as you, friend. Especially when you have knowledge of our direction and intent. But I did not detect anyone in pursuit until this morning when I saw you at a distance. N'Khael?"

"No," she answered, wiping her face and shaking her head. "The forest was quiet with our passing. I definitely would have noticed if we had been followed from Ny'we Adye. Why would Dredaius send us to Hemel and then have us followed?"

Nightfall frowned. "There is a lot here that doesn't make sense. What can you tell us of your mission to Hemel?"

Avanstel took a deep breath and then exhaled. "What we know comes from Dredaius," he started. "So, considering what you've shared, I am uncertain of what is truth and what is falsehood. If reality is the former, I am glad for your company, and if the latter, I am even *more* glad for your company. Though I dread putting anyone in further danger. I would, in truth, take on this burden myself rather than cause more risk to any of you."

"I will not let kings, nor kingdoms, separate us again," Luinedhel said. "Regardless of the danger."

Avanstel smiled. For a moment, he looked like the young *ort* that Luinedhel remembered him to be, happily tending bar at The Pig & Lamb, friend to everyone and admired by all for his charm and wit. But then his face turned serious, and he looked more like Dredaius.

He leaned back and took another deep breath. "As you have been told, deep within the Barrens lies the city of Hemel. Hemel was the capital of a vast elven empire, which was ruled over by an ancestor of mine, of the J'Onsal line, the first emperor."

He looked at N'Khael and Hathar. "Though you may know some of this, I have not shared the full story with you. I swore to Dredaius to keep this within the J'Onsal family. I tell you this now, and break my vow to my half-brother, because I can no longer discern if he is as deceitful as his Adelyn, or if he is sincere and simply a pawn in her game ... as we may all be."

"The emperor possessed a scepter, said to grant him supernatural power to rule the lands, conquer his enemies, and safeguard his people. Dredaius told me that this staff is most likely buried with the dead emperor, in his tomb, below the palace at the center of Hemel. This is a closely guarded family secret. That's why nobody has heard of its existence, for if they did, there would have been many who had sought it before us ... though it would have been useless to them, as only one truly descended of the J'Onsal line can wield its power.

"The stories passed down by our family from each generation to the next say that anyone touching it that is not of the J'Onsal line would instantly die. There are even secret prophecies recorded in books in the Ade's personal library that speak of the weapon returning from the dead to bring about the ruin of the enemies of the J'Onsal line."

"The Arcana Sephyrie," Nightfall said.

Avanstel raised his eyebrows. "You know of it?"

Nightfall nodded. "As did Lord Omaga." He looked meaningfully at N'Khael.

"But Van," Luinedhel said. "*Akan'gott* has long since disappeared from the realm. And if this scepter were *omu'gott*, it would have long ago faded, and would be nothing more than a walking stick."

"It is neither *akan'gott* nor *omu'gott*, Luin. It's a forgotten magic — *eer'gott*."

Luinedhel frowned. "The Seer made no mention of this magic."

"It has become a myth too, Luin. Just like Hemel. Disregarded and wiped from the histories of our people. But my family knows of the hidden truths. The staff is special. It was created when *akan'gott* flowed from all living things, before the magic disappeared. Those who created it channeled the *akan'gott* into it. When *akan'gott* faded from the world, the staff kept its powers. This magic is known as *eer'gott*, which is what remained of *akan'gott* after it vanished from the other things of the world.

"When the magic left the realm, and the First People saw that it yet remained inside this scepter, they sought to recreate it, to extract what little *akan'gott* could still be found in the natural world and to place it into created things. That is *omu'gott*, which we know was weak and faded long ago. But the power of the staff did not …

which means it *must* be *eer'gott*. And that is why Dredaius is sending me after it." Luinedhel nodded. "If it's true, and if what we suspect of Questelle to be true, then we need to ensure that this relic does not find its way into her hands … if it exists."

"Agreed."

"Did Dredaius give you any more information or direction to where we might find Hemel amid this giant swamp?" Luinedhel gestured to the land on the other side of the river.

"We have a map," Hathar said. "There are some landmarks in the swamp that we need to look for to guide our way. If we were seeking a city built by men from thousands of cycles ago, I would say that we have little hope of finding anything. But this was a city of the First People, so we may yet find something recognizable deep within the marsh. And now we have two more pairs of eyes to help us look!"

N'Khael stood up. In the course of the conversation, she had transitioned from the weeping child grieving the loss of her father to the bold warrior and protector that they had all known her to be. She sniffed and breathed deeply, shutting away her sadness. She wouldn't allow her own sorrow to endanger them. "Let us make haste to find this weapon then. I am eager to return to Ny'we Adye and put an end to the schemes and planning of our Ade and his Adelyn. I will take my seat on the Elder Council in my father's place, and I will work with Lady Alle and Lady Shaal'Elonthra…" She turned to Avanstel and nodded. "And our Aetheling … to end these deceptions."

Avanstel nodded in return and stood up. "Yes. It is time to bring light to this darkness."

Luinedhel thought back to the night in Caerbexsys, looking up at the ceiling of the Maw, reflecting on the discussion with Nightfall about light and darkness. Avanstel would be a good Ade. He would lead the Weode from their darkness and into the light. And maybe the staff was just the thing that was needed to help bring about these kinds of massive changes to the Weode people. There was no one better than Avanstel to wield such a powerful tool.

Luinedhel was certain of it.

CHAPTER 23: GRAVENWILDS

They forded the river, which was deeper and wider than they had expected. The difficult crossing exhausted everyone, including the horses, so they arrived in the Barrens soaking and tired. The marshland before them was even less welcoming. The ground, which had appeared to be lush and dotted with scrub brushes, was mostly a tangle of floating reeds and other vegetation, with the occasional remnants of dead trees sticking out of the murky soil. The horses had difficulty finding purchase in the swamp, and they stumbled slowly through the muck and underbrush.

Hathar suggested they make their way toward the woodlands directly in front of them. The forest perched on the edge of the lake, covering most of its eastern shore.

"Must be better ground than this if the trees can grow there," he said. "Perhaps we can make it by evening, and camp on less soggy ground." The others agreed and adjusted their heading towards the distant and dark woods.

The day brought biting flies, swarms of gnats, and other buzzing annoyances. No matter what they did to swat them away, the insects found a way to their soft flesh. It was futile to try to avoid getting bitten. Even the horses grew agitated at the pests, squealing and tossing their heads in frustration. Although it was autumn and the day had started cool, the sun had risen high in the sky and seemed to be intent on roasting the small group traveling across the marshes. It felt like midsummer. The choice between sweltering in layers of their sweat-soaked clothes or removing some garments and exposing more skin to the biting flies was a difficult one to make. Luinedhel, resigning himself to the heat, pulled his hood over his head to prevent the midges from entangling themselves in his thick, dark hair.

By evening, the party reached the edge of the forest. The ground here, only slightly elevated from the swampy morass, was by no means ideal for setting up camp, but they were too exhausted to go deeper in. They collapsed on whatever high ground they could find, ensuring that the horses had enough space to move and graze before selecting a place to rest.

Although the evening and shelter of the trees brought relief from the blazing sun, it also meant that their source of warmth had disappeared. A frosty chill soon replaced the day's heat, leaving them shivering in their damp garments. Avanstel and Luinedhel gathered what dry wood they could find as Hathar and N'Khael attempted to light a fire. After numerous attempts, they both gave up.

"Nightfall?" Hathar said as he sat back, exhaling and falling back against a tree. "Might need a little help here."

Nightfall reached into his cloak and pulled out an object that looked like a small orange sphere of glass. He set the marble on the ground, in the middle of the leaves and dry moss that they had gathered, and arranged some twigs and small branches around it. He crouched over the pile, cupped his hands, and whispered something in an unfamiliar language. Then he released his hands towards the small mound and blew gently.

Luinedhel leaned forward, intrigued.

The orange glass glowed brightly, and soon there was a wisp of smoke rising from the kindling. A flame came to life briefly, illuminating the nether-elf's face as the small sphere shattered and disintegrated. A few dried leaves caught fire, and soon several twigs and sticks smoldered with the heat from the meager flame.

"Best I can do, I'm afraid."

"It's enough." Hathar leaned forward and blew lightly on the flames until the twigs had dried enough to catch fire. He gingerly built upon the fire, each branch releasing its stored-up dampness and drying enough to burn.

"You can make fire with magic? Are you a mage?" Luinedhel frowned, cocking his head slightly at Nightfall. In all their travels together, he had never seen the *drivrid* do anything like that before. In fact, never in his life.

Nightfall laughed and swatted away a fly. "There are no such things as wizards. *Omu'gott* is long gone from this world, and the wizards along with it."

"Then it's *drivrid* magic? I did not know they were a magical race. My studies never mentioned it, although there is not much information available."

"No, nothing of the sort. The nether-elves have no more magic than the Weode … or the humans." Nightfall added a few damp leaves to the fire, creating a cloud of smoke. Luinedhel coughed, his eyes stinging.

"Smoke to keep the bugs away. At least some of them," Nightfall said, waving a dark hand in front of his face. "I purchased a few fire marbles when I was in the southlands, from an old enchanter I know there. He has made me charms before; *creer'gott.* In fact, you have been the beneficiary of them on several occasions."

Luinedhel's eyes grew wide. "You have charmed me?"

Nightfall chuckled. "No, no, *sondartin.* It is not like you imagine. Many refer to the magic of *creer'gott* as charms. They are simple magic, insignificant things that are often used once and then they are spent. Like these fire marbles, or the charms of sleep … which I have used to help you rest. In fact, if I had one, I would use it tonight on all of us, for it has been a long, grueling day and we could use some sleep."

"You … you…?"

"I assure you there was no ill intent. I have committed myself to your well-being from the start."

"Nightfall's charms have come to my aid many times," Hathar said. He smacked his arm where a midge was biting him. "He often has something up his sleeves to help when needed."

Luinedhel looked at the cleric and then back at the *drivrid*. "I just never knew such things existed."

"There is much more to this world," Nightfall said, smiling softly. "Much more than Chark and Ny'we Adye. Halbrun offers an entire continent of things you have never experienced or imagined. And then there are the lands beyond Halbrun – all of Naveis Orthea, filled with things both familiar and unfamiliar. Perhaps you'll join our travels after we overcome this Weode crisis. We would welcome you."

"Indeed," Hathar said, slapping Luinedhel on the back. "Especially now with your fancy blades and your training in the Dance! And you apparently can ride better than Nightfall now." His white teeth flashed beneath his bushy beard. "We could add a fourth to our troop. I'm sure Scorpio would not protest, since he rarely says anything." He chuckled at his own joke.

Luinedhel sat back, leaning against his pack, and looked over at Avanstel. He seemed lost in thought, his eyes directed at the small fire, but unfocused and distant. Luinedhel had never considered parting from Avanstel or taking a different path than his friend. Nor had he ever thought much about anything beyond Ny'we Adye and the Weode. With Selyndar's invitation to be part of House Omaga, he had assumed his future lay with the elder elf and the kingdom of his adoptive father. And of course, with Avanstel.

But now that Selyndar was gone ...

"We shall see," Luinedhel said. "My first obligation is to Avanstel, and House Omaga."

"Of course," Nightfall said, "I didn't mean to ..."

"No, it's all right," Luinedhel interrupted. "All of that is far away, so who knows what the future holds. I have centuries ahead of me; my life is only beginning."

Nightfall nodded and smiled. "The blessing and the curse of the *accentation* of elven-kind."

"Which is why we work hard to enjoy every day!" Hathar said. "But I will confess, today was a lot harder to enjoy than other days. But look, we have a fire – and somewhat dry ground. And we have made it across the first part of the marsh in one piece. The only blood we have lost today is to these biting insects."

"Allow me," N'Khael said. She slapped the side of Hathar's face where a fly had landed – perhaps more forcefully than required to kill the bug. The look of surprise on the cleric's face caused Luinedhel to burst with laughter. The others joined in, including Hathar.

"It's time to rest," she said. "I will take the first watch and tend the fire to ensure that we keep most of the pests at bay; flying, biting, or otherwise."

"You rest," Nightfall said. "Let sleep wash away some of the heaviness in your heart. The news we have brought has been grave. I will take first watch tonight."

N'Khael did not protest. She inclined her head. "Thank you," she said. "We still have a long journey ahead and we will need our strength if the days ahead are anything like today."

Hathar said he would tend to the horses and then take the second watch. The rest of them settled down to sleep, lying as close to the meager flames as they dared. Luinedhel wondered how he would be able to sleep as he shivered in the cold damp of the swamp and swatted away at an insect buzzing near his ear.

He faced Avanstel. "Are you all right?" he said quietly.

Avanstel shrugged. "It's a lot. All of it."

"I know."

After a moment, Avanstel said, "I'm glad you're here, though. To be with me. I don't like putting you in danger, but I wouldn't want to do this without you, either. I'm torn."

Luinedhel smiled. "I wouldn't be anywhere else, Van. Something deeper is going on, and if being here with you leads to my death, then I've done the right thing. I'd rather die with you anywhere than back in the comfort of House Omaga, far away from you."

Avanstel smiled back. "I've never had a better friend, Arrac … I mean Luin."

They both laughed as quietly as they could. Avanstel closed his eyes, with a smile still lingering on his face.

A moment later, the sheer effort of the day overtook Luinedhel, and despite his concerns over whether he could rest, he was asleep almost instantly. No sleeping charm needed.

Questelle shed the clothes as a snake does its skin and tossed them into the burning fireplace. Flames spread across the elegant fabric, turning the gold and white pattern to brown, black, and then to ash. Best to leave no traces.

Although she had taken precautions and thought she had covered her tracks sufficiently, her recent activities had drawn too much attention. Now, both Lord Y'Vellian and Lord Kellendaer were looking into the bodies. She couldn't risk another discovery. They had to think that the danger had passed. That's why she had shifted strategies and had begun to use the Delve, far below the castle, where nobody would discover what she left behind. Thank

Enos she had spent her time, while N'Athero was alive, mapping the secret passages within the palace walls. That had proved a useful pursuit.

The clothing, along with anything that would connect her to Tretarilus, had to be burned. There would be too many questions if his garments were found in her quarters – especially after his absence was noticed in the coming days. The constant changes were becoming exhausting and annoying, and of course, left behind more bodies that heightened her chances of discovery. She was done with *this* deception. It served no further purpose.

She had caught hints that her influence over Dredaius wasn't as absolute as she had initially thought. He had started to confide in the Steward more, and some of the inquiries and comments he made, though not directly about her, could imply that he was becoming distrustful of his bride ... something she would have to fix. She couldn't play both Adelyn and Ade – she needed him to stay alive a little while longer. She made a mental note to meet with him tomorrow as she picked up the silver necklace and placed it around her neck. She touched the charm and smiled to herself.

Her time had been productive. She had learned what she wanted, whispered in both ears of the Ade, gotten him to send Avanstel to fetch her weapon, and ensured her privacy in the abandoned tower. It was time now to set the rest of her plan in motion; time to gather the army she wanted for her new kingdom and ensure her victory over the Weode, and eventually the Th'arule. The elves, all of them, would face the consequences for their rebellion.

She had had millennia to plan for this. Ni'Ilyan's legacy would finally end.

There was a chill in the air the next morning. A fog hung over the lake, its misty tendrils winding their way into the edge of the forest. Luinedhel's clothing was still damp, though slightly less so than when he had fallen asleep. He awoke with a pain in his shoulder where a stone had pressed into his back during the night, something he had overlooked when clearing the spot.

Avanstel stirred next to him and opened his eyes and looked around the campsite, his blue eyes meeting Luinedhel's hazel ones. A smile crossed his face. "I thought for sure I would wake up before you. I was out instantly."

"I was not awake long after that," Luinedhel said.

"You snored loud enough to alert every hungry creature nearby," Hathar chided. "In fact, the both of you did. But *you*, worst of all." He looked at N'Khael. She flushed and punched his arm.

"And you, too," Nightfall said. "I could hear you loud and clear while I was on watch – though I have grown used to your noise over the cycles. The sounds of you all must have scared off every forest creature around. There was nothing besides the flies bothering us last night. Cleric, what direction does the map say we should take?"

Hathar stretched and yawned. "I believe we are in the Gravenwilds," he said. "They are southwest of Hemel. We should continue into the woods. To higher ground." He loosened the cord that bound his sleep-mussed hair at the back of his head. His long brown mane fell around his face before he gathered it up and tied it neatly. "We are off our original route. But I think we made the best decision. It's not as direct, but we are still heading in the right direction. Hemel lies at the center of the Barrens, so we should go further in and then we can go north."

"Sounds good. Aetheling, anything to add?"

Avanstel shook his head. "Dredaius said nothing about the forest. I don't think he intended for us to go this way, but I agree with Hathar. Let's climb to higher ground if we can, get away from these midges, and then head toward Hemel."

Plan determined, they broke camp. The horses had recovered enough overnight to carry their riders through the unknown terrain. Luinedhel found he was looking forward to riding; not just to avoid having to walk the entire way, but because he was enjoying his time with Aelduin. The mare seemed to know what Luinedhel wanted without needing direction. He rubbed her neck and offered her an apple from his pack, and then he climbed into the saddle.

Hathar led the mounted group away from the edge of the lake and deeper into the forest. Luinedhel followed Avanstel, with Nightfall behind him. They rode in silence, each of them still tired from the day before and uncomfortable in their perpetually damp clothing. The farther into the forest they went, the less light they had, but also fewer biting, bothersome insects. The ground continued to rise, and soon it was dry, and the horses were surefooted.

Luinedhel noticed after an hour or so that the forest had grown steadily quieter, and the low groundcover had given way to mostly dead leaves and pine needles punctuated by dark grey, almost black, tree trunks. The usual sounds of birds from the branches overhead had long disappeared, and now even the buzzing of the flies and crickets seemed to have faded away. The light was dim, casting everything in a dull grey color. Luinedhel looked up into the trees. Overhead, dark branches faded into dark masses of interconnected tree limbs. Slivers of grey sky peeked through the choked treetops.

Ahead of him, Avanstel sputtered and waved his arms around him. "That's the second time I have ridden through a web! This wood is thick with them."

Luinedhel heard Nightfall whistle behind him. He pulled on Aelduin's reins and directed her to the right so the nether-elf could ride up beside him. "What is it?"

"It's not right. It is too dark, and too quiet." Nightfall's golden eyes darted up into the dim canopy.

Luinedhel looked around him. He couldn't detect any danger, but the only deep forest he had experienced was Belkin Wood, and only on the outskirts of Ny'we Adye, which was highly patrolled by the Green Guard.

Nightfall pulled Nyx to a stop and made another bird whistle that echoed through the woods. Ahead, Luinedhel saw Hathar turn his horse around and exchange words with N'Khael and Avanstel. They joined Luinedhel and Nightfall a moment later.

"I feel it," Hathar said without Nightfall saying a word.

"I also." N'Khael looked around at the gloomy woods surrounding them. "Do we continue forward?"

"Do we have other options?" Nightfall asked.

Hathar shook his head. "We could continue east to the other side of the woods. But that is marshland, according to the map. Most likely, the same as we saw yesterday. It would be difficult terrain. It's why I pressed forward."

"Ahead then?"

The cleric nodded. "Just be on your watch." He turned his horse and headed back the way he had come.

Nightfall gripped his reins. "N'Khael and I will flank. You won't see us, but we will be there. You two follow Hathar at a distance. Keep him in sight. If there is trouble, turn immediately back. We will find you. Don't engage. It's important that you both stay safe."

Luinedhel nodded. Nightfall and N'Khael rode off in opposite directions, leaving Avanstel and Luinedhel in the shadowy forest alone. They exchanged uneasy glances. Ahead they could see the dark form of Hathar weaving amidst the blackened trunks.

"We should follow," Avanstel whispered.

Luinedhel stretched out his arm. "Hold a minute." He stared into the forest ahead of them. Seconds passed. He could still see

Hathar's cloak, dark grey now in the dim light, sliding in and out between the trees. A few more seconds passed, and then Luinedhel lowered his hand and nudged Aelduin forward. Avanstel fell beside him, and they rode on in silence.

Luinedhel squinted, trying to keep Hathar in sight, while simultaneously trying to scan the forest on either side of them for any signs of movement, from friend or foe. An eerie hush blanketed the woods. Even the footfalls of their horses seemed muted. Luinedhel could sense Aelduin's unease. The horse continued forward only because Luinedhel urged her to do so.

The ground was rising upward. Ahead, he could make out the form of Hathar, stopped at the top of what looked like a ridge. He motioned for Avanstel, who drew his horse up close next to Aelduin while they waited. Avanstel was breathing heavily beside him. Luinedhel reached out a hand and placed it carefully on Avanstel's forearm. Avanstel looked at him. Without words, Luinedhel tried to assure his friend, motioning for him to be calm. Avanstel nodded in understanding, exhaling slowly.

The sound of a bird echoed through the forest. Though muffled, Luinedhel recognized it as Nightfall's signal.

"Follow me. But stay alert," Luinedhel whispered, and nudged Aelduin forward toward the ridgeline. The horses hesitated, as uneasy as their riders, but then continued toward the frozen figure of Hathar. N'Khael appeared from the dark woods ahead of them to their left. She joined the cleric on the ridge.

Luinedhel could perceive a dim green glow outlining the duo. It grew stronger the closer they came. Eventually, he could tell that something in front of them was illuminating their silhouettes with an acidic light. He frowned. The unnatural luminescence was unsettling. He looked to the forest on their right to see if Nightfall had joined them, but he saw no sign of the *drivrid*.

"What is it?" Avanstel said, his voice breaking the heavy, peculiar silence.

As they reached the ridge, Luinedhel directed Aelduin to the right of Hathar. Avanstel drew up beside him. Now they could see the source of the strange light clearly.

Below them, in the center of a large basin lined with trees, sat a stone structure. It appeared to be a tower, three or four stories high, made of blackened slabs that were outlined with a pale green glow, as if some strange unearthly mortar had been used to hold the glistening stones together. A moat of dark, viscous liquid that seemed to move of its own accord surrounded the tower. A lone bridge spanned the moat and ended at a tall door. Flanking the bridge stood two large pillars, made of the same stone as the tower, with the same strange green glow between the rocks. At the top of each pillar was a large metal brazier, in which burned an unnatural fire, sickly green light illuminating the crater before them. Between the ridge and the tower, a mist had gathered, low, thick, and winding between the dark trees, obscuring the ground beneath it.

"Hemel?" Luinedhel asked quietly. Aelduin shifted uneasily beneath him.

"No," Hathar replied. "This is not on the map. Hemel lies beyond."

"We aren't going there," Avanstel said. It was a statement, not a question.

Before Hathar could respond, there was a shout behind them. Luinedhel turned his horse around and saw Nightfall racing through the forest towards them. Nyx dodged left and right through the trees. "Go!" Nightfall shouted.

Hathar leaned forward and grabbed Aelduin's reins from Luinedhel's hands before he had time to react. The cleric kicked his horse, and they leapt down the side of the caldera, dragging Luinedhel and Aelduin behind them. Luinedhel clamped his thighs down on his mount's sides and grabbed Aelduin's mane for purchase. He risked a glance behind him, trusting Hathar and the natural instincts of his horse to keep him on whatever path the cleric had suddenly directed. Behind him, he saw Avanstel's mount rear in fright, Avanstel clutching the horse's neck to stop himself from being thrown. N'Khael pulled her horse alongside and reached for the reins. Avanstel clung to his horse as it bucked wildly. After an agonizing, hectic moment, N'Khael was successful. She jerked the reins, pulling the horse forward, and galloped them both down the side of the ridge just as Hathar had done with Luinedhel's mount.

Luinedhel looked ahead and saw that the light of the green fires on the stone columns was rapidly approaching. They were heading for the tower. He kicked Aelduin's sides, and the horse leaped ahead, drawing aside of Hathar. The cleric flung the reins toward Luinedhel, who caught them and pushed Aelduin forward, across the wooden bridge that spanned the dark moat below them.

Ahead of them, the doors to the tower were closed, and he pulled hard on Aelduin's reins to avoid crashing into the barrier. Hathar drew up beside him, dismounting in one smooth motion. He pushed hard against the black wooden doors. They would not budge.

Luinedhel jumped from his saddle and joined the cleric as they heaved against the doors. Finally, they gave way and opened with a loud creaking noise. Hathar shoved him hard to the side and out of the way, just in time for N'Khael and Avanstel to race through the entrance and disappear inside.

Luinedhel turned to see Nightfall on the far side of the bridge, Nyx galloping full-out and clearing the distance swiftly. Luinedhel felt the rush of air as the *drivrid* and his mount raced past him into the tower.

"Inside!" Hathar commanded, grabbing Luinedhel by his tunic and shoving him into the darkness within. The cleric took his massive hammer from his back, taking a stance in the middle of the doorway, prepared to do battle with whatever danger had been in pursuit of Nightfall.

"Get the doors closed, Thelo!" N'Khael leaped past Luinedhel towards the door to his left. He sprang toward the opposite door and shoved it with his entire weight. It slowly yielded, and Avanstel ran to join him, forcing the door to creak on its massive hinges as it moved forward. Nightfall and N'Khael had gotten the other door closed, leaving only a shrinking gap between them.

"Hathar!" N'Khael called, and the cleric stepped backwards quickly, still hefting his hammer in both hands, ready for the fight.

Luinedhel caught a brief glimpse of what was going on outside before the doors closed. He saw what seemed to be a mass of figures, countless pairs of bright red eyes staring down at them. They stayed at the edge of the caldera, moving in and out among the trees, their many-limbed forms illuminated by the green fires that burned at the top of the pillars. He couldn't discern how big or how many, or what kinds of creatures they were, but just the glance he had filled him with dread. The creatures vastly outnumbered his small group, and if Nightfall had urged them forward with such ferocity, the enemy was something even Nightfall, Hathar, and N'Khael wouldn't be able to overcome. The shelter of the strange tower was infinitely preferable.

Avanstel collapsed against the door as Hathar and N'Khael lifted a large bolt in place above his head. "What are they?" he asked, breathless.

"I have only heard rumors," Nightfall said. "I wasn't even sure they really existed."

"Like Hemel … or the *drivrid?*" Luinedhel dropped to the floor beside Avanstel and looked up at the nether-elf.

Nightfall looked down and grinned. "Well played, *sondartin.* Though I am afraid these creatures are more … unnatural … and even more deadly than my kind. Though their origins are lost to time, many legends persist. They are called the Urnean … the Lost Ones. Shadow creatures. Twisted and deformed beings that were once something human, or elven, and now are living somewhere between beast and man. An abomination to nature itself. They vary widely in appearance, some more bipedal, and some that walk on four legs, and some with even more. Perverted and distorted creatures bent in repugnant ways. Some have forms and faces almost recognizable, while others resemble amalgamations of creatures whose skin and fur have been melted by acid or burned by fire. Heads, limbs, and various body parts twisted and placed together monstrously. Vicious and bloodthirsty, with an inexplicable hatred of all that is natural and living. It drives them, obsessively, to kill and devour.

"Stories describe them as roaming the empty countryside and lonely places, encountered only in small numbers. Terrorizing remote villages, slaughtering anyone they encounter that is not strong enough to defend themselves. Eight powerful warriors might defeat a group of three or four Urneans, for they fight with a rage driven by unnatural power. It is as if they feel no pain or fear. With our skills, we may be able to overcome a few of these creatures, but this … this was an entire army of them, unstoppable in those numbers without the full force of Ny'we Adye.

"I should have sensed it earlier – the lack of living things in the wood. The Urneans devour any living creature that is unfortunate enough to stumble across their path. They have stripped the land. That is why it is so silent here. No game, no birds. Not even insects. Nothing remains; the ground is barren. It is likely they have devoured their own kind to stay alive. It was good fortune to find a refuge from them."

"Good fortune? That has yet to be seen." Hathar said as he peered around the gloom of the strange tower.

CHAPTER 24: KEYS

Luinedhel looked around the dim interior. Dull, gloomy light filtered in through several arrow slits overhead, providing little illumination to the space. He could discern the shapes of objects around the room, vague variations in the darkness, but it was challenging to determine what they were. The way the sound echoed around the chamber hinted they were in a large room, likely taking up the entire first floor of the building.

Nightfall used a fire marble to illuminate the shadows enough to locate a couple of torches in sconces nearby. Luinedhel could see the remnants of what might have been horse stalls to their right, with a stone staircase to their left leading up to a landing overhead.

"A guard tower," Nightfall said, answering his unspoken question.

"Here? In the middle of nowhere?" Avanstel stood up and helped Hathar with the horses. They led them to the remnants of the stalls and removed their saddles. "Guarding what?"

"Do you think it belongs to the Lost Ones?" Luinedhel asked.

"No. The Urneans don't build structures, they have no homes other than whatever shelter they can find in the wilds." Nightfall lifted a torch up and moved to the wall, sliding his hand over the dark stone. "It is old."

N'Khael stepped beside Nightfall and traced her fingers over the joints. "The inside joints don't glow like those on the outside. What do you think it is?"

"Unnatural!" Hathar stepped forward next to the others, lifting the other torch. The torchlight made the stone glisten as if wet. "And the strange fire upon the bridge pillars! I have seen nothing like it before."

"*Creer'gott?*" Luinedhel said.

Nightfall frowned. "I don't think so. This is much more powerful."

Luinedhel reached out and cautiously touched the wall. It was dry; not what he had expected. A shiver ran down his spine. "Odd."

"Indeed, *sondartin*. This stonework looks almost …"

"Elven. But different than what is in Ny'we Adye," N'Khael said. She turned to Hathar. "Could this belong to Hemel?"

"According to the Ade's maps, we are far from where the city was. Hemel lies to the north. We are still within the Gravenwilds."

"Then a guard tower for Hemel, perhaps. How could this place still be standing after all this time?"

"How indeed." Nightfall turned from the wall and stepped toward the back of the large room, nearing the stairs. Beneath the stairs, there were what looked like remnants of crates and barrels against the wall, rusted weapons scattered amongst the broken debris, so old they had become useless.

"Do we go up?" Luinedhel peered into the darkness above.

"Better than going out," Avanstel answered.

"I will go," Nightfall said. "Maybe I can reach the top of the tower to get a better look at our enemies. It is probably safest for the Aetheling and Thel Omaga if –"

"We are going with you," Luinedhel interrupted. "We will not separate again." He looked at Avanstel for confirmation and received a nod.

Nightfall turned around and met Luinedhel's gaze. He looked over at N'Khael and Hathar and then shrugged lightly. Luinedhel could see the hint of a smile tugging at the corner of the *drivrid's* mouth. "As you wish, *sondartin*. We will remain together."

He led the way up the stone stairs to the second level of the tower. They reached the landing and stopped at a gap in the wall where a door once stood. The wood had fallen apart; the metal hinges rusted and bent.

Nightfall squatted down and peered at the dust on the floor. "No tracks. Nobody has been here for a long time."

"Then the Urneans haven't come here?" Avanstel asked.

"The green fires must keep them away." Hathar said. "Or the glowing mortar ... whatever the magic may be. That's why they have not attempted to attack the gate."

"Protection. But protecting what? Whom?" N'Khael peered into the darkness of the room beyond. "If no one lives here, how do the fires still burn?"

"A refuge?" Avanstel offered. "A way station?"

"For those who wander the swamp? Not likely. But perhaps it was home to someone long ago."

Nightfall stood up and raised his torch again. He stepped across the threshold and into the dark room. The party followed.

Racks of rusted weapons and miscellaneous pieces of decaying armor littered the room. It was considerably smaller than the chamber below, nothing more than a wide hall, with two doorways on either side. At the far end of the room, opposite the entrance, was another stone stairway leading upward.

They explored the four rooms on the sides of the main hall and determined they had once been barracks for some unknown team of soldiers. Remnants of cloth that could have been clothing or bedding lay shredded and scattered among pieces of wood and straw that might once have been beds. Other than the scraps, there wasn't much of anything else to discover.

As they ascended the stairs to the third floor of the tower, Luinedhel felt the hair rise on his neck. He paused.

Avanstel bumped into him from behind. "What is it?"

Nightfall turned around, holding his torch aloft. Luinedhel listened intently, but the only sound he heard was their breathing. "I don't know," he said. "Maybe I heard something, but it's gone now. I just … it's nothing."

"Are you sure, *sondartin*?"

Luinedhel nodded. "It's gone." He shivered and exhaled. "I'm fine."

Nightfall climbed the stairs again. Luinedhel saw the *drivrid* reach for his dagger, and Luinedhel did the same. As he wrapped his hand around his sai, he listened for Marek's voice, but there was only silence. He took Adesh in his left hand, but again, no counsel or remark came. Behind him, he heard Hathar pass his torch to Avanstel, followed by the soft sounds of the cleric and N'Khael preparing their respective weapons. His heart raced.

"*Sere'eden*," he repeated to himself. "*Stay calm. Control your emotions.*"

The third-story landing was small, barely big enough for all of them. Before them stood a door that was unlike the doors on the previous levels. It was made of stone. On the door, Luinedhel could make out carvings of a forest scene, interwoven with a flowing script. It harkened back to the carvings he had seen at the Shadow Gate. He shuddered. N'Khael moved up beside him.

"Similar to elven, but old. Ancient. Before Weode or Th'arule. Maybe the First People."

The hair rose again on Luinedhel's neck.

N'Khael stepped toward the door. "Do you see a way forward?"

"I do not," Nightfall answered. "There is no bolt or lock, but it must open by some mechanism. Here, on the floor, you can see where the door's grating and passing feet have worn the stone. And there, if you look closely, those are stone hinges built into the wall and disguised as blocks."

Luinedhel peered closely at the relief on the door, shadows shifting with the movement of the surrounding torches. A large circle, bisected by a vertical line to form two neat hemispheres, had been carved into the wall. The right hemisphere showed a beautiful city, engraved with domed towers, arches, bridges, and winding stairs. Draping vines clung to the buildings, and a large fountain stood in the middle of a plaza, surrounded by statues of figures and forest creatures.

On the left side of the circle, a large solitary mountain took up the top of the carving. Its form dominated the landscape, and there was little around it. Luinedhel thought it resembled the Mountain of Woes, as it stood alone in the middle of a flat plain. The bottom half of the left hemisphere appeared to represent the netherworld with a scene like Caerbexsys – engravings of stalactites and stalagmites and large stone columns, dotted with geometric shapes of large crystals.

A river flowed between the two hemispheres, on the right carrying fish, and on the left bearing salamanders and other multi-legged creatures.

Circling the entire circumference of the relief was an etching in an unfamiliar script. He had learned the basics of Weald-speak from Selyndar, but he couldn't make out any of the words here. "Can you read it, sister?" he asked N'Khael.

"No. It looks similar to Weald-speak, but the words are unfamiliar to me." N'Khael turned to Nightfall. "Pry it open?"

Nightfall placed his dagger in the thin break in the stone on the left side of the door and pushed. The wall did not move. He tried again, but nothing budged.

"Do we go back?" Avanstel asked. "Maybe the Urneans will give up and disperse, and we can find our way past them."

N'Khael shook her head. "They won't leave. The strange fire may keep them at bay, but their hunger will keep them close by. As capable as I believe we are, we could not face that foe in such numbers. We cannot risk it."

Nightfall moved to the side, examining the wall to the left of the door. "Perhaps there is a hidden latch or catch that would release the door." The others began pressing various blocks, but nothing gave way.

They attempted everything they could imagine. Hathar tried his hammer, but the stone did not give. The blows did not even damage it. N'Khael tried to translate the ancient elven words, but the results were scrambled, rambling, and nonsensical. Nightfall attempted to pry it open again with the help of Luinedhel's blades, but nothing moved.

Defeated and frustrated, they returned to the first floor to care for the horses and retire for the evening.

"Perhaps a night of rest will provide us some additional insights," Nightfall offered. There wasn't much else they could do at that point.

Knowing the tower was long abandoned, and the unearthly fires outside kept the Lost Ones from advancing, they felt secure enough not to set a watch for the night. Hathar assembled a small fire using the broken scraps of wood littered about and one of Nightfall's fire marbles, careful not to build it too big, as only the arrow slits above allowed the smoke to escape the room.

Luinedhel tried to make himself as comfortable as possible on the cold stone floor. He watched the trails of smoke make their way lazily toward the small windows high in the walls above them. Beside him, Avanstel's breathing became slow and rhythmic, and then he started to snore lightly.

Sleep evaded Luinedhel. He felt skittish. The uneasy feeling he had as they approached the third level clung to him like spiderwebs. He rolled over to his side, placing his back toward Avanstel, and closed his eyes and willed himself to sleep … but it wouldn't come.

A few hours passed in this restless manner, and eventually he gave up. He sat up and looked around the room. Across from him, Hathar and N'Khael were sleeping soundly. Nightfall lay with his back towards the fire and facing the stairwell. No doubt the nether-elf was ever vigilant and not completely asleep. The horses remained in the broken stalls. Nyx and Aelduin were standing, one hind leg resting on the tip of her hoof. The other horses were lying on the floor. Selyndar's horses were a different breed from the ones that even the Ade called his own.

Accepting that sleep would not come to him tonight, Luinedhel stood up. He figured he would spend his time examining the door once again to see if there was any clue that maybe they had overlooked previously, or any other way to get past the obstacle. Perhaps there was an alternate way of entry. Doing *something* was better than lying here doing nothing.

He quietly stepped over Avanstel and crossed the room toward the stairway. He glanced back at the fire. No one had stirred, not even Nightfall.

As he reached the second floor, the light from the fire below disappeared, leaving him in darkness. He wished he had a light crystal or had taken a torch. He felt his way along the wall, past both open doorways, and to the base of the stairs leading up to the third story. Without another light source, he could now discern a faint glow from above. It was yellow-green, like the phosphorescence they had seen between the dark stones on the outside of the tower. He felt his skin prickle again.

He cautiously mounted the stairs until he found himself once more in front of the impassable stone door. The glow he had seen from below was emanating from the thin gap at the base of the door.

Dim though it was, it lit the small landing, and since his eyes had adjusted to the darkness, it gave him just enough light to see by. He drew both daggers, their familiar forms molding again to his hands.

"*We can open the door.*" It was Adesh and Marek in unison.

Their voices startled Luinedhel. He stifled a gasp. When his racing heart slowed, he whispered into the darkness. "How? We have tried already to pry it open."

"*We are the key.*"

"I don't understand."

"*There, on the right. In the center,*" Marek said.

He placed Adesh on his belt and ran his fingers over the city scene. He touched the sky and clouds, working his way downward. The rough stone scratched his fingers. He ran his hands over the bridges and the towers and the hanging vines, and then over the fountain and the statues, tracing each one carefully, then finally, over some of the details of the buildings, the walls, and the doorway. There he felt the stone, suddenly smooth and slippery beneath his finger. His hand jerked back involuntarily. He stepped closer and peered at the carving, tracing his finger over it again to find the smooth spot. It was a triangular-shaped doorway carved into one of the domed towers, barely noticeable amongst all the other lines of decoration.

"There?"

"*There!*"

Luinedhel frowned. "I still don't understand."

"*We are the key. There is our lock.*"

Luinedhel hefted the sai and placed the tip at the smooth spot. To his amazement, he met no resistance, and Marek slid into the stone as if it were not there, embedded to the hilt. Luinedhel heard a click and a release, and the grating of stone on stone. He stepped back from the door, expecting it to swing inward, but nothing happened. He pushed on the door, but it did not give way. He frowned.

"The other dagger." The voice came from behind him, startling him. He withdrew Adesh in one swift motion and spun around to strike. Nightfall caught his arm. "My apologies, *sondartin*. I should have announced myself. I saw you climb the stairs and followed."

"Of course you did." Luinedhel shook his head and turned back to the door.

"Try the other dagger," Nightfall repeated. "Is there another slot?"

Luinedhel stepped toward the door again and placed his fingers on the left side of the carving. He started at the bottom of the design, in the river, and moved toward the cavern, feeling the outlines of all the underground features, all rough against his fingers. He moved to the top of the carving, tracing the rocks of the mountain and the edges of its massive form. Nothing. Then, finally at the very top of the mountain, he felt a smooth spot.

"*There!*" Adesh's voice echoed in his head.

He pressed the winding dagger against the smooth spot in the door, and, like before, Adesh slid into the stone as if it were not there. There was another click and a grinding sound. This time the door shuddered and swung inward, recessing an inch or so and then coming to rest. Luinedhel looked at Nightfall. The strange yellow-green light that flowed from the opening made the *drivrid's* countenance look frightful.

Luinedhel swallowed and tried to calm his pounding heart with the mantra Adine had taught him. It took him a moment, but he grew calm and finally asked, "Should we get the others?"

"It is probably best. We don't know what lies beyond."

Luinedhel nodded. He stepped forward and retrieved the daggers from the door. "I don't understand why they didn't speak to me before." He held Adesh and Marek in his hands, turning them over in the alien glow. There were no scratches or marks on them, as one might expect from a dagger that had been driven into a solid stone surface.

"Some things are without explanation," Nightfall said. "Perhaps they were waiting for you to be alone. Perhaps you weren't ready to hear what they had to say. Perhaps there are other reasons only known to them."

"If this tower is from the First People, and these daggers open this door, then perhaps the daggers are connected somehow to the First People."

"It makes sense. Maybe that is why the Seer could not tell us much about the daggers. Their existence may precede any of the written records of the Weode. When Scorpio returns to Ny'we Adye, we may find out more about these unique weapons you possess. Until then, we only know what the daggers themselves will share with you."

"If they are of the First People, I wonder how they got from here to the Undercroft."

"How indeed, *sondartin*. I am certain the daggers have many secrets yet to reveal."

CHAPTER 25: DOOR

Beyond the stone door lay a large room, which occupied the tower's upper floor. Hanging on the far wall was a strange object. It resembled a large mirror or a door, though it was unlike any door Luinedhel had seen before. Silver-blue *estrayaed* metal, polished to a high luster, surrounded the object's edges. The opening was an equilateral triangle with three overlapping segments, each with a triangular form on the end. Each segment resembled a large, stylized metal femur. The bottom segment stood a hands-width off the floor. At the top, in the center, was a large glowing yellow-green crystal about the size of a fist, surrounded by a triangle of *estrayaed* that resembled the shape below. The crystal emanated a sickly yellow light. The wall behind the object resembled the walls outside of the tower: dark, slick stone outlined by the strange glowing mortar. The light that filled the spaces between the stones radiated outward from the crystal.

The surface of the object was a material that looked like a shifting and slow-flowing mutable liquid, something that existed somewhere between glass and metal. It rippled and flowed as if moved by some unknown current; at one moment it appeared solid like metal; the next, transparent like glass; then, murky and fluid, like an oil with a rainbow of colored swirls moving over it. Though they could see their reflection, it appeared fuzzy and distorted due to the constant movement of the surface. An almost imperceptible pulsing hum filled the room and seemed to pulse along with the surface of the object.

Avanstel was the first to speak. "What do you think it is?"

"Some kind of scrying device, maybe." Hathar scratched his beard and arched an eyebrow.

"I've not seen anything like it before," Nightfall said. "I think we would all agree that whatever the object is, it's definitely magical … though different than any magic I have seen before. And I would say *that* may be the source of the magic of this entire place." Nightfall pointed his dagger at the glowing crystal at the top of the doorway.

"It's not elven," N'Khael said. "Though it's made of *estrayaed*, it's unlike anything Weode or Th'arule. Do the *drivrid* use crystals like that?"

"Yes, many kinds of crystals in Caerbexsys are used for different things, but nothing like this. Only living flesh activates the crystals. Without that contact, they are inert. Pretty, but not useful. I've never seen a crystal glow on its own, and certainly never one that could power an entire building."

Hathar took a step closer to the object, his hammer in his hands. "So not Weode, nor Th'arule, nor *drivrid*. And certainly not from human hands." He looked again at Nightfall. "Groundlings?"

"They oppose magic. Even Arial, whom her people would say has a rebellious disregard for the traditions and ways of the groundlings, would not deign herself to create anything powered by magic. To them, *creer'gott* is an abomination of the natural world – and anything more than that is reprehensible."

Luinedhel stared at the object, mesmerized by the alternating reflectivity on the surface, listening to the low hum filling the room. The doorway shifted its pattern almost imperceptibly, along with the sounds of their speaking.

Avanstel stepped beside him. "So, we don't know who made it. Is there a way to find out what it does?" He stepped towards the shifting plane.

N'Khael placed her arm in front of him, stopping his advance. "Aetheling, I insist. Please stay behind us." Hathar stepped closer to N'Khael and blocked Avanstel's path forward. Avanstel shot a frustrated glance at Luinedhel. He smiled and offered an apologetic shrug.

"Yes," Nightfall echoed. "As much as the Ade feels it is appropriate to place you in danger, we don't need you to take such risks. You are the heir to the throne. I will approach it to determine if it is safe for the rest of you."

Nightfall took a step towards the object. There was no change in the sound, or light, or pattern. Another step. Still no change. When he was in front of the wavering surface, he turned his head to look at the others and then reached out carefully to touch it. Luinedhel turned his face away and closed his eyes.

Nothing happened. He cracked his eyes and turned back to the object, half expecting to see the *drivrid* vanished, but he stood there running his hand over the surface. "It feels smooth," Nightfall said. "Warm to the touch, but not hot."

"*Use it.*" Adesh's sharp voice echoed in Luinedhel's head. He looked down at the serpentine dagger in his hand, which he had drawn instinctively.

"How?"

"What do you mean?" Avanstel asked.

"It's Adesh; she says to *use* the object, but I have no clue how."

"If your daggers know of a way forward, *sondartin*, perhaps they can provide further instruction." Nightfall stepped to the side and motioned Luinedhel forward.

Luinedhel stepped up to the object. He could see that along the sides of the smooth frame there were geometric shapes and lines of differing numbers and orientations. Fine etching on the polished metal showed squares, triangles, diamonds, and other polygons. He looked them over carefully, trying to discern their meaning or even a pattern, but they did not repeat, and were different on each side of the frame. The placement appeared random. Other than the etchings, no other discernible marks were visible.

He looked at Nightfall. "Should I touch it?"

Nightfall gave a nod, stepped back, and withdrew his daggers.

"Use it! It's the way out," Adesh urged again.

He took a deep breath and reached out a trembling hand towards the mirror. His heart was racing as his hand contacted the strange, shifting surface. *"Sere'eden!"*

He expected a shock or a surge of energy or a burst of light, but again, there was nothing. It was just smooth and warm, like Nightfall had described. He ran his hand over the surface, looking for an imperfection or a rough spot, but couldn't discern any differences. The pattern continued, shifting with the pulsing hum. He looked at Nightfall again.

"You must choose. The choice is always yours."

Luinedhel sighed. As much as he liked the daggers, their cryptic directions confused him. Interpreting their meaning was often a frustrating exercise. "Adesh says it's a way out. It must be a portal, some kind of door. But I'm not sure how to activate it, nor do I have any idea where it leads. She just tells me that I have to choose."

Avanstel let out an audible sigh of relief behind him. Nightfall placed a hand on Luinedhel's shoulder. "It will come to you, *sondartin*. The blades have guided you well so far."

Luinedhel nodded and looked again at the patterns on the left side: three lines stacked vertically, an oval, one wavy line horizontally, a triangle, a two-ended arrow, and a pentagon. He looked at the pattern on the right side of the doorframe. On this side, there was a triangle, two wavy lines vertically, a diamond shape, four lines horizontally, a square, and two lines crossed.

Of all the etchings, only two were of single lines; on one side, the oval, and on the other, the triangle. Every other pattern contained multiple lines – either joined or crossed or parallel. The triangle caught his eye. It was the same shape as the smooth doorway on the stone door's carving where he had placed Marek, and the same shape as the mirror in front of him. He touched it.

At his touch, the shape glowed chartreuse, matching the color of the crystal above the door, which was now pulsing. The low hum in the room changed to a higher pitch and oscillated. Before him, the plane of the mirror became cloudy black, losing its reflective quality. There was a whoosh, and the mirror became a dark opening. He couldn't see what was inside.

Luinedhel looked at Nightfall. "What do we do now?"

"Do you trust your blades?"

Luinedhel looked down at Adesh, resting in his hand, its serpentine surface reflecting the pulsing light above. The blades had led him from the Undercroft; they had provided him guidance during his training with Selyndar; they seemed invested in his safety, in him. Though he still was not sure of their motives, they had always acted in a manner to aid him and lead him away from harm. "I do."

"Then I think we go through." Nightfall's golden eyes glinted in the pulsating light. "But … I will go first." He smiled and then stepped through the doorway without further discussion or a chance for Luinedhel to raise an objection.

Immediately, there was another whoosh, and the doorway returned to its previous state. The pulsating crystal became a steady glow. The low hum replaced the high-pitched oscillating sound. He touched the surface of the portal again, and it was solid, shifting once more between states. He stared at the surface, but all he saw was his brief, distorted reflection. There was no sign of Nightfall.

N'Khael came up beside him. "We all must go through quickly, Thelo. If Nightfall has stepped into danger, we should be at his side."

Luinedhel nodded and touched the triangle again. The portal jumped to life, and the dark matte surface returned along with the pulsing light and high-pitched thrum. N'Khael looked over her shoulder. "Hathar, take the rear. Send Avanstel ahead of you, and come in swinging, just in case we are in danger. We will move out of the way to prepare for you."

"I will," the cleric said, hefting his oversized hammer in both hands.

"Follow me, brother," N'Khael said. "The three of us will set up a defense for Avanstel." She stepped through the portal and disappeared as quickly as Nightfall had.

Luinedhel wasted no time in resetting the door, pressing the triangle once again. He looked back at Avanstel and offered a smile. Hathar was beside him, poised for battle. "I will see you soon."

Avanstel managed to smile, although Luinedhel could read the concern on his face. Luinedhel turned toward the portal and stepped through. The world became silent darkness.

And then there was noise again. But it was different from before. The dripping of water and the whispering whistle of wind had replaced the throbbing hum of the tower room. Everything was dark, but somehow, he knew he had crossed through the portal into another place.

"I'm here, Thelo. Step away from the portal." Luinedhel felt N'Khael's hand touch his arm and pull him to the side.

He heard a muffled noise like stone grating against stone, and then a bright light appeared. It was almost blinding after the deep and profound darkness. Luinedhel raised an arm to cover his eyes and stumbled forward. An arm caught him and steadied him.

"My apologies. Let me direct you, Thels Omaga. Give your sight a moment to adjust. Sit here while you wait. I will go back for the others." Nightfall guided him toward the light, up a couple of stairs, and out into the open. When he paused, Luinedhel reached down with his free hand and felt a cold, hard, moss-covered stone surface. He sat down and waited for his eyes to adjust to the light.

After a moment, he was able to look around and inspect their new surroundings. N'Khael sat across from him, squinting and blinking. They were both seated on large stones that had once been walls, the ruins of a triangular room. Between them, the ground looked as if it had once been a tiled floor, but was now overtaken by vegetation. Through the mist, he could see the dark stone forms of ancient buildings that lay beyond the walls. To his left, the grey stone rose, and there in the center of the wall was an equilateral triangle, just like he had seen on the carving in the stone wall. Nightfall had pushed a large slab of stone back from the entrance and was emerging from the darkness beyond. Avanstel and Hathar were on either side of him, arms raised to shield their eyes.

Luinedhel stood up, crossed the space between them, and grabbed Avanstel's arm. "I'll take him."

"Luin?" Luinedhel could hear a thread of relief in his friend's voice.

"I'm here." He took Avanstel's arm and led him toward a seat. "Where are we?"

"I don't know. We are outside. There's fog all around us. I think I can make out the shapes of buildings when the mist parts, but I don't know where we are. I assume it's Hemel." He helped Avanstel sit down. "Rest here. Your sight will adjust in a second."

N'Khael was standing in the remnants of the doorway at the edge of the fog. She peered into the white mist.

"Do you see anything, sister?"

"No. The mist is too thick to see far. But this building, or rather what's left of it, continues on. I am going to scout around." She turned to Nightfall. "Assuming, of course, you have not had the chance."

The nether-elf shook his head. "It took me a moment to figure out how to get out of that room. Thankfully, my sight was able to adjust to the darkness before the rest of you came through."

N'Khael nodded and withdrew her daggers, and then slid silently out into the pale haze.

Luinedhel looked at Nightfall, who was pushing the slab back over the entrance. "Did you try the door? To go back to the tower, I mean."

"It's nonfunctional, I'm afraid. The crystal on this side of the doorway is shattered, though the doorway is identical in every other way."

Luinedhel frowned. He hadn't considered their journey could be a one-way trip. Not only were they trapped here now – wherever they were – but they had left the horses in the tower … protected from the Lost Ones, but also unable to leave the building and escape. The thought of Aelduin and the other horses left there to starve put a knot in his stomach.

"We'll find a way back," Avanstel said. "We won't leave them." He smiled, trying to make the best of their situation. It was something that Luinedhel loved about his friend – he was usually optimistic, always trying to find the silver lining in whatever circumstance they found themselves in. Avanstel's compassion and empathy would make him a good leader for the Weode.

N'Khael reappeared in the ruined doorway. "There's no sign of the Urneans here," she said. "At least not right now. But I think I've found something else. Cleric, let's look at the map."

Hathar stood up and pulled the map from his pocket. He unfolded it and sat it on the wall. It was the first time that Luinedhel had seen it. He had expected it to be old, faded, and brittle, but the ink was crisp and dark, and the parchment was supple. He looked up at Hathar. "When was this made? It looks new."

"I don't know. The Ade Gerent gave it to us. I'm not sure where he got it."

On one side of the document, Luinedhel could see the familiar shapes of Belkin Wood, the rivers, and the boundary of the Barrens. A four-pointed star marked the location of Hemel, northeast of the lake, and the Gravenwilds.

The other side of the map looked to be a more detailed chart of the city of Hemel itself, with streets and buildings, public plazas, and markets. The city's design resembled a wheel, almost like a Haven Chase board, but with only three primary spokes. The three large avenues radiated out from a large central circle in the middle of the city. Smaller roads created concentric rings connected to the main spokes. A wide river, crossed by many bridges, wound through the city and intersected the center circle where it divided into two parts, each curving to the sides and making a kind of moat around the central hub. Inside the city center, the roads became a spiral, winding inward to what Luinedhel assumed was the palace. The river continued through the rest of the city and disappeared off the map.

"That's where we need to go?" Luinedhel asked, pointing at the center.

"I believe so. And I think we are here." N'Khael pointed to a spot on the map that showed a large, open plaza with a fountain in the middle of it. It was along the main spoke that pointed directly south and was not too far from the central circle. "There's remnants of the fountain, though most of it is underwater." She turned to Luinedhel. "And the carving on the door in the tower. The doorways of this structure are in the shape of a triangle, like the one above the portal, and I don't see any other ruins with stonework like this."

Hathar scratched his beard. "We can follow these roads that spiral around the palace, or we may be able to cut through and go directly there. Either way, we'd have to make our way north. The royal tombs will be under the palace at the center. That's where Dredaius told us to look."

Luinedhel looked up at him. "Dredaius seems to know an awful lot about this forgotten city hidden in an impassable swamp that nobody else knows about, not even the Seer. Doesn't it seem odd to you that the map is new and so detailed, even though the city sank into the marshes long ago?"

Hathar considered this. "Perhaps it is a copy of an old map that only House J'Onsal has access to. Or perhaps there are other reasons. To be honest, there's been so many odd happenings in the palace and within the city over these past months, I suppose I have gotten used to inexplicable things. Are you concerned, friend?"

"Only for Avanstel's safety." Luinedhel looked at N'Khael. "You don't think Dredaius would send Avanstel here on this errand to have him killed? Somewhere far away from Ny'we Adye where curious people would not notice and it could all be just explained away?"

"Fears of the Th'arule invasion preoccupy him. I think he sincerely believes that this relic is the only way forward. There are always cunning and treacherous things going on within the palace, but I think the Ade was genuine in his need for the scepter to defend our kingdom."

"Against what? There's no invasion coming. Why does he need this relic?"

N'Khael shrugged. "Perhaps against the Peytriad. Or maybe for something else."

Luinedhel shook his head. They all seemed too trusting of Dredaius, but he was confident that N'Khael and Hathar would protect Avanstel, so who was he to oppose them? Besides, what would they do? Refuse to retrieve the artifact and just run away? And how would that benefit Avanstel, the heir to the Weode kingdom?

He nodded, pushing aside his worry. "Lead on, then. It doesn't look like it's that far away."

They attempted to follow what had once been a wide avenue heading north to the center of the city, but most of the roadway had sunk into the swamp, leaving small irregular hillocks of soggy turf dotted with paving stones scattered amongst pools of stagnant water. They traveled along the dry ground, looking for signs of the lost road, and listening for movement in the mist. Everything remained silent, and they stayed roughly on course. The farther north they ventured, the wetter the ground became. However, Luinedhel was able to catch a glimpse occasionally through the mists of a large dark mound ahead of them that rose above the wetlands, promising drier ground.

The road stopped at the remnants of a bridge that ascended from the surrounding swamp to the top of the mound. On either side, off in the distance, they could see the remnants of the other two bridges. The one before them looked as if it could crumble at any moment and join its companions. Several sections of it were missing, but it looked like there still might be a way up.

The mists were thinning, and they could clearly see the collection of fallen buildings that made up the center of Hemel. The circular protective wall had since crumbled to piles of rubble, but Luinedhel could imagine that it once stood high and proud, overlooking the vast city below.

Nightfall and N'Khael pulled ropes from their packs.

"We are climbing the bridge?" Avanstel asked. "It looks like it might fall apart at any moment."

"We will go on," Nightfall said. "You can stay here … with the Urneans. Though, I recommend you come with us." He looked at

Avanstel. "You are the Aetheling. I cannot make you do anything … nor would I try. However, if what Dredaius tells you is true, then only you can retrieve the scepter."

Avanstel had no retort. Nobody wanted to stay here in the swamp. Up looked like the most promising direction.

They began the ascent, using ropes and hooks to help them cross the open sections successfully. It was exhausting and slow-going work, and not without moments of trepidation as parts of the bridge would collapse beneath their steps, but they reached the top of the bridge as night closed in around them.

Here at the edge of the city center, they could see clearly the ravages of time on Hemel. Because of its elevation, it had not sunk into the marshes like the rest of the city, but that had not spared it from decay. The towers and buildings had crumbled for the most part, but they still offered some shelter, though no one felt quite comfortable entering the unexplored ruins in the dark of night. Although there had been no signs of the Urneans during their travels through the ruined outer city, and the welcome sounds of insects and frogs and occasional bird calls had filled the air, they agreed it was best to wait until daylight to continue forward. The Urneans could still be within the old city.

They set up camp beneath the enormous arch that had once been the gate at the top of the bridge. With scraps of scavenged wood, Nightfall used one of his fire marbles to create a small fire for them. N'Khael insisted they keep watch and volunteered Luinedhel for second watch after herself.

Accepting his duty, Luinedhel cleaned away some rubble to get a few hours of rest, so he could stay awake while it was his turn to watch over them. Thankfully, the biting flies and bugs remained in the swamp below, leaving only an occasional buzzing near his ears to irritate him. Eventually, the sounds of Avanstel's rhythmic snores lulled him to sleep.

CHAPTER 26: HEMEL

Urneans slunk around them in the darkness, quietly watching the visitors, those who had come to their dead city. Their red eyes glowed in the darkness. They would move closer occasionally, taking a step and then waiting, and then another … steadily and systematically moving closer to him.

Luinedhel watched them, paralyzed with fear, waiting for them to rush forward all at once and overwhelm them. He reached for his daggers, inching his hands ever so slowly so as not to draw attention. His hand was almost upon Adesh when a hand covered his mouth and stopped him from screaming and alerting the others. He fought against it, and the creature spoke … and this time, he understood the words.

"Thelo! Wake up! It's just a dream," she said.

N'Khael was beside him, her hand over his mouth as she shook him gently awake. He looked around the camp, seeing the others resting peacefully. There were no red eyes peering at him from the darkness. He inhaled and then exhaled and nodded. She released him.

"I'm sorry, Thelo. You were dreaming fitfully, and I didn't want you to wake the others or cause alarm." She motioned for him to follow her to the edge of their camp. He moved slowly, his heart still pounding in his chest as he shook off his grogginess.

They sat on a fallen pillar, out of earshot of the others, and spoke in low voices.

"You are still having the nightmares?" she asked.

"Yes, but not every night. Some nights I am able to sleep well, and others …" He looked up at the night sky. Eyama was high above them, directly overhead. Normally, the light from the little yellow moon was dull compared to that of her large lover, Relos, but this night, her light was bright and illuminated the surrounding grounds.

He looked over his shoulder at the camp. "He can sleep through anything. It has always been like that. I envy him." He looked out over the city that lay below them. Strange lights moved through the shadowy swamp. One moment they looked connected, organized in a line, and the next they dispersed and scattered, each moving at a different speed.

He rubbed his eyes. "Urneans?"

"I don't think so. Maybe other nighttime wanderers. Perhaps will-o'-the-wisps or fool's fire. Swamp gases, maybe. Or insects that light up at night. Probably not the Urneans, though I don't know enough about them to be fully certain. I've never actually seen the creatures until the tower. Father would sometimes tell me stories of the Lost Ones when I was a child …" She trailed off.

Luinedhel touched her shoulder.

She reached up and clasped his hand. "I apologize for accusing you. I know you loved him, I —"

"Say no more, sister. Let's focus on bringing justice to those who did this. Let's cleanse Ny'we Adye of the Peytriad and focus on bringing light to the darkness in the city. Together."

She nodded silently and rubbed a tear from her eye.

"Any disturbance in the city behind us?"

"Nothing. It has been quiet."

He thought about his dream of being stalked by the Urneans. He couldn't shake the feelings, though he knew it was only night terrors. "Do you think they're there … ahead of us?"

"It's possible," she answered. "But I would have expected to encounter them by now. If they are here in the city center, we will evade them. If they are below, they will have trouble reaching us because the bridge is almost gone. I think we are safe – but keep watch." She smiled. "Don't fall asleep on us."

"I won't, sister. I promise."

She hugged him briefly and then headed back towards the camp, leaving him alone in the darkness. Luinedhel glanced back and saw that she had taken the place he had vacated next to Avanstel, ever the diligent protector of the Aetheling. He found comfort in her strength and assurance, knowing her commitment to guarding his dearest friend.

He sat down on a rock to watch the weaving lights below him. Some of them were green, some blue, some yellow, and some orange. He pulled Marek from his belt and turned the blade over in the moonlight.

"Any thoughts you want to share with me?" He smirked at the lack of response and set the blade down on the rock. He pulled Adesh from his belt. "What about you?"

Silence.

He picked up both his blades, twirling them in his hands. They had become so familiar to him, like an extension of his own body. Their soft grips fitted exactly to his hands, their balance exquisite, their instruction helpful – even though Selyndar had insisted that he learn to fight without their aid.

He looked again at the bluish metal and wondered what its connection was to the stone door and the strange portal. They had told him they were keys, and indeed had functioned so, opening the immovable door. But they were *more* than just keys. They were fine weapons, and imbued with spirits … or personalities, or intelligence of some kind. Were they made first to be weapons, with the door later fashioned to use them as keys? Or the other way around? Were there other sets of blades — more keys like Marek and Adesh? Or other ways of opening that door? Surely these two blades could not be the *only* keys, or that door would have remained sealed forever if he had not found them in the Undercroft.

As he spun them in his hands, he looked once more at their odd pommels. They were concave, and looked as if they had once held a stone or a gem that was now missing. They weren't rounded or pointed like a typical dagger. Luinedhel had always wondered why they had hollow pommels. Perhaps that was the fashion when they were originally made, but he considered the design useless now. With a solid end, one could use them as a secondary attack, but with a design like these, that additional strike would be much less effective.

A noise from behind him broke his train of thought. He turned to look back at the fire. Everyone was still sleeping soundly, and no one had moved. He stood up and turned around, moving as quietly as possible across the broken pavement and back toward his friends.

Beyond the small fire and the low glow of the embers, he could see the shattered remains of buildings, gilded in the yellow moonlight. They rose towards the large crumbling towers in the center of the city, which Luinedhel assumed were the palace ruins.

He heard another noise, small and barely discernible. Low and drawn out, fading into the darkness. He shivered and tightened his grip on his daggers.

He made his way past his sleeping companions until the fire was at his back. The moonlight illuminated the faces of the first few buildings on the wide road that curved away to the right. He remembered from his view of Hathar's map that the roads inside the wall spiraled counterclockwise towards the palace. He looked back over his shoulder and considered for a moment whether he should leave his companions to find the source of the noise or wake them to help him investigate. Avanstel snored softly between Hathar and N'Khael; Nightfall, back toward the dying fire, had wrapped himself in his cloak.

Luinedhel listened intently. He heard the noise again, distant and faint. It didn't seem that his companions were in any immediate danger, so he decided against waking them. Suddenly though, he felt a presence at his side. Without needing to turn around, he knew it was Nightfall.

"I hear it also. I will investigate."

"I will go with you."

"Thel Omaga –"

Luinedhel stepped forward, cutting off further discussion. He gripped his blades tightly and walked toward the dark, ruined city. He sensed Nightfall hesitate, whistle quietly, and then move in behind him to his left. Luinedhel glanced over his right shoulder and saw Hathar sit up in response to Nightfall's signal. The cleric looked their way and then stood up and reached for his hammer. Nightfall whistled again, and the cleric nodded. Hathar remained with N'Khael and Avanstel.

The scouting pair crept along in silence, avoiding the rubble that littered the street. Parts of broken facades had fallen over the centuries, leaving hollowed-out husks of buildings on either side of the road. Even in decay, Luinedhel could tell that this city must have once stood strong and fine and proud, a majestic testament to a kingdom with abundant resources, one that boasted many talented builders and artisans. The splendor of the architecture was still present in its fallen stones. Hemel was similar to the architecture of Ny'we Adye, although more like a distant cousin than a sibling. Something about the way the stones fit together – and the remnants of elegant arches – was undeniably elven … or elven-like.

The road continued to wind to the left, and Luinedhel noticed the moonlight shifting ever so slightly. It had once illuminated the edges of the buildings in front of him, but now it had swung behind him, causing their long shadows to darken the road. Not being able to see that far ahead of them around the bend of the road put him on edge. Anything could lurk just around the curve of the next building, just out of sight. Luinedhel wondered if the city had been designed this way as an innate form of protecting the palace, forcing enemies down circuitous roads where defenders could easily ambush them … assuming they made it this far. The lack of obvious entrances to the city center, the high bridges that needed to be crossed from the lower city, and the general construction of the roadways made Hemel a highly defensible location.

Ahead, Luinedhel could see a wall rising above the ruined buildings. There was another low, drawn-out sound. Closer now. It was a long and mournful wail. Luinedhel felt Nightfall's hand on his shoulder. He stopped and looked at the nether-elf, who motioned for them to split apart and make their way to either side of the road. He nodded and darted into the shadow of a building to the left, watching as Nightfall slid into the darkness on the opposite side of the street.

As he crept forward, his foot struck a small pile of bones, and he cringed at the noise they made as they tumbled into the darkness. For a moment, he panicked. Were the Urneans close by? But then he realized the bones were old and long stripped of any flesh. If the Urneans had done this, they had done it decades – or maybe centuries – ago.

He paused for a moment, intentionally slowing his breathing. *"Sere'eden! Sere'eden!"* He listened intently for the noise to repeat. He could not see Nightfall amidst the darkened ruins, but he was certain the *drivrid* was there, cautiously making his way forward, and likely doing better at avoiding stumbling over old piles of bones.

He crept ahead, blending into the darkness as Selyndar had taught him. As they rounded the curve, he could see the remains of a large stone gate. The massive slabs of granite lay shattered on the broken road. Beyond them rose the ruined towers of the palace, the center of the city. Eyama shone down brightly on the pale stone, illuminating the entire area. If they were going to continue on, they would need to step out of the shadows and onto the open street. He paused and waited. Another wail echoed through the ruined city, fading away into the night. Whatever it was, the source was ahead in the palace ruins.

As the sound dissipated, Nightfall emerged from the darkness on the other side of the road and stepped up on top of the fallen gate. Luinedhel matched his movements, looking at the nether-elf for direction. They stepped through the large opening in the wall and moved into the darkness beyond.

A large space opened before them, what had probably once been a courtyard, but was now filled with fallen columns and other broken debris that had tumbled from the heights above them. Across the littered ground, he could see stairs leading into the towering palace. Luinedhel looked upwards. The massive structure, lit by the bright yellow moon, was still impressive despite being a shattered ghost of itself. He estimated it was maybe twice or three times the size of the palace in Ny'we Adye.

He tilted his head. The place looked familiar, as if he had seen it somewhere before, but he knew that was impossible. He had never been to Hemel; he hadn't even known of its existence until days ago. Nobody did. How could he ever have seen this place before? Perhaps it reminded him of some place in Ny'we Adye that he couldn't quite pin down.

There was a sudden numbness and tingling in his hands, as if something had cut off the circulation and it was just returning. He frowned and turned his blades over, flexing his grip.

"What is it?" Nightfall whispered.

Luinedhel shook his head, unsure how to explain the sensation or the familiarity of the tower overlooking the city.

Another wail broke the silence. The sound was coming from the darkened opening ahead of them. This time, Luinedhel thought it sounded like a cry of agony, like that of a trapped animal, or a mother who has lost her child. It was heavy and full of sorrow. It dragged on his heart.

Nightfall motioned for them to move toward the doorway. They made their way around the debris and toward the dark opening, pausing at the threshold. The tingling in Luinedhel's hands had intensified, but he pushed it from his mind.

"Do you have anything to light the way?"

"Best to stick to the shadows," Nightfall said. "We don't know what lies within."

Luinedhel nodded, although stepping into potentially treacherous ruins in complete darkness was not something he preferred. He lacked the *drivrid's* night sight, but he trusted Nightfall. If he thought it was best to remain hidden, then he was probably right.

He placed Adesh back in his belt and used his left hand to feel along the walls, stepping slowly and cautiously forward. Nightfall disappeared again into the black shadows. Luinedhel listened for him, for the slightest sounds of his boots scraping along the floor or his breath echoing through the stillness, but he couldn't hear anything. The nether-elf had long ago mastered the art of moving silently. It was something Luinedhel needed more practice to do well. Selyndar had taught him much, but there hadn't been time to learn everything.

They reached the end of a long corridor. Luinedhel felt a wooden door blocking their way forward. Unlike the deteriorated wood they had seen throughout the city, this door was surprisingly solid and intact.

Another wail. Louder. It was coming from beyond the door. They waited for the sound to fade before moving.

"Through?" Luinedhel whispered.

"Follow me."

He heard the screech of rusted metal as Nightfall pulled a latch, and the hinges groaned. What had been closed for thousands of cycles resisted the call to open, but was still functional enough to give way under Nightfall's insistence. Luinedhel could see a faint light ahead that was different from the pitch blackness of the corridor. It was the same tint of the strange yellow-green light that they had seen in the guard tower.

His right hand was burning as if pricked with a thousand needles. He shifted Marek to his left hand and noted that the sensation followed the blade, fading from his right hand as his left began to throb. He placed the sai into his belt, flexing both hands until the sensation finally receded. Nightfall had watched the entire exchange without comment.

"The blades are vibrating ... or something. I don't know. But it is unpleasant to hold them."

Nightfall nodded. He handed Luinedhel one of his blades. Luinedhel took it, half expecting it to vibrate and prick his skin, but the strange sensation did not return.

The *drivrid* stepped forward and through the doorway. Luinedhel followed.

The room they entered was massive. It was like the hall at the palace in Ny'we Adye, but on a much larger scale. On either side was a tall row of columns, extending far into the distance, where the faint chartreuse light was originating. Luinedhel listened for a hum like that of the portal in the guard tower, but there was nothing. He looked at Nightfall, who gestured for them to move cautiously.

The light grew brighter as they moved down the columned aisle. They reached a point where the columns ended, and the hallway joined a room with a domed ceiling high above them. Two other corridors, lined with columns like theirs, led away from the central circular space, splitting the entire room in perfect thirds at precise angles – just like the roads leading into the city on Hathar's map, and the triangle symbol over the portal. The architects of Hemel must have been obsessed with the number three.

In the middle of the floor was a round dais, and on top of the dais was a massive cluster of yellow-green glowing crystals, each one about twice the height of a man. Luinedhel counted at least eleven large crystals, with multiple smaller shards jutting out from the mound. Whatever destruction had befallen the rest of the city had spared this place. There were no signs of damage. He wondered if it had something to do with the crystals. Perhaps the crystal at the guard tower had kept that building from crumbling as well.

Nightfall motioned for Luinedhel to circle to the left while he moved along the right side of the dais. Luinedhel nodded, raising Nightfall's dagger in a defensive pose. As he reached the hallway leading away from the crystals, he turned in that direction, prepared for something to leap out at him. Whatever had made the forlorn noise had come from this place, and he expected to encounter it at any moment. *"Sere'eden!"* he said to himself to keep calm.

He peered down the line of columns that faded into the darkness. He could not discern any movement. After a beat, he turned slowly back around to examine the giant crystalline cluster and gasped aloud. Nightfall leapt from the darkness, closing the distance between them quickly and flashing his blade. Luinedhel pointed toward the center of the room with his dagger.

What they had taken for an unnaturally large formation of crystals was the backside of an immense crystalline throne. The shards that Luinedhel had counted made up the back of the enormous throne. More crystal shards jutted from the pile, making arms and a seat, and framing the entire thing in sharp-angled brilliance. Crystalline steps had been carved into the dais, ascending upwards to the throne. On top of that structure that towered over them sat the long-decayed body of Hemel's once powerful emperor, still dressed in his royal armor. A crown made of yellow-green crystal had fallen from the skeleton's head and now lay at the feet of the dead ruler. The figure clutched an *estrayaed* staff, which was topped by a multifaceted sapphire that sparkled in the pale green glow from the throne.

"I would venture to say, *sondartin*, that we have found the artifact that we have come for. The emperor is not in a tomb, but still upon his throne."

Luinedhel nodded in agreement.

At that moment, the mouth of the skeleton opened, and a mournful wail filled the chamber. Luinedhel froze in fear.

CHAPTER 27: WOE

No matter how much Luinedhel protested, Nightfall insisted on approaching the crystalline throne alone. He advised Luinedhel to shelter behind the nearest column and to only come out when he called for him. "I cannot put you at risk, *sondartin*. Just as you place the value of your friend's life above your own, I value *yours* above mine. I swore a pledge to Lord Omaga, and I will fulfill my vows."

Luinedhel relented, returned the dagger to Nightfall, and retreated to the cover of the nearest stone pillar. He watched anxiously as the rogue stepped onto the stone dais and made his way toward the crystal throne. As he stepped onto the lowest translucent stair, the nether-elf paused, carefully placing his weight on the step, ever-alert for a hidden trap.

Nothing happened.

He took another step and glanced over his shoulder at Luinedhel. The idea of climbing the throne and stealing a powerful magical item from an undead ruler wasn't a choice either of them would make if they had it. But completing Dredaius' mission was the only way to ensure Avanstel's safety. If doom awaited, better it be them than the heir-apparent.

Luinedhel instinctively touched the daggers at his side. The discomforting tingle ran through his hand again, and he realized that the closer they had drawn to the throne, the stronger and more painful the sensations had grown. He wasn't sure he would be able to withstand the pain for any length of time, but steeled himself to do so, if he needed to use the weapons. He would defend Nightfall if required, with whatever weapons he had, *estrayaed* or otherwise.

The *drivrid* took another cautious step.

Nothing.

He repeated this process until he stood directly in front of the throne. Nightfall stopped there, frozen. He carefully examined the scepter and the throne for hidden dangers. Simply taking the staff would be too simplistic – there had to be more to it. Nightfall was a master of many skills, and Luinedhel was confident he had the expertise to locate any hidden dangers. The *drivrid* had survived many of Selyndar's missions, and one did not survive long without the skill to avoid even the deadliest of situations.

The mouth of the skeleton opened, and another wail echoed through the large chamber. It startled both of them. Nightfall leapt down the steps and raised his weapons in one smooth motion. Luinedhel closed his hands around his *estrayaed* weapons and withdrew them in a defensive pose. His palms burned with pain.

"*Focus*," Marek's voice echoed. "*Rise above the pain. You have it within you.*"

"*Now* you have something to share?" Luinedhel closed his eyes and concentrated, trying to climb above the shooting pain that traveled up his hands and into his arms, incrementally rising higher. "*Sere'eden!*" he said to himself.

"*Don't be weak!*" Adesh said. "*Master the pain! Rulers remain strong in the face of opposition.*"

As he focused and visualized the pain subsiding, it slowly moved from his upper arms to his forearms, and then to his wrists, hands, and fingers. He exhaled and opened his eyes.

The *drivrid* was standing directly in front of him. "What did you do?"

Luinedhel looked at him quizzically. "What do you mean?"

The nether-elf motioned to the throne and the skeletal emperor. Luinedhel looked up to see sparking arcs of blue lightning jumping around the large sapphire atop the *estrayaed* staff. There was a crackle in the surrounding air, and Luinedhel could smell a strange metallic-like scent. The blue stone had come to life with an energy that seemed to fill the entire room.

"I don't know."

"Drop your blades."

Luinedhel looked down at his hands and saw jagged blue light arcing from the blades to his hands and chest. Although he had closed his mind off to the pain, the energy that had caused it was still very real. Shocked, he opened both hands, and the blades clanged to the floor, crackling and sputtering as the light racing along them faded and disappeared.

He looked up at Nightfall in wonder and confusion. The nether-elf grabbed Luinedhel's hands and turned them over in his own, looking for signs of damage or burns. There were none – his hands were unharmed. Nightfall held Luinedhel's face in his hands and turned it from side to side. "Are you all right, *sondartin*?"

"I'm fine, I think."

Nightfall exhaled sharply and turned around to look at the throne behind him. The sparks had disappeared from the staff as well. The skeletal ruler had not moved, remaining frozen in his dead state.

"Well, I think we've established beyond a doubt that there's a connection between your weapons and the scepter. Although I'm not sure if that's because they are both made of *estrayaed*, or if something else is involved."

"*Eer'gott.* Do you think it's true what Dredaius told Avanstel?"

"It must be. And perhaps why the Seer could not discern the power of your blades. A forgotten magic that isn't in any records. And it must be why Dredaius wants the scepter."

Luinedhel reached down to pick up his blades.

"Careful. I think it's best that you don't touch them. Best that *no one* touch them while they are near the staff."

Luinedhel wrapped his hands in the end of his cloak and cautiously grabbed Adesh from the floor. The blade remained lifeless. He placed it in his belt and repeated the process with Marek. Whatever enchantment was upon the blades and the scepter, it was clear that to activate it required contact with the skin, like the *drivrid*'s crystal lights and fire marbles. If he kept from touching his daggers with ungloved hands, he should be safe from the blue lightning – and, perhaps, they could even take the scepter this way, despite the warnings of death to any non-J'Onsal making contact with it. Nightfall noted this.

"Here, take these," Nightfall said. He removed his black leather gloves and handed them to Luinedhel. "I need you able to fight, should the need occur."

Luinedhel slid the supple gloves onto his hands and grabbed Marek from his belt. There was no reaction, no blue lightning. He had guessed correctly. He looked up at Nightfall and nodded. The nether-elf walked across the room and slowly climbed the dais again.

This time, when the eerie groan filled the room, they stood ready. Nightfall sheathed his own blades and removed his cloak as he reached the top of the stairs. He wrapped the cloak around his left hand and cautiously reached towards the staff. He paused momentarily, looking over the emperor and his throne once more. Luinedhel held his breath as the *drivrid* began to slide the scepter from the skeletal grip.

At the movement, the emaciated head turned to look at Nightfall. Its jaw opened, and a loud voice emanated from somewhere within the ancient remains. It was haunting and breathy

– and it was the same language from his dreams, the one he knew but didn't understand. As the voice spoke, the carvings on the side of the scepter glowed bright blue. The symbols at the bottom lit up first, and the more the skeleton spoke, the more symbols illuminated. They were words, a language, and the skeleton was speaking a chant or a spell.

Just as Luinedhel was about to shout at Nightfall, the *drivrid* yanked the staff from the emperor's bony clutch. A louder, more mournful wail reverberated around the room, rising in pitch to almost a scream. It was painfully loud and shrill. Luinedhel dropped his daggers and clapped his hands over his ears as the lament turned into a shriek. The entire place shook. Rubble and parts of the ceiling fell around him. He looked across the room and saw several pillars begin to sway.

Nightfall was at his side in an instant. He had wrapped the staff in his cloak and secured it to his back with a strap. "We have to get out!" he shouted above the rising whine and the roar of crumbling stone.

Luinedhel nodded as the wail continued. He picked up the daggers from the floor, stowed them in his belt, and raced behind Nightfall back toward the entrance. A large pillar fell across the corridor, knocking another over and blocking their escape. A third column shifted forward and fell towards the crystalline throne. It slammed into the structure, and shards of yellow-green crystal sprayed into the surrounding air. Luinedhel ducked just in time to miss an enormous chunk that hurled towards him. "This way!" he shouted, pointing toward the third corridor.

Nightfall nodded and sprinted ahead, with Luinedhel close behind. Looking over his shoulder, he saw the crystal throne rotating, spinning around in a circle atop the dais at an increasing rate. The skeletal figure at the top had stood up and was attempting to descend the stairs, but the speed at which the dais was turning made him stumble. He stood up and continued down the stairs, oblivious to the chaos around him as entire sections of the ceiling fell and crashed onto the tiled floor.

Luinedhel tripped over a chunk of stone and landed face-first on the ground. Directly in front of him was a lime-green fragment of the crystal throne. Luinedhel grabbed the shard as Nightfall helped him to his feet. He held the crystal up to show the nether-elf. "The doorway!" he shouted above the din.

Nightfall nodded and pulled him out of the way as another column fell. They raced toward the corridor. The wail reached a crescendo. It was immediately drowned out by an enormous roar as the entire building above them began to collapse. An enormous cloud of dust and rubble rushed towards them. They raced forward toward the door at the end of the arcade as they dodged falling columns and debris.

At the end of the passage was another wooden door, similar to the one they had entered. They flew out of the opening and continued running through the courtyard beyond as the palace crumbled around them. The roar was almost deafening now, as the ancient structure collapsed in upon itself. Enormous chunks of the towers rained down around them, falling with tremendous booms as the two of them raced to escape the destruction.

One final, thunderous boom erupted behind them, then a cloud of dust enveloped them, and they were showered with a pelting of small stone fragments. They reached the white walls surrounding the palace, and Luinedhel stopped to catch his breath. Nightfall grabbed his arm and dragged him forward. "It's not safe yet. Keep going!"

Luinedhel pulled upon his last reserves to continue running through the city and its spiraling roads. Suddenly, he heard the cracking of the palace walls as they tumbled over and poured out into the streets behind them. He pushed forward until he could run no more and finally fell down, collapsing in exhaustion as he lay in the middle of the roadway. Gasping for air, his lungs burning, and his legs trembling, his heart pounded loudly in his ears. He closed his eyes and tried to swallow.

He felt Nightfall's hand on his chest and, above the throbbing in his ears, he heard the *drivrid* say, "Well done, *sondartin*. Well done."

Luinedhel kept his eyes closed, but a smile crept across his face. They had retrieved the relic that Dredaius had sent them for *and* kept Avanstel out of danger. He finally felt as if he had done something meaningful, something that would have made both Adine and Selyndar proud.

Because the city's design was a spiral with the palace at its center, they estimated that heading roughly southwest would eventually lead them back to their camp, where they could catch up with the others. This was easier said than done, as they had to traverse the remains of the ruined city. Much of the city remained standing, and many walls, several stories high, blocked their way. Going through these obstacles was the best option. They spent most of the morning looking for passages and unblocked alleys between the collapsed buildings that would lead them in the right direction. By midafternoon, they had found their original route and backtracked to the camp.

Avanstel was there to greet them as soon as they appeared. "Arrac … Luin … Praise Enos that you are alive! We heard the sound and felt the tremors in the night and woke to discover you both were gone. We couldn't tell what had happened until this morning when the sun rose. The palace is …?"

"Destroyed," Nightfall answered.

Avanstel's smile faded.

Luinedhel took his friend's face, held it in his hands, and locked eyes with him. "Do not despair. We did not fail you. We have what we came for."

Avanstel's eyes lit up. "You did? How?"

"There's more." Luinedhel said. He held out the fist-sized shard of crystal that he had retrieved from the exploding throne. "We might be able to use it to power the portal and return to the guard house."

"Amazing!" Avanstel hugged Luinedhel, squeezing him tight. "But more importantly, are you hurt?"

"I'm well. Nightfall made sure of that." He looked over at the nether-elf, who had handed the wrapped scepter to Hathar. Avanstel followed Luinedhel's gaze.

"Is that …?"

"It is."

Before he could say more, N'Khael stepped in front of him and hugged Luinedhel briefly and then punched him sharply in the shoulder. "Don't do that again, Thelo!" Her face was stern. "You may think that sneaking off into the night is acceptable behavior for a little brother, but now that I have one, I don't like the thought of losing him! *We* are the only family that we have. Don't put yourself at risk again."

Luinedhel smiled. "I will remember to take you with me next time." She smiled back at him and shoved him lightly.

Hathar pulled back a corner of the cloth covering the scepter.

"Don't touch it," Nightfall warned. "There is a strange magic at work here. It must be *eer'gott*, as Dredaius had explained. It is more powerful than anything I know."

Hathar nodded and flipped over the last piece of Nightfall's cloak that covered the relic. In the sunlight, the large sapphire atop the scepter was brilliant, shimmering from cerulean to a rich midnight blue. The way the light caught the gemstone made it sparkle and dance. The bluish metal shone with a sharp polish, like it was new. Luinedhel leaned in for a closer look.

N'Khael looked up at him. "Thelo, it's *estrayaed*!"

"Yes," he said. "Do you see the words there?" He pointed at them, careful not to touch the metal. "Do you know what they say?"

"It looks like the writing on the stone walls at the guard tower. This first word is like Weald-speak. It could be '*thanele*,' similar to the Weode word '*thaen el*,' though we don't use that word now. We just say '*tanel*.'"

"That means dread … or sadness … or woe," Luinedhel said, remembering his lessons with Selyndar.

"Yes, woe." She frowned. "Maybe the first word of a warning?"

Luinedhel looked at Nightfall. "We don't know, but from what we saw, this may be the enchantment that unlocks the power within the scepter."

"I don't like it," Hathar said. "It feels … cursed. Even through the cloak, I can feel the chill of the metal. Even here in the sun, it feels cold."

Nightfall reached out and covered the scepter again. "You may be right, cleric. What Luinedhel and I experienced was not of the natural world. An undead emperor from a long dead kingdom caught somewhere between life and death."

The *drivrid* relayed the tale of traveling through the city and retrieving the scepter. Luinedhel opened his mouth to tell them about the blue lightning that had come from his blades, but he caught a quick glance from Nightfall that suggested he keep that to himself. He frowned, but didn't say more.

"No Urneans?" N'Khael asked.

"No," Nightfall answered. "If they had been here once, they have long since abandoned the city center. The collapsed bridges make it difficult to enter here, and there is nothing alive within, so there's no reason for them to try. As far as I am able to discern, this place is dead – an empty shell of what it once was. And now, its sole remaining occupant has finally found his rest."

"Do you think this was their city? The Urneans?" Avanstel asked.

"No," Luinedhel answered. "It was not the Urneans. They came later. The First People built Hemel. They had structure, knowledge, and civilization. They were able to build this city, the palace, the portals, even the guard tower. The Urneans could not have built all this."

"So, the Urneans killed the First People?"

"I don't know, Van. Nobody knows what happened to the First People. It's possible, but … I think something else happened here. I don't know what. I'm not sure anyone will ever know."

"Well, I'm glad to be gone from this place," Avanstel said. He looked back toward the center of the city. "Even in the daylight, this place has a haunted feeling to it."

"It does," Hathar said. "Let's see if that crystal will power the portal so that we can get back to the guardhouse and out of The Barrens."

They spent the rest of the day navigating their descent over the bridge from the city center to the marshes below, and reached the triangular doorway as night fell on Hemel. Luinedhel placed the shattered crystal into the three crossed bones at the top of the portal, and a familiar thrum began, the shifting surface coming to life. The pulsing glow washed over the small room, illuminating all their faces with its sickly chartreuse light. Luinedhel looked at the symbols on the side of the frame and found that these were different from the portal in the gatehouse. There was only one symbol on each side. On the right was a rectangle, and on the left was a spiral made of three lines. He pressed the rectangle, and the door became a black void, the low hum shifting to a pulsing beat.

Nightfall stepped forward. "I will lead."

"No, I will go first," Luinedhel said. He removed the daggers from his belt. "You have risked enough for me today."

Nightfall moved away from the portal, motioning for Luinedhel to proceed. As Luinedhel stepped through the portal, momentary silence enveloped him. He emerged where he had expected, in the stone room in the guard tower. Everything was as they had left it.

CHAPTER 28: FLIGHT

Aelduin, Nyx, and the other horses were happy to see the party return. The thought of their entrapment here in the tower had weighed on Luinedhel's mind the entire time in Hemel, but until the moment they reunited, he hadn't realized how much. Aelduin nickered when he saw Luinedhel descend the stairs and trotted over to him, nuzzling his neck. He patted the mare and smiled.

They started a fire with the last remaining fire marble. Their provisions were running low, so the meal was meager. The trip back to Ny'we Adye would be a long one, and until they left the swamps, they would need to ration their food. Nobody had brought a bow to hunt with, so they would need to scavenge for berries and roots on their way.

N'Khael and Luinedhel helped Hathar remove the heavy bar across the entry of the guard tower and opened the door enough for Nightfall to slip through to scout the area. As expected, driven by their hunger, the Urneans had remained near the tower, waiting for the inevitable desperate escape of their prey. Nightfall returned shortly with the bleak news.

"They are roaming the area," he said, "not really in any organized patrols, but certainly lingering and waiting us out. When we go, it will have to be under cover of night and as stealthily as we can. I think I have a plan."

Nightfall shared that he intended to ride out and serve as a diversion, drawing the horde away from the tower and deeper into the woods, which would allow the others to escape after the Lost Ones had taken pursuit.

"They won't expect that?" Avanstel asked.

"From what I know of them, their motive is to devour, to satiate their unending hunger. Their attacks are with animalistic force and vicious rage, not with strategy or planning. I don't believe they have the rational mind necessary to calculate the outcomes of their actions, nor to anticipate the response of those they prey upon."

Luinedhel frowned. "But what about you?"

Hathar chuckled and patted Luinedhel on the back. "You need not worry about our friend. He is more cunning and sly than anyone I know. If Nyx cannot outrun the Urneans – which is unlikely – Nightfall will find a way to slip their noose. We will see him again in Ny'we Adye, eventually. He has never failed to escape even the most dangerous circumstances we have found ourselves in."

Luinedhel looked at the nether-elf, who nodded in affirmation, and smiled. "Do not concern yourself over me, *sondartin*. I have survived similar situations. I can see clearly in the dark, an advantage I have over you and the others, and perhaps even our foes."

"The horses of House Omaga are the finest in the kingdom," N'Khael said. "Mother saw to that." She patted Nyx's neck. "He will carry Nightfall past the Urneans. I have no doubt they can escape."

"Let's focus on *your* path out of here, instead," Nightfall said. "Hathar, can you show the map?"

They reviewed Dredaius' map and discussed strategies. Eventually, they aligned on a route that took them southward along the waters of the lake and towards the Idar Mountains. They figured that higher ground would make it easier to travel with the horses. It was a less direct route, but it seemed like the best plan – better than crossing the swamp with the Urneans a continuous threat.

"Thel Omaga, will you bear the scepter?" Nightfall asked. "Should anything happen, N'Khael and Hathar will need to protect the Aetheling as their first duty. We cannot risk the relic, nor the heir, falling into the wrong hands. Can we depend on you to get the scepter back to Ny'we Adye … even if Avanstel is not with you?"

Luinedhel looked at his friend. Avanstel nodded in agreement. As much as he didn't like the thought of leaving Avanstel, he knew that there was a greater purpose in all of this, and it might require the sacrifice of their separation yet again. "Yes," he said. "I will get the scepter back to Ny'we Adye. You can depend on me."

Nightfall passed the package to Luinedhel and gave him a knowing glance. There was something more to this request than the *drivrid* explained, but he wasn't willing to discuss it further at the moment – whatever the reason.

They gathered and prepared their horses and waited for darkness to fall. N'Khael scaled the wall of the storeroom and monitored the activity outside through the arrow slits above them. When she gave the signal, they opened the doors, and Nightfall shot from the tower. He raced across the bridge, past the green fires, and disappeared into the dark woods.

Everything was silent for a heartbeat, and then a chorus of bestial snarls and growls echoed through the forest, pierced by the occasional bark or roar. There was a low rumble of heavy footfalls and breaking branches as the Urneans took pursuit. N'Khael descended from her perch and mounted her horse. They waited a moment for the noises outside to fade, and then she told them to follow her. She led them out and away from the tower and into the night.

The journey through the forest was slow. Luinedhel did his best to avoid the many gnarled branches that swatted him as they rode through the underbrush. As the sun rose, the trees eventually thinned. They descended toward a river, forded it, and climbed again into the woodlands. Here, the sounds of wildlife flourished. Insects and birds, and an occasional rustle in the bushes as they passed by, indicated that they had passed through the hunting grounds of the Lost Ones. Luinedhel took comfort in these sounds after the eerie silence of the desolate lands of the Urneans, and he eased himself back into the saddle, enjoying the leisurely pace.

The ground grew rocky and more challenging to navigate as they neared the mountains, forcing them to slow down even more. Eventually, they dismounted and led their horses across the hard terrain. As the sun was waning into evening, they came into a clearing in the woods, and Luinedhel could see the mountains looming overhead. He had never been this close to mountains before – save the Mountain of Woes – and their sheer size and number left him in awe. It was autumn, but there was snow on the peaks and crags high above them.

"It's already winter up there?" he asked.

Hathar followed Luinedhel's gaze and then smiled, teeth flashing beneath his beard. "It's *always* winter up there, friend."

Luinedhel shook his head in amazement. "Someday I would like to go there. To touch the snow in a place where it never melts."

"I will go with you," Avanstel added. "It would be a grand adventure!"

Luinedhel smiled. "We will go together!"

"It is not a simple journey," Hathar said. "It may look beautiful, but it is a harsh environment and a dangerous voyage to make."

"Indeed," N'Khael said. "It's not as innocent as it looks. Some go and never return." Something in her voice sounded heavy and sad. Luinedhel looked at her.

"Have you been, Sister?"

"Not I, Thelo. My mother." She paused.

"Oh." Luinedhel bowed his head. "I am sorry. I did not intend to bring more grief upon you, Sister."

N'Khael looked up. "Thank you, Brother. It was long ago, and not that mountain. And I was young. Time has dulled the pain of a life without her."

"Still, I grieve for your loss."

"We are the same, Thelo. Our parents have gone on to the next life. We are orphans together – but we have each other. And the memories of those whom we loved remains in our hearts. Let us cherish those thoughts, for each day has enough troubles of its own. Miring in past heartache just makes it that much more difficult."

Luinedhel nodded. He touched the small pouch that hung on his belt and thought of Adine. He had unfinished business back in Chark. Did he have the words yet to give her? Had he learned what to say that would convey what she had meant to him? And Selyndar … he hadn't had a chance to honor him with a farewell either – things had moved so swiftly, and there hadn't been a ceremony for him yet.

N'Khael continued, "And we each have found new purpose, and new companions to distract us from our grief, no? When my mother did not return as expected, that was when Nephinae and I became close friends. We enlisted in the Green Guard together, and her companionship helped ease my sorrow. And you, you have the Aetheling and the others. I might even be fortunate enough to be numbered amongst those who have helped you on your path."

"You have. More than you know. You, and our father."

She smiled. "And having *you* by my side has helped me with my own sorrow, brother. I know he loved you. Having you beside me is like having a little of him with me."

Luinedhel felt a lump rise in his throat. "Thank you." He wiped a tear from his cheek.

"Let us make camp here in this clearing. I will take first watch," N'Khael said, shifting the topic and addressing the group.

"No. Allow me." He wanted to show N'Khael how much he appreciated her, and maybe to find some time to sit with his thoughts a bit and reflect on the loss of his parents ... and possibly find some words that he hadn't yet been able to find.

She looked at him, first in surprise and then in understanding. "If you'd like."

They made camp and scrounged through their rations. Hathar divided the remaining stores, saving enough for one last meal before they reached Belkin Wood. They made no fire. They didn't want to call attention to themselves in this unfamiliar place. These lands were close enough to the dead forest that the return of the Urneans was a high possibility ... and there were other dangers that they may still be unaware of.

After the meal, Luinedhel found a perch at the base of a dead tree that gave him a clear view of the surroundings and made ready for watch. Avanstel wandered over and sat beside him.

They remained that way for a while, the two of them watching the fading sun together, looking up into the sky as the stars appeared above.

"Do you miss Chark as much as I do?" Avanstel said.

The question surprised Luinedhel. Avanstel was the heir to a royal throne and would one day be the ruler of the Weode nation. He lived in the palace and could have anything he wanted. Luinedhel assumed Avanstel was happy with his new life of luxury and comfort. What could he miss about Chark, the stinky, dirty city where they were outcasts and lived in poverty? "Why do you miss Chark?"

"Not Chark, I guess," Avanstel replied. He was silent for a moment. "I guess I miss the days when things were simpler. When it was just you and me, and Danvaren. And there were no armies and invasions and magical relics and duties and responsibilities. I mean, we had to work – but we worked together at The Pig. It was … well, it was hard, but it was good, too. Right?"

Luinedhel smiled. "Yes, it was good, Van. But we are together now, and we have a future ahead of us that was beyond anything we could have dreamed of back then. You, the ruler of the Weode, and I, Thel of House Omaga. Who would have imagined?"

Avanstel sighed. "My day on the throne is a long way away, Arrac. Dredaius has only just ascended. And he is Weode. The *accentation* in his blood is much stronger than mine. I may never be the Ade. He may outlive me by centuries."

"Then you will have more time for adventures," Luinedhel said, trying to find the positive in the situation – the way Avanstel always did. "We have many days ahead of us … and many more games of Haven Chase." He reached out and put his hand on Avanstel's. "Like N'Khael said earlier – let's not worry about what may happen in cycles, just think on today."

"Fair," Avanstel said. "Perhaps a little of Lord Omaga has rubbed off on you. You sound wiser than the friend I remember from Chark."

"You also," Luinedhel said. "And maybe a little more serious than I remember. I miss your laughter."

Avanstel did not respond immediately. "The weight of the kingdom is a heavy thing to bear."

"I understand. *Namartha t'undel,* friend." Luinedhel squeezed Avanstel's hand.

He squeezed back. "*Namartha t'undel.*"

Avanstel lingered there a while longer until the orange and purple light faded and then stood up and made his way back to camp.

Luinedhel watched him go and thought to himself about how their time with the Weode had changed them both — for better and for worse. Like Avanstel, he missed the simpler times, when they had only the worries of the day and each other's constant company.

These days, life was much more complicated ... but what could be done about it? Run away from it all? Reject everything they had received? And what would that accomplish? Questelle was still up to something devious, and their futures seemed tied to the Weode, whether or not they liked it. They would accomplish nothing by fleeing the situation. They needed to go forward strongly, and boldly ... and together.

The others eventually fell asleep, and Luinedhel was alone in the darkness with his thoughts. He removed his daggers and set them across his lap, watching how the moonlight of Relos glinted off their blades. He held them each for a moment, waiting for Adesh or Marek to speak to him. There was nothing but the sound of crickets to fill the cool night air.

His mind wandered as he thought about N'Khael's words. Orphans, both. Selyndar had mentioned Elisryn, N'Khael's mother, on a couple of occasions, but the conversations had been brief, and he had given no details about her death. Luinedhel knew she was an interesting and unconventional woman, an explorer with a passion for discovery. And of course, that she and Selyndar could not have children — which is why they had adopted N'Khael. But he knew little beyond that.

N'Khael had rarely mentioned Elisryn, so he wondered whether they had had a difficult relationship — or if simply the passage of time had separated them.

Luinedhel and N'Khael had each lost Selyndar, a wonderful man, the father who had taught them so much and had been so kind and generous and wise. And he had lost Adine, his mother, who had rescued him and cared for him as if he were her own. Loved him, taught him to control his emotions and pain, to not let them be his master, but to master them.

So much loss … so much pain.

His hand went instinctively to the moonstone pin tied to his belt. It was her last gift to him, his last remembrance of Adine. He had seen more of Halbrun than he had ever imagined, traveled farther than he ever had before, witnessed legends coming to life in Caerbexsys and the Barrens and Hemel. Learned the histories of the Th'arule and Weode and the city of Ny'we Adye. Trained with ancient blades that spoke only to him. So many adventures since his humble beginnings in Chark. Did he now have the words that she deserved?

Perhaps.

But maybe he was still learning what his place was in this ever-expanding world. Maybe there was more to learn about who he was, what he felt, what he thought, and where he belonged in all of this—other than at Avanstel's side. Maybe when he figured out his place, he would be able to tell her what she meant to him – and thank her for her gifts in helping shape him into who he was.

The route grew more difficult towards the mountains, so they stuck to the forest for as long as they could. Eventually, they changed course, heading due west across the plains. Occasionally, they would hear cries and howls coming from the woods behind them, which led them to believe that the Urneans might have been smarter than they had estimated … or their hunger was stronger. They took extra measures to cover their trail, though that proved more difficult out in the open. They remained vigilant and pushed forward without stopping to rest unless they had to.

Nobody mentioned Nightfall. His fate weighed heavily on Luinedhel as they traversed the grasslands and made camp next to a river that ran northward into the lake.

"Don't look so glum, friend." Hathar took the saddle off his horse, placed it on the ground next to him, and brushed his mount down while she ate the lush grass at his feet. "He will find his way back to us."

Their eyes met over the backs of their horses. Hathar's chestnut eyes were warm with compassion. He was speaking from his heart, not attempting to distract Luinedhel with false hope. The cleric sincerely believed Nightfall could escape the Urneans. Luinedhel nodded and turned his thoughts to what lay ahead at Ny'we Adye.

What would he do with the scepter when they arrived? Should he go directly to Dredaius and just hand it to him? Or should he deliver it to the Council instead? He assumed N'Khael would take Selyndar's position as an Elder on the Council when they returned; perhaps *she* should be the one to take the relic to the palace. Or perhaps Avanstel should take it to Dredaius for a private meeting. It was the Ade who had charged Avanstel with the retrieval, and the mission had been his in the first place.

But what about the connection the scepter had with his blades, or the blue lightning that he and Nightfall had seen in the palace at Hemel? Who could he trust with that information? He wondered again why Nightfall had avoided sharing those details, and whether he should tell the others now that he was gone. He decided that if Nightfall didn't appear before they reached Ny'we Adye, he would tell N'Khael what they had witnessed. She would know what to do. She, of all of them, had the most experience with the Weode.

For their dinner that night, they ate some mushrooms that Hathar had found, along with some berries that Avanstel and

Luinedhel had foraged at the river's edge. Although sparse, the meal was at least something in his belly. Avanstel reminisced about Caty's stew and the fresh bread she made at The Pig & Lamb, but they knew that even if they had had the means and supplies for a hot meal, a fire here on the open plain was ill advised. The Urneans could be following them.

The evening was warm for this late in the cycle, and soon the night music of crickets and other buzzing insects filled the air, along with the gentle songs of the night birds. They took turns bathing in the river, glad to wash the stench of their travel and the fetid waters of the Barrens from their clothes, skin, and hair.

Luinedhel volunteered again for first watch, but Hathar insisted he get some rest. He didn't protest, collapsing onto the grass next to Avanstel. He watched the fireflies dance around him until he heard Avanstel's familiar snores, and then he closed his eyes and fell asleep.

A shout from Hathar and the thudding of horses' hooves woke him from his sleep. Although it was dark and neither moon was in the sky, he knew the Urneans had found them. The air was thick and foul with a noxious scent. He heard Hathar roar loudly, followed by the sickening sound of flesh and bone giving way beneath his hammer.

"N'Khael, on your right!" Hathar cried.

Luinedhel heard the elven warrior's blade slice through the air and connect with something that let out a squeal and a gurgle, followed by a heavy thud as it hit the ground.

Avanstel stirred beside him and sat up with a yawn, unaware that they were under attack. "What's happening?"

"Stay down, Van," he shouted and leaped to his feet, drawing his blades. Blue lightning sparked around him, illuminating the night. He realized too late that his hands were bare; he had removed the gloves when he had bathed. Pain raced up his arms, but he pushed back on it, concentrating and containing it as Adine had taught him. *"Sere'eden! Sere'eden!"*

Avanstel cried out. "Arrac! You're on fire!"

"I'm fine," he shouted. "Stay down!"

The sudden flash of magical light had drawn the attention of the Urneans. One of them pivoted away from N'Khael and lurched toward him. The creature had four legs and two arms, and it was half as tall as he was. It lumbered toward him, red eyes glowing maliciously in the moonless night. As it drew closer, Luinedhel could see it had green-grey skin, scaly like that of a reptile, and a mouth full of pointed teeth like a shark. Black spiked hair spilled from its head and ran down its back, becoming fur that covered its insect-like legs. The creature raised its arms. The left arm resembled a giant crab pincer, while the right arm was like that of a man, and held an old, rusted blade. A hideous cry escaped the beast as it closed in.

Luinedhel drew his blades up in front of him.

"The corrupted will fall before us. The abomination will be cleansed!" Adesh's bloodthirsty voice rattled in his head.

"Strike strong and true and let these unnatural things be granted peace," Marek added.

Blue lightning arced between the blades and up his arms, but he kept the pain locked away. He grimaced in determination, pushing back the sting, refusing to let it have a hold on his body.

The blades glowed blue with lightning, and the creature stopped short. It hissed loudly, watching the light flash and dance before it. It hesitated and squinted with its strange eyes at the blue sparks. There was a guttural noise from its mouth that sounded vaguely like Weald-speak. *"Thanel el uhtrack —"*

Before it could say more, N'Khael's blade connected with the creature, slicing smoothly through one of its legs. It howled and lurched to the right, swiveled, and swung its massive claw toward her. She parried with her sword, but the force of the blow knocked her off her feet.

Instead of jabbing at her again, the Urnean turned back to Luinedhel, curiously watching the lightning dance across his forearms for a moment. Luinedhel readied himself for an attack, raising the daggers as Selyndar had taught him. He bared his teeth, funneling the pain in his arms into rage, and met the creature's gaze.

In those dull red eyes, there was a sudden shift, as if of recognition or understanding. The beast hissed once more and then pivoted and staggered unevenly away on its three remaining legs. An inhuman call rang out as it disappeared into the darkness, and Luinedhel was suddenly aware of movement in the shadows all around him, just beyond his sight. Clicks and thuds and growls receded into the night, moving away from him.

He maintained his defensive pose as he shuffled in a circle, keeping Avanstel at his back. The sounds were fading; the Urneans had retreated.

A moment passed, though he wasn't sure how long.

"Thelo?" It was N'Khael, who had regained her footing and was standing several feet away from him, taking in the spectacle.

"Sister, are you alright?"

"I'm injured, but the fight has not left me. What is happening?"

Luinedhel dropped his pose and placed the daggers into his belt. The blue lightning immediately disappeared. N'Khael grabbed his forearms, turning his hands up in front of her. "Hathar?" she called. "We need you."

It was too dark to see anything, so she gently ran her fingers over his palms, feeling for injury while she waited for the cleric.

"I'm here." The voice was off to their right. It was markedly strained, unusual for the high-spirited cleric. Luinedhel knew from his tone that something was wrong.

"Avanstel?" N'Khael called.

He appeared behind Luinedhel. "I'm here. Unhurt … save for my pride."

She exhaled in relief. "Go to Hathar. I will look after Thelo's wounds."

Luinedhel took her hands in his. "I am fine, sister." He met her gaze. "I'm not injured. It is you who needs tending." He pushed a strand of copper hair from her forehead, revealing a large gash and dark blood running down her face. "Let's sit so I can look at you."

She pushed him away and scoured the grass around them for her sword. "No time. They'll be back. We need to be ready. We need to get you and Avanstel to safety and —"

"They won't return," he said.

N'Khael looked at him, one eyebrow raised.

"The Lost Ones. The creatures are gone. They won't be back."

She frowned. "I don't understand, Thelo. Why do you say that?"

"Here, sit … please. I will tell you what happened in the palace at Hemel, and it will all make sense, but first, let me have a look at your wounds."

She agreed, and they sat down on the cool grass. Luinedhel pressed his hand to his sister's head. Avanstel appeared from the darkness with Hathar leaning heavily on him, an arm wrapped around Avanstel's shoulder for support. He had a large wound on his leg, along with a few other smaller injuries. He dropped to the ground next to N'Khael, landing on his back and panting.

"My bag is with my saddle. Thank Merces I removed it from my mount before they spooked and ran away," he said between breaths.

Avanstel nodded and headed into the darkness to find the cleric's knapsack. He returned shortly and offered it to Hathar. The cleric propped himself up and dumped the contents onto the wet grass. He sorted through them, grabbing several items. Popping the cork on a bottle, he sprinkled the contents from a pouch into it, then added ground leaves and mixed a poultice. While he worked, Luinedhel relayed the missing pieces of the story to the others, pausing to help spread the concoction onto N'Khael's forehead and assist with Hathar's bandages. He explained how the lightning had only appeared when the daggers were close to the scepter and when held in direct contact with his skin, and how Nightfall had given him the gloves to wear.

"Only those of the J'Onsal bloodline can touch the scepter without being killed," Avanstel said, setting down the bottles to tie a bandage around Hathar's leg.

"He didn't touch it. That's why it's wrapped in his cloak."

"Right," Avanstel said. "Maybe that's the magic. It's like the lightning from your daggers ... but more powerful. Powerful enough to kill. How is the scepter related to your daggers?"

"I don't know, Van," Luinedhel replied. "I don't know what the connection is between them other than they are both *estrayaed*. But there are other things made of *estrayaed*, right N'Khael?"

She nodded. "Yes, Thelo, there are other things. Maybe everything made of the star ore reacts the same way when close to the staff. We will have to investigate more when we return home. We should take it to the Seer."

Avanstel frowned. "But Dredaius ..."

"We will deliver it to him, but not immediately. I think we need the Seer to examine it first. This is probably why the *drivrid* withheld this information. Perhaps he was waiting for the opportunity to show us this *eer'gott*. He likely wanted to prevent the staff from being given to the Ade prematurely, before learning more about its powers. There's wisdom in that approach. What do you think, Thelo?"

Luinedhel nodded. "I agree. Dredaius might be speaking the truth, but there is more at work here. Maybe only the J'Onsal bloodline can touch the scepter without dying, but there might be more to it." He looked at N'Khael. "Learning what we can about the relic would be beneficial to all of us. You included, Avanstel."

Avanstel shrugged. "You're right. I don't understand it all. I'm not sure if anyone does. But I trust you … all of you. So, let's do as you say and take the scepter to the Seer."

They heard a neigh nearby in the darkness.

"Perhaps our mounts have returned," Hathar said. "This is a blessing from Merces! This leg will take a while to heal, and I did not relish the thought of making the rest of the trip by foot."

"Blessing indeed," came a voice from the darkness. Nightfall appeared, holding the reins of Aelduin and the other horses. "A blessing that I happened upon them and followed their trail back to you. For had I not, I would have spent several more days scouting these prairies for the lot of you, and I'm sure the Urneans would have caught you by then."

Hathar chuckled. "I think we are safe from the Urneans for the moment, friend." He turned to Luinedhel and smiled. "Did I not tell you he would return? And comes bearing gifts on top of it!"

Luinedhel smiled and shook his head. The nether-elf never ceased to surprise him. "It is good that you are back, Nightfall. We have quite a story to share with you."

CHAPTER 29: SEPARATION

The following day began with a frosty morning that dissolved into a dreary, drizzly day. Gusts of northerly winds drove the chill deep into their bones. By daylight, the party could see that Hathar's injuries were more serious than they had first thought. He tried to brush their concern away, but there was a greyness to his face that said otherwise, and the pallid look in his eyes made them all agree to watch him closely. They carefully helped him up onto his horse, securing him well, and then they set out, heading west.

Though Luinedhel had only glimpsed the Urneans in the darkness of night, he had seen enough to know that they all varied, no two seemingly the same. Some were small and others large; some had multiple limbs, while others were bipedal. If the Lost Ones had any similarities, he could not discern what they were. They all seemed to be malformed pieces of other creatures, randomly warped and melded together in unnatural ways. Whatever type of Urnean that had attacked Hathar, it had infected him with some kind of sickness. The poultice that the cleric had made was helping N'Khael's wounds, but it didn't seem to help Hathar. The sickness he carried was unlike anything they had seen before.

As Luinedhel thought about the Lost Ones, he understood why the tales portrayed them as a horror and a blight, seemingly unstoppable. Had the creatures pushed their advantage, they most definitely would have bested them all, devoured them without a second thought, leaving no one left to finish their quest and return the scepter to Ny'we Adye. But the lightning from the daggers had changed things. It was almost as if the Urneans had recognized it, knew it.

Luinedhel brought Aelduin into step next to Hathar's horse so he could keep a watch on the cleric while Nightfall led the way westward across the plains towards Belkin Wood. N'Khael and Avanstel brought up the rear. There was an unspoken agreement among them all that the most direct route was necessary to get Hathar aid as soon as possible. Nobody suggested a pause for a break, despite the rumbles in their stomachs. With no supplies remaining, stopping for a meal would have meant spending time scavenging, and that kind of delay wasn't worth the risk. They pressed on as quickly as they dared. The sooner they reached Ny'we Adye, the better – for Hathar, as well as everyone else.

The cleric became increasingly confused as the day passed. Their conversation would meander into nonsense, and he had twice almost fallen from his saddle before being rescued by Luinedhel. After the third time, Luinedhel suggested they move the cleric to Aelduin and double up. Nightfall agreed. Aelduin was a sturdy horse. As N'Khael said, one of the finest in the kingdom. If she had to carry the weight of two men Hathar's size, it might break her. Since elves weighed less than humans, the two of them would only slow her down.

Hathar put up no resistance. N'Khael and Nightfall got the cleric up onto Aelduin, and he situated himself in the saddle as best he could in his disoriented state. Nightfall handed Luinedhel the wrapped scepter, and he secured it to his back, adjusting the strap to give him as much arm movement as possible, then climbed up and sat behind Hathar.

"When we reach Belkin Wood, we will most likely encounter the Green Guard," Nightfall said as he climbed back into his saddle. "Dredaius will have the border of the kingdom set to high alert, to watch for the Th'arule. We may not find a warm welcome – a *drivrid*, an *ort* and a human entering the wood while the Th'arule linger about outside. It would be best to let N'Khael lead. She can secure safe passage for us through the forest."

Traveling in this manner would put Luinedhel's newly gained riding skills to the test, but he was confident he could keep Hathar from falling. N'Khael could protect Avanstel should the need arise. And the Aetheling was separated from the relic in case of ambush. It was a good plan.

He trusted Aelduin to choose the least difficult terrain and to carry them as swiftly as possible. Thankfully, the edge of the great forest was visible now on the horizon, so the ride would be short if they kept up the pace. With daylight fading, they agreed to press ahead without stopping, hoping to reach the area known as the 'boot heel' before the sun sank below the horizon.

N'Khael passed the reins of Hathar's horse to Avanstel and turned back to Luinedhel. "Are you secure, Thelo?" He nodded. "You chose wisely when you picked this horse from father's stables. She is … was … one of his favorites."

Luinedhel looked at her. Although she was strong and hid her pain, he knew her well enough to know that losing Selyndar and the thoughts of what lay ahead for them both in Ny'we Adye weighed heavily on her. "We will do this together, Sister. *Namartha t'undel.*"

A weak smile crossed her face. "*Namartha t'undel,*" she replied with a nod, and mounted her horse.

Luinedhel urged Aelduin forward. Nightfall turned Nyx westward. N'Khael and Avanstel followed him across the gloomy grassland toward the dark shadow of Belkin Wood looming in the distance.

Hathar was feverish. Luinedhel could feel it through his clothes. The cleric was burning up and had slipped into a delirium. He mumbled incoherently and shifted his weight frequently. Luinedhel slowed the pace so that the cleric wouldn't fall from the horse. Hathar's declining state made Luinedhel anxious. He wanted to let Aelduin ride swiftly, but he knew that keeping Hathar in the saddle at a gallop would be impossible. Going slower meant there would be a greater delay before they could get help. N'Khael and Avanstel were riding hard, racing to reach the edge of the wood before the light faded. The distance between them had grown as they had sped up and he had slowed down. To make matters worse, the overcast sky had turned to storms. Distant rumbles sounded above the rising wind.

The land grew dark, and although he could no longer see the forest, Luinedhel was sure they were drawing close. Occasional flashes of lightning gave some signs that he was near the edge of the wood, but those momentary glimpses of the landscape were brief and ever-shifting.

He paused, pulling Aelduin's reins hard, as he caught the ragged call of a voice over the rumbling and the whistling wind. He heard it again.

"Thelo!"

The shout was coming from his right. Aelduin immediately veered in that direction, her ears swiveling.

"I'm here!" Luinedhel shouted. The wind was whipping his hair around his face. The rain suddenly broke loose from above and poured thunderously down on them. "N'Khael, where are you?"

He didn't hear a response. Lightning flashed, and he glimpsed the shapes of trees looming directly in front of them. He nudged Aelduin forward through an opening between two of the enormous trunks and into the shelter under their branches. The pelting rain dissipated into a low but persistent drone. The intensity of the wind died down, but it was still enough to buffet him about. Hathar moaned and fell forward.

"Sister!" Luinedhel shouted into the dark forest, but only the sound of the storm answered him. He looked about desperately, but couldn't see more than occasional glimpses of trunks, like the giant pillars of the palace in Hemel, blinking in and out of existence with each flash of lightning. Hathar slid off Aelduin, and Luinedhel jumped off the back of the horse to catch the cleric as he fell.

Although he knew Hathar was burly, Luinedhel had not fully appreciated how sturdy he was until that moment. Hathar's robes concealed his physique, giving the impression he was smaller than he actually was. Hathar fell heavily into Luinedhel's arms, his mass knocking Luinedhel off his feet. Luinedhel stumbled backwards, his heel catching on a tree root, sending them both sprawling onto the forest floor. Hathar fell on top of him, knocking the wind out of Luinedhel. Although he had succeeded in cushioning his friend's fall, the sharp pains that wracked his body made him wonder if he might have broken a rib or two in the attempt.

He lay there for a moment, catching his breath, with Hathar on top of him, his dead weight pressing him into the damp leaves of the forest floor. Slowly, Luinedhel recovered his breath and was able to wriggle out from under the cleric. He knelt beside Hathar, placing the man's head in his lap, and bent over to confirm his chest was still rising and falling with breath. He was alive, but Luinedhel couldn't rouse him.

"Hathar!" He shouted and gently slapped the man's bearded face.

The cleric moaned in reply.

Luinedhel exhaled in relief. He *was* still alive, but possibly not for long, unless he received help. He looked around them, growing desperate. Where were N'Khael and Avanstel? He didn't see any sign of them, just dark, damp trees, and the sound of the storm and Aelduin's breath close by.

Lightning flashed again, and a figure illuminated in front of him. It was a Green Guard standing at Hathar's feet, blade drawn and pointing directly at him. Luinedhel gasped and leaned defensively over Hathar's body.

"Please!" he said. "He's injured and needs help!"

There was another burst of light. Luinedhel saw a dagger at the guard's throat. A shadowy figure was visible over his right shoulder. From the darkness, Luinedhel saw a flicker of golden eyes.

"Lower your blade. We are allies," Nightfall said in Weald-speak. "We are on an errand for the Ade Gerent. We are *taven'sanct*, and we have an injured man. It's urgent we get him to Ny'we Adye."

The guard adjusted his sword, now pointed at Hathar's chest, which rose and fell in an ever-decreasing rhythm. "We are under orders to protect the border," the guard said. "No one is to enter, especially not outsiders."

"Has the Aetheling passed by here?"

The soldier's weapon dipped. "The Aetheling? Do you have word of him? You know where he is?"

Nightfall removed the blade at the elf's throat. The young guard stepped to the side, keeping the strangers in front of him, his sword still raised. He whistled what sounded like a bird call.

An answer came moments later from somewhere in the forest. More Green Guard appeared almost instantly from the trees and surrounded them. One of them stepped forward and took the report from the young scout that Nightfall had exchanged words with. Luinedhel exhaled loudly. It was Nephinae! They were saved!

She turned to them. "My men say you have knowledge of the location of the Aetheling. He has been missing from the palace for almost a week now."

"He was with us, with N'Khael," Luinedhel said. "They were ahead of us. Hathar is injured. Can you get help for him? He needs medicines."

She signaled for the other Green Guard to lower their weapons and knelt next to Luinedhel to examine Hathar. Leaning in, she spoke in a low, muted voice so that the others could not hear her. "Lady Shaal'Elonthra sent word through her network. I know of the Aetheling's quest, but the others do not, as it is a secret kept to only the Council's inner circle. The official word from the palace is that the Aetheling is missing, possibly abducted by the Th'arule or the Peytriad, so the entire kingdom is on high alert."

She looked at Luinedhel. Her icy blue eyes sparkled with an inner life – even here in the darkness. "I have not seen N'Khael or the Aetheling, but I know this is his Second. You are right, if we don't get him help, he will not be the Second for much longer."

She stood up and spun around, addressing the others in Wealdspeak. "This is the Aetheling's Second. I recognize him. *Taven'sanct* has been declared and the Aetheling's Second is hurt, perhaps in defending the heir from those who took him and seek him harm. We must get him back to Ny'we Adye with haste, for the truth of where the Aetheling is may lie in his very words."

"Sergeant!" Four of the Guard snapped to attention and stepped forward. They adeptly rolled the cleric onto a cloak, each grabbing a corner and, without another word, swiftly disappeared into the dark forest. Nightfall reached out a hand to help Luinedhel off the forest floor.

"They will travel swiftly," Nephinae said. "They know the woods and will ensure that your friend gets to the city as soon as possible. I don't know if it will be soon enough to save him. He looks to be at death's door." She bowed her head slightly. "It is nice to see you again, Thel Omaga, though we seem to only meet under desperate circumstances. You say N'Khael should be nearby with the Aetheling?"

"They were right in front of us," Luinedhel said. "Did they not pass this way?"

Nephinae shook her head. "We have not seen them, though there are other contingents patrolling the woods. Perhaps another has encountered them."

Luinedhel exchanged glances with Nightfall.

"I will retrace our path," the *drivrid* said. "The rains have slowed, but the storm will have erased most signs of their passing. It may be challenging to find their trail." He turned and nodded curtly to Nephinae. "Demestre Kydel, I will entrust you to ensure Thel Omaga reaches Ny'we Adye without harm."

Nephinae looked at Luinedhel and smiled. "I will guide him myself. If we cross paths with others, I will inquire about the Aetheling and the Protector. Meanwhile, my men will search for them." Nephinae turned to the remaining Green Guard and gave directions. They nodded and slipped into the forest silently.

Nightfall looked at Luinedhel. "I will find you in Ny'we Adye. I trust your safety to those of House Shaal'Elonthra." He flashed a glance at the wrapped scepter tied to Luinedhel's back. Luinedhel understood. Nightfall gave one last nod and disappeared back the way they had come.

"I am indebted to you, Demestre Kydel."

"Nephinae," she said. There was a softness in her voice that put him at ease. "Please, call me Nephinae, Thel Omaga."

"Luinedhel," he said. "Thel Omaga is so formal, and any friend of N'Khael is a friend of House Omaga. Please call me Luinedhel … or Thelo if you'd like. That's what N'Khael calls me."

She smiled. There was a look on her face that Luinedhel was unfamiliar with. Something between amusement and …

"Let us go," she said. "I don't have a mount. Will you walk with me?"

"Yes," he said. "Of course."

She seemed pleased with that answer. He took Aelduin's reins. "Lead on."

She turned and started into the forest. He followed.

This was not the return he had hoped for. He was separated again from Avanstel … and now without Nightfall or Hathar or N'Khael at his side.

But at least Nephinae was here, and if he couldn't have Avanstel or the others with him, she was as close as he could get to being with friends.

CHAPTER 30: WEODE

Nephinae led him through winding routes that seemed to manifest immediately in front of them. Several times, Luinedhel was certain there was no way forward, only to be surprised when Nephinae stepped to the left or right and a path would appear. He wondered if the trees were moving, opening a way before the Green Guard, or if the shadows of the forest were playing tricks with his mind. Regardless, without his guide, he would have immediately become lost, and the trip through Belkin Wood to Ny'we Adye would have been impossible. He wondered how long one had to travel the wood to know these strange paths with such familiarity.

The rain ended, but the night remained dark and cold and wet. Nephinae would randomly signal for them to stop. She would whistle a bird-like call, and an answer would echo back from a hidden location around them. Luinedhel found it hard to determine where the returning sounds were originating. They seemed to come from all around them. Each call was slightly different, an entire language in itself. He marveled at the complexity.

"Where did you learn to speak with bird sounds?" he asked.

She laughed. "They're not bird sounds – at least, not birds from Belkin Wood. They're signals used by the Green Guard. They taught them to us as part of our training."

"It's fascinating." He stepped over a large tree root and made his way around the enormous trunk, following behind her.

"It's not difficult to learn. N'Khael or I could teach you."

Thoughts of his sister raced through his mind. Where could she and Avanstel be? Nephinae looked at him with concern, as if she could read his thoughts. "She is a strong woman," she said. "One of the best amongst us. You need not worry Thel Omaga … Luinedhel. I have known her for almost her entire life, and she is more than capable of making it back to the palace on her own. She will bring the Aetheling to safety." She moved around another enormous tree and jumped over a small creek. She looked back over her shoulder to ensure he wasn't having trouble following her.

"How did you meet N'Khael?" He tugged on Aelduin's reins as the mare stopped to eat a tuft of grass. He didn't want to lose Nephinae in the forest.

"Ah," she said. "That is a story that I will let *her* tell you. I'm not sure she'd appreciate me sharing it without her permission." Her tone was light and playful. "I will tell you though, that she wasn't always an obedient child. She gave Lord and Lady Omaga many a grey hair over her behavior." She laughed. "Oh, it was so long ago, but I remember it like it was just yesterday. I grew up in Lady Shaal'Elonthra's home. I am from House Kydel, and our House has maintained an alliance with House Shaal'Elonthra for at least the last two thousand cycles. My parents believed an education with the Lady Shaal'Elonthra would help improve our House's place at court. So, when I was young, I traveled everywhere with the Lady and learned the ways of the palace and the court. Watch your step here."

He stepped to the side, avoiding a hole in the forest floor that was covered in dark shadow. Aelduin had already moved to avoid it.

"Did you have to memorize the lineage of House J'Onsal? Father would quiz me on it incessantly."

"Oh, yes! That and so much more. Because I was with the Lady as her ward, I was with her wherever she went. That included her visits to House Omaga. As you know, a strong alliance exists between our Houses."

"For that, we are grateful."

She raised an eyebrow and gave him a strange look. She opened her mouth to say something, but then changed her mind. "It is a beneficial alliance for everyone," she said formally.

Luinedhel frowned at the shift in her tone. Had he said something improper? He turned the conversation back to N'Khael. "So, you met my sister on your visits to House Omaga?"

"Yes, and we became close friends because of all the time we spent together. We are almost the same age. She, a decade older than me. And Lord Omaga sent N'Khael to be tutored alongside me. I believe he thought I would be a positive influence on his irrepressible daughter because I was demure and obedient, while N'Khael was more boisterous."

Luinedhel laughed. "I do not find that hard to believe. That sounds like my sister!"

"Oh, she is much better at following the rules now," Nephinae said. She smiled again. "Though she does like to break them when it suits her." She stopped and looked around the dark forest. "If we go this way, it's faster, but a little more challenging." She pointed to the right.

"I'm up for it. I'm eager to get back and find news of Avanstel and N'Khael."

"Very well." They headed in the direction she indicated and started up a steep, tree-covered hill.

Nephinae was right. The way was not easy. She seemed to sense his exhaustion, and they paused for a rest at the top of the climb. They sat across from each other, perched on large boulders that littered the forest floor. In the dim light, and in her Green Guard armor, the resemblance to N'Khael was strong. Aelduin lingered close by, finding grass to chew on.

"So, you joined the Green Guard together?" Talking with Nephinae took his mind off things, and she was easy to speak with. She seemed genuine and practical – something he had experienced little of in his dealings with other Weode.

"Well, that was N'Khael's idea." She took a drink from her canteen and passed it to him. "I think that instead of me rubbing off on N'Khael, she had more of an impact on me that either Lord Omaga or Lady Shaal'Elonthra expected. When she announced she wanted to join the Guard, I went too. We had grown so close over those decades that we became inseparable ... much to the disapproval of House Kydel. Father and mother wanted me to have a position at the palace someday, but they had thought it would be with the court, not in the Guard. They eventually forgave me, but I believe they still hold out hopes that someday I would be a Lady of a prestigious House with the favor of the Ade – not just a guardsman in the *service* of the Ade. Are you ready to continue?"

He nodded and handed the canteen back to her. "Lead on." He checked the strap tied around his chest and shoulders, confirming the weight of the scepter had not changed, and then gathered Aelduin's reins.

They walked through the rest of the night, talking as they circumvented large boulders and crossed streams. When they reached a clearing, Luinedhel could see that the storm clouds had dissipated, and the heavens were alight with stars. To the east, he could see the very first hint of the sun rising. It was spectacular. He looked up at the sky in wonder and then over at Nephinae, who was watching him curiously. When their eyes met, she looked away, but the smile remained on her face.

"The city is not far now," she said. "Maybe an hour more."

In the dim light, he could make out the remains of ruins around them, overtaken by shrubs and vines and other vegetation. He wondered what the Weode had built here and why they had abandoned it, and then considered that maybe others had built it to start with. Perhaps they were even the same people who had built Hemel. There was a serenity and calmness to the place. It felt almost sacred. He didn't want to disturb the moment, so he didn't ask about it as they passed by, leaving the ruins to their slow decay.

Eventually, the sun rose, and light filtered through the canopy above. He could spot several trees whose leaves were turning from their rich green color to a beautiful bright yellow. Fall had arrived at Belkin Wood. The trees around Chark turned color too, but they were less uniform; here it was almost completely yellow, with a few spots of brilliant orange or a tinge of red.

Aelduin nudged him from behind, looking for something to eat, but Luinedhel had nothing for her, so she nibbled a few leaves off the trees as they passed by.

"We are nearing the city," Nephinae announced. She paused, turning to look at Luinedhel. "You have kept good pace. I am impressed."

He smiled at her. "I am in your debt, Nephinae."

She shook her head. "You are N'Khael's brother, and she is like a sister to me. There is no debt."

"Well, I thank you, regardless. You made the journey pleasant."

Her cheeks turned a deeper shade of pink. "And you also, Luinedhel."

His neck felt warm. He cleared his throat and looked away. "Do you think Hathar – the Second – would have arrived by now?"

"He would have arrived sometime during the night. My men would have taken other paths impossible for us with your steed. Some ways are intentionally narrow so that only those on foot can approach the city. That allows us to monitor and control the comings and goings."

"I see."

"Do not worry. They would have taken him directly to House Shaal'Elonthra, and I'm certain the Lady would have called for the healers."

Luinedhel looked back over his shoulder at the way they had come and could not discern their path. He wondered again whether the trees had moved around them, flowing like a stream parted by a stone, or if Belkin Wood still contained a bit of *akan'gott* from the world's creation. How would Nightfall be able to find them?

"You are worried about your dark elf companion?"

How did she do that? She seemed always to know what he was thinking! He nodded. "Yes."

"The *drivrid* knows the way. I have seen him slip in and out of the city many times. Unnoticed by anyone other than me." She smiled wryly. In the morning sunlight and with a smile on her face, she looked very different from the taciturn N'Khael. There was a lightness about her that his sister did not have. He noted again the twinkle in her blue eyes that reminded him of the sparkle of the sapphire strapped to his back.

"Will you report this to the palace?"

"I serve the interest of the Weode," she said.

She hadn't answered his question directly, which he found interesting. "The Weode?" he asked. "You mean House J'Onsal?"

The smile evaporated, and she lowered her eyes. Her silence was answer enough – she was not blindly loyal to the Ade or his House. Her devotion was to her people – the Weode – regardless of who sat on the throne. He was similarly inclined and felt a connection with her immediately.

"Nephinae," he said. "I will need to see Lady Alle before going to the palace."

Her head snapped up and caught his gaze. "I … The Lady …"

Luinedhel met her eyes and did not flinch away. He spoke with measured words. "It is in the interest of the Weode."

She paused, and Luinedhel could see that she was reasoning it out in her head, trying to determine the best path and where her loyalties might lie. Finally, she nodded. "All right. I will take you to Lady Alle, but then I must report to my Lady … as is my duty."

"I understand. Thank you, Nephinae."

She looked at him, studying him silently. The silence between them lingered long enough to make Luinedhel uncomfortable. He became self-conscious, looking down at his clothing and brushing it off. He pushed back a strand of his dark hair from his eyes and looked back up at her.

The smile had returned to her face. "Let us go," she said. She started forward into the forest.

Luinedhel pulled on Aelduin's reins and followed.

As they were nearing the city, she paused and turned to him. "Luinedhel … I hate to ask … to suggest … but…"

"What is it?"

She hesitated. "We must not draw attention," she said. "For your own benefit, would you raise your cowl?"

"Of course," he said. "I am used to this."

She looked embarrassed. "I wish it were not so."

"It's all right, Nephinae. Thank you for your kindness."

She nodded and walked toward the city in silence. He stepped after her, Aelduin behind him, and soon they were at the edge of Ny'we Adye. Luinedhel left Aelduin at the stables, with instructions for the mare to have nothing but the best care — whatever the cost. The horse had served him well, and he was sure that N'Khael would allow the expense for one of Selyndar's favored horses.

True to her word, when they entered the city, Nephinae led him directly to House Alle. Though her route was unfamiliar, as convoluted and clandestine as his first visit had been with N'Khael, he recognized the front of the house immediately. He climbed the steps to the front door. As he raised his hand to knock, the door opened. T'Antalius greeted them, and they stepped inside.

"She awaits you in her workshop," the boy said to Luinedhel. He turned to Nephinae. "Will you attend? No? She thought not. Please convey Lady Alle's gratitude to Lady Shaal'Elonthra for bringing Lord Omaga safely to her home." He turned to Luinedhel. "Please follow me, Lord Omaga."

"Please," he said quietly. "I am not ready to take the place of such an amazing man as Lord Omaga. I am hardly worthy of being called Thel to his house, though to be called his son was an honor."

T'Antalius bowed in acknowledgement, and Luinedhel caught another brief and calculating look on Nephinae's face.

"I will leave you, Thel Omaga," she said. There was a twinkle in her eye. She found this amusing for some reason. While they had traveled, she had called him by his given name, Luinedhel, but here she was more formal. "I will deliver the report of your safety to the palace … and others who will want to know."

Luinedhel nodded. "I await your return."

Her eyebrows arched in surprise. "*My* return?"

"I assume the Lady will want to speak with me?"

A wry smile crossed her face. "Oh, yes, of course. As will others of the Council. I will return should she direct me. Otherwise, perhaps, I will see you at the palace, *Thel* Omaga."

She bowed and departed.

Luinedhel watched her leave. She was different from the other Weode he had encountered. More accepting of his mixed heritage, and there was something else there, too. She was … interesting. There was something about her, something he couldn't put his finger on.

T'Antalius ushered him through the entrance to the stairwell in the back and down into the protected workshop below. Seer Alle was sitting at a desk, her white eyes poring over a scroll unrolled in front of her, a fire crackling in the hearth, illuminating the entire workshop in warm orange light. She looked up as Luinedhel's foot left the last stair. "The wayward child returns! Oh ho! And with such a prize!"

Luinedhel had but a moment to look at her quizzically before a large, dark figure erupted from the shadows beside him and engulfed him. He pushed against the restraint for a second, unable to free his arms or reach his weapons, but then lit up in recognition and returned the embrace.

"Scorpio!"

The giant man broke the hold and stepped back, his dark stubbled face split by a white grin. He clapped his hands against Luinedhel's shoulders, and they placed their foreheads together. Luinedhel smiled. "It is good to see you have returned! So much has happened, and I've missed having you along."

The warrior grunted, and Luinedhel laughed.

"We should share stories. You go first. I'm sure you have a lot to tell me."

Scorpio laughed, a rare but not unwelcome sound from the usually silent man. It was a deep and rumbling sound, and infectious. He had really missed the warrior – more than he had realized.

"There is much to tell," the Seer said. "So much! Come, Thel Omaga, come. Show us this prize you bring. I can discern the powers radiating from it. So bright. So bright! I have not seen such in all my cycles." The Seer moved to a table nearby, shuffling its contents and clearing the space.

Scorpio squeezed Luinedhel's arm one last time and stepped aside. Luinedhel pulled the strap over his head and sat the scepter down on the table, carefully removing Nightfall's cloak. Based on the Seer's words, he expected there to be blue lightning racing over its surface, but the staff just lay there. A polished and beautiful *estrayaed* weapon, but with no trace of the brilliance that the Seer allegedly saw with her milky eyes … and no blue lightning.

She stepped back, gasping. "It is true, warrior. It is true! I would have never thought such things still existed. Never in thousands of cycles."

Luinedhel looked at the scepter sitting dully on the black cloak. He looked up at Scorpio and then back at Lady Alle. "There is more," he offered. "Nightfall and I retrieved it from the hand of the emperor. From the throne in the fallen city."

The Seer clapped her hands like a child. "Yes! Yes! This must be it! I saw something coming from far away once it had left the Barrens. Powerful magic must have hidden it there, protecting it from scrying and other means, or someone would have discovered it long ago. It still contains a power that prevents it from being understood or detected. I sensed something had been freed, but I didn't know what. It appears so small and insignificant; it wasn't until you stepped foot in my workshop and my wards diminished its magic, so it could be seen for what it is."

"*Eer'gott?*" Luinedhel asked.

"*Eer'gott* indeed! The lost magic! And oh, so powerful. So powerful!" She hovered over it, scanning it with her sightless eyes. Luinedhel noticed she did not touch it and kept her hands hovering above its surface.

"The dead king. Who was he?"

"The first king. The first emperor," she said.

"The first Ade?"

"No, no. Before the Weode. Before the Th'arule. The ancestors of the elven people. From before the line of J'Onsal. Little is known of them."

"The scepter was clutched in his hand. He was sitting on a crystal throne. The crystals had power in them. Even Nightfall had not seen such things. The emperor stood up and spoke and the scepter came alive with power … with blue lightning."

She gasped and clutched the amulet that she wore around her neck. Scorpio stepped back from the table at her reaction, his hand immediately going for his weapon.

"No, no," Luinedhel said. "It does nothing on its own. You must touch it, and perhaps recite these words here, engraved on the side of it, for anything to happen."

The Seer leaned toward it cautiously. "Touch it? Explain."

Luinedhel relayed his experiences with the sapphire weapon both in the throne room at Hemel and during the fight with the Urneans on the plains. The Seer peppered him with questions, and he answered them as best he could. At one point during the interrogation, she leapt from her stool and began scuttling about the workshop, pulling down books and scrolls from various cubbies and bringing them to the already overflowing table.

She turned to him. "And your blades? You still have them?"

"Yes."

"They are tied to this scepter." It was a statement, not a question, but he answered it anyway.

"I believe they may be." He explained how the lightning had sparked from them when they were near the scepter.

"Ha!" she exclaimed triumphantly. "The warrior has brought more information from the Library."

Seer Alle spoke of the place as if he should know what it was. Luinedhel looked at Scorpio, who only nodded in agreement, but offered no additional information.

"What is the Library?"

She stopped bustling about and turned to him, surprised by the question. "I thought you knew. No?"

He shook his head.

She glanced at Scorpio, shrugged, then turned back to Luinedhel. "It is a guarded secret. Perhaps I should have said nothing, but maybe it is good that you know. The Library may lie in your future."

Luinedhel frowned. Lady Alle spoke in riddles, like his blades. He looked at Scorpio again, hopeful for help, but the warrior, true to his nature, said nothing.

"Please explain," he begged.

She grimaced, sitting down again on the stool across from him, the scepter lying on the table between them.

"The Library of the Mystics sits in Q'Serath," she explained. "At the top of the Mountain of Woes. A hidden city, protected by powerful *akan'gott*. Yes, yes, *akan'gott*. It is one of the few places in Halbrun where the original power still flows. There are people there, the Mystics. They are called to the city … by the city. The place allows them to find the hidden ways and to enter, because they are chosen. Those who try to find Q'Serath will not unless the city wants them to. I, myself, have never been, but there are some …" She looked over at Scorpio. "Some who the spirits of Q'Serath have allowed in. And others …" She turned to Luinedhel, blank eyes scanning him. "… Like Lady Omaga, who they have not."

Luinedhel thought back to the conversation with N'Khael about her mother. She must have tried to scale the Mountain of Woes, to go to Q'Serath, and had not made it. He understood now why she did not like the mountains.

"The Library holds histories of Halbrun. Annals and journals, scrolls, and books, records as far as the eye can see. The Mystics have become the guardians of those histories and have taken up the job of keeping the account. They scry Halbrun with their tools and magical machines of *akan'gott*, seeing all from their perch on the Mountain, and they spend their time recording notable events of the lands. Nobody knows who the original Librarians were or for what purpose they recorded these histories, but the Mystics do it now. They say it's because that is what the city wants from them.

"I sent the warrior to learn about the blades. Hoping he could discover more about these strange *estrayaed* weapons."

She paused and then stretched out her hands to him. "Let me see them."

"You will need to cover your hands," he said, pulling out the leather gloves that Nightfall had given him. "They react when so close to the scepter."

"They will not react here," she said confidently. "My wards are strong and confound all magic. This is a safe space."

Luinedhel looked at Scorpio for confirmation. The fighter nodded in agreement, but Luinedhel hesitated. He had seen both the scepter and the blades alight with lightning, and was wary of unleashing that kind of power in such a close space. Trusting the Seer, he slowly withdrew Adesh and Marek. Their hilts did not conform to his grip like they usually did. And there were no sparks or lightning, as he had expected. Her wards *must* be powerful indeed! He flipped them over and handed them to her, grip first. They sat dormant in her hands.

"Look here," she said, sitting Marek down on the table and turning the empty inset in the pommel of Adesh toward him. "Curious, is it not?"

Luinedhel nodded. "I have thought so before."

"And now, look here," she said, placing Adesh down on the table in front of her and pointing at the top of the scepter near the large, brilliant sapphire. A thick *estrayaed* collar ran around the bottom of the gemstone, attaching it to the rod. Within the collar, placed opposite each other around the circumference, were two metal protrusions of the same size and configuration as the inserts in the daggers' pommels. Luinedhel straightened, his eyes wide in amazement.

"Aha!" she exclaimed. "As I thought. You see it too?"

"They look like they go together, but ..."

"But how? Maybe more importantly, why?"

A noise sounded from the stairway that led upward from the workshop.

"My apologies, for interrupting, Lady Alle." T'Antalius stood in the doorway, a serious look on his face. "The Green Guard is at the door. They are asking for Thel Omaga." He paused. "And what he has brought with him."

"The Thel will come immediately," she answered. The boy nodded and disappeared up the stairs.

The Seer draped Nightfall's cloak back over the scepter and tied the straps around it. She pushed the blades across the table at Luinedhel.

"You must go. You will need to deliver the staff to the Ade. There is no way to avoid it. He knows it is here." She placed the wrapped staff in his hands. "But the rest of what we have discussed, keep to yourself. We will learn more when we are able." She grabbed his arm and led him to the doorway. "I will send the warrior with you, and I will do what I can within the Council. For now, go with haste. Don't give the Ade reason to doubt your loyalty or be suspicious."

Luinedhel nodded. He climbed the stairs with Scorpio. An entire squad of Green Guards filled the main hall. There were many more than were necessary to escort him to the palace. Behind him, he heard Scorpio grumble in disapproval.

"Lead on," he said. He wanted to act before Scorpio could turn this into a confrontation.

The leader of the group nodded curtly, spun on his heels, and headed out the door. Luinedhel followed with Scorpio at his side. This time, he did not put his cowl up. It was time for Ny'we Adye to acknowledge his heritage – Omaga or otherwise. The Ade had summoned him directly to the palace. An *ort* – on his way for an audience with the Ade.

CHAPTER 31: DELVES

The audience with the Ade was held in the throne room. An entire contingent of the Green Guard accompanied Luinedhel, flanking him and closing off the entrance behind him. He thought it humorous that they thought he might even consider trying to escape. That was the last thing on his mind.

Scorpio shifted uncomfortably by his side. Luinedhel caught his eye and shook his head slightly. Whatever was going on, it was best not to start an altercation with the Guard. Their battle today would be with words, not swords.

Other Weode were present. Most he did not recognize. The two figures standing to the left of the throne he knew well: Lord Y'Vellian and Lord Kellendaer. As he entered, they whispered to each other, leaning close to conspire. The Seer and Lady Shaal'Elonthra were noticeably absent.

Dredaius sat on the large throne. Questelle stood at his right side, electing to vacate the smaller throne made for her. The wolves that made up the arms of the throne looked darker and more threatening than he remembered, as if they were ready to leap forward and devour him. The eyes of the wolf's head carved into the back of the chair glared at him. If the throne had been made to intimidate and cause fear, it was working. Luinedhel shuddered. He was in the wolf's den, and there was no escape.

The Ade looked pallid and perhaps a little sallow. He had dark circles under his eyes and was hunched over slightly, as if bearing a heavy weight. The last time Luinedhel had seen him in this place, Dredaius had been lively, arrogant, and confident — a man full of himself and his newly acquired power. In stark contrast, he now looked broken, somber, and exhausted with worry. The responsibility of protecting the entire kingdom and the legacy of the Weode had worn him down.

Questelle, however, was as Luinedhel remembered her. She looked at him, barely containing a sneer. Her eyes flashed with contempt, an anger that he did not understand. Did she hate the *ort* that much? He was barely worthy of her attention, so he didn't understand her vicious glare. Or was there something more to her intense dislike? It was as much as he could do to keep his expression calm as he reflected on their last meeting: the casual nature with which she had spoken of killing Danvaren, and how she had spat his name like a curse. His heart pounded in his chest, and his stomach knotted with the memory.

"*Sere'eden,*" he thought, and closed his eyes. He knew he needed to tread carefully. Selyndar was not there to help him navigate this, nor were his allies. He was on his own. Opening his eyes, he nodded politely to both Dredaius and Questelle and then dropped to one knee. Scorpio grunted beside him in disapproval but begrudgingly followed suit.

"I greet you, Ade and Adelyn," Luinedhel said. He kept his tone even and calm.

"My Champions tell me they found you in the southeastern part of the Wood with the Aetheling's Second, gravely injured." Dredaius spoke in a measured tone, neither accusatory nor overly friendly.

"This is true, my Ade. May I inquire of the cleric's state?"

"You may not!" Questelle shot. "Do not interrupt the Ade, *ort!* Do not speak unless he asks you to."

Luinedhel bowed his head respectfully. He caught a flicker of annoyance cross Dredaius' face as he looked at Questelle. The look spoke volumes. There was trouble between them. Something deeper was going on beyond Luinedhel's ken.

Dredaius cleared his throat. "What were you doing with the Second in that part of the kingdom? More precisely, do you know the whereabouts of the Aetheling and why the Second was not with him?"

Avanstel was still missing? How could that be? He had been with N'Khael when they had parted, and surely, she knew the way back to Ny'we Adye. He tried to focus his thoughts on the situation at hand and not get distracted with worry about his sister and his best friend.

Why had Dredaius called him into question in such a public forum? He was pressing Luinedhel into a challenging position. He dared not lie to Dredaius or be caught in a falsehood, but he didn't think revealing their mission publicly would please the Ade Gerent. They could have spoken privately, or even in the Council chambers, but he had chosen this place to ask about their mission with so many witnesses around.

"I do not know where the Aetheling is, my Ade. Though if he is in any danger, it is not by my hand, nor his Second's." He paused, then added, "If there is anything that my Ade could ask of me with regard to the Aetheling, or ensure his safety, my Ade has but to mention it, and I will immediately oblige." That was all true.

Dredaius sat back in his chair and folded his hands in front of him in his typical manner. He appeared satisfied with the response. The look on Questelle's face, however, showed she was not. She started to speak, but Dredaius held up a hand, cutting her off. She frowned at him and bit her lip.

"Thel Omaga, I return to the first question, what were you doing with the Second in the boot heel?"

Thel! So, the news of Selyndar's death had not reached the Ade. This was good news. Luinedhel thought for a moment. If he were to explain how he arrived with Hathar, their trip to Hemel and the fight with the Urneans, it would not only raise more questions, but questions that may require him to reveal the scepter in front of this large group of people … and that was something he would rather do in private with Dredaius.

He studied Dredaius and Questelle. The Ade was unreadable; he looked detached, though Luinedhel guessed that behind that passive look, he was pensive and quite engaged. Questelle narrowed her eyes and furrowed her brow. She glared at him. Luinedhel thought she looked like a predator, waiting for an opportune moment to pounce on her unwitting prey … like a wolf.

"My Ade," Luinedhel began, bowing lower. "In truth, we were seeking after the Aetheling, concerned for his well-being … as I am sure you are. We ran afoul of savage creatures, and Hathar, the Second, was injured in the skirmish. I was returning him to Ny'we Adye for aid." Again, all of it was truthful, none of it revealing their true quest.

The Ade nodded. Questelle's frown deepened.

"And what are your purposes now, Thel Omaga?"

"I would continue to seek after my friend, the Aetheling," he said. "With your permission, of course, my Ade."

"Of course." Dredaius stood up and addressed the room. "But before I dismiss you to that, I will have private words with you." Luinedhel caught another glance between the Ade and the Adelyn. Dredaius turned his attention back to Luinedhel. "I will reveal to you what we know of the events surrounding the disappearance of my brother, the Aetheling. To aid you in your quest to find him. Come now, to my chambers, and we will speak."

He descended the steps before the throne, and without pausing, he turned and disappeared through a door behind the dais. Questelle lingered a moment longer, scrutinizing Luinedhel. Her sharpened nails clicked on the side of the stone throne. The silence lingered in the air. Luinedhel kept his expression neutral, though he felt the pressure of Questelle's harsh gaze. *"Sere'eden!"* He tried to calm his breathing.

A guard stepped beside him and motioned for Luinedhel to follow Dredaius out of the room. He took a couple of steps toward the door. Scorpio began to follow.

"Just the *ort*," said the guard. He put his hand in front of Scorpio. Luinedhel saw the man's hand trembling. The contingent of Guards behind him gave him enough courage to challenge the warrior … just barely.

"Stay here, Scorpio," Luinedhel said. He turned around to look at his friend, exposing his back to Questelle.

When he turned around, he saw recognition on Questelle's face. Her gaze was fixed on the package strapped to his back. She snarled, descended from the dais swiftly and exited through an opposing door.

His heart sank. She knew he had the scepter. Nothing good would come of this.

Dredaius dismissed his guards, leaving the two of them alone in his private audience room. The room was dimly lit and decorated in emerald green and silver, the colors of the Green Guard and House J'Onsal. There were several rooms leading out from the main chamber, but Luinedhel could not discern their purpose.

The moment the door closed, the Ade turned to Luinedhel. The passive and disengaged look he had worn in the throne room disappeared immediately. He looked over Luinedhel's right shoulder where the top of the wrapped scepter rested.

"You found it." It was more of a statement than a question.

Luinedhel nodded. "We did."

"Show it to me." His concern for Avanstel had evaporated instantly. The scepter was the focus of Dredaius' attention.

Luinedhel hid his disgust. He lifted the strap over his head and placed the relic on the table in front of them. He untied it and parted the covering, revealing the silver-blue *estrayaed* staff with its sparkling sapphire gemstone on top. His eyes went immediately to the strange extrusions that the Seer had pointed out to him just an hour before. Could it be that the scepter and his daggers were part of the same weapon? That would mean his daggers were not Weode or Th'arule, but from the First People. Could they be that old?

"It's just as I was told," Dredaius said, snapping Luinedhel from his thoughts. "The destruction of the Th'arule is now within my grasp." He reached for the scepter. As he touched it, blue lightning sparked around his fingers. He jumped backwards, clutching his hand in pain.

"What deceit is this? You have placed a ward on it!" He looked at Luinedhel with rage.

"No, Dredaius … Ade … I assure you. I have done nothing of the sort. It is the power of the scepter. This is exactly how it was when we found it. The power is unlocked when your skin touches it. Here, take these." He proffered Dredaius the gloves that Nightfall had given him.

Dredaius stared at him and did not take the coverings. "Have *you* touched it?"

"No, not at all. Avanstel told me that only the descendants of Ni'Ilyan, House J'Onsal, could touch it and live. Anyone else would perish. I dared not touch it."

The Ade squinted at him. "Did *he* touch the scepter?"

Luinedhel shook his head. "No, my Ade. We retrieved it from the palace of Hemel, wrapped it in this cloak, and brought it to you. Not a soul has touched it since …"

"Since?"

He shifted uncomfortably before answering. "Since my *drivrid* friend took it from the hands of the awakened ruler."

Dredaius took another step back from the table. He looked at Luinedhel incredulously. "The emperor was still alive?"

"Not alive. He was animated, but the decay of his body showed he had been dead for many centuries. Perhaps the power of the scepter kept him bound to this world long past his time. Or perhaps it was the crystal throne. He was a wraith, a specter. Dead, yet not dead." Luinedhel shivered, remembering the encounter.

Dredaius's eyes were wide, though there still lingered a hint of doubt. He stepped toward the table, looking down at the beautiful but now inert staff. His voice was hushed, carrying with it a new appreciation for the magic within the relic. "I doubted the full truth of her stories. I know she's hiding something … but it seems in this, she speaks truthfully. This surely must be the Nwi'Diad! The scepter with which the First ruled his entire empire."

"Her?"

Just then, the door to the room burst open and Questelle entered, with two Green Guard behind her. "Apprehend this *ort*! Take him to the Delves and lock him there. As I told you, he brought a magical weapon to the palace to strike down the Ade Gerent. See here, he waits for a moment alone to attack. It is just as I had said. He is Peytriad!"

Luinedhel looked at her in confusion, and then at Dredaius. The Ade's stoic face had returned, noncommittal and detached. He nodded at the guard, and they stepped next to him and took his arms. Luinedhel stared at Dredaius in disbelief.

"But I —"

"Silence, Peytriad deceiver!" Questelle said. She turned to Dredaius. "Had I arrived but a moment later, I fear that the assassin may have harmed you. I noted the weapon strapped to his back as he exited the throne room. We will no doubt discover it is the same tool used to slay the Aetheling when we find his body. This Peytriad loyalist surely had the same ill end intended for you, my love." She stroked the silver pendant on her neck.

She turned to the guards holding Luinedhel. "Take his weapons and send him below! The warrior, too. We shall not allow any Peytriad, or their sympathizers, to go free. We must protect the Ade and the line of J'Onsal."

Luinedhel's arms were bound behind him, and his daggers removed. He held his breath apprehensively, expecting the blades to spring to life when the guards touched them. But there was no blue lightning, despite being in proximity to the scepter. They remained lifeless blades. He frowned. Why didn't they react to being held by the Guard when they were so close to the Nwi'Diad? Had the wards in the Seer's workshop damaged them permanently?

As guards escorted him from the room, he cast a last glance at Dredaius and received a blank stare. In the hallway, he saw Scorpio, his arms tied behind him in the same manner. Nephinae was beside him.

A guard held Scorpio's long blade awkwardly. It was an unwieldy weapon to anyone who didn't match Scorpio's stature. The warrior raised an eyebrow at Luinedhel, but the *ort* shook his head. They both knew that Scorpio could easily break free and take out the Guard before being overwhelmed, but to what end? Best to play this out and wait for N'Khael and Avanstel to return. They would not leave their friends to an unknown fate.

One of the guards shoved Luinedhel forward. He stumbled. Nephinae caught his elbow before he fell flat on his face. She helped him to his feet, leaning in and whispering in his ear, "Don't resist. Help will come."

He gave her a small, silent nod. She stepped back from him, not wanting to draw attention.

The guards led their prisoners through the winding labyrinth of the palace and down several flights of stairs. As they descended further beneath the palace, Luinedhel noticed that the stonework became rougher, less maintained, and a dank smell permeated the air. Making their way through several torch-lit passages deep below, they stopped at a large iron portcullis. Beyond the gate was darkness.

One of them produced a keyring, unlocked the gate, and swung it open. The other guards grabbed torches from the walls and lit them, as only darkness lay below in the bowels of the palace.

Luinedhel had completely lost his sense of direction by the time they had reached his cell. He wondered if they had taken a route intentionally designed to confuse escapees, or if the maze of passages, doorways, and stairwells simply resulted from a city built upon the ruins of another over millennia. In any case, should he free himself from his cell, it would be almost impossible for him to find his way to the surface.

A gate opened before him, and he was unceremoniously shoved inside. Rough stones, like those in the Undercroft, formed the walls of the small room. There were two straw pallets on the stone floor, a meager comfort for them. A small, shallow stream trickled along one side of the room. Luinedhel took it to be their source of water for both drinking and the removal of waste from their cell.

The guards moved to push Scorpio into the chamber, but he growled at them. They stepped back, and he willingly stepped over the threshold. The bars were closed and locked behind them. Without further word, they turned and headed back the way they had come, leaving the prisoners bound and taking the only source of light they had. Darkness enveloped them.

After the sound of their footsteps faded, Scorpio spoke into the darkness. "Are you alright?"

"I am. Are you?"

Scorpio grunted, which Luinedhel interpreted to mean that he was fine.

A weak voice came out of the darkness outside their cell. "Thelo? Is that you?"

Luinedhel stepped toward the voice and smashed into the doors of their cell. He felt the warm flow of blood from his forehead and his nose. "N'Khael? N'Khael, I'm here. We are here. Scorpio and I."

"Praise Enos you are safe! I thought for sure …" Her voice trembled.

"N'Khael, what is wrong? You don't sound right. Are you injured?"

There was a long silence.

"They ambushed us, Thelo. There were too many of them for me to fight alone, and it was dark. They … they took Avanstel … and I could not stop them. They overwhelmed me, though I fought … my injury from the fight with the Urneans has weakened me. It turned bad. And I could not …" He heard her voice crack, and he wanted more than anything to be there beside her to offer her comfort. "I am sorry, Thelo. I am so sorry."

"N'Khael, don't apologize. It wasn't your fault."

There was only silence.

Luinedhel felt Scorpio step beside him. "Did you see who your attackers were?" His deep baritone echoed through the darkness. He spoke so seldom, his gentle eloquence always took Luinedhel by surprise.

"It was her," the quavering voice answered from the darkness. "Questelle. Questelle and her followers – the Peytriad. I saw their mark. She's their leader. She's here in Ny'we Adye to destroy the throne and erase the line of J'Onsal. It's been her all along."

A pause.

"And she killed my father ... our father. By her own words, she confessed to it – even gloated over it." Another pause. "And she meant to kill you too, brother."

Luinedhel stepped backwards, leaning against the wall, and sank to the floor. Questelle had taken so much ... Danvaren, Selyndar, and now she had Avanstel. And who knows what she intended for him! Even Dredaius was under her control – either by threat or counsel or some other power. Stinging tears of anger, loss, and frustration welled in his eyes.

He heard Adine's voice in his mind, coaching him again. *"Sere'eden,"* she was telling him, encouraging him toward peace, control.

He did not want any of it. Questelle had taken too much from him. He let loose his tears.

He would find a way to stop her.

CHAPTER 32: BROTHERS

He woke to darkness, the same inky blackness that he had left. Nothing had changed except that his arms were free. The ropes must have slipped off while he slept. He felt tingling in his hands, like the tingling he felt when the daggers were near the Nwi'Diad. He looked down and saw the blades. But how …?

Then he saw the dark flower before him, unfolding over and over and calling him in that strange language. Four bands spun around it, glowing with blue runes. The fifth ring lay dormant on the floor; the light faded from the strange symbols. Then suddenly, there was an ear-splitting crack, as if lightning had struck next to him. The flash of light was so bright it blinded him. He shielded his eyes and turned his head away.

There was a lone voice whispering in his ear, speaking the foreign tongue that he only heard in his dreams. "Vengeance has corrupted her. We must stop her."

Then a low moan that became a howl of pain. He clasped his hands over his ears and grimaced at the sound of the horrible cry. It died slowly. The wail lasted longer than any mortal being could sustain.

When he opened his eyes again, he saw the undulating blossom before him, the rings spinning around it. One ring, however, wobbled off its axis, the etchings on its surface now dull and faded. It spun slower than the remaining three, and as it rotated around, Luinedhel could see there was a crack in the band that hadn't been there before.

The voice whispered in his ear once more. "She is coming to destroy you. Destroy you all. And she will not fail. Woe. Woe to the children of the shifter and the children of the realm. Woe to all."

He gasped and opened his eyes. He was back in the Delves, the dungeon beneath the palace. His hands were still bound. He could hear the trickling of water from the stream that ran through their cell.

"Scorpio?"

"Dreams?" The voice came out of the darkness from his right.

He exhaled. "Yes. Again."

The warrior did not respond.

"N'Khael?"

She did not answer. He called again, and this time her voice came from the darkness, but it was weak. She was fading. "Hang on, sister. Nephinae told me help would come. She won't leave us here."

"She won't. If she can find her way here, she will come."

"Do you think she knows where we are?"

There was a long silence before N'Khael answered. "The Delves are dark and deep. There are many passages and rooms down here. And we are far below – in the oldest parts of the palace. I don't think many have come here, maybe in thousands of cycles. It may take her time to find us, but she will come. She is a sister to me. She will not leave us."

Hours passed, but none of them could tell how many. Perhaps it was days. The passage of time was impossible to gauge without the natural cycle of day and night. Here, there was just inky black, unending darkness – not even the faded illumination from fungi like there had been in Caerbexsys. They slept and woke and slept again several times. N'Khael, when she spoke, sounded weaker as time passed.

"I don't know what else to do," Luinedhel whispered into the darkness.

"Perhaps it's best that she rests," Scorpio answered.

"She needs help. Soon."

Scorpio grunted in agreement. "The rope is *retten*. It's elven, and they tied it well. And the bars are Weode metal. Beyond my strength to break."

Luinedhel exhaled and leaned back against the wall. "I know."

More time passed.

He drank from the small stream that ran through their cell, trying to ignore the pangs of hunger running through his gut. No guards came to bring them food.

As he sat in the darkness with his thoughts, he wondered where Avanstel was and whether he was safe. He reflected on his vivid dreams. They were connected – always through that unknown language, and always with darkness and dread. But it was nothing he could make sense of, and he had never had these visions before he left Chark – before he saw the fearful carvings in the Shadow Gate. Yes, he had had bad dreams before, but not like this.

More hours passed, and still nobody came to check on them or bring food. Those who had placed him here with Scorpio must have been the same ones to bring N'Khael here. They knew the way and could have stored him in many other cells. What had persuaded these Weode to imprison the Thelyn – Lady – Omaga?

The Weode were deceitful, and distrustful and even wicked, but N'Khael was a Green Guard, and a Lady of a Founding House.

Surely, there was at least a shred of decency amongst them; something that might pass for honor here in the elven realm.

But still, no one came as the hours spun by.

"Why N'Khael?" Luinedhel asked into the darkness. "She has done nothing but to protect Avanstel. You and I are outsiders, dispensable. And I am *ort*, so I understand that. But not N'Khael."

"Questelle has gained their obedience," Scorpio answered. "Either through promises, or bribes, or threats. Perhaps to their family, or to their lives. There are many places in the realm where injustice and darkness are common, but none I have seen more than in Ny'we Adye."

Luinedhel thought about that for a long time. Nightfall talked about how darkness and light often coexist. And Luinedhel had hoped that Avanstel would bring light to the darkness of the Weode … but perhaps it was too much to hope for, too much to put on the shoulders of one man. Perhaps the corruption of the Weode was beyond fixing; it was just part of their blood, their *accentation*.

"Then why hasn't she just killed us all? Why keep us alive?"

"*That* is the question," Scorpio said.

Time passed. The three of them spoke little. Scorpio, because that was his nature. N'Khael lacked strength, her vigor fading. And he, because there was little to say other than speak of the anger that continued to grow inside of him, the dread of what fate awaited Avanstel, and Hathar, in the wicked world far above them.

He was on the verge of giving up hope, figuring that Nephinae had also met an unkind or untimely end at the hands of the Adelyn, when there was a distant sound of footsteps.

"Do you hear it?" he said.

"I do. There are two of them. One in armor. The other is not."

Luinedhel didn't wonder how Scorpio was able to discern such things from such distant sounds. The warrior just knew.

"N'Khael. Someone is coming," Luinedhel said into the darkness. There was no response. He felt his heart pounding in his chest. "N'Khael?" He said louder, his voice cracking.

"Thelo?"

"Sister, someone is coming." He heard movements in the darkness coming from her direction. At least she was still alive. He exhaled in relief.

He made his way to the front of their cell. Scorpio did the same.

"How long do you think we've been down here, Scorpio?"

"Hard to tell." The warrior shifted uncomfortably. Between the tone of voice and his restlessness, Luinedhel could tell that it was taking a significant amount of effort for Scorpio to remain calm. He was used to sleeping under the stars and roaming free, not being locked in a dungeon to waste away.

"Take heart, friend," Luinedhel said. "We still have allies above. Surely someone will come."

Scorpio grunted.

Minutes passed as they listened to the footfalls in the darkness growing closer. Luinedhel heard them coming in their direction, winding through the labyrinthine passages of the prison. Eventually, he could make out two distinct voices, but he couldn't hear what they were saying.

"It must be Nephinae," Luinedhel said. "But who is with her? Can you tell if it's Avanstel or Nightfall?"

"No. It's not Nightfall." Scorpio's answer was definitive, delivered with heaviness and something akin to dread. Although he spoke little, the tone was unusual for the warrior. He couldn't quite place the emotion it carried. Was it relief? Hope? Anger? Concern? Scorpio didn't elaborate, and Luinedhel knew that even with prodding, the warrior wouldn't offer much more.

He waited at the bars and soon he could discern enough variance in the blackness to know that their visitors carried a light with them.

"Shield your eyes," a voice called. It was Nephinae. "Your sight will take a moment to adjust."

Luinedhel felt relieved. He closed his eyes and, through his shut lids, he saw the patterns of red and flashes of phosphenes. He heard their visitors pause outside their cell, waiting.

"Nephinae? I was —"

"I'm sorry it took so long," she said. "The palace is in an uproar, and everyone is in a frenzy. The Ade has assembled an army, and we are marching to the Idar on the morrow. Between that and my responsibilities for the Lady, it was a while before I could break away to find you. And when I did, it took me ages to comb through the dungeons. I didn't know this part of the Delve was still in use."

"How long have we been here?"

"Almost four days now."

"N'Khael," he said. "She's in a cell nearby."

The light source moved a little, dimming slightly, and he heard Nephinae move away from their cell. He eased his eyes open, adjusting to the blinding brilliance of the torch. As his vision focused, he was able to make out the shape of Nephinae. She was squatting against the wall of the cell a little further down the passage, across from his own.

"N'Khael?" she called.

There was no answer.

Luinedhel saw Nephinae stand up quickly and heard the jingle of keys and then the sound of a lock being loosed. She handed her torch to the other figure standing nearby and disappeared into the blackness of the cell across from them. There was a sharp gasp, and Luinedhel's heart fell. N'Khael was dead!

He pressed against the gate. "Nephinae! Nephinae! What is it?"

"It is not her." Her voice echoed back from the dark cell. He heard her armor moving, and then she stepped back into the light. Her face was pale, and she looked as if she were about to vomit.

"What is it?" Luinedhel asked. Concern tinged his voice.

"Bodies," she said. "Like we heard about in the Council chambers. Eight of them, by my count. Shriveled and blackened in unnatural ways."

"Why would they be here?"

She shook her head. "I don't know. As I said, nobody uses this place. Maybe they have been here a long time, but …"

"N'Khael?"

"No, she's not one. I am certain of that."

"Then maybe the next cell?"

She moved to the next cell, unlocked it, and disappeared into the darkness inside. Luinedhel watched apprehensively. The moments passed, but they felt like an eternity.

"She's alive," Nephinae said. "Barely."

"You must help her!" Luinedhel said. "She can't die here. She can't die at all!"

Nephinae appeared in the doorway and crossed over to his cell. "I won't let her die, Luinedhel. No matter if it means my own life, I will take her from this place and get her the help she needs."

The figure next to her cleared their throat. Luinedhel had been so focused on Nephinae and N'Khael that he had ignored the other person with her up to that point. Nephinae nodded. "You have a visitor, warrior. He convinced me to bring him here, but we had to do so in secret so those above do not know of his arrival or his purposes."

She stepped back from the gate.

In the dim light of the torch, Luinedhel could make out the man's features. He bore a striking resemblance to Scorpio. They both had the same raven-dark hair, dark skin, and strong jawlines. The man smiled slightly – it was the same smile that Scorpio had.

"It's good to meet you finally," the stranger said. His voice was deep and with the same accent as the warrior's. Luinedhel looked again at Scorpio, an eyebrow raised quizzically. Scorpio did not offer an explanation.

"My apologies," the stranger said, stepping toward the cell. "I should have introduced myself. I can see from your confusion that Zuralion hasn't spoken of his past." He chuckled, looked at Scorpio and shook his head. "Though that doesn't really surprise me much." He bowed to Luinedhel. "My name is Hythorn. As you may have surmised, Zuralion is my brother. Though I believe he prefers to be known as 'Scorpio' now." A smile tugged at the corners of his mouth.

"Have you come to free us?" Luinedhel asked.

"Unlikely," Scorpio stated bluntly, and turned away from the bars.

A pained look flashed across the stranger's face as he watched his brother retreat into the cell and lean against the far wall. Hythorn turned to Luinedhel. "I am a Librarian."

Luinedhel looked at him blankly.

Hythorn cleared his throat and continued. "I am sorry. I see that you don't understand." He looked at Scorpio disapprovingly. "Let me start at the beginning."

Luinedhel was becoming annoyed. "We don't have time for stories. We need to escape."

Hythorn bowed his head and took a deep breath. "I understand. Let me explain. I am a Librarian at the Library of the Mystics, in Q'Serath where my four younger brothers and I have served for over one hundred cycles."

Luinedhel peered intently at the man. There was no hint of elven heritage that he could discern, no signs of *accentation* running through his blood. There were those of the *ort* whose elven heritage was less prominent, but there were no half-breeds who escaped the telltale signs of their elven blood and appeared fully human.

Hythorn was most definitely human – and so was Scorpio. He looked at the warrior, and saw what he always saw: Scorpio was a muscled, rugged man in his mid-thirties, scarred from battles, and with a few wrinkles that showed around his eyes when he smiled.

He was incredibly fit, definitely human, and definitely not over a hundred cycles old.

"Is this a deception? Are you in league with Questelle?" His voice rose.

He sensed Scorpio step up behind him. "This is no deception, friend. My brother speaks the truth." He looked at Hythorn. "I did not tell him of my past, nor of my recent visit. He doesn't know that the Seer sent me to Q'Serath to find out more about the blades."

Luinedhel looked at Scorpio. "You went to Q'Serath?"

The warrior nodded.

"And you *are* over a hundred cycles?"

He nodded again. "There are mysteries still about Q'Serath that even the Librarians do not fully understand. And one thing that has yet to be fathomed is that while you remain within the city, you do not age — or if you do, it's imperceptibly slow. Those who live in Q'Serath outlive even the elves."

It was more than Luinedhel could understand, but he trusted Scorpio, so he took him at his word. "Then why did you leave?"

"The Librarians have an oath. It is at the core of their beliefs, their first directive. We are allowed, even required, to record the events in Halbrun, but we cannot interfere with them. Fate and history must be allowed to take their course. We … they assume that those with access to the Library, the first Librarians, may have caused a past disaster by intervening in events in Halbrun. Perhaps even the very thing that brought the downfall of the First People. Therefore, they strictly prohibit interference."

Scorpio's tone shifted, and Luinedhel again sensed the tension in the air. "So, they scry. They observe and record the events of the world in their journals and tomes, from the safety of their mountaintop. They note the pain, the suffering, the tragedies, the devastations, the wickedness, and corruption and deceit. Disconnected and silent observers of all the injustice of the realm, never taking action to ease the despair. Forbidden to do so."

Luinedhel saw another flash of sadness cross Hythorn's face as he looked down at his feet, not challenging his brother's words.

"A long, possibly eternal life. Safe from the dangers of the world," Scorpio said. He paused. Sadness tinged his voice as he continued. "That may appeal to some, but it was not for me. The things I saw as a Librarian enraged me, and I could not continue to stand by and do nothing. I left Q'Serath to see what I could do to right some of the wrongs. To free the enslaved and battle the corruption I spent cycles recording."

He approached the bars again, and Hythorn met his gaze. Luinedhel watched the brothers, so like each other, but also so different. Something passed between them, and when Scorpio spoke again, his tone was softer. "I am assuming you are not here to free us. No, I thought not." His words were not angry but colored with an echo of disappointment.

"You are here on Library business? Coming to Ny'we Adye is dangerous. You are at risk. You know the kingdom here is not stable." He motioned around the cell, indicating their current state. "You must have something important to share. What news do you bring, Brother? Is it about the invasion of the Weode kingdom? The Librarians wouldn't allow you to interfere with these events, I know that. Unless … did you get leave from Octar, or are you here without his blessing?"

Hythorn looked up. Once again, their resemblance amazed Luinedhel. Though Scorpio was slightly taller and much more muscular, there was no denying that they were brothers.

"Octar *sent* me, Zee."

Scorpio's eyes widened, and he stepped back from the bars. "It must be important. He wouldn't allow you to break the oath without cause."

Hythorn nodded. "It is the Nwi'Diad."

"The scepter," Luinedhel said, remembering the words Dredaius had used.

"And the blades," Hythorn added.

Scorpio approached the gate again. "What is it, brother? You have discovered more? I knew there was more to the Nwi'Diad! What did Pedron find?" Scorpio's face lit up, and excitement filled his voice. Luinedhel found himself amazed at the transformation. Gone was the silent, taciturn warrior who would only occasionally offer a grunt in response to a question, even when prodded for more. He was now an animated, intelligent, and curious man ... a man who had once been a Librarian, and now a warrior.

"After you left," Hythorn said, "Pedron took his findings to the Heads of the Order for consultation. They agreed that the scepter and the blades warranted a special investigation into the archives. What they found there was confirmation that the relic is *eer'gott*, and so few of those items are still in existence. Because of that, we took the information to Arcanist Nuyora. He and Zon-Ar met to review what Pedron discovered."

He paused, shifting back and forth on his feet. Scorpio placed both his bound hands on the bars and leaned closer. "If the Nwi'Diad has caught the attention of the Stone Wardens, there must be more to tell. What is it? What do we need to know?"

"It's not the scepter nor the blades, Brother," Hythorn said. "It's not just the Nwi'Diad that has brought me here." His voice lowered, though there was nobody else nearby who could hear him. "It is the sapphire that rests atop of the staff. They believe it to be another Stone, maybe the first one. Older than both the Opal and the Hematite."

Scorpio whistled and stepped back from the bars. "It is a Stone?"

Luinedhel looked at Scorpio, confused. "What does it mean, Scorpio?" he asked.

Scorpio turned to Luinedhel. "I'm sorry. This must sound like riddles to you. Let me explain what I can, as we truly know little about the Stones. Currently, there are two other Stones in existence.

Octar, Arcanist Nuyora, is the Warden of the Hematite, and Zon-Ar the Opal.

"The first stone discovered was the Opal. Zon-Ar, the first Chief Librarian, found it when we came to Q'Serath. Then Octar, the current Arcanist, found the Hematite sixty cycles later. Pedron, our brother, has a bit of an obsession with the Stones, and he believes there are more Stones in Halbrun, but that was just a theory … until now."

"The stone on the scepter? What does it do?"

"The Wardens believe the stones are amplifiers. Somehow, they channel the innate abilities of those who wield them and intensify them … maybe to unknowable limits. Those possessing a Stone may have immense powers, perhaps even powers that could destroy all of Halbrun. Since the Opal and the Hematite are in Q'Serath, and the Wardens are bound by the Librarian oath to not involve themselves in the happenings in Halbrun, the realm has not been in danger from either of the wielders of the Stones. But a Stone in the hands of someone out here in Halbrun, someone not under the Oath, could have unforeseeable consequences. Possibly changing the course of history itself."

Luinedhel's head was spinning. Giving extensive powers to Dredaius and Questelle most definitely could change the entire realm, far beyond the consequences of this alleged invasion by the Th'arule.

And he had delivered this weapon directly into their hands.

He fell against the stone wall of the cell and sank to the floor. What had he done? What could he do to rectify it? There was much more at stake now than the lives of his friends, N'Khael and Avanstel and Hathar. The fate of the entire Weode people, maybe all of Halbrun, was at risk. If Questelle had that much power, she would be unstoppable, and who knew what her true intentions were. He leapt up, crossed to the gate and grabbed a bar with his bound hands.

"You must free us! We have to stop her!"

Hythorn opened his hands before him in a motion of helplessness. "Master Arracnoth, please understand, I am bound by the Oath. I cannot act. Were it not for the direction of the Wardens, and these unique circumstances, I would not even be here."

Luinedhel clenched his fists tightly around the door's iron bars and shook them. "But don't you understand? N'Khael needs help, and we have to get out so we can stop Questelle and Dredaius!"

Scorpio placed his bound hands on Luinedhel's shoulder. "He understands. That is why he is here. He cannot do more." He turned to Hythorn. "Thank you, brother, for coming."

Hythorn nodded. "If it is within my power, Zee, I will always be there for you. You know that we all watch you, Calessio most of all."

Scorpio nodded. His eyes were moist. "Tell the littles that I bid them well and look forward to the day when I can share meals with them again. Even Artesh … I mean, Zon-Ar."

"I will, Zuralion." Hythorn turned to Nephinae. "Thank you for bringing me here. It was not by chance that I found you, and not by chance that you brought me here. You have heard what is at stake. Do what you must, now that you know."

She nodded and immediately withdrew the keys from her belt. She fumbled with them for a moment, found the correct key, and unlocked their cell. The door swung inward, making a terrible screeching sound as it moved. Scorpio stepped out of the way and motioned for Luinedhel to exit first.

As he stepped out of the cell, Luinedhel breathed deeply. The air in the passageway did not differ from that of their cell, but it somehow seemed to fill him with a feeling of freedom. Nephinae's hands worked over the knots on his bindings and freed him, then she turned to the *retten* that bound Scorpio.

Luinedhel crossed swiftly to N'Khael's cell and disappeared into the darkness. He returned moments later with his sister in his arms. She was frighteningly pale, ghostly, and almost translucent in the wavering torchlight. And lighter than he expected. Luinedhel could see red streaks beneath her pale skin, running from her forehead and down to her neck. They were from injuries she had received in the battle with the Urneans.

"We have to go, now. She's not well."

Scorpio nodded. He was back to the silent warrior that Luinedhel was familiar with. Gone was the excitable scholar. It had been interesting to see a different side of him, to get a peek into who the man was. He would have to ask the giant more about his time in Q'Serath, and the Library, and his brothers, when time permitted.

He turned to Nephinae. "Can you lead us out?"

"Yes, follow me. Few know the way."

The fair-haired elf turned toward the passage from which she and Hythorn had arrived. He turned to follow her, his eyes lingering a moment on the dark space across from them where Nephinae had reported she had seen the bodies. Was that the fate that awaited them? Was that why they had been kept alive? For some horrific purpose?

He looked back over his shoulder and saw Scorpio and Hythorn embracing. Whatever philosophical differences existed between them, they were brothers, and the bond of family was a hard one to break.

His gaze shifted to his sister. Her eyes fluttered open momentarily, and she smiled weakly in recognition, and then closed her eyes again.

She was his family. All the family he had.

He refused to let this be how it ended.

CHAPTER 33: LORD

Nephinae led them back through the maze of corridors, stairwells, and doorways, up and out of the Delves. Luinedhel could not determine if they were retracing the route that had taken them to their cells or if she was taking them a new way, but regardless, he was grateful she was their guide. He wondered how they might conceal themselves and escape the palace once they emerged from the Delves, but getting out of the dungeons was the first obstacle.

As they entered a long, narrow corridor that was lit at regular intervals from a dim light above, Nephinae extinguished the torch. It took a moment for their eyes to adjust to the soft illumination, but they did not stop moving forward. Luinedhel brushed against the wall to steady himself, and felt the chilly dampness of the stone penetrating through his tunic. The moist air coming in from above mixed with the smell of mildew and rot. As they made their way down the passage, he realized they were in a storm sewer, and the light shining into the tunnel was that of Relos and Eyama through the grates of the storm drains. He exhaled in relief. They were near the surface.

Nephinae paused beneath one of the grates.

"House Omaga is nearby," she whispered. "This is as close as we can get through the tunnels. They turn away and run in the opposite direction from here. I will lead Librarian Elliot up and out near the edge of the city so that he may return to Q'Serath, and then I must return to the palace as swiftly as possible. The Guard could be looking for me by now."

"Are you sure you shouldn't come with us?" Luinedhel asked.

"No," Nephinae answered. "I must return to the palace and take my place with the army. I am at risk now, being absent for so long, and the longer I am gone, the greater the chance of being noticed. If they discover your escape, they may start an investigation. That will prompt questions, and my absence will raise suspicions. You must go now. I will send word to the Lady about the bodies and the Nwi'Diad and the Stone. She will assuredly take what action she can to determine the connection between them all and what the Ade and Adelyn have planned."

"All right," Luinedhel agreed. A moment passed in silence as they listened for noise from above. Hearing none, Scorpio placed a leg on either side of the narrow tunnel and pushed himself upward toward the ceiling. He grunted as he placed his back against the grate and lifted it carefully, pushing it to the side. He looked down at the group and nodded to Hythorn. "Until next time, Brother." He breathed out into the frosty night air, his breath turning to mist.

"Wait, Zee. I almost forgot. This is for the nether-elf. Please give it to him." The Librarian passed a metal-plated book to the warrior. The silver glinted in the dim light. "I think this is the volume he's been looking for."

It caught Luinedhel's eye as it passed before him. There were strange figures carved into the surface that reminded him of those on the Shadow Gate. He had seen a book like this before ... in his dreams, but also ... somewhere else. Where?

Scorpio nodded and placed the book into his belt, then disappeared up the hole. A moment later, his face appeared in the darkness above them. "Hand her up to me."

Luinedhel raised N'Khael up. Scorpio caught her under the arms and lifted her through the opening. She woke momentarily, looking around in confusion. Her pale face was surrounded by matted red hair, and her eyes looked tired and drawn. Luinedhel turned to Nephinae once N'Khael was through.

"I know you will say this is nothing, but I find myself in your debt yet again," he said.

She flung her arms around him in a gesture that surprised him and hugged him tightly. "Take care of our sister, Thelo." She dropped the embrace and pulled away. "And take care of yourself … please."

Luinedhel didn't know how to respond. Her actions had caught him off guard.

His confusion amused her. She smiled and then turned to Hythorn. "Let's go." They turned and disappeared back through the tunnel, leaving Luinedhel to stare after her.

"Are you coming?"

Luinedhel looked up to see Scorpio's thick forearm reaching down for him. He grasped it, and the warrior lifted him up onto the street. He immediately went to N'Khael and picked her up off the cobblestones as Scorpio replaced the grate. N'Khael felt cool to the touch, which concerned him. He leaned in and could still sense her breath, though it was shallow and slow. He looked at Scorpio with urgency. "We have to get her to House Omaga fast. And she needs medicine."

Scorpio ducked into the shadows at the side of the street. Luinedhel followed close behind. Since both moons were up, there was sufficient light to see by as they navigated their way. But this also meant anyone walking down the street could see them just as easily. They remained in the darkness as much as they could until they reached Selyndar's home ... *his* home.

They opened the iron gates and stepped briskly across the portico. Anafelen had bolted the massive entry doors shut, as was customary. Scorpio banged his hands against the entry doors, and they waited for a response from inside. Luinedhel looked down at N'Khael and felt the urgency well up in him again. *"Sere'eden,"* he reminded himself, slowing his own breathing.

Anafelen appeared moments after they knocked. Their presence startled him, and the sight of N'Khael limp in Luinedhel's arms shocked him even more. He swung the door open and hastily ushered them inside. They strode swiftly down the length of the main entry hall, ignoring the stairs to the private quarters. Instead, Luinedhel carried N'Khael directly to the library and laid her down gently on the leather sofa there. He directed Anafelen to stoke the fire and to bring blankets and tea.

"What I wouldn't give for some of Hathar's foul-tasting medicines right now," he said to himself absently, wondering for a moment where the cleric was and how he was faring.

"I will fetch the Seer," Scorpio said and turned toward the doorway.

"Scorpio, you must remain hidden. You are supposed to be imprisoned. You're accused of being a conspirator with a Peytriad and an attempted assassin of the Ade. If someone spots you, Nephinae will be at risk."

"I will avoid detection," he said. He turned away before Luinedhel could argue further.

Anafelen returned with blankets and warm tea. Luinedhel made N'Khael as comfortable as possible and coaxed her to drink the tea, though it seemed almost impossible for her to swallow. She opened her eyes for a moment.

"Thelo? Where are we?" Her voice was thin.

"We are home, Sister. At House Omaga. Scorpio has gone to fetch the Seer. Help is coming." He grabbed her hand and patted it. "Stay with us."

She placed her hand against his cheek. "Thelo, our father was right."

Luinedhel frowned. "Right about what?"

N'Khael smiled weakly. "He saw things in you. Things others cannot see. You have the heart of an Omaga. He was right to bring you into the family."

"It is an honor, sister. It is a blessing to carry the name. Our name."

"Brother, if I don't make it …"

"Don't speak like that, N'Khael. I don't know anyone stronger than you, more determined. Maybe even a little stubborn."

She shook her head.

"You will fight, right? You are going to keep fighting. I need you to keep fighting," he said to her, urgency in his voice.

"For you. But if I don't make it, I want you to know that father would be so proud of you. You must carry on his legacy – uphold the ideals of House Omaga. Continue the battle."

"I will."

"Promise me, brother. Promise me you will work to set right the wrongs. Like an Omaga would – like father would."

He placed his hand on hers. "Of course, but that's enough of this talk. The Seer will come with her medicines. Scorpio has gone to fetch her. I'm sure she will help. She helped me, and kept me from the gates of Parvanor. She'll do the same for you."

She nodded her head slowly; her eyes fluttered again. "So many things I need to tell you, Thelo. I haven't had the time. So many things you need to know."

"You'll tell me when you're better, N'Khael. We have time. Look, here's the Haven Chase board. You have yet to beat me. And I will let you be the white wolf, or the white sword, or even the dark horse … whatever token you want." It sounded ridiculous upon reflection, but he was grasping at anything that might give her a reason to continue to fight until Lady Alle came and brought the medicines.

Her smile trembled. She took several breaths before she continued. "In the chapel, there's a hidden door. And upstairs, in the south wing, you need to know about the secret rooms and the treasury. And even here – in the library – that bookshelf opens to Father's hidden study. Thelo, there's so much more to tell you." Her voice was getting weaker even as her words grew more urgent. She clutched his hand desperately. "I think … I think …"

Luinedhel looked desperately toward the dining room, hoping that Scorpio's figure would appear there with the Seer at his side, but the doorway remained dark.

"And the Arcana Sephyrie," she said. "He was right …"

"Shhhh," he said. "Just rest, N'Khael. Save your strength."

She moved her hand to her head, touching it gently. "I … I'm having trouble, Thelo. I'm not sure I …"

Luinedhel placed his hand over hers. "N'Khael, stay with me. Fight. You're a fighter, a strong one. Fight, now. Just hold on a while longer." His throat was tight, tears pricking his eyes. "The Seer will give you medicines. She saved me from the poisons; she can save you! Just fight! You're strong, you're a warrior. Fight!" His voice was desperate, and he felt panic rising in him. Even *sere'eden* would not send it away.

"Thelo." Her eyes shut, and her voice was almost a whisper now. "I'm not sure how much more I can …"

"Fight, N'Khael!" His voice cracked, and a hot tear rolled down his face. "I need you, Sister. I can't do this alone. We need to do this together."

He felt her squeeze his hand gently. Her breath came slowly. Her voice was almost inaudible. "Not … alone … Brother."

He rubbed her hand, squeezing it again. Tears were flowing freely down his cheeks, landing on her pale ivory hand. He looked up and around the room. The servants had gathered around the edges of the study. Anafelen must have roused the entire house. They looked at him, their faces clouded with sadness; it seemed all hope was lost.

He touched her face again. Her skin was cool. "Please, Enos," he whispered. "Please don't let her die. I need her."

Finaly, Lady Alle appeared with Scorpio and T'Antalius in tow. Luinedhel moved aside so the seer could examine N'Khael, but he did not let go of his sister's hand. The woman's white eyes scanned over N'Khael. Luinedhel watched as the Seer touched N'Khael's forehead where she had been injured, her chest, her arms. She bent over to listen to her breathing. With T'Antalius' help, she leaned back and perched on a stool at N'Khael's side.

"You can give her medicines," he said. "To make her better. How long will it take? What else does she need?"

Her blind gaze looked up to meet his. Sadness enveloped her face, and she shook her head.

"But … your magics, your *creer'gott*?"

The Seer's gaze fell. She didn't respond.

"There's nothing? Nothing? Hathar's medicine. It is strong. He can help." His voice was louder than he had intended. "Scorpio, go find Hathar. Bring him quickly!" He refused to accept that there wasn't anything that could be done for N'Khael. The Seer had brought him back from the edge of death. Hathar had helped Avanstel. Surely there was something!

There was a whisper from N'Khael. Both the Seer and Luinedhel leaned forward to hear what she was saying. She was reciting something, but he couldn't tell what it was. Her words were faint and becoming indiscernible.

Luinedhel looked up at the Seer with a frown. "What did she say? I don't understand the words."

The Seer sat back with a thoughtful look on her face.

N'Khael's grip tightened, and she pulled him closer, suddenly alert and strong. "Thelo?" Her eyes opened and focused on him. Through his tears, he looked into her warm brown eyes. "He … loved you. I love you … Brother. Lord … Lord Omaga."

And then her eyes closed, and her hand fell limp. Her chest stopped moving.

"No! No!" Luinedhel wailed. He squeezed N'Khael's hand. "You can't leave me! You can't." He fell to his knees at her side, his body wracked with sobbing, still clutching her hand.

He was only slightly aware of the sounds in the room, of others who had known N'Khael much longer than he had. Perhaps some of them had witnessed her *anneming*. They had been there when she was a child. Had been beside her during the loss of her mother. Watching her grow from a small elven maiden into a powerful warrior. These same people had just recently bid farewell to Lord Selyndar as he passed to Parvanor, and now were losing the next member of their family, with such a brief period between. Grief and muffled cries surrounded him.

He felt a hand on his shoulder. Scorpio lifted him from the floor, wrapping his arms around the *ort*. Luinedhel groaned with sadness. Aching sounds originated somewhere deep in his soul. He felt as if he were going to fall apart. Scorpio squeezed him harder, and Luinedhel thought maybe that was the only thing that kept him from completely shattering into a thousand pieces.

"*Namartha t'undel*," the warrior said quietly. "I am with you."

Luinedhel felt a wave of grief wash over him, and he gave himself over to it. "*Sere'eden be damned!*" he thought. He sobbed and screamed in despair while Scorpio held him.

At some point, he remembered letting go of N'Khael's hand, though he did it with much hesitation. He also recalled vague impressions of being helped to his quarters by Scorpio before falling into his bed, where anguish overtook him and his world faded to black.

There were no dreams that night, simply a world of nothingness.

"Lord Omaga?"

Luinedhel opened one eye. He was awake, had been awake for hours, but had refused to get out of bed. The room was dark, the shades drawn, but he could make out enough details to know that he was in his room, upstairs on the north side of the massive mansion that was House Omaga. The voice was Anafelen.

"Lord Omaga, are you awake?"

"What is it?" Luinedhel did not feel like moving. If he lay here long enough, he hoped he might fall back to sleep and escape this new reality. Sleep was the place where none of the last four days – or the last few months – existed. Sleep was a sanctuary from everything. Unfortunately, it was also elusive. His mind simply would not be silent.

"I'm so sorry, my Lord. Lady Shaal'Elonthra and Lady Alle asked me to wake you. They say it's urgent. They are waiting in your study."

Selyndar's study ... Now his.

Luinedhel exhaled. He was not ready. Not ready to face the day, to face what lay ahead. N'Khael was gone, and though he may now be Lord of House Omaga, he was also an accused assassin ... and an escaped prisoner ... and alone.

What did they want with him? Did they expect him to take Selyndar's place on the Council? Would they even allow him to replace his father, given his alleged treason against the throne?

He was not ready to push aside his grief yet again for the necessity of what lay ahead, what was required of him by the Weode and their political machine. If Selyndar or N'Khael were here, they would urge him to rise and face the challenges ... but they were not here ... and he lacked the energy – and even more, he lacked the desire – to meet their demands.

He wanted to be left alone.

"Shall I tell them you will be down shortly?"

"Tell them to go away, Anafelen."

"I understand." His tone was sympathetic. They had both lost N'Khael ... and Selyndar before her. All of House Omaga felt the loss. "As you wish, Lord Omaga." He closed the door.

Luinedhel could hear Anafelen's footsteps receding down the hallway.

So much had been running through his head in the last few hours. Most of it had been reflections of N'Khael and Selyndar, of the family that he had gained and lost again. Of what these events meant for him, his future. And of Nightfall and Scorpio. And Avanstel and Hathar; their fates were still unknown. So much darkness, so much loss.

There was another knock on the door.

"What is it, Anafelen?"

The door opened.

"You need to get up."

Luinedhel rolled over and looked at Scorpio. He wore his cloak tied around his broad shoulders, showing he was headed somewhere or had just returned.

Luinedhel took a deep breath. "I appreciate you trying to rally me, Scorpio, but I –"

"Get up," he repeated.

Luinedhel frowned. Scorpio had never talked to him this way. He typically spoke little, if at all. What was going on?

"Get up and fulfill your duty. You are Lord of House Omaga now. Be worthy of that title, that honor. Both Selyndar and N'Khael believed in you. Trusted you. Wanted you to be part of their family. And with that honor comes the responsibility to take care of House Omaga. You are Lord of a founding House now. An Elder on the Council. Advisor to the Ade, and eventually the Aetheling. You cannot sulk, no matter what loss you feel today. The world doesn't stop because N'Khael is not at your side."

"Scorpio, I –"

"I have just returned from the House of Maidens. I carried your sister's body there alone. I did it for you because I know the pain you feel, and you are a friend. But it was your responsibility to do it, to make arrangements for her burial. I could do that for you, but I cannot act as Lord of House Omaga, nor council with the other Elders. That is something *you* must do. Get up now and do what is expected of you. What is needed of you."

Luinedhel looked at the warrior incredulously. He was angry with Scorpio for chastising him. The tenacity of the man! He considered shouting at him to leave but realized that the warrior had come to do and say what needed to be said, and he wouldn't be dissuaded. Scorpio's words stung and upset him.

But ... he was also right. Those things that he didn't want to do, he had to do them now. And not just today. Many more things would likely be ahead of him he would have to do – whether or not he wanted to do them. He *was* an Elder now. Lord of an important Weode House. The blessing of it came with the accountability of doing what Selyndar and N'Khael could no longer do.

Luinedhel cleared his throat. "Tell them I will be down momentarily. Please have Anafelen see that the Lady and the Seer are comfortable."

Scorpio grunted, stepped out of the doorway, and closed the door behind him.

Luinedhel lay there a moment longer, gathering the strength to extract himself from the bed. He looked at his reflection in the mirror; pale lines streaked down his face where his tears had washed away the grimy reminders of his time in the Delves. His long dark hair was disheveled, and he looked gaunt, like a haunted version of himself. The events of the last few weeks had changed him in many ways. He did not recognize his own reflection. The face of a stranger stared back at him.

He washed in his private bath and selected an appropriate outfit from his wardrobe, thinking back to the time when Nightfall had given him his first Weode clothing. He wondered where that blue outfit had ended up. It was likely put away in his wardrobe after laundering, and he'd forgotten its location. He picked up the small blue pouch and moonstone pin that rested on the table at his bedside. He ran his thumb over the stone. So much loss! So much pain!

He never said a proper goodbye to Adine, never had the chance to say farewell to Selyndar. And now, N'Khael. A lump rose in his throat. It was so much, almost too much.

"*Sere'eden*," he said reflexively, and tied the pouch to his belt.

The white sword Haven Chase token sat on the table. He picked it up also and tucked it into his pocket. Where was Avanstel? And was he okay? Perhaps the Seer and the Lady brought news of him, or of Hathar. Scorpio was right to push him to meet with them, and he was right that he needed to play his part in all of this. He could not shirk those responsibilities. He was Lord Omaga now.

He exited onto the grand balcony that surrounded the entrance hall below and glanced across the enormous room to the south wing, where Selyndar's rooms were. He imagined for a moment seeing the tall, gentle figure of the elf coming to meet him. How unfortunate that the former Lord Omaga would never again walk the halls of his beautiful house. Luinedhel sighed and made his way down the stairs and onto the main floor. He strode through the entry hall and stepped inside Selyndar's study.

Lady Shaal'Elonthra and the Seer sat in large brown leather seats facing Selyndar's massive desk at the far end of the room. Beyond the desk were ornate leaded windows that looked out onto a private garden off the dining area. The design of the glass was the same as that in the chapel – the three vertical circles intertwined in the symbol of House Omaga. Something that would now represent him.

His guests rose to greet him as he entered. Lady Shaal'Elonthra took his hand. He could tell she had been weeping, although she still looked elegant and her beauty had not diminished. "Lord Omaga, you have my deepest sympathies on the passing of both your father and sister. They have given so much to our kingdom." Her eyes welled up. She cleared her throat and exhaled. "I will miss them deeply."

"Indeed," echoed Seer Alle. "It is a grave time for not just House Omaga, but the entire Weode nation. Two brilliant stars have begun their journeys to Parvanor. Our skies will be duller for their absence. But rest assured, our Houses continue to stand united with House Omaga."

"Thank you both," Luinedhel said as he moved toward the chair that had been Selyndar's. He stood next to it, looking at it in silence for a long moment before taking his seat. His guests remained standing until he motioned for them to sit.

Scorpio knocked gently on the door and entered the room. He had discarded his cloak and wore his signature red outfit. His dark hair was clean and combed back. Freshly shaven, he seemed recovered from his time in the Delves. A look passed between them. Luinedhel knew that although the warrior looked composed and presentable on the outside, the errands of the morning had been a heavy burden to him. So had the conversation they shared upstairs.

Scorpio remained standing by the door, with a concerned look on his face.

"Thank you for joining us, Scorpio," Luinedhel said. They both knew what he meant.

Scorpio nodded, relief on his face. He bowed to the Seer and the Lady.

Luinedhel sank into the worn leather chair. It felt enormous … and he felt small and unprepared. Selyndar was – had been – such a regal and intellectually imposing figure. Luinedhel wasn't sure he could fill Selyndar's role within House Omaga, let alone within the other places of Ny'we Adye. He shifted in the chair, trying to find a comfortable position.

He cleared his throat and folded his hands in his lap, the way he had seen Selyndar do a thousand times before. "How may I help you?"

The Seer looked at the Lady with her white glazed eyes, waiting for her to begin. Lady Shaal'Elonthra leaned forward and smiled softly at him. "Lord Omaga, let me start with some good tidings. Your friend, Hathar, is safe and healing at my home. I have had healers with him around the clock. Lady Alle has even come to visit him with some of her medicines. It may be a few more days yet before he can leave his bed, but we are seeing all the signs that he will indeed recover."

Luinedhel exhaled, relief washing over him. "I cannot thank you enough, Lady. He is a close friend and loved by many." He shifted again in the chair. "And Avanstel?"

Lady Shaal'Elonthra shook her head. "No news, I'm afraid. Nephinae scoured the palace for signs of him, but she could find nothing. The Guard are preparing to march so the south, so I'm afraid she won't be able to continue the search."

Luinedhel looked down and touched his pocket where the white sword token rested. Where could he be? "I see," he said. "Is there other news?"

Lady Shaal'Elonthra looked at the Seer and then back at him. "Lord Omaga, I am hesitant to bring this topic forward, but it is of significant importance. Lady Alle has some information that we both feel you should know."

"Go on."

The Seer cleared her throat. "Last night, while we were with Thelyn Omaga …" She hesitated as if she could see the flash of grief that shot across Luinedhel's face. "She said something that gave me pause."

Luinedhel did not answer. He was trying to keep his grief from overtaking him. "*Sere'eden*," he thought to himself. "Go on."

"*Through winding ways, to long-lost stone*," the Seer said.

Luinedhel swallowed and tried to stop his voice from trembling. "I remember. I didn't understand it. Does it make sense to you?"

The Seer looked again to the Lady and back at Luinedhel. "It is a line from a volume of the Arcana Sephyrie, an ancient text written by a groundling named Gravlin Groundstone. He's said to be a soothsayer by few, though most would consider him simply a madman. The Weode disregard the Arcana Sephyrie as ramblings of a lunatic drunk on *drekannen,* so it's not a respected source, nor is it spoken of often. Hearing Thelyn Omaga quote the words from memory was highly unusual. Given her father's penchant for ancient texts, perhaps I should not have been surprised. I had only read it recently myself, during my search for information on your daggers, so I had to double check, but it is certainly of the Arcana Sephyrie."

She sat back in her chair and adjusted her robes.

"I don't understand the significance." His tone was a little sharper than he had intended. His emotions this morning were raw.

Scorpio shifted his weight at the back of the room and caught Luinedhel's eye. There was something here, something that Luinedhel needed to pay attention to.

"Go on," Luinedhel said, more calmly than before.

"Read him the whole passage," the Lady said to the Seer. "The whole thing."

The Seer nodded. She reached into her robes and withdrew a small book. The book's exterior was polished silver metal; its cover featured a carving of a creature that was part dragon, part wolf, and part bird. It was the book from his dreams. The one with the figures carved from the Shadow Gate.

Luinedhel gasped as he suddenly remembered where he had seen it before. Arial, the Groundling, had given one to Nightfall back when they were fleeing Chark. She had told the *drivrid* that it was something of interest to Selyndar. And Hythorn had given one to Scorpio just the night before, and had bid him to give it to the nether-elf.

The sunlight from the windows behind him reflected off the book and lit up the room. The Seer unlocked the bindings and opened it, scanning it with her blind eyes as her fingers raced over the words she could not see.

"This is volume eight. Here it is in quire eleven," she said and read aloud:

"In hushed depths, dark shadows linger.
In catacombs, a soul does stir.
Whispers darkness, starlight shimmer.
A never-king, his vision blurred.

Winding tunnels, forgotten lore,
Birthed in darkness, ancestral call.
Foreseen and known in times of yore,
They usher forth their rise and fall.

Usurpers' wish, as dark as night,
Outsider from the depths does foil.
Repeat old thirsts for power and might.

Plans and plots and dark schemes they spoil.

Through winding ways, to long-lost stone,
Seeking nothing, yet finding all,
Purloins starlight from hands of bone.
Unknown of fate, destruction's call.

Unearth the truth that cannot hide!
Three hands, no more, land's fate they hold.
The first finds they cannot abide.
The second holds death, the third seeks gold.

The roots of blood, with forms unbound.
The shifter's seed, which now does bloom.
Two kings to fall, none to be crowned.
One to be lost, a kingdom's doom.

An heir revealed, fate's bright decree,
An orphan, a scion, a Lord.
Darkness and light both set them free.
Though exile is the end reward."

The Seer closed the book and looked up at Luinedhel, waiting for him to respond. He stared back at her blankly, unsure what to say.

Finally, he offered, "I might agree with those that think Gravlin Groundstone was a drunken madman. I don't understand what it's supposed to mean. And why would my sister have memorized it?"

Lady Shaal'Elonthra leaned in again. "Lord Omaga, it's about you. It's as Selyndar believed … *You* are the heir of J'Onsal."

It was time to leave this place. What was required had been obtained.

Based on their research, the moons would meet in just a week's time, and it would take them that long to reach the tower. They needed to leave now.

They wished it could be done here – or anywhere; it would be easier and faster. But they needed the old powers, and the old powers were only found in the few remaining places from the First Age. And what they wished to accomplish would take all the old power they could find. After all, the old power had kept them imprisoned for thousands and thousands of cycles, and had only just recently begun to weaken. Enough might remain, along with the scepter, the meeting of the moons, and the only other doul'zur blood left in Halbrun. They hoped it was enough to do what was needed.

It had only been done once before, and the fool had destroyed the empire. But this time, it would be done right, and it would *create* the empire … *their* empire. They would have their revenge, and they would birth a new kingdom, a new people to rule the realm, and perhaps this time, they would move beyond Halbrun to the other continents – as had been the original plan.

They touched the silver pendant at their neck, as they walked into the Ade's bedchamber. He had fallen in line. Men, whatever their race, were weak to the charms of a beautiful form, something they had mastered at the dawn of time. He would send the army tonight, as they wanted, to the Kragdenmal-Err. And they would arrive in time for the lunar conjunction. In time for them to complete the ritual and speak the words that would begin their reign and demolish this usurper's.

"Hello, love," they said as they slid beneath the sheets.

The Ade kissed their neck and touched their face.

"The army must depart in the morning, at the first light of dawn," they said. "You need your sleep, my love. Conserve your strength for the march south. There will be other opportunities in the future to indulge your desires."

"As you wish, my love," Dredaius said. He groaned in disappointment, kissed them once again, and then turned on his side and put his back to them.

They looked at his back, breathing in and out, and thought perhaps they could kill him now and take his form. Was there really a need for both of them to lead the army south? The Ade, or his semblance, may be enough.

But doing that would leave a body, and they had been so careful lately. Why ruin it now? There wouldn't be time to hide it. It was more convenient to maintain the charade. Soon, they would eliminate him, the last of the abominations, and this pathetic excuse of a kingdom.

CHAPTER 34: PLANS

He tossed the book down on the table. "It's nonsense," Luinedhel said. "Just the ramblings of an old drunk groundling. Anything there that is true of me would also be true of Avanstel. I am no Aetheling. I have only just become head of this House, and I have my doubts that I'm even capable of managing that responsibility. I'm not sure I can even step into the role that Selyndar filled within this kingdom. These words … they mean nothing." He pointed at the copy of the Arcana Sephyrie Hythorn had given Scorpio before they had parted.

Scorpio did not reply, but continued to watch Luinedhel pace back and forth.

Luinedhel spun on him. "Say something, please! I need your advice, Scorpio. I cannot do this alone."

The warrior opened his mouth to speak. There was a knock on the door.

Anafelen entered. "Your *drivrid* companion has returned. He is on his way up. I will bring a meal, my Lord."

"Thank you, Anafelen."

The serf disappeared through a side door just as Nightfall entered the common room.

Scorpio stood up and greeted the *drivrid* with a powerful clap on the back. "I started to worry. I am used to your absences, but you were gone long this time and much has happened."

"Apologies." Nightfall looked over at Luinedhel. *"Sondartin,* you look … changed."

Luinedhel brushed his hair back from his face. "Time in the Delves will do that to you. That, and …" He looked down at the floor, fighting back sudden tears.

Nightfall crossed the room and clasped his shoulder. "Say no more, *sondartin.* I received the news. It is a tragedy. I have known the Omaga family for many cycles. I have watched N'Khael grow from a kidling. She was a skilled fighter, and a staunch ally. I grieve alongside you for her loss." He made a fist and placed it firmly in the middle of his chest.

"Thank you." Luinedhel's voice cracked as he swallowed back the tears.

"The Arcana Sephyrie, Volume Eight," Nightfall said, noting the silver book sitting on the table behind Luinedhel. There was a tinge of surprise in his voice – something that was unusual for the nether-elf. He eased himself into the chair next to Scorpio and unlaced his boots. "I've been acquiring volumes for Lord Selyndar. He and I had many long conversations over their contents late into the night, on many occasions. I will miss those discussions." He looked sideways at Scorpio. "He didn't have this one. Where did you get it?"

"Scorpio's brother."

"His brother? Here? Calessio?"

"Hythorn," Scorpio answered.

Nightfall let out a low whistle. Luinedhel noticed the surprise on his face. "There must be an important reason."

"The scepter we brought back from Hemel," Luinedhel answered. "It has a stone at the top of it. Do you remember it? The blue stone?"

"I do."

"They think it's a special stone."

"*A* Stone," Scorpio corrected. "*Eer'gott.*"

Nightfall sat back in the chair. "I see." He was silent for a moment and then looked intently at Luinedhel. "Then the Arcana Sephyrie is even more relevant than before. I understand now how these events might stir the interest of the Librarians, but for Hythorn to leave Q'Serath ..."

"It's ramblings," Luinedhel said. "*Through winding ways, to long-lost stone* ... it means nothing. Almost *all* of it means nothing."

"It meant something to Selyndar."

Luinedhel didn't reply. He had profound respect for his adoptive father, a learned, wise, and revered man among his people. If this nonsensical prose meant something to him, then there *might* be something there. Something beyond Luinedhel's understanding.

Anafelen entered with a large tray of food and drinks and sat it on the table between them. Luinedhel sat down and picked up a fruit and a handful of nuts. The others joined him.

Nightfall took a glass of the elven wine and sipped it. "The Arcana Sephyrie was one of the reasons that I held back in Chark while my companions went ahead with your friend. Yes, the writings are vague and confusing and wrapped in enigma, it is true. But to me, they are like a puzzle to be worked out. As I said, I spent many long nights in discussion with Selyndar, discussing their meanings, looking to the signs, matching his knowledge with mine to help decipher their potential truths."

"Lord Omaga felt strongly enough about how we interpreted them to send us to retrieve the heir of N'Athero J'Onsal in Chark. And *I* felt strongly enough about their words to think that perhaps it was not Avanstel who was the true heir, but instead it might be you. There have been other signs too, along the way ... if you will interpret them as such."

"But most of it makes no sense," Luinedhel argued. "I understand how some phrases might lead you to a conclusion, but they are open to interpretation." He picked up the book and opened it to the marked page. "Here… '*An orphan, a scion, a Lord.*' Perhaps I am the orphan, and Avanstel the scion, and we are … were … *taven'sanct* of Lord Selyndar, but …"

"Perhaps *you* are all three," Nightfall stated flatly and took a sip of his wine. "Born an orphan, now twice-over orphaned, to our extreme sorrow. But you have become a Lord now, and, a scion may yet be true – as the heir to the throne of the Ade Gerent."

Luinedhel closed his eyes and shook his head. "But Avanstel is …" He paused. "Do you have news of Avanstel? Do you know where he is?"

"I'm afraid I do not, *sondartin*. I tried to find out but was unable to locate him. That was the reason for my delay in returning. I spent several days searching around Ny'we Adye. I even ventured to the sewers – the favored travel route of our Peytriad Adelyn. Even to the parts connected to the Delve. But there was no trace. Dredaius and Questelle must have hidden him somewhere inside the palace. I have limited ability to navigate unseen there. I hoped that perhaps … others … would have been able to aid us to find him."

Luinedhel thought for a moment. "Nephinae looked, but the Lady said she could not find him either." He stood up and walked to the windows that overlooked the gardens below. "My sister might have …" His voice trailed away as the memory of training with N'Khael flooded his mind. His heart ached. He turned away from the window and looked at his companions. "What now?"

Nightfall placed his glass down on the table and touched his fingertips together in front of him. "Unless you would like to end our arrangement, my companions and I will continue to serve at the will of the Lord of House Omaga," he said. "We do what you direct."

Luinedhel sighed. "I was afraid you would say that." He stepped over to the fireplace and put a log onto the embers. "My priority is to find Avanstel … and to stop Dredaius and Questelle. Whether I am the heir or Avanstel is, it doesn't matter. But from what Scorpio's brother has shared – if it's true – they have a Stone. And that could be very dangerous. Especially since we know what type of people they are – and we don't know what they plan to do with it. The only sure thing is that no good will come from it. We must retrieve it … and my daggers."

"The daggers," Nightfall said thoughtfully. "*Whispers in darkness, starlight shimmer?*"

Luinedhel frowned. "No time for the riddles of the Arcana Sephyrie, Nightfall. We need to find Avanstel, and the scepter, and get them far from the reaches of the Ade and his Adelyn. And then we can figure out the rest. To that end, we will go to the palace tomorrow. I will confront Questelle's lies and declare my innocence, and bring some light to this darkness just as Avanstel would, were he here. I will demand to see him because we *know* they must have him somewhere. This time, Scorpio, I grant you permission to take whatever action is needed to keep us from ending up back in the Delves, or worse. You also, Nightfall. We will fight against this darkness."

The warrior grunted in agreement.

Luinedhel dreamed of Avanstel that night. But it wasn't Avanstel the Aetheling; it was Avanstel, his childhood companion and best friend. They were younger, both of them, racing around the alleys of the Blundt. They hid from Danvaren – a game they often played together as children. They had found a hiding place, or so they thought. At the end of the backstreet, behind some old barrels, there was a gap in the stonework just big enough for the two young *ort* to sneak through. They had scampered through the hole just as they heard Danvaren's footfalls racing down the alley behind them.

The boys pressed together in the darkness, listening intently for their pursuer to give up the chase. Danvaren called them both, but couldn't find them. The dim light from the break in the wall illuminated their faces. Arracnoth mimicked his friend, covering his mouth so a giggle would not give them away.

He looked into Avanstel's blue eyes, and suddenly they were no longer children, but grown men, somehow wedged into this confined space under the stairs leading to the second story of the apothecary's shop. Arracnoth flinched as he remembered his last time there ... when he had gone to retrieve the medicines for his mother, who had become rapidly ill. Avanstel put a finger to his lips and motioned that they should crawl under the stairs to peer into the main room of the store. They did so together.

Elred, the herbalist and shop owner, had his back to the stairs, and was mixing something with his mortar and pestle. He was humming a familiar tune from Arracnoth's childhood. It was one that Adine had sung to him on those nights when he could not sleep and had been afraid of the darkness. Even now, here in this strange dream, it brought him a measure of comfort.

A bell rang, and someone entered the shop and approached the counter. It was a woman ... a human woman – which was unusual for this place in the Blundt. She wore a hat, from which escaped stray strands of golden hair, and which obscured her face. He did not remember seeing her, and he was almost sure he would have remembered a human woman in the Blundt. Still ... there was something in her voice, something familiar, but he could not place where he knew her from. Perhaps a customer he had met at The Pig & Lamb.

She exchanged words with Elred, reading from a list of herbs she needed and inquiring whether he had them. He moved around his workspace, packed some leaves and spices into a bundle, and handed them to her. He told her the cost, and instead of reaching for her purse, she reached up and tucked a strand of hair back into her hat. There was a flash of light as the silver stone around her neck caught the sunlight from the shop window. She rubbed the stone lightly.

Arracnoth inhaled sharply and turned to Avanstel, but Avanstel was gone and Arracnoth was alone. Had Avanstel ever been there, or had he come here alone? Why was he hiding under the stairs of the herbalist's shop?

Another bell, and another customer entered the shop. He recognized this one. It was himself! He remembered this interaction. Adine had sent him to the shop to fetch some dewberry and soldier's cress to make some tea to soothe her stomach. It was just days before she passed. But he didn't remember the woman being there. He had never seen her before.

He watched himself approach the counter where Elred greeted him. He told Elred what he needed. The woman lingered at the counter. The herbalist nodded and pulled two jars from the shelf behind him and placed a scoop of each onto brown parchment paper and tied it up. The woman reached up again and stroked the silver stone around her neck.

From this vantage point under the stairs, he watched her switch the packages, exchanging the papers that Elred had given her for the one containing the tea ingredients for his mother. Neither he nor Elred had noticed. They … he … couldn't have seen it. It had been a quick movement, obscured by the various jars on the countertop.

He watched as his other-self gave Elred two coppers and left the store.

Poison! he thought to himself. The woman had exchanged the dewberries and soldier's cress for whatever melodious concoction she had gotten Elred to sell … or give … to her. And it was that very package of 'medicines' that had caused Adine to fade so quickly and to die. But to what end? Why had this old woman wanted to poison Adine?

Then, it happened. The woman placed her hand on Elred's arm. The look on his face moved from confusion to shock and then pain. He tried to pull his arm back from her, but her grip was strong, and she held his arm down on the counter. Her nails dug into his flesh, drawing blood. He protested and again tried to pull away but was restrained. He tried to push her, but she did not move.

Then Arracnoth heard her speaking. *"Thanel el uhtrack da'vael omvadla eral'datu."* And he knew where he had heard those words before, though he had never read them completely, and certainly never heard them spoken aloud. They were the words on the Nwi'Diad! The words that the skeleton king had spoken, and the words that had filled his other dreams. Words of the language of the First People.

Elred collapsed on the floor, and the woman leaned over him. A frightening sound arose somewhere between a screech and a wail. Cries of pain and of elation mixed with the sounds of bones crunching and flesh shifting. Then it was over. There was nothing but silence.

The woman stood up, her back to the stairs, and adjusted her clothing. She removed her hat, and Arracnoth could see that her hair was no longer blonde, but a rich auburn color. She knotted it, tying it to rest on the back of her neck. She stepped over the corpse and moved from behind the counter.

Elred lay there on the floor, emaciated; a withered skeleton, drained of life. His skin was grey and dull, and stretched too tightly over the skull beneath it. His head faced the stairs, and his empty eyes peered into the space where Arracnoth watched in horror. Arracnoth clasped his hand over his mouth and scrambled backwards, bumping into a small shelf holding various jars and bottles. They rattled loudly enough to give away his position. The woman turned toward the noise. Her eyes narrowed, and she laughed.

He knew that laugh. He knew those eyes. The woman had transformed from a human woman to a young, beautiful, and vibrant *ort* girl. One he knew as Questelle.

He opened his mouth to scream, but he couldn't.

"The shifter devours. That is their nature," came a voice in his ear. He turned, and he saw Nightfall's face – golden eyes that pierced his mind. "It's all in the words. If you had only understood them before."

Luinedhel sat upright, muffling a cry, and looked around the darkened space. Slowly, he recognized where he was and relaxed. He was home, in his bedroom, at House Omaga. Safe, but unsettled by the vivid dream.

CHAPTER 35: FEINT

Luinedhel could not return to sleep. He slid out of the bed and pulled on a robe, a little warmth against the chill of the night. He exited his room and crossed to the room that Avanstel had occupied before being taken to the palace. He sat on the edge of the bed, thinking of his friend, wondering where he was and whether he was safe. He rested his head on the pillow, hoping the familiar and fading scent of Avanstel would still his restlessness and allow him to return to the world of sleep, but his mind kept racing over the dream.

He wandered from Avanstel's room and down the balcony that overlooked the main entrance. It was dark and silent below, Anafelen and the others having long ago retired. He paused for a moment, taking it all in. This was to be *his* now ... his home ... as Lord Omaga.

If he could overcome Questelle's plans, whatever they were.

He wandered further through the north wing, pondering the meaning of the dreams. They all seemed related, like parts of a story. The tower, the bloom, the Stone, the lightning, the withered bodies, the cries and howls, the words, and of course, Questelle.

Were they just worries and thoughts of the day mixed with fears and the strangeness of the dream world, or was there more to them? Were they revelations of the past, or things from the future? And what was his part in all of this? If they were not simply nightmares, what else could they be? Nothing made sense. But then again, dreams rarely did. They had all been so vivid, so real.

Luinedhel remembered that Questelle's appearance had changed between her days in Chark and their meeting at the palace here in Ny'we Adye. He had attributed those minor changes to some *creer'gott*, to the silver stone amulet she wore around her neck. He had assumed it was a disguise charm, and that's how her appearance had changed. But this dream seemed to hint that a different, deeper, more sinister power granted her the ability to transform. Something deeper than *creer'gott* was at work here.

Did the bodies stored in the Delves belong to *her*? The same kind of bodies that had been discovered in the forest and in Ny'we Adye that Lord Y'Vellian and Lord Kellendaer were investigating? If his dream were true, not only had Questelle intentionally poisoned his mother, but she had used her magic – whatever it was – to transform, to shift into something else. That might explain the bodies … but there were so many in the dungeon. That would also mean she could be anybody – even the Lady or the Seer, or Nephinae, or even Nightfall or Scorpio.

There were so many unanswered questions, and he needed answers, not more mysteries.

He found himself at the door to the room that Scorpio, Nightfall, and Hathar shared at the rear of the north wing. He could hear Scorpio snoring lightly and decided he didn't want to wake them or pass the burden of sleeplessness onto their shoulders. So, he stepped into the large common room where they had talked and shared a meal before retiring for the night.

The silver-plated Arcana Sephyrie was sitting on the table where he had left it. Luinedhel absently picked it up and flipped through the pages again. It still looked like nonsense to him, words that were open to any interpretation by anyone.

He paused and read through the lines again. *"The roots of blood, with forms unbound. The shifter's seed, which now does bloom."*

"Shifter," he said aloud. That was the word that Nightfall had used in his dream. *'The shifter devours.'* Maybe these words had fueled his dreams, and this was all just wild speculation, the vomit of the day's events.

He slipped the book into a pocket in his robe. He opened the doors leading to the balcony that ran the length of House Omaga. Below him, he could see the gardens and the green where Selyndar had taught him the Dance. He strode into the moonlit night, lost in thought. The weaver, Eyama, was high in the sky. Her diffuse yellow light brought a warm glow to the landscape below. Relos was setting, just visible over the tops of the pines near the chapel.

If Questelle was a changeling, able to alter her appearance without the aid of *creer'gott,* then that meant that she was not Weode nor Th'arule. She was something else. Whatever she was, she was an enemy, as confirmed by her actions. She was behind the deaths of Danvaren, Selyndar, and N'Khael … and if the dream was to be believed, even his mother, Adine. She was a master of poisons and deceit. And instigator, insurgent, traitor. Founder of the Peytriad, whose goal was to take down the line of J'Onsal. Which included Avanstel … or him, if Nightfall and the Seer were correct in their interpretation of the Arcana Sephyrie.

But Questelle could be even more than all of that. If she were a shifter, she would be a more powerful enemy than any of them realized. Somehow, she knew the words written on the Nwi'Diad without ever having seen it. He had only glimpsed them himself … yet he knew them too. Perhaps they were from something he had heard long ago. He wasn't sure how he recognized them, but there was no doubt they resided somewhere deep in his mind … long before he had heard Questelle speak them in his dream.

He shivered. The night was chilly, but his shudder had not come from the frost that had formed on the stone balustrade or the brisk night air.

He closed his eyes and breathed in deeply.

"*Sere'eden*," he exhaled. "Mother, where have I found myself?"

He thought of the last time they had spoken as she lay wasting away in her bed, in their shack in the Blundt. She had encouraged him always to find peace and not to let his anger take control of his actions.

But this was different. Peace would not save him, nor Avanstel, nor the kingdom of the Weode. There was a time for peace, just as there was a time for everything. But now was the time for action, for confrontation, and for truth. He needed to expose Questelle for who she was, and let Dredaius and Avanstel, the entire kingdom, know of her deception.

Lady Shaal'Elonthra met him at the foot of the bridge that crossed to the main gate of the palace. Seer Alle was at her side, one hand resting on the Lady's arm. It was just as they had arranged that morning, through various letters exchanged between the Houses. Each of them had brought several members of their household. Altogether, Luinedhel guessed that there were about twenty of them. That was enough: a small crowd of functionaries that included Anafelen, Nightfall, and Scorpio from House Omaga, T'Antalius, and a few others from Seer Alle's home, and a handful from House Shaal'Elonthra. It was unusual for a group this large to gather at the same time, but Luinedhel had a purpose.

He stepped forward to greet the Seer and the Lady. They bowed to him. "Lord Omaga," they said in unison.

Like it or not, the mantle of House Omaga was indisputably upon his shoulders now. He returned their greeting, bowing in turn. He saw another figure over the Lady's shoulder.

"Hathar!" Luinedhel exclaimed. He was both comforted to see his friend and surprised that he had joined them, knowing the sickness that he was recovering from.

"I could not persuade him to stay and rest," Lady Shaal'Elonthra said. "He insisted on joining us and would not relent, regardless of what I advised. You can see by his bearing that he's not fully healed. As an outsider, I expected a certain level of disregard for the ways of the Weode. He did not disappoint. He is difficult to reason with."

Hathar smiled as he leaned on a staff for support. Luinedhel stepped up and embraced the cleric, who returned the hug with one arm.

"It is good to see you are healing," Luinedhel said. "I was concerned."

"Merces watches over fools and babes," Hathar said. "And apparently, also over those who fight for the future king." He winked.

Luinedhel shook his head. "Not you, too."

Hathar grinned and glanced over at Nightfall.

The mood of the group seemed light, but what lay ahead of them tugged at the edges of Luinedhel's mind. He knew their plans would eventually lead to a confrontation with Questelle and Dredaius, and that experience would not be pleasant. But he had to do what was necessary to stop their plans, and to bring about justice for his family ... all of them. He had to end this darkness.

And find Avanstel.

And the Nwi'Diad. Before they used it.

He turned to the Lady. "Nephinae?"

"The army moved south last night. She could not remain. She's with them now."

"Well enough," Luinedhel said. "As long as she is safe."

"For now." The Lady looked across the bridge toward the palace. "What is to be, is yet to be seen."

Luinedhel followed her gaze. "Let us begin." He stepped forward toward the gates. The Lady and the Seer followed behind him, arm in arm, and the three of them strode across the bridge toward the palace entrance. Those gathered followed behind them.

A small contingent of Green Guard greeted them on the other side. Lord Y'Vellian and Lord Kellendaer stood at the center of the line. The guards eyed them warily, anticipating trouble. Luinedhel turned and looked at the Lady. It was as they had expected. She nodded. He turned his attention back to the palace and stepped forward to meet the line blocking the entrance. He stopped before Lord Y'Vellian.

"I am here to see the Ade," Luinedhel stated. "Lady Shaal'Elonthra, Lady Alle, and I request an audience."

Lord Y'Vellian sneered at him. He didn't even attempt to hide his contempt for Luinedhel. "Well, *ort* child, the Ade is not taking visitors. The palace is closed." He motioned behind him. "As you can see, the hall is empty."

Luinedhel frowned. "Still, we need to speak with him. As Council Elders."

Lord Kellendaer stepped forward. "The Ade is in the south, preparing the army as we speak. They march to Orevael and on to Grevyn Pass, where they will slay the Unwritten and all their kin."

Lord Y'Vellian snapped his head to the side and bared his teeth, as if he were a cat. "Lord Kellendaer, it is unnecessary to share such information with this *ort!*"

Luinedhel's frown turned into a scowl. He stepped closer to Lord Kellendaer and tried his best to look intimidating. "Is the Adelyn here? Or is she on the front lines with the Ade?"

Lord Kellendaer took a half-step backward and seemed to shrink in upon himself. His bluster was gone. "I believe so." There was a slight tremble in his voice.

Out of the corner of his eye, Luinedhel noticed a Guard shifting his hand to their sword.

"I see. And all this done without the advisement of the Council?"

"*We* have advised him," Lord Y'Vellian said, stepping in front of Lord Kellendaer. "That was all that was necessary. We have his ear, and his trust, along with the Adelyn."

Luinedhel feigned defeat. "I understand. Very well." He stepped back and adjusted his belt. Several more guards shifted their hands to their weapons, assuming he was reaching for one of Selyndar's daggers that adorned his sides. He heard Scorpio growl behind him. Luinedhel placed his empty hands in front of him, palms up. There was no point in engaging these soldiers – he wasn't here for that today. And aside from Scorpio, those behind him carried no weapons. His fight was not with the Green Guard. Other things were in play.

"Please deliver the Ade a message from me … and from the other three on the Elder Council." He looked at the Lady and the Seer. "We seek an audience with him, if he is able to break away from his activities at the front lines. It is of utmost importance."

There was a twitch at the side of Lord Y'Vellian's lip. "We will send word, but do not expect a response. He will return to the palace when our foes are vanquished."

Luinedhel nodded curtly and turned away, walking back across the bridge. He could hear the large doors to the palace closing behind him, followed by the sound of the portcullis being lowered. There would be no entry to the palace for anyone, Council or otherwise. Dredaius had given his cronies orders, and they had remained behind to enforce them.

On the far side of the bridge, Luinedhel could see that a crowd of onlookers had gathered. Word must have spread about the strange events going on at the palace, and the curious Weode had come to see what was happening. He heard whispers pass among those gathered around. He assumed it was more prejudice aimed at the *ort* in their midst, but their attention seemed focused on the Lady Shaal'Elonthra and Lady Alle. The crowd seemed shocked by the inner workings of the Council of Elders. It was scandalous that the two men had denied the two women access to the palace. Whatever the gossip, it captivated them and kept their attention elsewhere, which was just what he wanted.

He distanced himself from the crowd so that they couldn't overhear him. Hathar and Scorpio followed him. The rest of those gathered broke off into smaller groups and chatted quietly among themselves.

Scorpio caught his eye and nodded. Hathar winked. Luinedhel scanned the crowds. He could see no sign of Nightfall. He was missing, as they had hoped.

"Good," Luinedhel said. "Let's pray that Merces continues to show favor to babes and fools … and those who fight for the future king. Our *drivrid* friend will need the blessing if he is to accomplish his purposes within the palace."

"Merces will," the cleric replied. "I have faith."

CHAPTER 36: TOWER

Cycle 739; Rime Wither; The Fifth Age.

Luinedhel paced the library. The fire was burning low; the room was aglow in a soft orange color, and filled with the familiar and comforting smell of hillstonas wood. The Haven Chase board sat on the low table in front of the sofa. A few dice rolls separated the dark horse from the tower, but the game remained frozen, never to be finished. He sighed, thinking about the many nights that he had sat in this room with Selyndar until the late hours, discussing Weode society and politics, learning the genealogy of Ni'Vahyan J'Onsal and stories of how the White Wolf had set them free. He would miss those days. The board was another grim reminder of the things stolen away from him.

The tall clock that stood on the far wall chimed softly, indicating it was past the mid of night. He took another piece of wood from the pile and placed it into the fireplace, stirring the coals. There had been no word from Nightfall, and Luinedhel wondered if their plans had fallen through and the *drivrid* had been discovered. Perhaps he sat in some cell deep in the labyrinth of the Delves, company to the grey and withered bodies.

Scorpio was sitting on the sofa, which fit his frame more like a chair. His thick arms were crossed over his barrel chest, his feet resting on the low table in front of him. Though his eyes were shut, Luinedhel knew him too well to mistake his resting pose for sleep. The warrior was just as eager for the return of their ally as Luinedhel. There was little doubt that Scorpio could leap into action at a moment's notice.

Hathar had insisted on coming with them back to House Omaga, much to the dismay of the Lady. He lay peacefully sleeping on the opposite couch, his breathing rhythmic and deep. The cleric would have been better cared for at House Shaal'Elonthra, and Luinedhel had tried to urge him to return with the Lady, but he would not have it. In truth, Luinedhel felt a yearning to be surrounded by his companions, so he relented and hadn't resisted Hathar's request. The cleric, though currently weak in body, was strong of spirit, and Luinedhel found his cheery persistence gave him added encouragement to keep fighting against the darkness and loss.

"*Sondartin.*"

Luinedhel stopped in his tracks and looked at the darkened doorway, exhaling with relief. Scorpio was already on his feet. Hathar remained lost in sleep.

"Did you find him?"

"Uncertain. There's something going on at the Summer Tower. He may be there."

"The Summer Tower? I haven't heard of it."

"It is on palace grounds, but it's one of the more remote buildings and has stood abandoned for some time. It's not used for anything now, but there's been some recent activity there. It stands on the south end of the palace complex near where the river plunges into the gorge below. It's impossible to access it from outside the palace walls because of the sheer drop, and it has only one approach from inside."

"You believe he is being held there?"

Nightfall crossed the room and stood by the fireplace, warming his hands. "I had to use some … persuasion … to loosen some tongues." There was a hint of something mischievous in his eyes.

Scorpio chuckled. "Unsurprising."

Nightfall smiled. "One of the guards told me they saw lights in the tower last week. When he reported it to his superior, he was told to ignore it. If Avanstel is not there, he may not be at the palace at all. The rumor persists that he is still missing and perhaps even fled his responsibilities as the Aetheling. The Ade and the Adelyn appear to have given up their search for him and turned their attention to the supposed Th'arule invasion."

"Of course they have," Luinedhel said. He stepped to the sideboard and poured two cups of wine. He handed one to Nightfall. "But why assemble an army in the south if there's truly no invasion?"

"To empty the city," Scorpio said.

Luinedhel considered the thought, taking a sip of his wine. "For what purpose? Dredaius is already the Ade, and Questelle the Adelyn – nobody opposes that. Their word is final, and they have the entire army at their command. Why call the army to the south if there's no invasion? And why would they need the Nwi'Diad? We are missing something."

"Speaking of missing pieces, I have something for you." Nightfall placed his glass on the mantel and pulled back his cloak, reaching around behind him. He withdrew the objects and passed them to Luinedhel.

"My daggers!"

"They were in the armory, left behind when the army moved to the south." Nightfall smiled. "Weode wouldn't take the *estrayaed* weapons with them. They were easy enough to retrieve."

Luinedhel held them in his palms, feeling their familiar warmth and the way they melted into his grip … something he had missed with other weapons. "It's good to have them back. Thank you!"

He listened for a moment, wondering if Adesh or Marek would speak, but there was nothing. As far as Luinedhel could discern, it was completely random when the weapons offered their help. They continued to be a mystery to him.

"When you are ready, *sondartin*, I can lead you to the Summer Tower." Nightfall looked at Hathar. "We may want to leave the cleric here so he can rest."

"Agreed. Anafelen will see to his needs. Scorpio?"

The warrior grunted, stretched, and cracked his knuckles. "Let's go."

The route to the Summer Tower was as convoluted as their journey had been to the Delves. Luinedhel was thankful that Nightfall was leading them. The *drivrid* knew Ny'we Adye well and was able to navigate the trio by roads and backways. It was still the depths of night, and most, if not all, of the Weode were sleeping peacefully in their beds. However, Nightfall kept to the shadows as a precaution. There was no point in drawing unneeded attention should a yet-awake resident stumble across three shadowy figures skulking about the city. With Ny'we Adye emptied of anyone who could hold a sword, there were no patrols, and fewer eyes to avoid. The chances of discovery were slim, but best not to take the chance at all.

They arrived at an enormous wall extending far in either direction. Luinedhel assumed the palace grounds lay beyond. Nightfall stepped toward the wall and moved his hands over the surface, pushing on various stones in a seemingly random sequence. There was a barely audible *click* somewhere deep inside the wall, and a section of it rotated inward, revealing a doorway. Nightfall motioned them inside while he glanced up and down the street one last time before slipping in. He closed the door behind him.

The darkness lasted only a moment before Nightfall produced a light crystal, illuminating the small room with a cold, pale light. Luinedhel looked around the room. It was empty, just a small square cube barely large enough for the three of them, with stone walls all around them on all sides. There was no apparent doorway.

"We are inside the palace walls," Luinedhel said.

"Indeed, *sondartin.*"

"I assume there is a way out?"

Nightfall moved to the wall opposite where they had entered. "A well disguised and smartly protected egress through the palace walls." He paused for a moment, examining the wall.

"First, one would have to know of its existence." He pushed a stone on the wall in front of him, and it slid inward. He reached high over his head and pushed on another with the same result.

"Then you would need to know the combination to unlock both doors; otherwise, the wall would trap you inside. The Omaga family had hidden that combination into a childhood story; I heard it many times over the cycles spent with Selyndar and N'Khael.

"Our time in the tower in Gravenwilds made me recall the story and I've been thinking on it since. I believed it held more meaning that what appeared on the surface. *The knight kicked the dark monster so hard…,*" he said as he pushed a dark grey malformed stone with the tip of his boot and it slid inward, "*that he flew into the sky and landed on a flat white cloud.*" Nightfall stretched to reach a rectangular, light-colored stone that was barely within his reach. It receded into the wall. "*He landed on his head and shattered his skull and was never seen from again.*" The *drivrid* pressed a roundish stone at eye level that vaguely resembled a skull with two shallow indents for eye sockets. There was a click, and the door swung open. The room filled with the scent of lavender.

"The palace gardens?" Luinedhel asked.

"Yes," Nightfall answered. "That was the last piece of the puzzle – the location. I searched N'Khael's quarters within the Green Guard barracks while looking for Avanstel and noticed that she had several bundles of dried lavender hanging around her room. Since her duties occupied her time at the palace, she wouldn't have been able to go to the market for such things. I have smelled it on her many times."

"Me too. I thought perhaps it was just a perfume."

"I surmised she had retrieved the herbs from the palace gardens, not a place a Green Guard would be in their normal line of work. So, I came to the gardens and found where the herbs grow: here, against the palace wall. And it all made sense then. I figured she used this egress in and out of the palace when she needed to reach House Omaga quickly, or unseen. Having all three pieces now – the existence, the location, and the code – I was able to use it to return to House Omaga unnoticed."

Luinedhel stepped out of the wall and into the gardens, inhaling the fragrant air and thinking about N'Khael. "I wonder what other Omaga family secrets are now lost." He sighed heavily.

"Take heart, *sondartin*. Lord Selyndar shared many things with me over the cycles, including the location of his private studies hidden within House Omaga. I'm sure you will have time to explore your estate completely once this is settled. You will most likely unearth many treasures – both material and intellectual. Although Lord Omaga was wealthy and could have lived a life of ease and comfort, he dedicated himself to seeking knowledge. He and Elisryn shared that in common. She was an explorer of the world, he an explorer of the mind. He was ever a student, always learning and trying to understand and unlock the mysteries of the world. I'm sure you will find many amazing things amidst all he has accumulated."

Luinedhel looked up into the sky and saw both moons had risen during their journey to the palace. "I didn't get to know him well enough. Our time was too short."

Luinedhel felt a hand on his shoulder.

"We should go," Luinedhel said, shaking the sadness from his mind. "We need to get Avanstel and get out of here before the sun rises."

Nightfall led the way through the gardens and across the palace grounds toward the southern part of the complex. Although they stayed concealed as much as possible, the open ground exposed them, giving them no place to hide. Luinedhel was anxious about this, knowing that being discovered here would land them all back in the Delves, and this time there would be no Nephinae to set them free. But Nightfall assured him that the palace was practically empty, and the risk was acceptable.

As they rounded the corner of a building, Luinedhel could see a tower ahead of them. It appeared to be a modest four-story building, unlike some of the other grand buildings within the palace complex. Walls defining the borders of the palace grounds rose on either side of the hexagon. Directly in the center stood a large, dark door.

"The Summer Tower," Nightfall said. "Are you ready?"

Luinedhel nodded, and Scorpio grunted. They raced across the open lawn toward the shadow of the tower. When they reached the door to the tower, they discovered a chain hanging around the handles and a large solid lock holding it tight. Luinedhel's heart sank.

"Why would an abandoned building require this much extra security? I don't suppose there's another way in?"

"Give me a moment, *sondartin*." Nightfall produced a set of lock picks and worked to open the lock, his dark brow knitting together. "This one is … different," he said.

"How so?"

"I'm not sure. I'm having trouble." He glanced back the way they had come. Luinedhel heard it too. There were footsteps on the gravel pathway, headed in their direction.

"Rounds," Scorpio said. His voice was deep and hushed. He slid his sword silently from the scabbard on his back.

Luinedhel reached for his daggers, and the moment his hands closed about them, he heard both Adesh and Marek speak as one. *"We are the key."*

The memory of hearing their voices in the Undercroft immediately overwhelmed him. Somehow, he had escaped that place by putting Adesh into the lock and twisting. And of course, the time in the Gravenwilds with the stone wall where both daggers had unlocked the door leading to the portal.

"Let me try," Luinedhel said. Nightfall slid aside, withdrawing his own blades.

Luinedhel placed the tip of the serpentine dagger into the opening.

"Both of us. We are the key."

He added Marek to the lock, and he felt something shift and change, and suddenly the lock broke free and opened with a clang that seemed far too loud. Luinedhel held his breath. The footsteps paused, and he heard a weapon being drawn.

"Inside, quickly!" Nightfall said. He opened the door swiftly, and Luinedhel cringed, anticipating the screech of rusty hinges, but it opened quietly and with ease.

"Greased," Nightfall explained. "I noticed it earlier. Someone didn't want to draw attention to their use of this place."

They slipped inside and closed the door behind them. Darkness enveloped them again. Luinedhel could hear the footsteps approaching through the closed door. Closer and closer they came. The three of them readied themselves for a fight. But the steps retreated without so much as a pause at the tower. When they had faded, Luinedhel exhaled.

"Didn't they notice the lock was open and the chain was down? I am losing confidence in the ability of the Green Guard to protect our Ade."

"Perhaps, like my friend with the loose lips, they have been told to ignore activity in the Summer Tower. They may have noticed but gave no mind to it, because that is their orders."

"Perhaps," Luinedhel replied.

He looked around the room. To his right, a stairway led up to the levels above, and to his left, another led downward. On the opposite wall was a large window, which provided a bit of light for the space. He crossed the room. Rusted iron bars hung over the window, but beyond them, moonlight illuminated the landscape, and the view took his breath away.

To his left, the river that snaked through Ny'we Adye suddenly plunged several stories onto rocks far below. The silver-lit water cascaded over the falls, and clouds of mist rose where the water met the rock below, obscuring the view. To his right, he could see the river continuing its gentle meander back into the surrounding forest.

"Spectacular," he breathed. "I have never seen falls before. They are beautiful."

"Indeed." Nightfall joined him by the window. "It is a shame that the Summer Tower is not in use. It has one of the best views in all of the city. Although, further downstream, there are even better views. We will go someday."

"Someday, perhaps." He glanced at the stairs. "Up?"

"I will go down," Scorpio said.

Nightfall nodded and moved to the steps leading up, his daggers still in his hands. Luinedhel followed.

They climbed the wooden steps up to the second floor. Someone had used it for storing old furniture. There was nothing of interest there. Nightfall indicated a path through the cluttered furniture leading to the next set of stairs. "Someone has been here recently, and more than once. The dust has been disturbed here."

On the next level, they found much the same, though this room had fewer and older items – some of which had been eaten away by time. Again, there was a path through the dust that led to the fourth and final story. They crept cautiously up the stairs.

Luinedhel's heart was beating in his chest. He wasn't sure they would find Avanstel, and what condition he might be in. His friend could be on the brink of starvation, or worse yet, Questelle could have used his body like the others to shift, to change into someone else, and he may be dead. Luinedhel refused to consider the possibility. He pushed the thought out of his mind. Dredaius and Questelle wouldn't go through all the trouble of finding the long-lost heir, protecting, and educating him, only to lock him away, to starve or kill him. Would they?

A door in the ceiling sat at the top of the next stairs. Nightfall paused there, and they listened intently for noise from above. They heard nothing, so Nightfall cautiously lifted the door. There was no sign of light or movement, so he pushed it open until it rested against the wall of the tower. They gingerly stepped into the room.

A large, ornate bed sat on one side of the room. It was in pristine condition, unlike the furniture on the floors below. Across from it, a large window overlooked the falls, and beneath that, there was a long table. Papers and books cluttered it, bathed in moonlight. On either side of the makeshift desk were bookcases filled with books. They appeared ancient – older than the books in Selyndar's library.

A map of the northern half of Halbrun decorated the wall next to them. It looked familiar, penned in the same hand as the map that Hathar had had, which outlined the route to the Barrens and Hemel.

Luinedhel crossed the room to the bed. In the moonlight coming through the window, the bed looked empty. "Nightfall, a light?" The white light from the crystal filled the room, casting sharp shadows on everything. Luinedhel pulled back the covers. "He's not here."

Nightfall's voice was beside him. "I'm sorry."

"It's not your fault. It was all the information we had. At least there is still hope that he is alive."

Scorpio appeared at the top of the stairs. "A storeroom below, and what looks to have been a prison once, but it is empty now save for one shriveled body. Though I have little experience with this, I believe it to be Tretarilus, the palace Steward."

"Do you think they kept Avanstel here?"

Nightfall moved over to the desk underneath the large window. There was a candelabra with four half-burned candles resting on the surface. He used a fire marble to ignite them and stored his light crystal. Warm yellow light washed over the documents.

Luinedhel picked up a book and scanned it. It was the story of Ni'Ilyan, the White Wolf, but not the way he had remembered Selyndar telling it to him. This book was much older and written in Th'arule. It was the same tale, but with some intriguing differences that changed the story in subtle but important ways. In this version, the Weode were not the repressed and downtrodden, but instead were ruthless and comprised mostly criminals, and violent ones at that. They had not overthrown their captors and emancipated themselves. They had instead gone on a bloody and horrific rampage through the palace during a festival and had been cast out along with their leader, Ni'Ilyan. The only similarity in the stories was that even in this one, he had transformed into a white wolf and killed his father.

Could he be a shifter, too? Was it more than just a legend?

He wanted to continue reading, but Nightfall handed him a book from the table. "Have you seen this before? In all my journeys across the realm, I have never seen such a language," Nightfall said.

"I have," Scorpio said, leaning over his shoulder. "In Q'Serath, but I do not know what it is or how to read it. Some of the oldest books in the archives use this script."

Luinedhel placed both books back on the table, noticing then a third.

"Look here. It's a journal, freshly written." It was penned in the same language, and in a script that matched the writing on the maps.

"This is not Avanstel's hand," Luinedhel said. "It is Questelle's. And this language is not Weode or Th'arule. It is the First People's – the language of the Shifters. The language on the Nwi'Diad, and the same on the Shadow Gate, and the doors in the guard tower and on the walls in the palace at Hemel. Questelle is a Shifter."

He looked out the window onto the cascading river, his eyes distant and unfocused. *"The roots of blood, with forms unbound. The shifter's seed, which now does bloom. Two kings to fall, none to be crowned. One to be lost, a kingdom's doom."*

He turned to Nightfall and Scorpio. "If she is in the south with Dredaius, then Avanstel is there with her. She intends to kill them both. We must go. *Now.*"

CHAPTER 37: EVER

The bard strummed his lute absently, fixing them all with his bright gaze. He took a breath and launched into his tale. His voice was rife with drama and suspense…

"The locals lower their voices to a whisper and make signs of warding when they speak of the Err, though most prefer not to speak of it at all … except when warning newcomers or the rare traveler passing through Orevael. There are some who dismiss the tales as superstition. Perhaps they think themselves cunning or brave, immune to the darkness that shadows this city. But most would call them brash, foolish, or filled with the ignorance of youth.

"The Err is the dark citadel perched precariously high on a cragged peak overlooking the entrance to Grevyn Pass. Kragdenmal-Err is its full name. At least, that's what it's been called since records have been kept in Orevael. No one knows who first named it, or who built it, or for what purpose. It's just an ancient, impenetrable fortress that was there before the first miners came to Orevael in search of the riches in the mountains.

"At the beginning, there was an interest in piercing the mysteries of the Err. Some wanted to unlock the secrets within – to discover the powers that were said to be held inside. But as with all fashions, the interest waned as the risks rose. Most who ventured near the Err simply disappeared, never to be heard from again.

"Foreigners come sometimes, seeking to travel through Grevyn Pass to the Southlands. Some come to see the Err. Any who dismiss the warnings of the Orevaelians, discarding them as rumors or old wives' tales, are usually never heard from again.

"Long ago, there was one who survived his encounter with the Err. A strong and brave young man – a man of faith in the old gods. He had taken an oath to rid Halbrun of all darkness – something we all know is impossible – but it was his mission, and he could not be dissuaded. He came from a far-away land, armed with nothing more than a mighty sword and a pure heart. He set out for the Err, intent on unraveling the mysteries and dispersing the curse, unswayed by the warnings and resolute in his purpose.

"A few days after setting out, people found him aimlessly wandering the lands surrounding Orevael, his mind shattered by what he had experienced. He spoke of a place where otherworldly things lingered just out of reach. Things he couldn't define, things that were best left undisturbed and unimagined. Creatures, figures, that limped, or crawled, or slithered, ever so slowly and methodically as though trapped within a thick black liquid, just on the other side of the razor thin veil that separates our world from theirs.

"He raved and cried out for two days before the madness overtook him completely and he drowned himself in the river in the middle of the night. The valiant man of faith is buried in the cemetery in an unmarked grave. Time has erased his name, but his voice still speaks warnings that echo through the cycles, reminding Orevael's citizens to give the Err a wide berth, and to keep out from its shadow.

"The only other who has survived the Err is a young girl. Her name ... or the name that the Sisters gave her ... is Clarana. Two cycles past, in the fall, she was found wandering the roads nearby – just as the holy man had been, many cycles ago. She mumbled nonsense and spoke of shadows and figures that she saw at the edges of her sight, of whispers and sounds that frightened her, sensations invisible to those around her. She flinches at the brush of grave-like coldness on her hands, or hot breath from something non-corporeal on the back of her neck. Most of what Clarana says is mutterings and shrieks of horror, of madness. Or else she sits alone, in hours of silence, rocking back and forth, her eyes staring blankly ahead of her.

"The Sisters of Yul'e care for her. They alone are brave enough … or perhaps have the faith enough … to watch over the cursed child. Some nights, if you listen carefully, you might hear her shrieks, carried on the wind that blows from the abbey. Though the sisters do not speak of what happens within their walls, they bring her out into Orevael where others can see her broken form – a reminder that nothing good awaits you at the Err. And some things are best left undisturbed."

Ever leaned in and said in a hushed voice. "She has not spoken in almost a cycle, now. A captive in the prison of her own mind, haunted by her experience at the Err. Her last words, an eerie omen for all who remain in Orevael: *'It is free'.*" The bard nodded toward the fireplace and took a long draw of ale before swallowing and setting the tankard down on the table in front of him.

Luinedhel shivered and looked where the bard had indicated. Through the throng of people moving about the large room, he spotted a withered old woman curled in upon herself, rocking in a chair near the crackling fireplace against the far wall. Her eyes were pale blue, almost white, reminding him of Seer Alle. There was no life behind that blank stare, only emptiness. Her wispy white hair was in disarray. She was a frail, old, and unremarkable woman. No different from any other old woman, save for the yarn that the troubadour had spun about her. Another woman, dressed in red, sat beside her. Luinedhel could tell by her garb that she was a woman of the faiths. "That is Clarana?" he asked.

"It is her," Ever said.

"She's an old woman – not a child. There's nothing special about her."

Ever leaned in and whispered. "Although I sometimes exaggerate my tales to delight my audience, I assure you this is true, sir. That is the child, Clarana."

Luinedhel looked at his companions. "Do you believe him?"

Hathar frowned dismissively and looked at Scorpio. "Anything that you might know about the Err from your … ummm… past life?"

The giant shrugged and turned his attention back to his tankard.

"As I thought. You're no help." The cleric shoved against Scorpio, intending to upset his drink, but the giant was immovable. He looked at Hathar out of the corner of his eye and smiled.

"It is irrelevant. We aren't here for entertainment anyway," Nightfall said. He slid a koara across the table. "You earned your coin, story weaver. Indeed, an unusual and frightening tale of your city. I haven't heard one like it before."

Ever picked up the coin with a smile, rolled it over his knuckles, and it vanished. He grinned, and Luinedhel smiled back at him, amused by his manner. "I'm pleased that you enjoyed my tale." He looked over at Luinedhel. "You, sir, should determine if my words are truth or falsehood, or somewhere in between." He shot a glance over his shoulder toward the fireplace. "You could ask the child herself, but I doubt she will speak to you." He winked.

"But now, dark elf," he said, turning back to Nightfall. "I am a spinner of yarns; I am always on the quest for fresh stories that I might add to my repertoire. If you don't mind me asking … what is *your* story? A *drivrid*, thought to be a fable by most, who has left the netherworld to roam the surface? An incredibly unique person, and I'm sure you have an incredibly unique story! What brings you and your companions to Orevael? You haven't asked about traveling to the Southlands, and by the looks of your party, I don't believe you are here for mining or trading. It's obvious you aren't with the Weode army; otherwise, you'd be camped in the valley below and subject to the same restrictions."

"Restrictions?"

The bard smiled and tapped his finger lightly on the table. It was an innocuous gesture that Luinedhel barely noticed. Nightfall placed another coin in front of him and hesitated a moment before sliding it across the table. Ever waved his hand over the coin and it disappeared like the one before it. Luinedhel was almost certain that although it looked like magic, the crafty bard was simply performing sleight-of-hand tricks … though the ease with which he did these things raised a doubt that there may still be some *creer'gott* at work.

"Only a few of the elvenkin have come into Orevael. And those that have ventured from their camp come to trade for provisions. They don't come to The Broken Well to enjoy our fine beverages or hear the stories and songs from the realm's finest storyteller!" He smiled and bowed his head. "Pity that. They don't realize what they're missing!"

"Provisions?"

Ever nodded, finished his drink, and motioned for the barkeep to bring another round to the table. The coin that Nightfall had just given the bard magically reappeared in his fingers, and he flicked it nimbly through the air. The barkeep caught it and turned to fetch more drinks.

"The elves have paid the merchants generously for the little they provided. Hence the gregarious mood that you see around you this evening. The Broken Well hasn't had this many customers since Usher, and even then, the drink was not flowing so freely."

Luinedhel thought back to the last Usher celebration when he was working at The Pig & Lamb with Avanstel. It seemed like centuries ago, in a distant land and a distant time. A flash of sadness crossed his face as he imagined Avanstel behind the bar, smiling in his disarming manner. Where was his friend tonight?

Ever continued, interrupting Luinedhel's thoughts. "You see, Orevael is a small mining town and does not have the resources that larger cities like Redwinds or Marinstarn have. We were not prepared to feed an army, nor did we expect one to show up on our front porch." He glanced around the room before leaning in again and whispering, "What Orevael was able to provide is not enough for an army of that size for any length of time, though the city leaders do not seem to have thought that far ahead. The coin has distracted them for a while, but …"

"That means the army did not bring provisions with them for a long campaign. They would not come this far, expecting that Orevael would have the supplies they would need for an extended stay. They are here short term." Nightfall's golden eyes flickered to the others. "Do you know the reason they have come south?"

"Ah, that is the question now, is it not, my dark friend?" He tapped the table again nonchalantly.

This time, Nightfall produced a coin inlaid with gold, silver, and copper. It was a coin that Luinedhel recognized … like the one that had started him on this entire journey. Nightfall held the coin in front of him so that Ever could see it clearly, but not high enough to draw attention. A look of surprise flashed across the bard's face as he recognized the value of the coin. "Let us be candid, friend," Nightfall said. "I think this should be enough to acquire whatever information I may have need of … and more."

Ever nodded slowly. "Indeed, sir." Luinedhel noted that the bard's tone had shifted from light and playful to somewhat serious. Ever cleared his throat and looked around the room, trying to be inconspicuous. He leaned in. "Perhaps we should take this conversation elsewhere?"

Nightfall exchanged glances with Hathar and Scorpio. The cleric and the warrior nodded. Nightfall stood up and announced to nobody in particular, "My companion and I are weary from travel." He patted Luinedhel on the back. "Bard, for a coin or two, would you come to our room and regale us with more of your fine tales, and perhaps a song or two to lull us to sleep?"

Ever stood up from the table. "Certainly, sir. My lute has been thirsty for a coin or four … or a purse of them, should you find my songs as delightful as my tales! Fear not, Tryane, I may have my debts paid this very night!" He waved to a gruff-looking man sitting in the back of the tavern with his arms crossed.

There were a few laughs from around the room. Ever had apparently been in Orevael long enough to establish a reputation for himself, though Luinedhel couldn't tell from the crowd's reactions whether the troubadour was considered a minor local celebrity or a grifter about to clean the purses of his new customers.

Ever turned back to Luinedhel. "I lost a small wager over a game of Haven Chase last week. Word of advice: never play against the black dragon token. We should have declared pieces before I took the bet. Won't make that mistake again." He smiled and winked at Luinedhel.

Luinedhel stood up, his hand brushing against the sword token in his pocket to confirm it was still there. He followed Nightfall and Ever across the common room to the stairs near the back of the building. He glanced over his shoulder to see Scorpio leaning back in his chair, positioning himself so that he had a view of the stairway. Hathar, too, had shifted in his seat and was now monitoring the coming and goings of those at the front door. Luinedhel considered for a moment whether he should offer to send the cleric up to rest, but Nightfall had clearly wanted Luinedhel to hear what the minstrel had to share with them. He turned and climbed the steps.

The room they entered was cozy. Not as nice as the rooms at The Pig & Lamb, but comfortable enough for the four of them. It was on the top floor of the three-story building built onto the back of The Broken Well to accommodate guests. Their room was the largest that the place offered, spanning the entire width and length of the building below. The proprietor had assured them it was the best accommodation in all of Orevael, and he proudly had proclaimed that the Alcade of Redwinds had resided here an entire month while negotiating with the Overseer of the Blackthorn Mining Company. The claims meant nothing to Luinedhel. The warm and dry room was a much nicer place to sleep than the ground he had slept on for the last ten nights.

Luinedhel closed the door behind him and latched it shut. He picked up the small metal bell that rested on the shelf next to the door. Without calling too much attention to himself, he tied the bell to the thin wire at the top of the door just as Nightfall had instructed him. The *drivrid* had placed the other end of the wire in a manner to give them notice of anyone coming up to the third floor. With the way the stairs creaked and groaned as they had ascended, Luinedhel wasn't sure an additional warning would be necessary.

Nightfall was stirring the fireplace. Ever plunked down in the chair next to a small table, which held a lantern on it. He leaned toward the light and examined the coin of Ni'Ilyan. He caught Luinedhel's eye.

"Is it real?"

"It is," Luinedhel said.

Ever whistled. "I've only ever seen one other. It was used to purchase my father's entire stable. Back then, I thought that was the best thing that could happen to me since it meant that I had an entire two months where I didn't have to shovel horse manure! But inevitably, a ship arrived with more horses to sell, and my Da was back in business … which meant I was back on shoveling duty. It didn't last long, but it was a good two months!"

Luinedhel crossed the room and sat down on the window seat. He looked outside at the dark and dreary night. Rain pattered against the thin, wavy glass, amplifying the warp and blur of the light coming from the stables where they had housed Aelduin, Nyx, and the other horses. He was glad that the mare had a dry place to stay tonight. The ride had been hard on them all.

Ever flipped the coin in the air, caught it, and it disappeared like the others had. "You're from Chark, right? I can tell by your accent." He smiled slightly. "And your ears."

"I am," Luinedhel answered. He reflexively pulled his hair forward, covering his ears. "I used to be. And you?"

"Harper, originally. Though I haven't called that home in a very long time. That's where my family is from."

Nightfall had the fire going now. The light and warmth were welcome. He pulled up a chair and sat across from the bard. "The coin should more than cover what we would need to know. Please, enlighten us."

Ever grinned again and leaned forward conspiratorially. Luinedhel found the mannerisms humorous. It was as if the bard had shared so many secrets in exchange for coin that it had become a habit to lean in and whisper even when there was nobody around to overhear. Maybe he thought it gave more credibility to what he was saying, or maybe it was all part of the showman's performance. Luinedhel leaned in, too. He listened intently, eager to hear the bard's next words. Perhaps there *was* some *creer'gott* at work here, after all. He realized suddenly the theatrics had played him, and leaned back, smiling to himself at how easily the bard had captivated his attention. He was taking a liking to this young man and his dramatic mannerisms. The two of them could be contemporaries if Luinedhel didn't have *accentation* running through his veins, making him over ten cycles older than the young human.

"They arrived here several days ago," Ever said. "They've stayed camped there in the valley. Rumor is that they're waiting for something. Someone heard that there is going to be a battle with someone coming through Grevyn Pass, maybe the elves from the south … but that's not likely."

Nightfall nodded. "Why is that?"

"The Kragdenmal-Err!" He exclaimed, then paused, frowned, and looked at the two of them, a pained look on his face. The coin appeared again in his hand, and he offered it to Nightfall. "Sirs, I have clearly failed to entertain. If this evening's tales did not enlighten you, nor capture your attention or leave you with things to ponder upon, then I must return your coin, for I have not done enough to earn it."

Nightfall laughed and sat back in his chair. "No, indeed, bard. You must keep the coin. It is I who have failed to discern the deeper meaning in the tales you have shared. I assure you they were most interesting. But I took them for mere ghost stories. You are saying there is more to them?"

Ever hesitated, looking at Nightfall curiously, and the elven coin disappeared once again without argument. "Grevyn Pass is guarded by the Err. Nobody passes through."

"That's not true," Nightfall corrected. "I, myself, have passed through."

Ever shook his head. "It's not possible, dark elf. I've seen the Err myself, from a distance of course ... and the dread that fills me from the very sight of it was enough to fill my dreams with fears for nights. How is it you have gone through unscathed?" He looked at Nightfall and then at Luinedhel.

Luinedhel stood up and stepped beside the fire to get warm. "Nightfall, when you went south, by what route did you travel?"

"I went through Caerbexsys."

"And our warrior friend? He's from the Southlands. How does he go?"

"He travels the Winding Pass to the desert ... or he goes by ship from Redwinds and meets a caravan in Oakhold, like many others."

"Then when was the last time you traveled Grevyn Pass?"

Nightfall frowned. "Maybe ... ten cycles ago. Has it been that long?" He stood up and paced the floor. "It was before I met the others. Before I became … employed." He exchanged a meaningful glance with Luinedhel. There was no point in revealing more to the bard than they needed to. Uttering the name of one of the Weode houses could give away more information than was necessary. "I guess it *has* been a long time. I know the netherworld well, and it is faster for me to travel those roads when traveling south, given the difficulties of the routes past the Idar. I have usually gone under, rather than overland."

Nightfall turned to Ever. "But I've seen this place you speak of. It's simply an abandoned ruin from the ancient days. As you said, it's a tower perched on a precipice at the entrance to the pass. A tower without a door."

"It was," Ever said. "Until two cycles ago. That's when Clarana appeared. There's a way in now … and a way out."

Nightfall frowned again. "You're saying the tower has a door?"

Ever shook his head. "No. The citadel is still faceless. But somehow Clarana went in and came back out, right?" He hesitated, looking from Nightfall back to Luinedhel. "There are also rumors …"

"Of what?"

"Rumors that she did not come out alone. She said, 'It is free.' Perhaps she went in, and by going inside, she released … something."

Luinedhel shot a quick glance at Nightfall. They both had come to the same conclusion.

Questelle.

CHAPTER 38: SISTERS

Before him was an opening. A dark black maw in the wall's side, surrounded by ancient glyphs and carvings – the words of the First People. Black tendrils of thick, strange smoke wound their way out of the opening, crossing the threshold and slithering slowly across the rocky ground before him. They moved like smoke, but were solid … and with purpose. A hiss filled his ears, obscuring the deeper sound of many voices speaking at once in low and guttural whispers. The smell of death and decay hit him like a wave, and he tried to turn away. But he could not move.

He could do nothing but watch as the winding coils snaked toward him. They were alive and dead, most definitely dead, simultaneously. Unnatural. Panic rose in his chest. He looked down and saw Adesh and Marek in his hands. The silver-blue *estrayaed* glinted in the light from Relos and Eyama, a stark contrast to the darkness in front of him that absorbed all the light. The reflection of the moons in the sai looked … different. Peering closely, he realized the moons were aligned. Eyama's golden yellow centered directly in the middle of Relos's white, like a giant eye looking down at him from the sky.

"The time draws close. You will have to choose." Marek's voice sliced across the cacophony of chanting voices. It held power, and the words dispersed the fog of confusion clouding his thoughts.

"Will he choose to embrace his truth ... or will he choose to flee and be consumed? He will have to choose," Adesh said.

"The choice is his to make."

Luinedhel could sense the urgency and importance in Adesh's voice, loud in his head, echoing. *"Plans and plots and dark schemes ..."*

The black tendrils overtook him, blocking everything from his view. They reached for him with hunger, and an unspoken need for something that he had, but he didn't understand what it was. He closed his eyes. Something like a low moan of distress leaked out of him as the dark strands enveloped him completely.

"Wake up, friend! It's just another dream."

Luinedhel opened his eyes and saw Hathar leaning over him. He offered a small cup of drink. "It's water," he whispered. "I didn't have time to make a draught, nor did I want to wake the others."

Luinedhel sat up and took the cup from the cleric, his hands still trembling.

"It's the citadel," Hathar said. "I can sense the darkness. I'm afraid that's where our path lies."

Luinedhel swallowed the water.

On the far side of the room, Scorpio lay on his stomach in his bed. His naked form took up the entire frame, one leg hanging off the side, with his foot resting on the floor. The enormous, intricate sun tattoo that covered his back looked almost red in the candlelight's glow. Luinedhel scanned the rest of the room, peering into the shadows, looking for twisting tentacles of black smoke.

There were none. In the opposite corner, he caught a glint of golden eyes peering at him from the darkness.

Hathar took the cup from him and sat it on the small table at the bedside. "It seems coincidental that Questelle and Dredaius would draw the Weode army southward to Orevael to simply sit here and wait for the Th'arule to come through. The Err plays a part in all of this."

"I'm sorry for waking you, Hathar."

"It is almost dawn, friend. I was already awake, praying to Merces for guidance for today's activities. We need his blessings every day, but I think today we will need it more than most. Nightfall told me what the bard had shared, of the changes in the ancient tower. I have never seen it myself, but have heard of it before, though only as a remnant from the First People."

The small bell at the door moved ever so slightly, and a single thin note rang out. There was an instant flurry of activity. Scorpio leaped out of the bed and met Nightfall at the door. Both had their weapons drawn. Nightfall slept in his black leather armor, a habit that the *drivrid* had picked up long before he had come to the surface. Hathar had stood up swiftly and hefted his hammer from where it rested beside his bed without even the slightest of sounds. All three of them stood poised for a fight, while Luinedhel had barely put his feet on the floor. He marveled at the trio's ability to react so quickly.

Luinedhel glanced over at his *estrayaed* daggers resting on the table next to his bed. If he reached for them, the bed would make noise. He was frozen, unprepared to meet their visitor.

There was a small and quiet knock at the door. "Are you up?"

Nightfall signaled for Scorpio and Hathar to stand down as he sheathed his daggers. "Come in, Ever."

The door opened cautiously, and the bard poked his head inside. He held a candle he had taken from the main room. It lit his face from below. "I didn't want to wake you, but three elves have arrived at the eastern gates just moments ago. Word spreads quickly through Orevael these days. They are inquiring after the Sisters of Yul'e, and I assume based on our conversations last night, they are here to speak about Clarana. I thought you might be interested." There was no hint of his asking for payment in exchange. Ever understood the value of the Weode coin Nightfall had given him.

The bard looked around the room, noting that they were all alert, armed and ready to act … save for Luinedhel, who still sat on the edge of his bed. Luinedhel couldn't help but smile as Ever's eyes passed over Scorpio with a hint of amazement mixed with a bit of envy. Clothed, the giant warrior's physique was impressive, but with every muscle exposed and illuminated by candlelight, he looked like a legendary hero from childhood tales, even more imposing than usual.

"You have time to dress," he said with a grin. "It's cold outside, and I don't think you'll want to go out like *that*, warrior."

"Thank you, Ever," Nightfall said. "We will come down."

"The gates are not open yet. The city defenders won't open them until the sun is up. Magistrate's orders. The elves will have to wait, but they've sent for Sister Ages. She is the head of their order."

Nightfall nodded. "Will you accompany us?"

"Most definitely. The more tales I can pen to entertain my guests, the more coin lines my purse. I have a feeling that the four of you may give me plenty of fodder for song and story. I wouldn't miss the opportunity to be a witness to whatever events are about to unfold. I'm betting they will be quite extraordinary." The troubadour ducked out of the room with a wink. They could hear the creak of the steps as he made his way back downstairs. Scorpio moved to his bed and pulled on his buckskins.

Nightfall closed the door and turned to Luinedhel. "Bad dreams again, *sondartin*?"

Luinedhel stood up and brushed his dark hair away from his face. "Yes. I wish I could make sense of them. A line from the Arcana Sephyrie this time."

"Not surprising."

"It feels ..." He was unable to put into words the rising urgency, perhaps anxiety, about this unexplainable shifting that he felt around him. The entire cosmos seemed focused on this time, place, and these events. He felt everything hinged on the next moment, and the next after that.

"I feel it too." Nightfall stood in front of him. His golden eyes stared intently into Luinedhel's, almost as if they were telling him something about what lay ahead ... things they knew, but could not be spoken.

Hathar appeared behind Luinedhel and gave him a friendly smack on the shoulder. The intensity of the moment faded. "Let's go meet these visitors from the camp and find out what the Weode are up to. Perhaps we can grab a biscuit or two from the kitchen as we head out." He made his way toward the door, with a slight limp in his step. It would be a season before the cleric fully recovered, but Luinedhel was glad he had come along with them to Orevael. It was encouraging for him to have his friends around him. If only he had his family, too.

"Nephinae!" Luinedhel exclaimed and crossed the space between them in three steps. He embraced her, and she returned the embrace enthusiastically. "It's good to see you." He broke the embrace and took a step backwards, noticing that the set of elven warriors behind her had shifted their hands to their weapons. He hesitated for a moment, remembering that to them he was still a wanted criminal for allegedly threatening the Ade.

Nephinae motioned for her guards to stand down. They placed their hands at their sides and nodded curtly. "Apologies, Lord Omaga. Stalle and Chendrelus are with me." She paused and gazed at him intently, her breath coming in puffs of mist in the sharp cold of pre-dawn. "They serve the interest of the Weode, also."

Luinedhel nodded.

"Welcome, Demestre Kydel," Nightfall said. "It is good to see you again. This time under … different … circumstances." A sly smile crossed his face. He bowed his head in greeting. Luinedhel wondered how their paths had crossed before. Something he would have to ask them about when the opportunity arose.

Nephinae glanced over Luinedhel's left shoulder. "Cleric, it appears you are recovering well, though I would say, it would be better for you had you remained in Ny'we Adye under the care of House Shaal'Elonthra. Surely, the journey will delay your full recovery."

"It is a delay I will endure. My place is here, beside Lord Omaga. I am well enough to swing my hammer, should there be need."

She nodded and shifted her gaze. "Warrior. You, too, look better than last I saw you. A spirit like yours was never meant to be caged." Scorpio grunted.

Her gaze fell on the most recent addition to their group. She raised an eyebrow.

"Nephinae," Luinedhel said. "May I introduce you to –"

"Orevael's finest storyteller," the bard said. "Perhaps in all of the northlands." He stepped forward and bowed low, his cape flaring about him dramatically. "Ever Silverleaf, my lady. I am incredibly pleased to meet such a lovely elven maiden, and a Demestre with the Green Guard in addition! I never guessed my day would hold such a fortunate event. My lady, your beauty, and brilliance shine like the sun. I would author such stories about your resplendence, sing such songs about your might! I am at your service."

A smile tugged at the corners of her mouth. Luinedhel could see that the bard's charms had an effect even on her. Nephinae turned to Luinedhel. "We should talk. … in private."

"The minstrel is in our employ," Nightfall said. "He has proven himself useful thus far and we trust him." He glanced at Ever, with a look of warning that should he prove otherwise, there would be dire consequences.

"Very well." Nephinae rubbed her gloved hands together. "Shall we find someplace out of the cold, then?"

Luinedhel nodded. They turned back to the gates of Orevael just as several figures appeared at the entrance. The tallest of the five appeared to be a town guard. Upon seeing them, he faded back into the shadows behind the gate and resumed his duties.

The four remaining were dressed in red from head to toe and covered in voluminous scarlet capes. One, a middle-aged woman, wore a tall crimson headdress that was embroidered with a single white rose. Though she appeared to be more diminutive than the younger ladies, the headdress was so tall and elaborate that it matched Scorpio's height. The woman marched directly toward Nephinae, boldly and purposefully. Luinedhel stepped aside.

"Weode." The word was blunt and filled with displeasure. The woman's lips pursed in indignation. "What is it you need?"

"Sister Ages?" Nephinae inquired.

"I am." The woman's eyes squinted at the elf.

"I must apologize. I didn't intend to pull you from the warmth of your home. Is there a place where we may speak that would be more comfortable for you and your attendants?"

"State your business, so we may return to ours."

Nephinae shifted her weight. She didn't want to engage the woman on adversarial terms, but her attempts at diplomacy were failing. The woman clearly had an unfavorable disposition, though Luinedhel couldn't determine if it was toward Nephinae herself or toward the Weode as a whole.

"Dear, dear Sister Ages," Ever said, stepping forward. "Our guests to Orevael seek information to aid them on their journey. They need the aid of the Sisters of Yul'e. They turn to you in their time of need. Your counsel, Sister Ages, as the wisest and kindest and most revered of all, is most valuable. Surely you, and your Order, wish to appear to have the most beneficent and important impact on the events of these days when the songs are written about them. The tales should tell of your kindness and goodness shown to those who seek to dispel the darkness, allowing the light to once again shine upon our lands. You could be the saviors of all, heroes of these most dreadful and troubling times. Should it not be told that way?"

Sister Ages' face softened. "It should, minstrel. Your songs are delightful."

"Well then," Ever said, clapping his hands together. "Shall we not find comfort, and perhaps some warm drinks, where we can talk without every eye in the city upon us? Curious minds may devise their own tales of these days. Whispers and gossip shared at the local laundry may overshadow the stories that I would pen. Whilst I would write with the most noble intents, of course, my words may come against the slanderous speeches that might paint our players in a less beneficial light."

Sister Ages considered a moment, then smiled. "Let us retreat to the abbey," she said. She gave a gentle nod to Nephinae and then turned to Ever. "Lead on, minstrel."

Ever offered his arm, and she took it. He directed her back toward the town, his silver tongue continuing to pour forth flowery and flattering words to the sister as they made their way back toward the gates. He winked at Luinedhel as he passed by.

Luinedhel exchanged glances with Nightfall. Putting the bard in their employment had been a wise strategy. His dramatic flair and eloquence were things they lacked.

They made their way down the main street of the town, Ever and Sister Ages in the lead, with her attendants following. The rising sun was bringing Orevael to life. Morning light sparkled across the frosted ground as the street filled with locals starting their daily routines. Winter was coming to the land, and there were last-minute preparations to take care of. Luinedhel saw several empty wagons being prepared to leave town. He assumed they were headed to Marinstarn, the nearest city, to fetch additional supplies. The party walked past the townsfolk, who did not spare so much as a comment or a greeting. Everyone was focused on his or her own business. Or, perhaps the activities of the Sisters were best ignored. He found their lack of attention to him refreshing. He was so used to the scrutiny of everyone in Chark and Ny'we Adye. It felt nice to be a little more anonymous here.

The group stopped in front of a stout building near the far end of the rundown city. Two stone columns marked the entrance to the yard. Red banners with white roses decorated the columns. The attendants disappeared inside, and Ever's ceaseless river of words slowed to a trickle as they approached. He stepped aside so that Sister Ages could welcome them to the Abbey of Yul'e of Orevael. Her demeanor had completely changed during their brief stroll through town. She now seemed warm and welcoming.

"Please, come in and find rest," she said. "I will have some tea brought for everyone. There's a fire going in the dining hall. Let us gather there to talk more about how we can aid you all in these troubled times." She paused and looked them over once again. "You will need to leave your weapons here before entering. The Abbey of Yul'e is a house of peace."

Luinedhel looked at Nightfall. He leaned in and spoke in hushed tones. "Are you comfortable with this?"

The *drivrid* seemed to consider for a moment. "No, but I'm not sure we have another option."

"What if this is a trap?"

The nether-elf tilted his head to the side.

"What if Sister Ages is Questelle in disguise?" Luinedhel said. "She could be anyone. Even Ever. We don't know if she's shifted again, who she is now, or what her purposes are."

"I share your concerns, Lord Omaga. But I think Questelle's attention is on the army and the Err – whatever may be happening there. You are right, we don't know her purposes, but I don't think they lie in Orevael. Our arrival here was unnoticed – it was even a surprise to Demestre Nephinae. I think we are safe from Questelle's attention for the moment. But it's wise for you to be cautious, *sondartin*. I will tell the others to remain alert."

Luinedhel nodded. He trusted Nightfall's counsel. The *drivrid* exchanged words with the others and then they moved toward the entrance. Nephinae's guards took position at the stone columns. They would remain outside.

Scorpio unsheathed his great sword and handed it to Stalle, who did his best to manage it. He leaned it against the column. Hathar handed over his hammer, and Nightfall his daggers. Nephinae withdrew her bow and short sword. They had accepted the conditions of their entry into the Abbey.

Reluctantly, Luinedhel placed his daggers into the hands of Chendrelus. The soldier looked at the blades distastefully. Luinedhel smiled at his reaction. Little did he know of the power within the blades … and that of the Nwi'Diad itself. Maybe someday they would learn. Maybe someday soon.

He followed the others through the stone arch and into the Abbey, noting that the minstrel did not follow them. When he glanced over his shoulder, Ever waved at him and turned down the street on another errand.

Luinedhel found himself impressed by how the bard had masterfully smoothed the way and was able to get them exactly where they wanted to be. He had done well, and done it swiftly and with ease.

He hoped they would finally be able to get answers about Clarana and the Err, and possibly also learn what was going on at the Weode camp. He might even be able to get news about Avanstel.

Ever had done well.

CHAPTER 39: CHILD

The dining hall had no windows. It was lit by a sizable fire burning in an enormous stone hearth that took up the entire end of the far side of the room. There were a few candles placed randomly around the room, their sputtering flames attempting to chase away the shadows that lingered in the recesses of the space. It was a wide and sturdy building, with low ceilings and stone columns that held up the roof. Luinedhel realized he had grown used to the light and expansive spaces of House Omaga and other places in Ny'we Adye over the cycle he had spent in Belkin Wood. The open architecture of the Weode stood in stark contrast to that of the Abbey. Here he felt a heaviness, an oppressiveness, as if the entire world was pressing against the roof, threatening to collapse in upon them. He hadn't felt this way in Chark, not even during their time in the darkness of the Delves below the palace. This was different. The heaviness seemed like he could almost touch it.

He looked up at the thick wooden beams overhead, illuminated dimly from below, listening for the slightest sound of a creak or groan … or worse, the sharp crack of a timber splitting. But there were no indications of impending doom, just the troublesome feelings of being caught beneath an immensely crushing weight from above.

"What is it?" Nephinae asked, stepping up beside him and looking towards the ceiling with him.

"Nothing," Luinedhel said. "Do you have news of –"

"The Aetheling is with the Ade and the Adelyn," she said, leaning in. "The three of them addressed the army last eve. I saw him with my own eyes. He is alive and safe … as safe as one could be."

Luinedhel exhaled. Knowing that Avanstel was still alive was an enormous weight off his heart. And knowing that Questelle was at the camp, and not here in the city, was another relief. He had no reason to doubt Ever or anyone else … for the moment.

"Why didn't he send word or try to contact me to let me know he arrived? We've been looking for him everywhere! It doesn't make sense. Why couldn't anyone find him in the palace?"

Nephinae shook her head. "I don't know. Would there be a reason he did not *want* to be found?"

Luinedhel raised his eyebrows. "Not that I can think of. The last time I saw him, he was entering the wood with N'Khael, and then he just vanished." He frowned. "I assumed the worst, of course, with all that is going on. Is he being held against his will?"

"Not from what I could tell. Though he's still in danger. The troops are making preparations for battle. The Ade has announced that we will be marching this evening through the pass to meet the enemy."

"At night?"

Nephinae nodded.

"But …"

"I know. It doesn't seem right. I have sent scouts on ahead, but none have returned. So, either the Th'arule has captured them, or …"

Luinedhel's frown deepened.

"Come now," Sister Ages said, interrupting their conversation. "Warm yourself by the fire and tell me how we may assist you."

Her attendants had moved chairs to form a rough semicircle near the hearth. Stray wisps of smoke escaped into the room, and the smell of the burning logs immediately brought Luinedhel back to long evenings sitting in the study with Selyndar.

"Hillstonas wood," Luinedhel mused to himself.

Sister Ages looked at him, her brow furrowed. "I'm sorry?"

"Nothing," Luinedhel said. "My apologies, Sister. I was just recalling …" He trailed off as he caught a hand gesture from Nightfall out of the corner of his eye.

The sister waited a moment, and when Luinedhel did not continue, she turned back to the others with a dismissive harrumph. "Please sit," she said. She motioned to an attendant, who brought them a tray of mismatched cups filled with warm, fragrant liquid. Luinedhel took one and sipped it, but not before catching a slight nod from Hathar that it was okay to drink. They had had enough dealings with poisons recently to know it was best to let their resident expert take the lead.

Sister Ages took a deep drink from her cup and rested it in her lap, then leaned forward and addressed Nephinae. "What can the servants of Yul'e do for the Weode?"

Nephinae cleared her throat. "We come to inquire about the tower and about the girl, Clarana."

Luinedhel hid his smile at her brashness; she was direct, not wasting time with pleasantries. It reminded him of N'Khael, and he experienced a pang of sadness. The smell of hillstonas wood heightened his longing for more time with Selyndar and his sister. It was curious how a convent on the edge of Orevael was burning wood from the heart of the Belkin forest. Perhaps that's why the *drivrid* had motioned for him to drop the inquiry.

Sister Ages sat back in her chair, her hands tightening around her cup, her body a little more rigid. "The girl is here, under our protection," she said calmly, although there was a sharpness to her response. "What is it you want with her?"

"No harm, I assure you." Nephinae's voice was sweet and reassuring. "Only to help her, and all of Orevael, to cast off the shadow that has befallen this land." She had caught on quickly to the way that Ever had managed this woman. Her alternative approach seemed to have the desired effect.

Sister Ages took another drink. "The child does not speak. Ask me your questions and I will see what aid we can offer you."

Hathar cleared his throat. "May I offer my services as a healer?"

Sister Ages looked at Hathar as if noticing him for the first time. "Brother of Merces, we welcome you to our humble home. We have not had a visit to Orevael from your order in several cycles. But I fear the child is beyond the aid of the servants of Yul'e *or* Merces. Perhaps even beyond the aid of Enos himself. What plagues the child is something beyond our understanding." She inclined her head toward him. "Though if you would think to call upon your god for healing, we would not turn away your offer." She took another drink of her tea. "But you should not be concerned should your god not answer your calls. Clarana's ailment is … unusual."

Hathar scratched his beard and leaned forward. "I would attempt to help. If you would allow me."

The sister thought for a moment in silence. "We will." She motioned to another attendant, who quietly disappeared into the darkened hall. "While we fetch the child, what questions do you have about the Err?"

"We have heard the tales of the tower," Nightfall said. "But I have passed by it myself unharmed as I have traveled to the southlands."

"It has changed in recent cycles, dark dweller," Sister Ages said, then she smiled. "But you feign interest in the tower. You are here for the child, are you not?"

Nightfall sat back. Her words surprised him. "I'm interested in both." His body was tense, like his voice. Something had shifted in their conversation.

"I knew you would come for the child," she said. "I've been expecting you."

Nightfall raised a brow.

"The Arcana Sephyrie," she said, as if that explained everything. She motioned to an attendant to refill her tea. "We may be from a backwater town on the edge of the civilized world, but two cycles ago when the Kragdenmal-Err came alive and Clarana became ours to care for, I did my own research to discern what could be done to heal her malady. I met a man in Redwinds, on the way to the Temple of Yul'e." She paused and looked at Scorpio. "You remind me of him. By his looks, and his accent, I could tell he was from the deserts. Drest most likely, though it's hard to tell them apart sometimes. Are you Drest?"

Scorpio grunted. "I am."

Luinedhel thought back to speaking with Hythorn in the Delves. The brother's accent was unmistakable. Perhaps the man Sister Ages had met was Hythorn, or perhaps one of Scorpio's other brothers.

"As I thought. This other desert man noted my garments and inquired where the Order of the White Rose of the Sisters of Yul'e was based. When I answered Orevael, he was keen to speak about the Err. He told me he'd heard rumors of its awakening and that the lands around our city were blighted. This was true, but had only recently occurred, and I was surprised the news had traveled so fast to Redwinds. Then he handed me some pages which he told me he had copied down from a book called the Arcana Sephyrie, an ancient Groundling prophecy."

"I studied them, and indeed, they seemed to speak of the Err, and the darkness that covers our lands. And of a child. And a dark dweller, a nether-elf, coming to foretell of the end." She shifted her gaze to Nightfall once again. "It is rare to see a *drivrid*, so when I saw you at The Broken Well the other night, I knew you'd come here to find the child, and it was just a matter of time before you showed up on my doorstep."

"I would like to see these papers," Luinedhel said abruptly, startling Sister Ages. A bit of tea spilled down her hands, and an attendant handed the woman a kerchief. "If I may." He paused. "I have been researching these writings, and I am keen to learn more."

Sister Ages looked at him in the dim light, studying him. From her stare, he wasn't sure she would let him see the papers, but if they came from the Librarians, then they might be important. If the Arcana Sephyrie was something that would help them stop whatever dark plans Dredaius and Questelle had, they needed everything.

"I will have them brought here for you to examine, but I will not part with them."

Luinedhel agreed. "Thank you, esteemed Sister."

Just then, a door opened on the side of the dark room and daylight spilled in from a window beyond, lighting up the space. Luinedhel shielded his eyes. There was a repetitive squeaking noise and some rattling, and then the door closed. Darkness returned to the room. The noise continued to grow closer until it stopped with a loud grinding noise. As his eyes adjusted back to the darkness, he noticed that there was a figure in a wheeled chair sitting to the side of their gathering. Behind the chair was the attendant he had seen with the old woman at The Broken Well.

He looked at the figure in the chair. He tilted his head in confusion. Before him sat a young girl, not an elderly woman.

There was a chuckle from Sister Ages. "Not who you were expecting?"

"No," Luinedhel said flatly. Had Ever lied to them after all? Had it all been a story to acquire coin from them?

"Clarana ... changes," Sister Ages clarified.

"I'm afraid I don't quite understand."

"You may see it for yourself," she said cryptically. "If the child shows us. Though it's not by her calling. The changes come upon her at the whim of some cruel power, which is out of her control. Out of *any* of our control."

Hathar placed his cup on the floor beside his chair, stood up, and crossed in front of Luinedhel. He grunted as he knelt down on his bad leg in front of the child. She continued to stare blankly ahead. Her eyes were blue, but clouded over, just like the old woman's that Luinedhel had seen at the tavern. She didn't react when the cleric took her hand. Hathar smoothed the girl's long hair, so blonde it was almost white. He touched the side of her face, and there was only the slightest flinch from her.

Then suddenly, her face bubbled, and the girl cried out, a terrifying yelp. Her face morphed into something ferocious and bestial and then, just as swiftly, blurred. Something was moving and rippling beneath the skin like a creature trapped inside her, searching for an escape. To his left, Luinedhel heard Scorpio shift his weight as if he was preparing to draw his weapon, though he remembered then that they had left their weapons at the door. Had they walked into a trap?

Hathar stepped back from the girl. Nightfall was beside the cleric in a flash, signaling him to hold off taking any action.

"Do not fear," Sister Ages said calmly, rocking back in her seat as if the strangeness before them was nothing remarkable at all. "She changes, but will not harm you. The poor dear is trapped within her own mind and body, unable to do anything but survive these episodes. Helpless when it comes to the world around her. There's nothing to be done."

Luinedhel thought back to his dream about the herbalist shop in Chark. Where the woman, whom he knew as Questelle, had switched the medicines for the poison that had killed Adine. The sounds coming from Clarana were the same cries of pain and … joy … he had heard in his dream. It was the same screeching, the sound of bones crunching and reassembling. Clarana must be a shifter, like Questelle! Could this changeling girl be in league with the Adelyn of Weode? Luinedhel stood up quickly, his cup spilling and rolling across the floor with a clatter. He stepped backwards, tripping over the stool that he had been sitting on. "She's ... she's ..." he stammered.

Then, just as in his dream, the transformation was over in an instant. And where the young girl had been, an old woman sat – bent over and motionless, save for her heaving chest as she caught her breath. Her pale skin, hair, and eyes were almost luminescent in the light from the fire. It was the woman they had seen at The Broken Well. The one Ever had told them was Clarana, the child who had wandered into the tower.

"Merces help us!" Hathar whispered.

"Merces, Yul'e, and all the gods together," Sister Ages agreed calmly. She had remained seated, gently rocking in her chair by the fire. She took a sip of her tea as if the horrific change had not just happened. "Please ... have a seat and calm yourself. I know it can be disturbing, but fear not, the change will not happen again soon. Although in recent days, it has been more frequent. The child takes some time to regain her strength between her cycles. This is her only saving grace. Her body must rest before another attack."

Luinedhel stood dumbfounded, staring at the old woman who had been just a girl moments before. He felt Nephinae's hand on his arm, guiding him to sit again, but he shook his head. Though the others had returned to their seats by the fire, he couldn't calm himself enough to join them.

"*Sere'eden*," he thought, willing himself to quench the fire of fear that rolled inside him. "*Sere'eden!*" But he could not take his eyes off Clarana. She did not look his way. Her gaze did not move from the fire.

"You see," Sister Ages said, "I am afraid that Clarana cannot be of any aid to you in whatever your quest may be." She motioned for one of the attendants to retrieve the spilled cup of tea and bring Luinedhel another. When the young lady presented the cup to him, he did not move to receive it. His eyes remained fixed on the old woman. After a moment, the attendant disappeared into the darkness, taking the cup with her.

Hathar took a long drink of his tea and looked at Sister Ages. "I understand now, Sister." There was a timbre in his voice that resonated with Luinedhel, echoing the storm of fear and dread bubbling up inside himself. "The girl is beyond healing. What haunts her is something I have not seen before … and I have seen many things in my travels. I can pray to Merces for reprieve, but I'm afraid other than that, she is beyond my aid."

"As I expected."

"Esteemed Sister, if we may ask?" Nightfall said. His voice was calm, despite the display they had just witnessed. Luinedhel found comfort in the steadfastness of the unshakeable assassin. "As my friend has shared, we are curious about these papers that were given to you in Redwinds. Perhaps we might see them? I'm not sure they could help your ward, but perhaps they might be useful to us as we seek to understand the origin of the heavy shadows cast over Orevael."

"Of course, dark dweller. I expect you will find them of equal interest and may help explain our situation, why we keep Clarana so close and have not abandoned her to the wilds."

An attendant came forward, holding a wooden box secured with a lock. Sister Ages reached inside her red robes and pulled out a small silver key on a chain. She unlocked the chest, opened the lid, and removed a parchment from inside.

She looked over the paper. "The child will raise her fist against the darkness … when the time has come." Satisfied, she passed the document to Nightfall.

He took a moment to look them over before showing them briefly to Scorpio, who nodded in understanding. "These are …

interesting," Nightfall said. He turned to Luinedhel and offered him the aged parchment. "My friend, I believe you should look at these."

Luinedhel tore his gaze away from Clarana. In Nightfall's golden eyes, Luinedhel saw something that gave him pause.

"*Sere'eden.*"

He exhaled and took the papers, his hands still trembling. He sat down on the stool next to Nephinae, angling the papers so that they caught the light from the fireplace.

The paper contained bold, elegant letters.

Arcana Sephyrie, Gravlin Groundstone
Quire Seven; Pretacten Twelve.
In shadows deep where no light treads,
Dark dweller walks, where silence spreads.
With skin, a hue of moonless night,
And eyes like embers, burning bright.

From caverns vast where light unravels,
Through hallowed wood and alleys travels,
Cross paths unseen by common eyes,
Begin as strangers, now allies.

Journeys taken within the gloom,
Seeking, reaching, to slay the bloom.
Darkness alight with fire blue.
Ancient whispers revealed as true.

Dark tower shadows land of blight.
Loosed power triumphs, armies of might.
Against such horror, no man can stand.
Yet child raises defiant hand.

Dark dweller heralds, 'the end is nigh!'
Be warned, be wary the light on high.
Cursed waves pound down, corrupt the land.
Brandished, banished by child's hand.

As he finished reading the last word, the old woman suddenly jerked her head towards him. Her cloudy blue eyes became clear and focused. She looked at him with fierce intensity and grabbed his arm. He dropped the papers on the floor and pulled away from her.

"Shifter's seed!" she said. Luinedhel knew that voice! It was the voice from his dream – the one where the fourth ring had broken. It had been Clarana's voice! He froze, and she continued, "The blood! The blood! You must stop them. Their hunger is insatiable, their eyes blind with malice and rage. The child comes with darkness and light in hand to stop them, to prevent the cataclysm, the next destruction. Run! Run as fast as you can! The time draws close, the eye peers down and watches below. The wolf, once hunter, is now the prey! Only the blood of the doul'zur can stop them. They are free. They are free and only the blood can stop them. They are coming to destroy you. Destroy you all. And they will not fail. Woe. Woe to the children of the doul'zur and the children of the realm. Woe to all."

She wailed an ear-piercing and horrific sound of pain and agony and fell forward, out of her chair and onto the floor, where her limbs continued to bubble and shift in frightening and disturbing ways. She kept clawing at Luinedhel's feet in jerking, uncontrolled motions.

Everyone jumped backward in surprise, tripping and stumbling over their seats in the rush. They reached for weapons that were not there. Nephinae moved in front of Luinedhel, automatically placing herself in position to defend him against whatever strange thing would happen next. Even Sister Ages lost her composure and ducked behind the chair she had been sitting in. Her attendants fled the room.

Luinedhel looked over at Nightfall, who was grabbing Hathar's arm to pull him back away from the withering figure on the floor. "Leave her. Leave it."

Hathar glared at him. "She's in pain. I can help."

"No," Nightfall answered. "We are going. We have to leave now." He looked over at Scorpio. Without another word, the giant grabbed Hathar's other arm and pulled him back from the figure, still twisting and writhing on the floor.

Luinedhel didn't need further instructions. He turned back to the door and crossed the room swiftly. Nephinae was beside him, and the others followed.

They raced out of the abbey and toward the stone columns where Stalle and Chendrelus stood. The elven soldiers reacted to the scene by quickly drawing their weapons.

"To arms!" Nephinae cried. "Get the weapons!"

They tossed Nephinae her bow. She immediately drew an arrow, spun around, and aimed at the door they had fled from. Luinedhel passed her and reached for the daggers that were sitting on the stone wall. They came to life in his hands.

"*An old one!*" Marek said. "*I can feel them!*"

"*How long? How long has it been since I've tasted the blood of an old one? Kill them now before they take your life!*" Adesh commanded.

Nightfall and Hather reached the wall and retrieved their weapons, turning back to face the abbey. Scorpio was last out of the building, having guarded their retreat. He was prepared to battle the creature hand-to-hand, should it pursue them.

But it didn't.

They stood there for several moments, weapons lifted and ready for whatever would come at them. Everything outside the abbey continued on without awareness of what had just transpired within. They held there, waiting for what seemed like hours, but it was probably just a few minutes.

Then the door of the abbey opened, and Clarana's attendant appeared in the entrance. "Sister Ages asks you to leave the premises. The meeting is over." She turned, retreated inside, and closed the door behind her.

Luinedhel looked at the others in confusion and disbelief. "That was …"

"Unexpected," Nephinae said.

"Strange," Hathar chimed in.

"Indeed, *sondartin*. Somewhat concerning,"

Luinedhel frowned. "I was going to say it was frightening."

Scorpio grunted.

"*They are there, but they are …*" Marek trailed off.

"*Injured,*" Adesh said. "*A damaged old one without the power to change at will. We should kill them now, in their weakened state while they are most vulnerable.*"

Luinedhel ignored them, still shaken, but more confused than upset now. "I don't think Clarana intended to harm me," he said. "I think she was trying to warn me. Although, her words were as confusing as the Arcana Sephyrie."

"Speaking of which," Nightfall said. The *drivrid* withdrew papers from his black leather tunic. "Let us retreat so we can study these words. Selyndar only has four volumes of the books, and I don't recall this Pretacten. I would like time to review it and ponder their meaning."

"The faster and further away from here we can get, the better," Luinedhel said.

They withdrew from the abbey slowly, ever vigilant against what might come after them, but it remained still and silent. Luinedhel glanced over his shoulder one last time and shuddered as they turned a corner and the abbey was out of view. He hoped he would never have to return there.

They felt it momentarily. Another of the five. Another had also escaped the confines of the prison. They couldn't tell which one it was, but they'd eventually find out.

Not all the others agreed with their goals, which was unfortunate, but also not necessary. They were the purest of the five remaining, and the most powerful. That's why they had ruled over the others since the beginning. The blood of their family remained untainted by intermingling with other races. That purity was something that justified their decisions and their rule. Something they could boast about … until their sibling had imprisoned them. Curse the betrayer!

They raged for a moment, but then pushed the anger aside. They focused their attention on what was happening before them. They would soon correct the past. No need to dwell on it. They would bring about justice, and tonight they would give birth to a new world, in their image and under their dominion, and they would regain what they had lost.

Whichever of the others that had escaped would either be an ally or a minor annoyance, but it was unlikely it would affect their plans. They had all the pieces they needed, and nothing would stop them.

They looked out over the ocean of elven soldiers below, and a smile crossed their face. Soon that army would be better, more powerful, and would rampage over the realm with a ferocity unseen in ages. They peered through the curtain that separated them from the rulers of the Weode. Their smile faded as they looked at the two brothers in disgust.

The Ade sat with his back to them. Across from him was the tainted one. They smelled the doul'zur blood in Dredaius now. It had been a faint scent at first, stronger within the father. But as they had drawn closer to the tower, the smell had grown, and it was undeniable.

But the tainted one still had no smell. They spat. His blood was so diluted with elf and human that there was not even the slightest whiff of doul'zur on him — even here, closer to the ancient power! He probably had so little left in him that it wouldn't aid much in the ceremony — but every bit of blood counted. And then there was restitution to consider. For complete restitution, they must erase the betrayer's entire line. Even one remaining would not satisfy their anger.

They touched the charm at their neck, rubbing it and loosening the last of the *creer'gott* that remained in it. Soon they would not need the magic to enhance the glamour, for the ultimate amplification would be within their hands and they could do as they wished. Their eyes darted to the wrapped package that sat next to the Ade. In just a few hours, the waiting would be over.

CHAPTER 40: SOLDIERS

Nephinae looked back over her shoulder toward the east, where the sun was climbing higher in the sky. "I have to get back. Thank you, bard, for retrieving these supplies while we spoke with the Sisters. These will support our purposes here, should anyone notice our absence and ask questions."

Stalle took the oversized bag and swung it over one of her shoulders. The bundle looked to be almost as large as the she-elf, but she exerted little effort in lifting it and positioning it on her back. Luinedhel glanced over at Ever, who had struggled to remove the package from the rear of the wagon and had resorted to requesting help from Scorpio. The bard shrugged and smiled, raised an eyebrow, and flashed a grin at the elven warrior. She did not return his smile. He shrugged again. "All business, no time for fun," he mumbled, only loud enough for Luinedhel to hear.

Luinedhel reached into the back of the small horse-drawn cart and handed several quivers of arrows to Chendrelus.

"Those blades ..." The Weode guard nodded toward the daggers on Luinedhel's belt. "Interesting design." He hesitated for a moment. "They seem to be very ... old."

"They are," Luinedhel answered as he passed wineskins to him.

"Lord Omaga, if I may ..." Chendrelus deftly took the sword from his belt and pointed it, hilt first, toward Luinedhel. "It would please me and bring honor to my House if you would accept my weapon instead. I have not yet named it, as I only received it a hundred cycles ago. You can name it yourself. Master Orrion Quirtris, the most talented smith in Ny'we Adye, forged it in his workshop's fires. It is a fine weapon, made of the best elven steel, which is stronger and better than what you have now. It's a much more fitting weapon for a member of the Council of Elders and from a founding House. I am sure your sister would have wanted it to be so. It was an honor to serve alongside her."

Luinedhel looked down at the blade that Chendrelus was offering him. He took the weapon and hefted it, admiring its balance and craftsmanship. He swung it twice and marveled at the sweet and sharp note that rang out as the blade sliced through the air. N'Khael would have loved such a blade, and would have encouraged him to swap out his aged *estrayaed* daggers for a sleek and well-crafted sword such as this. However, as beautiful as it was, holding it was less comfortable than holding his daggers. The handle did not mold to his grip the way Adesh and Marek did.

"It *is* a fine sword, Chendrelus," Luinedhel said, and he handed the weapon back to the swordsman. "And I am honored by your offer. However, my daggers are familiar to me. They have been with me through many adventures thus far and I am disinclined to part with them even for a blade as excellent as yours." He patted the weapons hanging from his belt. "You should also consider that there may come a need for you to swing your own steel in the upcoming battle. You should keep it close."

Chendrelus caught his eye, acknowledging the comment with a slight nod of his head. "Yes, my Lord."

Nephinae tossed the final large sack over her shoulder. The smell of freshly baked bread wafted through the air. Ever had retrieved this one from the baker. "Shall we go then? We will need to travel swiftly, as we've already spent too much time away." Stalle and Chendrelus, with their arms and backs burdened with Ever's hastily gathered morning treasures, turned and headed towards the mountains and away from the eastern gates of Orevael.

Luinedhel looked at Nephinae, her pale hair glowing in the sunlight. "Please, be careful."

A smile crossed her lips. "Fear not for *my* safety, Lord Omaga." It was her way of subtly reminding him she was a Green Guard, and like N'Khael had been, was fully capable of handling herself in any circumstances – seemingly indestructible. He looked down at his feet. He had once believed the same about his sister.

"Nephinae, I ..."

"I will see you back in Ny'we Adye," she said firmly, clasping his hands in hers. She leaned in, pulling him forward, and kissed his cheek, her lips warm against his cold skin. "Or possibly this eve, should our paths cross again," she whispered, and quickly turned and sprinted after her companions.

Ever was at Luinedhel's side. "At least one of them has time for fun," he said.

Luinedhel felt his neck and face warming. He kept his eyes down and would not look at the minstrel. "We should ready ourselves," he said abruptly. He turned to see his companions watching him, and he knew by their faces that they also had witnessed the brief interaction between him and Nephinae. His face turned fiery.

"Indeed," Nightfall said, stepping forward and motioning toward the gates. "Best to review the new verses from the Arcana Sephyrie and make our plans in private."

Luinedhel was grateful for the change of subject.

As they made their way back through the city gates and toward The Broken Well, Luinedhel brushed his cheek with his hand and smiled.

The sun had sunk low in the sky, hovering over the flatlands to the west. One last wagon, a dark silhouette against the orange and purple sky, was teetering slowly down the road toward Orevael's western gate. Three guards waited there, prepared to close the gates for the night after they admitted the final traveler for the day.

Luinedhel watched the scene astride Aelduin. To his right, Nightfall was on Nyx. Their horses were motionless and silent. Selyndar's stable master had trained them well. To his left, however, Ever sat atop a gelding that fidgeted and continued to prance around anxiously, flicking his tail and shaking his head.

"Ever! Be still," Luinedhel hissed.

The bard pulled on the reins sharply. "I'm trying, but this horse has a mind of his own. We shouldn't wait much longer," he said. "They will close the gates as soon as they inspect the wagon."

"A moment more," Nightfall said.

As soon as he finished speaking, Ever's horse bolted forward. Luinedhel grabbed for the reins, but missed them. The horse sprinted ahead until it reached the hard-packed ground in front of the gate and then reared back, letting loose a loud neigh. The guards reached for their weapons, assuming they had somehow just come under attack from within their own city. They scrambled toward Ever and his horse to capture them.

"Whoa! Whoa!" Ever shouted, pulling back on the reins. The horse slammed its front feet down and raced out the gate and past the wagon, which had just reached the entrance. The pair of horses pulling the cart were spooked and bucked against their harnesses. They took off running down the main street of Orevael, dragging the wagon behind them. The wagon driver shouted for them to stop, his voice fading away as they raced deeper into the town.

A pair of guards raced after the wagon, shouting for it to halt, leaving the remaining man to watch the entrance. He looked at the enormous gates and scratched his head. There was no way he could close it by himself. He would have to wait for his cohort to return.

"Not what we had planned, but just as effective," Nightfall chuckled. He clicked his tongue, and Nyx stepped forward out of the shadows and toward the gates.

The guard raised both hands in warning. "I'm going to need you to wait a moment," he said. "We've just had an incident, and it's past sundown. Gates need to be shut. Nobody goes in. Nobody goes out."

"I understand," Nightfall said, drawing up beside the man. Luinedhel watched the nether-elf make a motion with his hand. In the air above the guard, faint pink dancing snakes appeared. They were barely noticeable unless one was looking for them specifically.

"*Creer'gott*," Luinedhel thought to himself. "Nightfall's weapon of choice."

The man yawned and rubbed his left eye. "What's your … business?" His voice slurred slightly.

"Going after a stolen horse," Nightfall said matter-of-factly. "A dun. Creamy with a black mane and tail. Have you seen anyone riding a horse like that?"

"Just … came … through." The guard motioned toward the gate. He paused and then, without ceremony, fell backwards, landing with a heavy thud on the ground.

Nightfall looked over his shoulder. That was their cue.

Luinedhel pressed Aelduin's ribs gently, and she walked forward out of the shadows and into the firelight. Hathar and Scorpio followed on their mounts.

"Easy," Hathar said. "Almost too easy."

"I wouldn't be concerned," Nightfall said. "You have grown used to the challenges that have come with being employed by Lord Omaga, which have usually required more … finesse. But this is

Orevael. Enjoy it. What awaits us ahead will likely challenge us more than enough."

Scorpio kicked his horse forward, heading out of the gates and in the direction that Ever had disappeared. The others followed.

As they slipped past the light from the fires along the wall, Luinedhel looked back to see the other two city guards returning from the chase. They shook their companion awake and dragged him away from the gates. One placed a foot firmly on his buttocks, gave a firm shove forward, and shouted something at him. The two men turned their attention to the gate. Orevael was closed for the night.

The party caught up with Ever shortly afterwards. His horse was walking along slowly as they circled the city and headed eastward, out of sight from peering eyes.

"I don't know what got into him," Ever said as Luinedhel pulled up beside him.

"Must be the rider," Hathar said from behind them.

Ever turned in his saddle to look back at the cleric. "I'm a fine rider, mind you. My father had a stable in Harper. I know horses!" The bard frowned and kicked his horse into a canter.

A wide grin split Hathar's face as he stifled a laugh. He held out his hand to Luinedhel. A long, thorny branch rested in his palm. He winked and tossed it into the darkness. Luinedhel chuckled. The cleric had taunted Ever's horse … and Ever himself. It was good to have a little levity in the group. They needed that. What lay ahead would be anything but lighthearted. Their destination was the Weode camp, and from there, on to the dark tower, Kragdenmal-Err.

Nightfall crept over the scattered boulders, Luinedhel in tow. From shadow to shadow, they made their way toward the elven camp in silence. Luinedhel could see torches in the distance, bobbing in an intricate dance that lacked any music or measure. Twice, the two of them had paused as they made their way forward, and Nightfall had signaled toward some distant point in the darkness ahead.

The first time, a small nocturnal animal had crossed their path before scurrying on without further incident. Although it had been nothing of consequence, Luinedhel had still felt his body tense and his heart pounding in his chest. The closer they drew to the Weode camp, the greater the risk of discovery. Their goal was not to engage with the elven army, but to scout the situation and then report back to the others. They needed to get in front of the troops as they made their way into Grevyn Pass.

The second time Nightfall signaled, Luinedhel knew it was more than a random night scavenger. He had heard the slightest scuff of a footfall at the moment the *drivrid* had motioned to him. Luinedhel held his breath and pushed against the boulder he was hiding behind, willing himself to be as small as possible. The Weode had keen sight, able to see much further than humans, but that gift had not been passed on to Luinedhel. Nightfall had the same gift as his elven cousins, but with the advantage of being able to see better than them in darkness – a talent that had given him an edge in his line of work.

Another barely audible sound behind them signaled the picket had passed them by, unnoticed. They were now firmly inside the Weode lines. They would have to be even more cautious moving forward and watch their backs to avoid discovery from behind.

The pair edged closer to the distant lights, slowly and methodically. Luinedhel could now hear voices as the officers barked commands to their troops to break camp and suit up for battle. The din from the encampment was subdued, and Luinedhel could sense the tension in the air as the soldiers prepared for what lay ahead. He wondered if they truly thought they were going to face off against the Th'arule, or if they suspected something different was at hand.

If Nephinae had connected with those in her network who were 'loyal to the Weode' and not necessarily supporters of Dredaius and Questelle, word may have spread far enough within the ranks of the army to put them all on alert. From the sounds coming from the camp, and from what Luinedhel could see at this distance, it seemed as if everyone was following orders.

Nightfall pointed to a small group of tents ahead of them. There was an exposed area between their current position behind a fallen tree and the edge of the camp. It was dimly lit by a fire burning between the tents. If they crossed that space, anyone looking in their direction would spot them. He shook his head, but Nightfall motioned again. Luinedhel frowned. He was not as skilled at silent movement, nor did he have night sight as the *drivrid* did, so he was not as confident in his ability to remain undiscovered.

Nightfall gestured again, more urgently this time. Luinedhel nodded, took a deep breath, and dashed for the tents as quietly as possible. He crossed the open space rapidly and flung himself into the darkness behind the tent.

"What's this?" a voice said to his right in Weald-speak. He had been discovered.

Luinedhel glanced up to see a Weode soldier staring at him. The elf had just finished relieving himself and was lacing up his breeches. He didn't have his armor or weapon on. The soldier took a step toward the side of his tent, where his sword rested against his backpack. Luinedhel reached for his daggers. This was turning out exactly how he had feared.

There was a sudden sound of movement, and then the soldier's head jerked unnaturally, and he fell to his knees. As he landed, Luinedhel saw Nightfall standing over the body.

"Quick, drag him behind the tent," the nether-elf whispered.

Without a word, Luinedhel scrambled to his feet, grabbed the legs of the soldier, and did as Nightfall instructed. Soon, the two were huddled in the shadows beside the soldier's unmoving body.

Nightfall started removing the man's tunic. He looked up at Luinedhel and whispered, "Take off your clothes."

"This was not the plan," Luinedhel responded. His fingers worked to free his cloak. "I can't —"

"You can. You must." Nightfall handed Luinedhel the shirt. "We can't make it to the tower before the army. There's too many of them and they're already assembling in formation. We are out of time."

Luinedhel slipped off his shirt and slid into the soldier's garment. "What about the others? It would be better if Hathar and Scorpio were with us."

"These uniforms fit elvenkin, not humans. Scorpio wouldn't fit. Hathar's bristles would be noticed instantly. The bard's beard too — and he wouldn't know to keep his mouth shut."

Nightfall slid off the soldier's boots and pants, and handed them to Luinedhel.

"What about you?"

"Get dressed. I will help you with the armor. Don't worry about me. I will follow you from the shadows. If my skin or eyes were spotted, they would draw attention. You're the only one who can do this."

"Nightfall, I …"

The *drivrid*'s golden eyes looked up and met Luinedhel's. His voice was soft, but firm. "You can do this. Your sister and your father have trained you in the Dance. You have been educated by the most honorable house in all the kingdom. You have seen lost and ancient places, touched magics that were hidden to mortals for millennia. You have seen more of the world than most of this entire army. You have companions who believe in you and trust you. You have blades that give you counsel and aid you in your battles. Merces and Enos and the other gods watch over these events. Even the hidden city of Q'Serath has stirred and taken interest. Fate intended you for this time and place, Luinedhel Omaga. Avanstel is counting on you. We are all counting on you, heir to the throne of J'Onsal."

As he spoke, a warmth had begun in Luinedhel's chest, building, burning, and now bursting and racing through his body. His heart was pounding.

"Sere'eden!" he whispered, trying to calm his thumping heart.

"No," Nightfall said. "Let go. Don't hold back. Unleash what you have fought against all your life. Let out whatever it is inside of you that you push down and lock up behind your fear, behind the mental barriers your mother trained you to build. Now is not the time for peace and serenity, but for action and strength. I have seen it in you since Chark, always there, lingering beneath the surface. Tamed and controlled, but wild, nonetheless. Let it go now, Luinedhel. Let whatever it is you were meant to be escape the fortress you have created around yourself. Use that fire inside of you to accomplish the purpose you were created for."

Luinedhel swallowed hard and nodded. He placed the Weode helm over his dark hair, his *ort* features disappearing beneath the shell of the elven armor. "For Adine." Luinedhel's voice held a new strength. "For Danvaren. For N'Khael and Selyndar. For Avanstel."

A smile crossed Nightfall's dark face. "For your kingdom. For your future." He stood up and offered his hand to Luinedhel. They faced each other, Luinedhel having transformed into one of the many nameless Weode soldiers, and the *drivrid* barely noticeable in the darkness.

Nightfall clasped his shoulder. *"Namartha t'undel,"* he said solemnly. "I am beside you. We are all beside you." The *drivrid* placed something in his hand. He looked down to see the white sword Haven Chase token.

"You are the white sword, Luinedhel. It is your destiny to bring light to the darkness. Go now, free your friend, and stop Questelle."

CHAPTER 41: PRETENDER

Luinedhel had observed N'Khael enough times to understand how to respond to the commands of the officers, what they meant, and where he should be. He fell in with the other soldiers as he made his way through the camp.

A light drizzle filled the air, intensifying as they moved eastward. Luinedhel looked up at the sky and could see dim yellow light from Eyama in the west. As the moon traveled across the sky, it eventually slid behind the clouds gathering in the east. He looked in that direction and saw the Idar Mountains looming darkly on the horizon. He shivered. He was cold and wet, but his reaction wasn't due to the weather. He swallowed his trepidation about what lay ahead and focused on getting to the front of the line, where he hoped to spot Avanstel or Nephinae – or even Stalle or Chendrelus. Just someone, anyone, who could be beside him through what lay ahead.

Thousands of Weode soldiers had gathered into formation in the large flatlands at the edge of the camp; lines of ten, in squares of ten, and then in larger squares of hundreds. Luinedhel estimated there were perhaps ten thousand troops between the foot soldiers and the mounted units. It was more than he had guessed that all of

Belkin Wood had contained. The Ade must have conscripted every able body from the entirety of Weode lands, save the handful Questelle had left to guard the palace.

His hunch proved more accurate the closer he drew to the formation. He noticed several soldiers who lacked the precision drilled into those who had served. These were being corrected by the officers to stand straighter, to form up beside the others, to hold their army-issued swords or bows in this way or that. The officers cursed in Weald-speak and grumbled audibly about the lack of ability in the newest members of their forces.

"The Th'arule will have no mercy! They will slaughter us!" A gruff general complained to his lieutenant as they passed in front of Luinedhel, ignoring his salute.

"They are merchants and craftsmen and bakers," the lieutenant answered. "If the Th'arule have brought their full force against us, we are doomed."

Luinedhel waited, watching them disappear into the rain, and then started forward. He was scanning the area and looking for the best place to insert himself into the ranks when he heard someone shout at him.

"You there! Hold!"

He turned to see an officer marching toward him. He looked to both sides to see if the Weode was addressing someone else, but he only saw other soldiers racing to fall into formation. His blood turned cold, and panic flooded his body. Had they discovered him? His hands reached for his daggers, concealed beneath the green sash that crossed his breastplate.

The officer was standing directly in front of him. His face was stern and rough. He was a veteran, perhaps as flustered with their situation as the other seasoned leaders. "Do you know how to ride?" the officer asked sharply.

Luinedhel saluted the officer and then grunted and nodded. He spoke Weald-speak enough for him to pass as a resident of Ny'we

Adye, but he didn't want to risk the man picking up on his accent. Now was an appropriate time to take a page from Scorpio's book and speak as little as possible.

"There!" The commander pointed to where a large tent stood. "Get mounted up and fall in with the others."

Luinedhel grunted, saluted sharply, and headed toward the tent. He was glad he had taken riding lessons with Selyndar. On horseback, he might have a better view of the landscape … and a quicker escape, should that become necessary.

They gave him a mahogany mare, fitted with elven armor that matched his own. His mount was the calmest of the three remaining in the tent. The other two were jittery and anxious, pacing around and snorting. He slid up into the saddle deftly and exited the tent, heading in the direction the groomsman had pointed. He saw the other members of the cavalry flanking the north end of the troops. As he neared the lineup, a soldier stopped him and handed a bow and a quiver of arrows. The woman had not asked him if he knew how to shoot, or if his aim was true. If you were Weode, you mastered the bow at an early age. It was just assumed that he could use the weapon. He took the items without comment.

Luinedhel looked down at the weapons and smirked. He recognized the fletching on the arrows. Ever had procured the quiver that morning. He swung the quiver over his shoulders, nodded to the soldier who had given it to him, and proceeded forward, falling in line with the other mounted troops.

He scanned the crowd, imagining, hoping he could pick out Nephinae or her companions. The rain was coming down harder now, making it difficult to see anything but what was directly in front of him. In the throng of identically armored soldiers, he doubted he would be able to pick them out, even without the rain.

Ahead in the distance, he could make out a wooden platform elevated above the masses with tents on it. Large braziers burned brightly in all four corners of the stage, despite the falling rain.

Figures moved about on top of the platform, but Luinedhel couldn't tell how many or who they were. As one of them stepped forward to the edge of the platform, the din of the crowd faded away.

"Peoples of Weode!" a shout came from the platform. Luinedhel recognized the voice of Dredaius as it echoed across the entire army assembled below. "This evening, we march on to fight against the Unwritten, our enemies of old, who would like to enslave us once again!"

There was a murmur from the crowd. The Weode were ready to fight for their freedom from the tyrannical rule of the Th'arule, though it had been thousands of cycles since they had had interactions with the southern kingdom.

"But I say to you," Dredaius continued, "No one will conquer the Weode, nor will anyone subjugate us! No, indeed! Like the White Wolf, like Ni'Ilyan himself, we will rise up against our oppressors. They will feel our bite at their necks as we tear away their lives. The children of Ni'Ilyan will rise once again to throw off the leashes of our former taskmasters!"

A cheer rose from the crowd, swelling to a roar. Soldiers banged their swords against their shields. Dredaius waited for the noise to die down and then continued. "We will not return to our past! We *cannot* return to our past! We look for a future of freedom and an end to the persistent threat of the Th'arule." There was another raucous cheer. "The Weode serve no one! The Weode are free! The Weode make their own destiny!"

The noise was deafening as the crowd erupted in shouts and whistles. The soldiers raised their pikes, banners, and swords above them. As if on cue, lightning flashed across the sky and a thunderous boom shook the ground. The army roared even louder.

Luinedhel could see movement on the platform as two figures stepped up beside Dredaius. He took each of their hands, raising them high. The crowd erupted again. A chant began, gaining with each moment as more joined in, until all those around Luinedhel began raising their voices. *"White Wolf! White Wolf! White Wolf!"*

Another flash of lightning arced across the clouds overhead, followed by a shaking blast. The chanting dissolved into a deafening cacophony, amplified by the marching of the troops. Luinedhel nudged his mare gently, and she moved along with the mounts on either side. As his regiment passed in front of the platform, he looked up, but the figures had disappeared. He could only assume that Avanstel had been one of those with Dredaius, and Questelle the other.

He looked around to see if he could spot where they might be in the army, but the jostling throng around him obscured everything. He spurred his mare forward into the rain and darkness.

He rode in silence; the rain pelted around him and rang off his elven armor. The rhythmic thrumming of the feet of the soldiers and horses around him pounded in his chest. The frenzy and roar of the crowd had died down as the reality of what lay ahead of them sank in. It was patriotic and honorable to put one's life on the line for one's country, but where the philosophical met the practical was ripe ground for the seeds of doubt to take root. These bakers and merchants thought they were coming up against the army of Th'arule – the older and wiser and larger nation of their ancestors. The army of Th'arule would undoubtedly possess superior equipment and training and would surpass the Weode in numbers. The idea that they might face their death replaced the chanting of *"White Wolf!"* that had filled the place just moments before.

Suddenly, there was a noise ahead: metal on metal. Luinedhel drew an arrow and notched his bow; he knew this much about the weapon. A sudden memory blossomed of days long past when

Avanstel and Danvaren had taken him on a hunting trip to the Cedars of Upper Geffam. The brothers had taught him the basics of the bow, though they were both much better at it than he was. Danvaren proved to be the best at hunting, providing all their meals on the trip. A pang of sadness raced through him, thinking of Danvaren's death at the hands of Questelle. His sadness turned to anger, which burned in his heart. She would pay.

The clamor faded. The troops had grown silent again. He looked ahead to see torches being lit on the front lines. They hadn't entered Grevyn Pass yet, but were drawing close.

"What's happening? Can you see anything?" A woman shouted to his left.

Luinedhel shook his head. "I'm going to find out," he said in his best impression of Selyndar, and nudged his mare. The horse bounded forward without hesitation, and he patted her on the neck. "*Good horse,*" he said in Weald-speak.

Others watched him as he passed them, assuming he was an officer or had been called forward. It was unthinkable for a Weode soldier to break rank without orders. Even newly indoctrinated civilians knew better than to disobey their superiors. Punishment would be harsh. No one questioned his movements. If he was there, they figured he must be there for a reason. He looked the part and did his best to act with the confidence of someone who was doing what he was supposed to. Having a horse, and knowing how to manage it, aided in the charade.

As he drew to the front of the assembly, a large flash of lightning streaked downward and hit the ground, illuminating the night for a moment. He saw then, up on the cliff side to his right, a tower outlined starkly against the black of the mountain behind it. They were practically in front of the thing. Had the sky not lit up, he would not have known it. Why had they stopped here, at the foot of the citadel? He didn't feel the dread that Ever had spoken about, so he was surprised that they had come so close to the place without even the slightest prickle of fear. Perhaps the Err had returned to its former state, like when Nightfall had passed by it long ago, when it was nothing more than a standing remnant of a long-lost civilization. Or perhaps there was some other reason.

In the distance, he saw a solitary torch moving up the path and toward the citadel. The crowds were watching it with rapt attention. Luinedhel nudged the horseman next to him and pointed at the distant light. "What is it?" he asked, saying a prayer to Enos that his accent wouldn't give him away.

"The Ade Gerent, the Adelyn, and the Aetheling went to the tower to get a better view of the land. They gave orders for us to stand our ground and wait for their return," the man said. He was shivering in the icy rain.

Luinedhel prodded his horse forward.

"Hey!" the soldier called to him. "The orders were to wait here."

Luinedhel spun around in his saddle. "I have an urgent message for the Ade," he said. "Word comes that the Th'arule are cowering at our might. I'm under orders to speak with the Ade immediately."

The soldier smiled and let him pass without additional questions.

The hubris of the Weode was a weakness that Luinedhel intended to exploit. They thought of themselves as superior to the other races in Halbrun. They were raised to believe that they were descendants of the First People – something he knew not to be true. The First People, he knew now, were shifters, Questelle's kind. The elves were merely their subjects, and when the empire fell, the elves claimed it as their own. Nobody was there to challenge or correct the lies.

The Weode also believed that Enos had blessed them above all other races, as proved by their *accentation* – their long life. They were special, and all other races were 'less than.' That arrogance was at the root of why they had no allies to fight alongside them now. And why they despised half-bred children like the *ort*.

They were Weode — favored of the gods.

Here they were, a mighty force of thousands upon thousands, armed and ready to slay their brethren to keep their kingdom free from the threat of 'other.' In their pride, it was inconceivable that anyone would be foolish enough to stand against them.

He shook his head. Such pride, such arrogance. Not only were the Weode corrupt and vicious, but they were blind, too. There were so few lights in the darkness. So few sparks of hope in the gloom of his people … the people of his father.

He kicked his mare into a gallop, trying to close the space between him and the torch making its way up the side of the mountain. When the ground rose sharply and became rocky, his mare slowed, unsure of her footing. He dismounted and proceeded on foot, leaving the horse to stand alone in the cold, dark night.

The elven helmet he wore interfered with his sight, and he no longer needed a disguise. He removed it and cast it off to the side of the narrow and overgrown trail. He gazed upward and allowed the rain to wash over his face. His long, dark hair clung to his face.

Above him, the clouds broke for a moment, and he saw Eyama high in the sky. He looked over his shoulder and could make out the fuzzy outline of Relos in the fog above. It looked like the Hunter would catch the Weaver tonight. It was a rare event that happened only a couple of times each cycle, and usually near the horizon. Tonight, it looked like they would meet high in the sky overhead, which would be a spectacular sight, the moons making a giant eye that looked down upon them.

The dream pushed its way to the forefront of his mind. He remembered the dark doorway with the tendrils of smoke that reached out to restrain him. He reached inside the sash where he had concealed his *estrayaed* weapons and pulled them out.

"*Your choice draws near,*" Marek said. "*And the choice will determine your path and change the world you live in. The time draws close.*"

Luinedhel shivered and looked to the tower, outlined by another flash of lightning in the sky above.

"Time for what, Marek?"

"*I smell an old one,*" Adesh said. "*This one is strong, even more so because they are here in the ancient place. You will need to kill them. Before they kill you … and those you love.*" Her voice was loud in his ears, despite the constant roar of the rain.

Luinedhel took off the breastplate and the greaves and the rest of the elven armor. He tossed it aside in favor of being able to move quicker and quieter over the rocks. He felt more like himself without all the extra weight on him.

With a dagger in each hand, he climbed nimbly ahead. The torch was moving not far above him. In its light, he could see three figures step off the rocky trail and onto a flattened area in front of the dark citadel. The one holding the torch was, without question, Dredaius. Questelle was at his side, and behind them both was a figure he recognized immediately.

"Avanstel!" Luinedhel said, though the rain drowned out his voice. Although Nephinae had brought word that he was alive, seeing his familiar figure here for the first time since their parting after Hemel brought tears to his eyes.

Avanstel looked down the hill into the darkness. For a moment, Luinedhel thought his friend had somehow heard his call, but Avanstel's gaze didn't rest on the shadows where Luinedhel crouched. Instead, he scanned the valley, at the army gathered below. Hundreds, thousands of torches fluttered in the rain. Avanstel turned back to Dredaius and Questelle and said something. Questelle motioned angrily at him and looked at the Ade, who only looked down at his feet. Avanstel relented, nodding his head, and they crossed the small space in front of the citadel.

Luinedhel crept forward. Questelle was standing in front of the tower's blank wall. The light from the torch flickered and sputtered in the wind and rain. The stories were true – the tower had no entrance – at least none he could see from this vantage.

Questelle reached out her hand to Dredaius. He grabbed the strap from his shoulder and lifted it over his head, along with a long, dark bundle. He sat it gently on the ground and untied the cloth. Avanstel stood behind him, looking over his shoulder.

Dredaius removed the fabric and then reached out and touched the contents. A blue crackle of light lit their faces from below.

The Ade lifted the scepter from its wrappings and held it in front of him. Blue arcs of energy flowed down his hands and over his arms and sparked around the sapphire at the top. Immediately, Luinedhel felt tingling jolts of energy from the daggers in his hands. He looked down and saw the same blue lightning that emanated from the scepter arcing around them, but much fainter and dimmer. There was no denying the connection between the three objects, but proximity seemed to be a factor. He placed them quickly in his belt, as even the faint blue illumination would be visible from above.

He looked back at the tower and saw Dredaius move toward the wall. Questelle stepped in front of him, blocking his way. She reached her hand out again, motioning for Dredaius to relinquish the scepter.

He hesitated, and they exchanged words, but her position did not change. After another exchange, this time joined by Avanstel, she stepped forward and slapped Dredaius on the face. She grabbed the Nwi'Diad from him, pulling it from his grasp and pushing him backward simultaneously. Avanstel and Dredaius turned their faces away in anticipation of her destruction.

A flash of lightning hit the tower, followed by a shattering crack of thunder. This must be what happened when someone not of the line of J'Onsal touched the scepter! But no … she was still standing there. Her arms raised. She had not fallen to her knees as the energy consumed her. Instead, she raised her arms higher into the air and laughed, her laughter cutting through the roar of the storm.

How could it be? Only those of the J'Onsal line could wield the scepter without being destroyed! They all knew that! Was it a lie invented to keep others away from the power of the Stone? Or was Questelle …

The surprise on his face was reflected in the faces of both Dredaius and Avanstel. None of them could understand what was happening. Was Questelle from the line of J'Onsal? How could that be? Was she another child of N'Athero? A third heir?

"Three hands, no more, land's fate they hold," he heard the Seer say in his mind.

Questelle pointed the scepter at the ground, and a blue bolt of lightning flashed out of it and struck the place where they stood. The air seared with a crisp metallic scent and a burst of intense heat. Around him, the rocks hissed and steamed. Luinedhel shielded his eyes a moment too late. The outlines of the three of them burned into his vision.

Then it was all dark. He was blind.

CHAPTER 42: SHIFTER

Luinedhel scrambled on his hands and knees, feeling his way forward. The jagged rocks cut into his flesh, but he pressed on, determined to reach the place where he had last seen Avanstel. The rain pounded around him. The ground shook with each roll of thunder.

As he climbed, his sight slowly returned, the lightning dancing in the sky above piercing through his blindness. He arrived at the place where Dredaius, Questelle, and Avanstel had stood. A flash of lightning revealed the scorched earth where the blue bolt had struck. Clumps of burned grass smoldered between the scattered rocks. The torch lay on the ground, barely alight. The others were nowhere to be found.

Luinedhel picked up the torch and waved it around wildly, looking for any sign of his friend. Before him lay the tower; dark and unmarred, a surface without a break. It wasn't smooth like glass, but didn't appear to be made of stone either — or at least not any stone that Luinedhel had ever seen before. It was alien and strange, as if from some other world. He could see why a place such as this fueled tales of strange events and brought fear to the people of Orevael. It would be easy and convenient to blame any missing people or unfortunate happenings on the mysterious Kragdenmal-Err; the place was unnatural and disconcerting.

He ran his hands over the black surface. He felt a vibration in his fingers, but he couldn't tell whether it was an echo of the storm or whether it came from something inside the citadel. He placed his ear against the surface, listening closely. He could hear a rhythmic thrumming, like that of a mechanism or the breath of a creature … as if the citadel was alive. There was a distinct sound that could either have been a growl or hum of something within the tower.

Luinedhel held the torch up high, scanning the surface for a sign of entry, but it looked solid, and he could not find a divide. In the sputtering glow, he picked out a few glyphs and symbols etched into the strange surface. He traced them with his free hand, not expecting he would recognize them, but trying to discern if they were even remotely familiar.

He inhaled sharply and stepped back from the wall. He recognized the symbols. They were symbols from the guard tower in the Gravenwilds and the journals in the Summer Tower. The language of the First People!

He set the torch on the ground beside him and reached for his belt. The daggers tingled in his hands. They throbbed in a slow, pulsing rhythm that was in sync with the tremors emanating from the dark wall before him.

Almost immediately, Adesh's voice was in his head. "*We are the key.*"

"I know." He traced his hands over the wall until he found a place where he thought the daggers would fit and slid them both into the slots. As before, he heard a click, and a door appeared in the tower's face. It swung inward.

"*Darkness and light both set them free,*" Marek said.

Luinedhel ignored the voice. He didn't have time for their riddle-speak; he needed to find Avanstel and stop whatever devious plans Questelle had. He pulled the blades from the wall and stepped inside.

He was in a room that was somehow bigger than the tower itself. At the center of the room was a brazier that burned with a preternatural blue fire. It danced and swayed in time with the rhythmic thrumming, which was louder now. The noise appeared to originate somewhere above him.

"*Darkness alight with fire blue,*" Adesh said.

He looked at his blades and could see occasional blue arcs of energy emanating from them. "Time to put an end to the Adelyn's plans," he said.

As he moved into the room, the door swung closed behind him. The noise of the storm outside immediately vanished. He found the sudden silence unsettling.

Across the room, opposite the door and beyond the brazier, was a large metal cage. The door of the cage was open. Luinedhel looked around the room, wondering what kind of creature the cage had contained. He assumed Questelle had released it and that it was lurking somewhere in the shadows, waiting to pounce on him. He raised his weapons in a defensive pose and pivoted slowly.

Thick pillars lined the walls of the circular room, stretching upward into the darkness beyond the firelight. There was no place for an adversary to hide, except in the shadows at the edge of the room. The dim and dancing blue glow revealed everything there was to see. Unless the released beast had the ability to remain unseen, he was alone here in the room. Where had Avanstel and the others gone?

He circled the room, checking for any doors that might lead away from the chamber, and found none. Though the sound of the storm had disappeared, the low and persistent throbbing continued. He looked up, noticing for the first time a long chain that reached down from the darkness, splitting into four smaller chains, which were attached to the corners of the metal cage. He walked closer to the enclosure.

The floor of the cage was a solid piece of metal. The bars on all four sides were spaced far enough apart for a person, or creature, to reach an arm through them. The same flat metal formed the cage's top. In the dim light, Luinedhel couldn't determine if the cage was made of *estrayaed* or a different metal, but based on his observations, he assumed it was the same as his daggers and the Nwi'Diad. There was a latch to hold the door closed, but no lock. If the cage were a prison, it would be an ineffective one. It had to have another purpose.

He stepped inside. Nothing happened.

When he pulled the door closed, the latch fell into place, and a whirring sounded overhead. There was a shudder as the cage lifted off the floor of the chamber. It ascended at a steady pace into the darkness overhead.

The strange blue fire faded below him, and darkness enveloped him. As he rose, Adesh and Marek glowed more vibrantly, sparks and arcs of light dancing around his hands. The tingling in his hands increased as they inched upward, but having felt this before in Hemel, it did not surprise him. He knew it meant he was drawing closer to the Nwi'Diad. And closer to Avanstel … and Questelle.

"*Sere'eden*," he said. He concentrated on blocking the sensation of pain in his hands. This time, doing so was much easier. He was getting accustomed to the pain that came with holding these *eer'gott* blades.

The cage ascended through the ceiling of the room, which had been much higher than Luinedhel had expected. Finally, it came to rest, and the cage door opened. Luinedhel looked around. The space was as wide as the one below, but the ceiling was visible here. In the center of the room was a raised dais surrounded by five smaller replicas of the brazier below. Three of the braziers cradled blue fires. The other two had burned out. The room was awash in azure light.

On top of the dais stood a strange mechanism, but one he knew well. Three enormous bands of *estrayaed*, each of varying widths, and each engraved with glowing blue glyphs, spun on various axes around a dark center of black smoke. Another lacked the glowing blue runes and rotated slowly, wobbling on its axis. A fifth ring, inert and dull, lay on the ground like a dead piece of metal.

The pulsing noise that filled the tower was louder here. It emanated from the inky cloud in the center of the mechanism. Luinedhel felt drawn to it, pulled toward it. He stepped out of the cage. The door swung shut on its own, and the whirring started again; the enclosure descended into the hole and down into the darkness.

Luinedhel took a step toward the whirling rings. Tendrils of the smoke would occasionally escape the center mass, reaching outward, probing carefully, but would violently retract when one of the *estrayaed* bands would intersect it. The magicked contraption contained the smoky sphere; the prisoner held within. He took another step forward, peering to see if he could discern forms within the darkness. Suddenly, the vapor shifted, and a pattern emerged. It became something coherent. Layers upon layers, peeling outward endlessly. Slowly, ever so slowly, moving outward and replaced by those on the inside, like a deadly black flower eternally blooming.

"The shifter's bloom," Luinedhel said aloud.

"*Beauty*," Adesh said.

"*Ruin*," Marek answered.

Luinedhel became entranced. He stepped closer to the undulating ebony flower, lifting a hand and wanting to touch it. He didn't understand why he wanted to; he felt … compelled. The wispy, shifting flower undulated in a never-ceasing and hypnotic pattern. He stepped closer. His foot knocked against something that rolled away from him, clattering over the floor. He looked down; the spell had been broken.

Around him on the floor were hundreds of blackened, withered corpses like those he had seen in the Delve – the same which had decorated the Shadow Gate. The bones were mixed with scraps of leather and shreds of cloth in a myriad of colors. The remains were scattered haphazardly around the room, not arranged in piles like in the Undercroft.

This was the graveyard of all who had come too close to the secret of the Kragdenmal-Err, their bones accumulating here over the millennia. They had fallen victim to the mesmerizing call of the magic emanating from the dark flower. And their life force had nourished the dark bloom, the thing – or things – that were caged inside the spinning rings of *estrayaed* marked with the language of the First People.

Voices filled the room, like a whisper multiplied upon itself. There were three of them he could discern, each different, but they spoke in unison and came from the dark smoke rippling and pulsing at the center of the room.

"Welcome, shifter child."

"We feel you. We know you. We smell your blood."

"You are one of us. A doul'zur like us."

"We have waited. Waited for an eternity for you to come and free us."

"We sense the old power. Have you brought it here? Set us free, so we can join you."

"Set us free. Let us join Kal'Rana and Ni'Shashti."

"Let us have our revenge on House J'Onsal for our imprisonment."

Luinedhel inhaled sharply and stepped backwards. The flower pulsed, reacting to his movement.

Ni'Shashti? She was the sister of Ni'Ilyan, the White Wolf. The pieces of the puzzle began to click into place: Questelle was Ni'Shashti, and she, like her siblings, was a shifter – shifter's blood and J'Onsal blood were one and the same. It all made sense. She was of the line of J'Onsal! *That* was how she was able to hold the Nwi'Diad and not be destroyed – she had the blood … the shifter blood. And that was why she had sent Avanstel to Hemel to retrieve the scepter – she thought he had the shifter blood in him too, so it was safe for him to touch it.

"Avanstel," Luinedhel said, remembering his purpose here.

There was a peal of thunder and a flash of light from above. He looked up and saw a stone stairway across the room that led to a hatch in the ceiling. Rain was pouring in, and he heard the storm raging outside the tower. He glanced again at the dark flower and moved away from the dais, giving it a wide berth as he made his way around the room.

Another flash of lightning. He looked up at the ceiling. He took the steps three at a time and peered cautiously over the edge above him when he reached the top. Questelle was standing there, her back to him. She held the Nwi'Diad above her head. Jagged arcs of blue light danced around the top of the tower. He couldn't see Avanstel or Dredaius.

It was like his dream – high above the city, high above Hemel – when the emperor had used the scepter to … what had he done? What was *she* trying to do? What had brought about the destruction of the first empire?

"What now?" Dredaius shouted. There was annoyance in his tone. He was angry, but not angry enough to challenge Questelle directly.

"Now … I make *my* army."

"What do you mean? We have an army already – the entire kingdom of Weode is here before you, ready to fight our enemies. What more do you want?" He yelled against the roar of the thunder and the howl of the wind. "Let us go through the pass and defeat the Th'arule. We will slay our enemies."

Questelle laughed. "Fool. *You* are the enemy. The *Weode* are the enemy."

He looked confused, and just a little hurt. "I am not your enemy, love."

She laughed again. "Stupid Dredaius." Luinedhel shuddered, remembering the meeting in the throne room when she had so callously mentioned that she had killed Danvaren. "Don't you see? You *are* the enemy. You and your entire line. All those who have descended from the loins of Ni'Ilyan … my wicked brother, who killed my father Ni'Vahyan and bore children with the Th'arule, tainting our line, weakening our power!

"You Weode disgust me with your worship of the White Wolf. My brother was nothing more than a coward, a deceiver, and a murderer. He ended our line, our future, because of his love for an *elf!* My father forbade the union, so Ni'Ilyan slew him, and imprisoned me and the last four doul'zur, here in this tower.

"But no more. I am free, and I will remake the world into what was supposed to be. I will reclaim what is rightfully mine – the Empire of J'Onsal. Now I have the power to remake the Weode into an army of *my* own, an army of Urneans. I will wipe the half-blood abominations, and *all* the elves, from this world. I shall restore the Empire!"

"You will not!" It was Avanstel's voice! Luinedhel couldn't see him from this vantage point, but this was confirmation that he was still alive.

Questelle laughed again. "*You* can't stop me. You and your half-brother will be the first to be unburdened of your pitiful forms. I will take the *akan'gott* that remains in your blood, and you will know what it's like to have your essence stolen from you, as Ni'Ilyan did to me and the others! I will use the Nwi'Diad to amplify the *akan'gott* that exists here, and within you, and you will be born again as Urneans."

Questelle raised the scepter above her head again. Blue lightning stretched down from the storm clouds and struck the rod. The sapphire atop the scepter sprang to life, the energy from the storm growing inside of it. Sparks and snaps of lightning appeared on the ground around her. The top of the tower crackled with blue bolts of energy.

Luinedhel launched himself out of the stairwell and onto the top of the tower. The power from the scepter connected to the daggers in his hands. The lightning danced away from Dredaius and Avanstel. The searing pain smashed into him, running through his entire body. The lightning jumped between the daggers and the scepter in an electric blue triangle, lighting up the entire tower. Energy danced around them, from sky to scepter, to blades, and back.

Questelle turned to him in surprise. "What is this?"

"Stop this, Questelle!"

She hissed. "You! I've spent far too much effort to rid myself of you. No more!"

She pointed the staff directly at him. A large bolt of blue lightning hit him square in the chest. The blast sent him flying backwards, landing just a hand's span from the edge of the tower.

"No!" Avanstel shouted. He ran across the tower and fell next to Luinedhel. "Arrac, what are you doing here?" He helped Luinedhel to his feet.

The daggers were glowing bright blue, having absorbed the energy from the blast. That was the only way he had survived it. The connection between the daggers and the staff was the key to withstanding her attacks. Blue lightning raced across their surface.

"Kill her now," Adesh said. *"Before they bring the devastation as before."*

"Strike true to their heart," Marek said. *"Or run!"*

"The blood is within you, child. Choose darkness and death. Use it for your power. Use me to strike the enemy down. I am at your side."

"Or choose light and life. Overcome the darkness with my blade. Overcome your blood. Use me to bring hope to the realm. I am at your side."

"The choice is yours. We are the key," they said in unison.

The pain from the energy was too much. He dropped the blades, and they clattered on the stone beneath him.

Questelle lifted the scepter toward the sky and chanted. *"Thanel el uhtrack da'vael omvadla …"*

"Ni'Shashti! Stop!" Luinedhel shouted above the crashing storm. The rain poured around him, over him, through him.

She turned and looked at him, surprised he had survived the blast from the scepter. Her face contorted with rage as her eyes fell on the daggers, dancing with blue lightning. *"Another* half-breed J'Onsal? Doul'zur blood runs through your veins, too. I smell it now."

She looked at Avanstel, her head tilted to the side and her lips curled into a snarl. "Cunning old Selyndar. He tricked me! He led me to choose the wrong one! You are just a common *ort*, like your brother. Unfortunate … but I will rectify that, now. I have no need of you anymore."

She raised the Nwi'Diad again and chanted. *"Thanel el uhtrack da'vael omvadla eral'datu."* The glyphs carved into the side of the Nwi'Diad glowed fiery blue. Bolts of blue lightning reached down from the clouds above, striking the scepter with an ear-splitting crack. The entire top of the tower was alight with the energy. It arced from the scepter and hit Dredaius, Avanstel, and Luinedhel. The energy surged through them and knocked them off their feet. The pain was more intense than before. Luinedhel could barely keep his breath.

She raised the scepter again, and another streak of power came from the sky, from the tower under their feet, and collected in the scepter. There was an audible hum, as if the entire tower was vibrating with the energy. The power collected in the scepter and then struck out at Arracnoth and Dredaius. Blue strands of lightning danced over him, pulling something from him. Something that was draining him. Pulling something from him – something he couldn't explain – that he didn't even know he had. She was siphoning his life, his … *akan'gott*. She would take it all – and leave him like those corpses in the Delve!

Questelle stepped to the edge of the tower and pointed the scepter at the army in the valley below. Lightning from the Nwi'Diad split into a hundred smaller bolts and hit the army. It arced from soldier to soldier. The sounds of their howls and cries rose into the night. In unison, they wailed, louder than the storm that shattered around them. The sound was not just pain; it was something deeper. It was terrifying, ferocious and … familiar. It was the sounds of the Urneans, the sounds that Luinedhel had heard Clarana make as she transformed. The sound from his dreams of the shifter.

"Yes!" Questelle said. "No more Weode, no more elves! Tonight, my army is born! An army of death that will sweep across Halbrun and then beyond! Tonight, the empire of J'Onsal is reborn! Come, Weode, take your forms as Urneans! Feel the power of the doul'zur! Embrace your new forms!"

"Questelle, stop!" Dredaius was writhing on the ground beside her. His hands reached slowly toward her as he pulled himself along the wet stone. "You have to stop."

She looked at him and shook her head. "I will not," she said. "I have waited so long to feel the power again. Power that Ni'Ilyan and his traitorous followers stole from me. I can feel it now … feel the power in your blood – the remnant of what was once the most powerful race in Halbrun."

She breathed in deeply and closed her eyes, a look of delight on her face. The lightning raced over her, but she smiled. She was aglow with the power. Dredaius trembled and shuddered. She reached out to him – the lightning snapping off her fingertips toward him. He cried out in agony, reaching up toward her in a feeble attempt to resist. She pulled the *akan'gott* from him and used his doul'zur life force to alter herself, extracting from him his essence to fuel her abilities. Her face rippled, and then there was the sound of bones crunching and skin tearing. She was becoming something hideous. Legs sprouted from her sides. Her abdomen shrank and became insectoid. Her face stretched and distorted, twisting into a draconian grin as her neck grew long and serpentine. Enormous wings unfurled behind her.

The figure on the Shadow Gate! Luinedhel gasped. The doul'zur, the shifters, were the ones who built the Shadow Gate! The connection was obvious now! How had he missed it?

Dredaius rolled over. His life force had been expended – consumed by the shifter. Where the Ade once was, a withered, blackened corpse lay unmoving, the face frozen in a grimace of agony.

Luinedhel caught the light reflecting off Marek and Adesh, which rested where he had dropped them on the pavers beside him. He closed his eyes and picked up the blades. *"Sere'eden,"* he whispered. Waves of pain flowed through him and moved into the *estrayaed* blades. He staggered to his feet.

"Now, child! Now is the choice before you. Make your decision. Light or darkness." They spoke in unison.

"Ni'Shashti!" Luinedhel shouted.

The creature jerked its head toward him and stepped forward. "You are next, child of the traitor. You will give me your *akan'gott* and I will build my army with your blood. A fitting end to Ni'Ilyan's line."

The creature moved toward him. Luinedhel held the daggers in front of him in the first pose that Selyndar had taught in the Dance. She swung the scepter around and aimed it at him. The blast from the Nwi'Diad pushed him toward the edge of the tower again. He fought with all his strength against the power of the Stone. Energy coursed through his body, overwhelming him.

"Sere'eden!" he shouted. The power of the Stone was too much. It was consuming him. He felt his body beginning to change, his sight growing blurred as his limbs faltered. He slid closer to the edge

of the tower. He was moments away from becoming an Urnean ... or falling to his death. The latter seemed like a better option.

"No!" Avanstel shouted and stepped in front of Luinedhel, taking the full blast of the lightning arcing from the Nwi'Diad. The power hit him with a resounding boom that echoed across the valley. Without the *estrayaed* daggers, Avanstel was defenseless against the power of the sapphire. He began to transform immediately, his face twisting, his teeth becoming fangs. He howled in pain.

The moment of reprieve was enough for Luinedhel to regain control.

"*Choose now! Light or darkness,*" Marek and Adesh shouted.

Luinedhel felt the bite of their combined power surge up his hands, through his arms and into his chest. He could bear the pain from one, but both? Which would he strike Questelle with? Marek, the light ... or Adesh, the darkness? He loosened his grip on the blades. He had to drop one. He had to choose a path. He lifted his right hand, ready to strike ... and then he brought up his left hand, looking at the blades once again. Which would hurt Questelle more? Light or darkness? He loosened his grip on Adesh. The doul'zur were wicked, so light was the best choice. Or were they? Clarana seemed to warn him against Ni'Shashti. She didn't seem evil like Questelle, just ... damaged.

Perhaps he should ...

He leaped over his friend and drove forward at the beast.

He would strike with both. He would choose both! Light *and* darkness.

The daggers struck into the shifter's flesh and plunged in deeply. He drove them to the hilt. They sliced through the creature without resistance. There was an enormous boom as another crack of lightning hit the scepter and arched towards the daggers, both stuck deeply in the creature. The full energy of the scepter, the stone, the blades, and the lightning struck deep at the monster. The beast let out a horrendous yowl of pain. She dropped the scepter and began clawing at him, trying to make him release the daggers. But he did not let go. He held on to both Adesh and Marek, bearing the pain as he pushed them deeper, as deep as they would sink. The blue lightning flashed from the sky, into his blades, and into the heart of the beast.

Finally, the creature's legs buckled and Ni'Shashti fell to the ground, flailing about in agony. She screamed, clawing and biting at him, but she could not reach him. Luinedhel let go of the blades and stumbled backwards, gasping for air, his lungs on fire. The Nwi'Diad rolled to a stop at his feet. He reached down and touched the scepter. The power of the Stone surged through him. He closed his eyes. "*Sere'eden,*" he said aloud, concentrating again to dampen its power, saying again those words Adine had taught him a lifetime ago.

The power faded, the energy died, the lightning ceased, and the thunder rolled away in the distance. Nightfall was right ... he was of the line of J'Onsal. The blood of Ni'Ilyan, the White Wolf, flowed through him, too. He was a doul'zur, like his father N'Athero before him, and before him E'Vestren, and before him Ni'Ilyan, and ...

The creature gurgled one last cry, "Shifter! You have betrayed your kind – the only family you have ever had. This will haunt you for the rest of your life." Ni'Shashti's body convulsed one last time and was still.

Luinedhel fell to the ground in exhaustion. The rain poured over him, washing the creature's blood from his face, his hands. The blood of a doul'zur ... his blood.

There was a small noise that was barely audible over the rain. Luinedhel opened his eyes and turned his head in that direction. Avanstel lay on the ground beside him, caught mid-transformation. His beautiful smile had contorted into a terrible snarl. His eyes, once filled with joy and laughter, were now dull and clouded and horrific. Luinedhel scrambled to his knees and pulled Avanstel's head into his lap.

"No! No! Avanstel, no! I can't … I won't …" His heart ripped open inside him. "It's too much! No!" He had never felt so much pain. He screamed into the darkness, letting out cycle after cycle of control – pushing away all the restraints and sacrifices he had made in his lifetime to be at peace. This wasn't possible! This was unacceptable! It wasn't right, or good, or fair! "NO! Van! Why did you do it? Why did you do it?"

The eyes rolled in the monstrous face and focused on him. "Arrac?" The voice reverberated with strange fluidic sounds, but it was Avanstel's voice beneath it all. "Arrac, is that you?"

Luinedhel gasped. "Van! I'm here! I'm here, Van. Stay with me. I will get you to Hathar, to the Seer … Maybe I can use the Stone to …"

The head shook. He smiled. As horrific as it was, it held the echo of what once had brought Luinedhel so much joy – to see Avanstel smile.

"No, Van. Please! Don't leave me! I need you! I need you."

"No, Arrac," Avanstel whispered. "You're the Aetheling. I knew it was you the moment you found the scepter. That's why I didn't contact you, why I hid away from you. I have been distracting them, acting the part so that their attention wouldn't be on you. I was protecting you … but it is you, Arrac. You are the Ade now. I'm sorry I couldn't do more."

"Why would you do that, Van? Why would you put your life in danger? We could have done it together! I'm nothing without you! Stay with me." Tears ran from his eyes, mixing with the streaks down his face.

Avanstel reached up with a deformed hand and touched Arracnoth's cheek. He pulled him closer. Their foreheads touched. "*Namartha t'undel, Arracnoth.*" Avanstel breathed his last breath. His hand fell onto the wet pavers.

Arracnoth screamed, his heart bursting into a million shattered pieces. The sound of his cry rang out through the valley. Soldiers below heard the wail, filled with agony that froze their blood. They looked at each other, wondering if they had imagined it, and turned toward the tower where the lightning display had been. The light show was gone. There was nothing but the sound of rain and the fading echo of the cry.

Arracnoth placed his hand on Avanstel's chest and closed his eyes.

"I love you, Avanstel. I have *always* loved you." He sobbed, clutching Avanstel and collapsing onto him. "*Namartha t'undel, Avanstel.*" He placed his hand on Avanstel's head, and then kissed his gnarled cheek one last time.

He looked up at the sky, unsure of what to do next. The clouds above him parted. Relos and Eyama were directly overhead, perfectly aligned, a large and ominous eye observing the events below.

CHAPTER 43: CONSEQUENCES

Lord Y'Vellian leaned over and whispered something into the ear of Lord Kellendaer. The hawkish man sneered and grinned, nodding his head in agreement. To the right, Lady Shaal'Elonthra stood, her hands resting on the back of her chair. She looked somehow diminished from the strong and powerful woman who had previously commanded this room, still a vision of noble grace, but subdued. Lady Alle was missing from the Council Chamber. There were rumors of her death, but with the kingdom in chaos, who knew whether there was any truth to them?

So many Weode had perished at the tower; so few had returned unscathed. It would take centuries for new craftsmen, bakers, horsemen, and scholars to learn their art and regain the level of advancement that had existed for the five thousand cycles since Ni'Ilyan had led his followers north and had broken ties with the Th'arule.

Questelle had failed in creating her army of Urneans to conquer Halbrun, but Ni'Shashti had devastated the Weode just the same. She had achieved her goal of destroying her brother's progeny and the kingdom they created, although not as thoroughly as she'd envisioned.

Lord Kellendaer stood up and cleared his throat. The noise sounded vaguely like the caw of a raven. "Considering your testimony ... ah ... Luinedhel Omaga ..." He looked back at Lord Y'Vellian, who nodded.

Luinedhel noted they had not referred to him as 'Ade,' 'Lord,' or even 'Thel.' He inhaled deeply and exchanged glances with Nephinae, who sat behind her patron. She smiled weakly. It brought little encouragement. They all knew where this was heading.

Lord Kellendaer continued, "With no witnesses to the alleged events ... and given the situation that we find ourselves in ..."

Lord Y'Vellian interrupted. "The Ade, the Adelyn, and the Aetheling went into that tower before you, and yet you are the only one to emerge ... with the scepter of the Ade!"

"Indeed," Lord Kellendaer bristled. His dark eyebrows came together in a frown. "And considering the accusations previously brought against you that you intended to harm the Ade with the very weapon that you now possess —"

"For which they imprisoned you," interjected Lord Y'Vellian.

"Yet you escaped," said Lord Kellendaer.

"Indeed," Lord Y'Vellian said.

Lord Kellendaer cleared his throat again. "For the theft of royal artifacts, and for what we can assume is murder of the royal family ..." He looked again at Lord Y'Vellian. The man sneered and nodded. "We sentence you to death, Luinedhel Omaga."

"My Lords!" Lady Shaal'Elonthra said swiftly. "I must protest. This has gone too far."

Lord Kellendaer flinched. He looked over at Lady Shaal'Elonthra as if she had struck him. Lord Y'Vellian nudged him, and Lord Kellendaer gathered his courage. "The Council has made their decision. The vote is two to one."

As if on cue, the far door of the chamber opened, and Lady Alle stepped into the room, escorted by T'Antalius. There was a grunt of disapproval from Lord Y'Vellian and a gasp of surprise from his co-conspirator, which the Seer seemed to enjoy. Her face lit up.

"If you've received news that I am dead, I assure you that information is erroneous," she said, almost cheerfully. Lord Kellendaer and Y'Vellian exchanged glances. Lady Shaal'Elonthra smiled. "The streets are in chaos. There is looting, and fires, and not enough guard left to contain the mayhem. It took me longer to reach the palace than I intended. Apologies for the delay." T'Antalius guided his patron to her chair at the large table. "What is the business at hand?"

"Lady Alle," Lord Kellendaer said. "We have just completed a vote. Considering the evidence presented, there is no other option than to sentence the traitor to death."

"Traitor?" the Seer snorted. "Certainly, you mean savior?"

"Now, now," Lord Y'Vellian said, "the facts are clear. The criminal holds the weapon that was used to attack the army of the Weode. He has either slain or imprisoned the royal family within that tower, which even our wisest sages and engineers are unable to breach. The criminal must face the punishment."

"An interesting assessment, Lord Y'Vellian. But, I fear, inaccurate."

"Regardless," Lord Kellendaer said. "The facts are obvious, and the law is clear."

Seer Alle paused a moment, considering. "The law …" She said it as if there were more meanings behind her words. They hung in the air for a pregnant moment. "The law …" she repeated.

"Yes!" Lady Shaal'Elonthra exclaimed. "The law of our people. The law of our entire kingdom, our foundation."

"Yes, yes," Lord Kellendaer snipped. "What of it?"

"As a member of the Founding Houses, and a member of the Council of Elders, it is my right to declare *taven'sanct*," Lady Shaal'Elonthra said.

Lord Kellendaer grimaced and glared from under his bushy brows. "You understand, Lady, that the law holds you now responsible for the actions of this *ort* … that you place yourself at the feet of our ruling. You take upon yourself the mantle of this punishment."

Nephinae stood up and touched her patron's arm in concern. The Lady's gaze remained turned downward. Her voice was somber. "If my death will mean life for Lord Omaga, then it shall be so. Our Houses have been allies for centuries. We will not turn our back on them. They have suffered enough loss. My son can carry on for House Shaal'Elonthra. Lord Omaga must continue to lead his House. There is no other."

"He is Lord no more," snipped Lord Y'Vellian. "He is — and never will be — Weode. He is an *ort*."

"If they only knew the truth of that statement," Luinedhel thought. He was not and never would be Weode. He was a shifter. At least part doul'zur … and the last of his line, save for those three others that remained locked away in the Kragdenmal-Err … at least, for now.

"Let us take private council and discuss this alone," the Seer said. "Without the Ade, the burden of the kingdom rests on this Council. We are responsible for the future of our people and there are pressing matters at hand. We need the wisdom of Lady Shaal'Elonthra to help restore the Weode, so her death, even though for an admirable cause, would have an impact that would echo for centuries. These things are not to be taken lightly. Let us retire to come to an agreement amongst the Council as to what actions will serve our people best. If you would excuse us, Lord Omaga." She pushed herself back from the table. T'Antalius came to her side and helped her to the exit. The other Council members followed.

Luinedhel stood up and watched them exit the room.

Lady Shaal'Elonthra went through last, glancing hopefully over her shoulders at him. Then the door shut behind them, and he sat down in his chair. He stared at the Nwi'Diad resting on the table in front of him. The blue sapphire still pulsed with remembrance of the power that had surged through it just days ago.

Nephinae crossed the room. "I can get you out of the city safely," she whispered. "If you come with me now, we can flee. You don't need to stay here to fight this."

He thought about her offer for a moment. "No," he said. "I will not run away. If it is to be my death, then I join my mother, Avanstel, Selyndar, and N'Khael in Parvanor. I have nothing left here in Ny'we Adye, so perhaps that is the better path."

"But, Lord Omaga …"

"Please," he said. He put his hand on hers. "Lord Y'Vellian is right. I am no Lord. I never was. Even when Selyndar brought me into his family. I was not intended to be an Elder. I was not meant to lead a people to whom I don't belong."

"But …"

"I had much time to think about this over the journey back here." He chuckled. "I had little else to do from the back of the prison cart."

"I'm sorry for that," she said. "I pleaded with the captain, but …"

"Do not worry about it. I expected nothing less. The *anneming*, my adoption into House Omaga, was a formality. Yes, it made me part of the Omaga family, but to the kingdom – despite my titles and right – I will always be an outsider, an *ort*, someone who does not belong here."

He pushed his chair back from the table and stood up. "House Omaga needs to be governed by a Weode, not an *ort*."

Her brow creased. "I don't …"

"You were a sister to N'Khael. You loved her, as I loved Avanstel."

"Yes, of course. We spent most of our lives together. I'm sorry …"

"And you know what she valued, how she thought. You knew her better than I did – perhaps better than even Selyndar, because she shared everything with you."

Her frown intensified.

"You have served under Lady Shaal'Elonthra as her Demestre. You have watched how she governs the kingdom, how she seeks to right the wrongs, how she works to bring light to the darkness."

"Yes ... but I don't understand why you say these things."

"And you know the legacy of House Omaga. How Selyndar was adopted into the family, and N'Khael, and then me."

"Are you saying ...?"

"Would you care for House Omaga? Would you watch over it? Would you take your seat here on this Council and work with the Seer and the Lady to do what is in the best interest of your people?"

"But ..."

"House Omaga has no heir. My future is in question. If you were to become Thelyn Omaga, you could take your place on the Council and help guide the kingdom. The Weode will need voices of reason to rule them ... especially in the absence of an Ade, and in the state of upheaval they are in. I'm sure that Lady Shaal'Elonthra would be happy that another wise counselor could join her and the Seer."

"I don't know what to say. I ..." Tears glistened in her eyes.

"Say yes, Nephinae. Say you will continue the work of House Omaga – for me, for N'Khael, for your kingdom."

She nodded and wiped the tears from her eyes. "Of course I will."

The door across the room opened, and the Council entered and took their seats around the enormous table. Lady Shaal'Elonthra remained standing behind her chair, a dark cloud on her face. Things had not gone to her liking.

"I speak for the Council," she said, motioning to the others who sat around the table. "The situation is not without its difficulties, as you know. Our entire nation is at the precipice of a questionable future. Since Ni'Ilyan, our nation has always had an Ade from the line of J'Onsal." She turned to Lord Y'Vellian and Kellendaer. "Despite the allegations … both the claim to your part in the disappearance of our Ade, Adelyn, and the Aetheling …" She turned to Seer Alle. "And claims that you are the heir that N'Athero sought, not Avanstel … some sort of response is required."

She cleared her throat. "To both uphold the law and to address the circumstances that our nation finds itself in … The Council Elders have reached an agreement."

He inhaled. "*Sere'eden*," he whispered.

Nephinae squeezed his arm.

"You will *not* be put to death."

He exhaled in relief.

"However …" She paused. Sadness clouded her face. "You are to be exiled from the kingdom by sunset this very day. You shall never walk in these forests again, *taven'sanct* or otherwise, unless invited by the full Council. Our word is final."

The silence hung heavily in the room.

Lord Y'Vellian waited for the words to sink in, his smile spreading slowly across his face. "And since there are no Thels in House Omaga, the Council will now comprise only four Houses."

"If I may," Luinedhel said.

"Yes?"

"According to the laws of the Weode, as an Elder of a Founding House – which I remain until I leave the kingdom …"

Lord Y'Vellian's eyes narrowed. "Yes?"

"I have the rights, within the law, for an *anneming*."

Lord Kellendaer bristled. "Well, yes, however –"

"Let him finish," the Seer said. She was already smiling. "It is his right … until sunset, as we agreed."

Luinedhel cleared his throat. "A ceremony will be performed at House Omaga this very evening. Demestre Nephinae Kydel will become Thelyn Nephinae Omaga. She will represent House Omaga and become Lady Omaga upon my departure from the kingdom."

"Your daughter?" Lord Kellendaer exploded. "You are half her age, and you are *ort*!"

"Nonetheless," Lady Shaal'Elonthra said. She was beaming. "It *is* the law. It is his right, and we agreed he would remain the head of House Omaga until sunset." The light had returned to her eyes. She looked like the brilliant woman he knew her to be. She nodded to him in acknowledgement and gratitude.

"So be it," the Seer said.

"Very well," Lord Y'Vellian said. "Do what you feel is necessary in your last few hours, and then be gone from our kingdom. We have much to repair that you have ruined."

Luinedhel swallowed hard. He was without a home once again, facing the prejudices the Weode held against those not of their race. Rejected by the people he had worked so hard to belong to, had worked to save them from the shifter and her plans of destruction.

"As you command."

He looked down at the scepter sitting on the table in front of him. "And the Nwi'Diad?"

"It will remain here, of course," Lord Y'Vellian snapped. "Something so potent must be kept securely." He folded his hands in front of him. "And of course, it belongs to the *Weode*."

There was a silence as the Council Elders exchanged glances. It became uncomfortably long.

He paused, looking at each of them intently. "The Nwi'Diad will go with me."

Lord Kellendaer and Y'Vellian exploded as Lady Shaal'Elonthra and the Seer began arguing with them.

"I will take the Nwi'Diad with me to Q'Serath, to the Librarians. They will advise what to do. And should it need to be secured safely, I know of no better location or people to watch over such an artifact."

"Ridiculous!" Lord Y'Vellian shouted.

"Child's tales!" Lord Kellendaer pounded the table. "House Omaga, of all houses … of all the Weode … knows that it's nonsense to seek after myths and fables of Q'Serath!"

Luinedhel smiled. "Some would say the Nwi'Diad was such a thing – a myth, a fable." He picked up the scepter. Small sparks of blue lit up his hands. He looked at the stone and the glow pulsating within it.

Lord Kellendaer and Lord Y'Vellian shrunk backwards. They had never seen the power of the Nwi'Diad in action before. Even Lady Shaal'Elonthra seemed surprised by the blue lightning. The Seer, however, smiled and nodded at him.

"I will be gone by sunset … after the *anneming*." He turned and walked out of the room, out of the palace, leaving the Council behind him. Leaving the world of the Weode behind him.

House Omaga passed to Nephinae, as it should. He was sure that she would lead the Weode to a better future alongside the Lady and the Seer. And perhaps someday, the darkness that was so prevalent here would recede. With the devastation of the kingdom, and the absence of a J'Onsal to act as Ade, their society was ready for new thoughts and ways. He hoped that the remnant of those who had survived Ni'Shashti's plans would rebuild on a better foundation.

As his time among the Weode ended, he felt it inappropriate to keep the name Selyndar had given him. He had asked for the Weode name so he could become part of their world, part of something that Selyndar and N'Khael were. But he had never truly been Weode … could never *be* Weode. The name Luinedhel would only serve as a reminder of something he could not be, and a family that had been, and no longer was.

He had aspired to be different from the *ort* child he was back in Chark. But what had changed in him had not occurred because of a Weode name. The thing that had changed him was the time he had spent with the people who loved him, and he loved in return. And the thoughts, words, and moments that they had shared.

And of course, the losses.

He thought back to the last moments on top of the tower, holding Avanstel as he passed to Parvanor. Even though Avanstel had tried to adapt to his Weode name, he had always been *Arracnoth* to him.

He was Arracnoth; son of Adine, son of N'Athero, son of an unknown noblewoman, son of Selyndar, brother of N'Khael, friend of Danvaren and Avanstel, adopted father of Nephinae.

He was Luinedhel Omaga no more.

He was just Arracnoth – as he had been born to be.

CHAPTER 44: FAREWELLS

Cycle 739; Darkening; The Fifth Age.

Arracnoth stood silently in the late afternoon light. Nightfall and the others stood to the right of him, somber, unspeaking, as the snow fell softly around them. It was cold, but he was not chilled. He was at peace. The din of Chark was barely audible in the background. Distant, like the memories of his life here.

He looked at the mound of freshly turned soil at his feet. His mind revisited the memories of the past cycle he had spent with Avanstel, Selyndar, N'Khael, and the others in Ny'we Adye and places beyond. Places he had never known before. Places that he would have never dreamed of visiting had he even known of their existence. One long montage of incredible experiences, punctuated by loss.

After a time, seconds and yet ages, Arracnoth felt a hand on his shoulder. "There is no rush," Nightfall said. "The mountain will not move, should we linger. Take your time, and we can leave whenever you're ready."

Arracnoth nodded slowly and placed a hand on his friend's arm. He raised his head and looked into the eyes of his companions.

They had all lost those close to them. In their faces, he saw both sympathy and resignation. This was the way of things for those who did not belong fully in any world. For those who did not have a place to call home, or a family to come home to.

"*Namartha t'undel,*" Nightfall said in Weald-speak. Hathar and Scorpio put their arms on Arracnoth's shoulders.

"Me too," Hathar said. "I am with you. No matter what happens."

Scorpio enveloped Arracnoth in an embrace. "We are all with you, friend. Until the end. Ours is a bond that is not easily broken."

A tear rolled down Arracnoth's cheek and moistened the ground. It was a long moment before he felt the strength to release his friends and stand on his own. He smiled at them as they nodded and turned away, departing into the wintry curtain. He watched them leave and then turned back to the grave.

"Avanstel, you are all that was good and bright in my world. I will miss your smile, your laugh. I will miss your encouragement and your companionship. I will miss our long talks deep into the night and, of course, beating you in games of Haven Chase. I will miss the warmth of your embrace and the mischievous twinkle in your eye. I do not leave you here in Chark. I take you with me, Avanstel. You go wherever I go."

He reached into the leather pocket on his belt and pulled out the white sword token he had carried with him. He kissed it and held it for a long time … unsure he could let it go. But he needed to release Avanstel to be able to move forward. Kneeling, he placed the fragile bone piece on top of the mound in front of him. "Rest well, friend. I look forward to the day when I join you and Danvaren in Parvanor and we can play again."

He moved to the grave next to Avanstel's.

More tears welled up in his eyes, and he brushed them away.

"Mother," he said, his voice trembling. "I owe you so much. You taught me to be brave, to be kind, to always have hope. You showed me that nothing was impossible and to never give up. You rejoiced with me when I accomplished something hard, and you cried with me when I could not. You always believed in me, believed I could do anything, be anyone. You gave everything of yourself. I learned to persevere from you. I learned to laugh at life and to take joy in the small moments." He shook his head and wiped his hand across his nose.

He pulled the small blue pouch from his waist and opened it up, letting the earth fall back onto the grave. He then took the simple pin from the dyed leather and held it for a moment in his hand. Compared to the treasures of the Omagas and other Ny'we Adye houses, it was simply made, but he considered it more precious than all that wealth. He brought it to his lips and kissed it.

"Goodbye, mother. I know you always loved me, and you know I always loved you. Thank you for everything you gave to me … your light, your laughter, your love." He clasped the moonstone pin to his cloak, letting it rest against his chest. "I carry you near my heart … until it beats no more. Thank you for your life, and for making me who I am today."

He stood up and looked down at the graves one last time. He slowly turned around and started down the path leading out of the cemetery. The others were waiting for him at the gates. Arracnoth untied Aelduin and gracefully climbed into the saddle, patting her neck. The mare shook the snow from her mane and snorted.

Arracnoth looked at the others. They waited for him to lead.

He pulled the reins and nudged Aelduin forward, heading toward the road leading out of Chark. The others followed.

He was grateful for his new family.

He was not alone.

EPILOGUE

Cycle 740; The Rising; The Fifth Age.

The Nwi'Diad sat in the middle of the table in front of him, along with Adesh and Marek. The center of the large circular room had no ceiling, allowing a view of the heavens more vivid blue than he had ever seen before. The sun shone down through the cloudless sky, illuminating the sapphire atop the staff. It sparkled brilliantly, sending refractions of blue all around them. Tall white columns framed enormous windows that lined the circumference of the room, filling the space with light. Scorpio and Hythorn sat on either side of him.

Two figures sat opposite them. Their appearance was striking to Arracnoth.

One, a dark-skinned man, had a glowing mark on his abnormally tall forehead. He wore goggles, the lenses of which looked almost liquid as they would move and shift, colors swirling over them like oil upon water. He had shoulder-length dark hair and wore a high-collared grey robe. Embroidered into the garment were intricate runes and designs in a silver thread that glowed like the marking on his forehead. On one hand, he had a ring with a large grey stone that both absorbed and reflected the light from the room. He rubbed it absent-mindedly.

The other was almost the opposite, a fair-skinned young man whose long hair was as white as alabaster, matching his beard. His blue eyes showed his youth, despite appearing to be old. His hair was perpetually moving in a breeze that didn't exist, reminiscent of Lady Shaal'Elonthra, but less subtle. He wore a white and beige robe that fluttered in the unfelt wind. A brilliant opal shimmered at the top of the wind-worn driftwood staff he held in his right hand.

"Without a doubt, it's a Stone," the goggled man said. "I can clearly see the *eer'gott* emanating from it. Can you feel it, Zon?"

"I do," the bearded man replied. "Even without the aid of your vision, Octar, I could tell it was not just a normal gemstone." He looked at Scorpio. "You were right to bring it here, Zuralion. It was as Pedron had suspected." He shifted his attention to Arracnoth. "What are your plans? Do you mean to return to Halbrun?"

Arracnoth hesitated. "I do," he responded. From the corner of his eye, he could see Scorpio sit back in his chair.

Octar exchanged glances with Zon.

"It's not what we had hoped to hear," Octar said. "The Stones are powerful, and we don't know what their presence in the world could mean. It could be dangerous for the Sapphire to be out in the realm."

"We had hoped you would remain here with us," Zon added. "We certainly would welcome you. You would have access to the entire Library – at least, every part the city has shown us. You could study here with us. We would accommodate whatever you need."

Arracnoth nodded. "I appreciate that, truly. However, my destiny does not lie here in Q'Serath – as beautiful and strange and exciting as it is. I would prefer to spend my time in Halbrun with my companions."

"They would be welcome also," Octar said. "Right, Zon?"

Zon bit his lip. "We could make accommodations. Typically, the city only allows those that it has called. The fact that you are here with the *drivrid* and the cleric would show that the city *has* invited you, even though Zuralion showed you the way."

Arracnoth put his hand on the table. He could feel the resonance of the Sapphire and the blades vibrating. "I came to seek your counsel," he said. "But do not intend to become a resident."

Zon sat back in his chair. Another look passed between the two Stone Wardens.

"This leaves us in a quandary," Zon said after a long moment. "We cannot retain you – even should we want to … and we don't. And we cannot take the Sapphire from you. As you know, it takes extreme will to master the power of just one Stone. Two would be impossible."

"We don't believe that whoever created the Stones intended for anyone to hold more than one," Octar said.

Arracnoth tilted his head to the side. "You believe there are more out there?"

Octar shot Zon a panicked look, readable even with the goggles covering his eyes. He had given away more information than they had intended.

"It is possible," Zon said. "But –"

"I will look for them."

Octar stammered. "We are not sure. You may waste your time searching."

Arracnoth smiled. "I have the long life granted to me by *accentation*," he said. "And companions who will join me on the journey. It will not be a waste of time. Even if we don't find another Stone, we will have made memories together along the way."

Octar raised a hand in warning. "You cannot wield it, if you find another."

"I do not intend to." He looked at the two of them. "But perhaps there are others, of similar mind, who would want to walk alongside me." He didn't want to risk their ire by adding his thoughts about their decision to remain separated from Halbrun and the needs in the realm.

Zon sighed. "I see you've decided your path, and we cannot dissuade you."

Octar shook his head. "We will watch you closely, Arracnoth. Know that our eyes are on you — and should we need to, we will intervene, for the sake of Halbrun."

"I would welcome it," he said. He leaned forward and picked the Nwi'Diad and the daggers from the table. He touched the hilt of Adesh to the scepter. It liquefied, stretching out and bending, and becoming one with the staff. He did the same with Marek, who transformed in the same manner. When complete, he held the Nwi'Diad in front of him, the *estrayaed* having transformed into a triangle surrounding the Sapphire, which sparkled now like a blue sun.

It was the symbol of the doul'zur, the shifters. His people.

"Let's go, Scorpio," he said.

His voice was firm, his visage resolute.

ABOUT THE AUTHOR

Asher has been wandering the realms of fantasy for over three decades — sometimes reading, sometimes writing, and occasionally (often) forgetting to come back to reality. He is the architect of Halbrun, a sprawling continent destined to serve as the backdrop for his planned nine-book Stone Warden series.

When Asher isn't plotting epic quests or wrangling wayward characters, he typically immerses himself in worldbuilding in his 'spot' on the couch in Indianapolis. A former business owner, web developer, and non-profit founder, he spends his free time playing "the world's most popular role-playing game" (alongside some of his characters), visiting with friends (usually talking about his books, much to his wife's chagrin), or — weather permitting — floating lazily in circles around the pool while pondering the mysteries of life (in every world).

THE STORY ISN'T OVER

Want More Secrets from the World of Halbrun?

In the shadowed wilds of Tyshin'Dael, Ni'Ilyan plots the unthinkable. To accomplish his desires, he will need to get rid of his own father and ensnare the remaining Shifter in an inescapable prison … forever.

It's the future he's dreamed of: a chance to protect the tender and ethereal elves from the doul'zur reign, to taste the freedom denied him from birth, and the opportunity to finally embrace his forbidden love. But when your trap is baited with ancient magic, one misstep can turn the hunter into the prey.

This is the lost tale of Ni'Ilyan's dangerous plot; the deadly and arcane truths that have been erased from time – now revealed to you!

Claim your bonus content at
asherhboyan.com/whitewolf
before the last circle falls and the Shifters are set free.